THE MORTAL FIRES

OTHER BOOKS BY ANNA DURAND

ANNA DURAND

JACOBSVILLE BOOKS JB MARIETTA, OHIO

THE MORTAL FIRES

ISBN: 978-1-934631-92-8 (pbk.)
ISBN: 978-1-934631-93-5 (ebook)
Library of Congress Control Number: 2017959859

Manufactured in the United States.

Jacobsville Books
www.JacobsvilleBooks.com

Publisher's Cataloging-in-Publication Data
provided by Five Rainbows Cataloging Services

Names: Durand, Anna.
Title: The mortal fires / Anna Durand.
Description: Lake Linden, MI : Jacobsville Books, 2017. | Series: Undercover elementals, bk. 2.
Identifiers: LCCN 2017959859 | ISBN 978-1-934631-92-8 (pbk.) | ISBN 978-1-934631-93-5 (ebook)
Subjects: LCSH: Magic—Fiction. | Spirits—Fiction. | Fairies—Fiction. | Shapeshifting—Fiction. | Women heroes—Fiction. | Romance fiction. | BISAC: FICTION / Romance / Paranormal / General. | FICTION / Romance / Paranormal / Shifters. | FICTION / Romance / Fantasy. | GSAFD: Love stories. | Occult fiction. | Fantasy fiction.
Classification: LCC PS3604.U724 M68 2017 (print) | LCC PS3604.U724 (ebook) | DDC 813/.6—dc23.

Chapter One

"I AM NOT YOUR SUPERNATURAL TAXI SERVICE." I LODGED MY HANDS on my hips and tried to frown at the leprechaun in front of me, but his pseudo-pleading look turned my frown into a half-suppressed smile. Tris was no stereotypical leprechaun. He wore no green felt hat, looked like a teenager, and stood average height—with a rangy build, buzz-cut brown hair, and bright blue eyes that glimmered with an uncanny light.

"Are you discriminating against leprechauns?" he asked in his very human accent, a cross between Chicago and the Bronx despite the fact this elemental being lived in a parallel world.

"Oh please." I lolled my head back, rolling my eyes at the heavens. It wasn't my fault somebody a long, long time ago created magical barriers to stop elemental beings from traveling more than one mile from any interdimensional portal. "Claiming discrimination is not going to make me do what you want. If I take you across the boundary, you might die. For real, for good, no coming back from it—not even for an immortal being like you. Getting my friend ripped apart at the molecular level would really ruin my day."

Tris had ambushed me outside the rock shop where I worked as assistant manager. I may have been the Janusite, a mortal gifted with the powers of a Roman god, but I still had to pay the bills.

I glanced at the corrugated metal building that hunkered alongside U.S. Highway 41 in a remote section of rural Mandan County, in the heart of the Keweenaw Peninsula. A colorful sign pronounced the shop "Rock the Keweenaw: Upper Michigan's Premier Geology Superstore." The building sported a fresh coat of barn-red paint. I'd come here on my day off to head for the Unseen realm and try to discover more about what being the Janusite meant, but the leprechaun had waylaid me.

"Come on," Tris whined. "You take Nevan over the boundary all the time."

Ah, Nevan. I couldn't help smiling every time I thought of my boyfriend. My immortal boyfriend. A sylph, no less. My mind rewound to last night, and the hours I'd spent ensconced in Nevan's underground lair in the Unseen realm, naked and wrapped in his big, muscular body, kissing and touching and—

"Hey!" Tris snapped his fingers in front of my face. "Don't go getting that dreamy look on your face. I'm talking to you, lady."

I folded my arms over my chest as a car whizzed past on the highway, twenty feet behind me. The morning sun glared in my eyes, peeking over the treetops and the roof of the rock shop on its daily journey across the sky. "I don't care to test the limits of a magical barrier or of my powers."

"You're gonna make me beg, aren't you?" Tris grumbled, screwing up his mouth, then sighed. "Lindsey Porter, would you pretty please take me over the boundary so I can check out your world?"

A warm tingle rushed through me, an awareness of a particular elemental approaching. My heartbeat accelerated, the fine hairs on my arms and the back of my neck lifted. Nevan was on his way.

"Sorry," I told Tris. "Gotta go."

Without waiting for his complaint, I sprinted around the back of the shop building, through the rock garden and past its concrete statuary of fantastical creatures, and straight down the trail into the woods. I reached the healing vortex, halting at the bench-shaped stones arranged in a semicircle around the empty space that contained invisible, healing energies. I'd once believed the vortex was a hoax, nothing more than a fiction to attract tourists, but I now understood it was real. The vortex could heal wounds and promote mental well-being, but it could also do so much more. It could resurrect the dead.

The warm, liquid tingle that heralded Nevan's approach mutated into a chill slithering down my spine. Not Nevan.

A breeze wafted past me, carrying with it a faint and unpleasant odor reminiscent of ammonia. It dissipated in seconds, though, and I hadn't gotten a good enough whiff to identify the smell.

I turned in a circle within the vortex, scanning the woods for the source of the false sensation that had drawn me here. The woods were quiet—too quiet. No chattering squirrels or rustling of the wind through the leaves.

How could someone or something fool me into thinking Nevan was coming? My connection with him fueled the sensation. I had no similar connection with any other living thing. Of course, I was living among magical beings who sneaked into the mortal realm undercover, often posing as mortals. I had no clue how many elementals walked among us mere mortals.

Twigs cracked at my left one after another, amid stumbling footfalls and the panting, whimpering breaths of a distressed individual.

I spun toward the sound and shoved my hand under my shirt to close it around the grip of the handgun holstered inside the waistband of my jeans. The Bond Arms Mini derringer was small enough to fit inside my palm but let me fire .357 rounds as well as shotgun shells, thanks to its interchangeable barrels. I hoped I wouldn't need either today, but I rested my hand on the gun just in case.

A girl staggered out of the woods and stopped several feet away, her body shaking, eyes wild and golden brown hair disheveled. Her large blue eyes flicked to me, and she froze. Her pallid skin grew whiter.

"Lindsey," the girl said, her voice dry and brittle.

"Do I know you?" Pretty sure I didn't, but she gaped at me like I was her long-lost relative.

A chill swept over my skin. This girl resembled me. Not like we were twins, but enough we could've passed for sisters. The pale girl gasping for air was more slender, where I had curves, and looked younger but otherwise…

The girl scuffled closer and stretched out one ghost-white, dirt-encrusted hand to me. Her face had transformed into a mask, as if she were drugged or entranced.

"You don't belong," she intoned. "You never will. Accept your fate or the forces allying against you will consume your power and your soul."

My power? She couldn't know about me being the Janusite.

The girl's knees trembled. She swayed on her feet, eyes rolling back in her head for a couple seconds before she seemed to return to reality, her gaze suddenly sharp and clear and locked on me. "You can't win. He won't choose you this time."

"What are you talking about?"

"The one you love. He won't choose you."

Finger-size marks bruised her neck.

I took hold of her shoulders. "Did someone hurt you?"

"He sent me to tell you. He made me come." She shuddered. "Swore he'd punish me if I disobeyed him. The way he punishes…"

She bit down on her lip, tears gathering in her eyes.

I studied her face, her bloodshot eyes, her skin that seemed drained of life. No human whackjob had done this to her. "Who hurt you?"

The girl swayed again, her eyes unfocused. "He calls himself N—"

She fainted into my arms. I hugged her to me with one arm, feeling for a pulse in her wrist with my free hand. The rhythmic surge of blood pushed against my finger, weak but there. I fumbled in my pocket for my cell phone, then remembered I'd left it in my purse back in the shop. *Dammit.* I shouted with all the volume my lungs could muster.

"Help! Somebody, help!"

Tris blipped into view beside me. One second not there, the next visible.

I jumped, my heart racing. "Thank God. Help me get this girl back to the shop. She's not well."

Tris glanced at the girl and his lip curled. "Cripes, lady, what'd you do to her?"

"Nothing. I found her this way." I glared at him and said, "Help me."

He slapped a hand on my shoulder and we zipped away, emerging a split second later on the gravel path right outside the shop's main entrance.

"There," Tris said, "that's my good deed for the day. I can't take you to the hospital, seeing as it's past the boundary."

"What about the vortex?"

His nostrils flared as his gaze bounced from the girl in my arms to the woods and back again. "Dark magic did this, I can taste it. Ain't no coming back from this kinda sickness."

"Please, Tris, can't you try?"

"Can't. Too dangerous." He gulped, his own face paling when he glanced at the girl. "I'm sorry."

The leprechaun vanished.

Motion in the trees snared my attention.

A tall, black-robed figure loitered at the edge of the woods, at the periphery of the parking lot. The hood of the figure's robe concealed his face.

Before I had time to wonder why I assumed it was a man, the figure winked out of sight.

In my arms, the girl began to twitch, foam spilling from her mouth.

"Stan!" I shouted. "Call nine-one-one! Hurry!"

Chapter Two

The ambulance rushed out of the parking lot and down the highway, taking away the sickly girl. I turned away from the road, my shoulders flagging. While I'd watched the paramedics loading the girl into the ambulance, I'd kept wondering what on earth had gone down here. Did the black-robed figure have anything to do with the girl's illness?

I'd stopped believing in coincidence the day I'd discovered the Unseen realm existed.

A tepid breeze ruffled my hair around my face and rattled the leaves of nearby quaking aspen trees. The sound imitated the pattering of a light rain, a strange contradiction to the clear blue sky above. My gaze drifted to a couple and their two small children navigating the path to the rock garden. It led up the hill into the woods and straight to the waterfall where I'd first met Nevan six weeks ago.

Why had I sensed him, if he wasn't in the vicinity? Another unanswered question.

"Am I boring you?"

Torn from my thoughts by the gruff voice, I turned to face the man behind me. Sheriff Travis Blackwell stood with hands on his hips, thumbs hooked inside his belt behind the .40-caliber Sig Sauer berthed inside a leather holster. Not long ago, I would've felt intimidated by his stance and the ease with which he could've whipped out his gun to threaten me. These days—thanks to both of us coming to terms with what really happened to Travis's brother, my fiancé Calder Blackwell—the sheriff and I had reached a state of tentative friendship, almost a return to the way we'd interacted before I met Calder.

It helped that Travis wasn't calling me ice princess anymore.

"Well?" Travis said. "You paying attention or what?"

His Texas twang truncated some words, turning paying into payin', but elongated others.

I sighed and rolled my shoulders back. "I'm listening. You're sure the girl's okay?"

"EMTs said she's severely dehydrated and exhausted, but the bruises don't look recent. Docs at the hospital will check her out to make sure, but yeah, they think she'll be fine once they get plenty of fluids into her."

"Thank heavens." I rubbed my neck, because it had begun to ache. I had a feeling I'd been gritting my teeth ever since I found the girl. "Did she say anything?"

"Just her name. Megan Kozlow. And the number for her parents. I called 'em and they're coming to pick her up." Travis frowned, shaking his head. "Damnedest thing. They say they last saw her in Copper Harbor, a good hour's drive way. The family was in an ice cream shop two days ago when she went to the bathroom and nobody saw her again. They reported it, but the Keweenaw County guys couldn't find any sign of the kid. Copper Harbor ain't exactly New York City, so I got no idea how somebody took her without anyone seeing."

"Was there a body of water nearby?"

"Lake Superior's a block away from the shop." One side of his mouth crimped. "Please don't tell me this has something to do with…all the freaky shit."

"That close to a body of water, any elemental could've abducted her. She was well within the one-mile limit." Natural water features concealed portals to the Unseen realm, but no elemental could travel beyond the one-mile boundaries that encircled every body of water on earth. With my newfound abilities, I could take elementals across the boundary, but only my closest allies knew about my skills. "Disappearing without a trace, in the blink of an eye, is a hallmark of the elementals."

"One of them must've taken her." Travis groaned, looking utterly miserable. "Wish to hell that was a surprise."

The girl's words to me replayed in my mind and a chill swept over my skin. I hugged myself, to no effect. The chill refused to leave. "How old is she?"

"Nineteen."

Christ. So young. I couldn't bear to think about what her unknown abductor had done to "punish" her, or that he seemed to have done it as part of a scheme to frighten me.

Travis let his arms drop to his sides, his shoulders slumped. "Did the girl say anything to you?"

I told him everything about my encounter with Megan, from the moment she staggered out of the woods until she collapsed in my arms.

Travis's eyebrows knit together. "Somebody whose name starts with N did this."

"Apparently."

He shifted his weight from one foot to the other, grimacing and scratching his cheek. "I hate to say it, but you and me, we do know somebody whose name starts with—"

"Nevan did not do this." Never mind that his name started with N, and that I'd sensed his presence right before Megan stumbled into me.

Travis held up his hands, palms out. "Hold up, Lindsey. I'm not saying it was Nevan, and you gotta believe me, this ain't jealousy talking anymore. I'm only looking at the facts we've got."

"I understand you have to consider it." Hugging myself tighter, I swallowed against a sudden tightness in my throat. "But you don't know Nevan like I do. He's a good man and he would never, ever hurt an innocent girl."

"Okay," Travis said slowly, "I get it. But listen, he was under some kind of spell when you met him, one that made him do things he didn't want to do."

"It was the result of a sucky bargain. And even when Skeiron had an iron grip over him, Nevan resisted the king's worst commands. He fought it with every ounce of willpower he had in him. Besides, Nevan is not bound by a magical bargain anymore."

"Are you sure?"

I tried to respond, but my voice refused to function. A cold fist gripped my heart. I knew Nevan wouldn't hurt an innocent willingly, but could I ever know for certain he hadn't gotten roped into another magical trap?

Travis settled a hand on my shoulder, his touch and his voice gentler than I'd ever known him to be. "I'm sorry, Lindsey. I'm a cop, and I gotta look at the simplest explanation first."

"Magic is the simplest explanation?" I almost smiled to hear Travis the logical cop suggest such a thing, but the worry gnawing at my gut squelched any humor.

"Crazy, ain't it? Guess I'm getting more used to this freakiness than I thought."

"Amazing what you can get used to when you have no choice."

Travis kicked at a rock. "I better get back to the office."

"Yeah."

He ducked his head and looked at me sideways. "You ever think about Calder?"

I shoved my hands in my jeans pockets and hunched my shoulders. "Yeah, I think about him sometimes."

Too often, actually. I had nightmares about my former fiancé, but I also suffered the occasional thought about what might've been if Calder hadn't stumbled onto a cougar and sustained fatal wounds from the attack, if he hadn't died and been reborn as something else. That sequence of events had altered my life too—and Travis's.

"You ever wonder," Travis said, "if we could've saved him?"

I shut my eyes. "Your brother was going to kill me. Nevan had to take him out."

"But you guys didn't even try to resurrect him. You brought back a frigging shoplifter, but you left Calder dead."

His words might've sounded angry, if not for the strain of grief in his voice.

I met his gaze, refusing to shy away from this moment. I'd known it would come sooner or later, when the shock of recent events dimmed and the consequences became baldly evident.

"Travis." I moved closer to light a hand on his arm. "We couldn't bring Calder back even if we'd wanted to, I'm sorry. There was no time. Nevan and Tris had to rush to get me to the vortex and heal me."

Travis nodded, his eyes glistening. "Can't believe my kid brother turned into a shapeshifting demon monkey."

"Neither can I." Unsure what to do with my hands, I stuffed them in my pockets again. "I wish we could've saved him, could've turned him back into himself. He didn't give us a chance to try. You know I would've saved him if I could."

"Yeah, I know."

I wanted to hug him, but that would've been weird. Travis had kissed me once, when he was drunk and freaked out by supernatural occurrences, and I didn't want to give him the wrong impression.

A familiar wave of warmth crested over me. Unlike what I'd felt earlier, this was strong and right and unmistakable.

"I have to go," I said. "Nevan's coming."

I bolted across the parking lot and through the rock garden, up the hill to the vortex. Just as I sat down on the nearest stone bench, Nevan poofed into view at the other side of the vortex. I'd gotten accustomed to the way elementals could poof in and out whenever they liked, and at times I envied that ability.

Nevan wore his favorite attire, a tan loincloth plastered to his hip and groin, the fabric seeming to blend into his bronzed skin. When he sauntered toward me, taut sinews flexed in his powerful thighs and across his sculpted abdomen. The sunlight glistened on his body, highlighting the metallic bronze sheen of his skin and the paler track of the scar that lanced across his heart.

I melted from the inside out, captivated by the sight of him. Would I ever get tired of admiring his exotic beauty? A sigh of appreciation whispered out of me. No, I never would.

He dropped onto one knee, settling his hands on my thighs. When he spoke, his Irish brogue lilted the words into a hypnotizing melody. "Good morning, love. Didn't want to leave while ye slept, but the tribunal—"

"Ugh. Can we not talk about the tribunal?" My thighs parted of their own volition, my body anxious for him to get closer. "I'm starting to think the tribunal keeps calling you in for meeting after meeting for the sole purpose of keeping you away from me as much as possible."

"Perhaps they do." He slid his hands up and down my thighs, and even through my jeans, his touch excited my skin. "But I have returned. As I always do."

My mind struggled to remain lucid, but the unnatural heat of his body enveloped and distracted me. I longed to plaster myself to his nakedness. "You could've woken me up to say goodbye, instead of dropping me off in my apartment while I was still asleep."

He smiled, one of those slow and sensual smiles he'd perfected, and eased my thighs apart to move his body between them. "You're angelic in slumber, and your snoring is adorably nasal. I hadn't the heart to disturb you."

"I'll ignore the snoring comment and forgive you anyway." I looped my arms around his neck and he slipped his arms around me, his hands roving my back. "How was your meeting?"

"Pointless."

"Sorry to hear it." The events of the day resurfaced in my mind, and I said, "A weird thing happened earlier. This girl—"

"Later." He nuzzled my neck, his breaths teasing my skin. "I would rather spend this time making love to you and convincing you to live with me."

"But the weird thing—"

"Tell me after, darlin', when we're both relaxed and thoroughly sated." His voice had lowered into a sultry register that never failed to arouse and entrance me. "First, tell me again why ye won't live with me."

The intoxicating nearness of him and the subtle, sensual way he touched me threatened to obliterate every thought in my head, but I couldn't let it. Not yet.

"Listen to me, Nevan." I planted my hands on his chest to keep him from cocooning me with his body and his mind-scrambling presence. "Something happened that's got me spooked, and it should have you spooked too."

He went still, his gaze searching mine. "Tell me."

I related my encounter with the dazed girl. "I don't know who this N person is or what exactly he did to her, but this was a message for me."

"No one will harm you, not as long as I live." He enveloped my hands with his. "And you have proven capable of defending yourself, as well as others. We will discover the culprit of this attack on an innocent girl, together."

"It's what we do, right? Hunt down evil." I suddenly recalled a part of the story I'd forgotten to mention. "Right before the girl showed up, I swore I sensed you coming."

"You would have. I had already crossed the veil at that point, and I paused in the cave to speak with Brennus. He had questions about his new duties as guardian of the falls."

"But you didn't find me until just now."

He raised our joined hands and kissed my knuckles. "I wanted to come to you immediately, but Brennus believed someone had breached the portal while he patrolled the woods. I returned to the other side to investigate, but found no evidence to support his concerns."

"What kind of evidence were you looking for?"

"Remnants of the magic used to open the portal or perhaps footprints."

"Somebody did come through. The man in the black robe."

Nevan's hand tensed around mine. "You believe Brennus detected his arrival, yet somehow the robed man concealed the magical evidence of it."

"Is that possible?"

"You should know by now, anything is possible."

"Sherlock Holmes would have an aneurysm if he were in my shoes, because logic has no bearing on the elemental world."

Nevan glided his hands up my arms and around to my back, roaming them in slow circles, urging me closer to the inviting heat of his body. "Before we delve into the riddle of the man in black, I would like to solve another mystery. Why will you not live with me?"

Pressed against his firm body, I threaded my fingers into his hair and moved them in lazy circles on his scalp. "We've been through this before. I'm not ready to relocate to the Unseen and shack up with you. I need more time."

Though I loved Nevan, like I'd never loved Calder, I'd known Nevan for a matter of weeks. He was immortal, insanely hot, and recently crowned king of the sylphs—all things that complicated our lives.

Nevan fixed me with his steady gaze, his amber eyes glowing from within and swirling with metallic shades of bronze, gold, and silver. "You still think of Calder, don't you?"

"Well…yeah." I hunched my shoulders. "He turned into a monster, literally."

"You fear I will do the same."

"No. Maybe. I don't know." Letting my head fall back, I growled in frustration. "I'm confused, okay? I've got a new job and my Janusite powers to figure out. I've been researching the mythology of Janus, but I need your expertise here. Then there's the tribunal, who want you to dump me. Most everybody in your world agrees with them I'm a filthy, worthless mortal."

His fellow sylphs called me "the king's mortal plaything." Only three elementals knew I was the Janusite—Nevan, Tris, and the shapeshifter Brennus—and the rest of them dismissed me as a puny, insignificant human. They had no clue I was a mortal gifted with the powers of the Roman god Janus, the only being in either world who could take elementals across the boundaries in this world.

"I will never leave you," Nevan said, "no matter what the tribunal or anyone suggests."

"You might be better off without me. Not that I feel unworthy, but really. How many times did you have to save my life when Skeiron came after me?" I dropped my chin to my chest, then lifted it again to gaze into his whirlpool eyes. "Like I said, I'm confused and I need more time. Please understand."

"I do understand." He peppered kisses along my throat. "But how much more time do you require before making up your mind?"

"Don't know. I..." My voice trailed off, thanks to Nevan nibbling at my earlobe. I tilted my head to the side, exposing my throat to his ministrations. He dragged his lips down my neck, his hands skimming up my back to splay over my shoulder blades, urging me closer until my taut nipples pushed against his bare chest through my shirt and bra. "This is so unfair. You know I can't think when you're—Oh."

With my arms around his head, holding him to me, I arched into his body as one of his hands drifted around to my breast.

"My sweet Lindsey," he murmured into my ear, "I want your delectable skin on mine while I dive into your slick heat."

Oh God, I wanted that too. "Right here in the vortex? What if a tourist shows up?"

"Then I shall whisk us away." He drew my earlobe into his mouth, suckling briefly before releasing it. "The healing vortex does more than heal. It can strengthen our bond and heighten our pleasure."

"Are you serious?" I pulled my head back, brows raised. "You never mentioned that before."

"Never had you soft and willing inside a vortex before."

I was soooo willing. Since the moment I'd given up resisting his seductive charms—on the fourth day we'd known each other—I couldn't say no to him. Didn't want to. He set me on fire, and I dissolved into him every time.

The crunching of footsteps on the fallen autumn leaves interrupted our interlude. Nevan leaned back, twisting his head around to glance in the direction of the sound. I slanted sideways to peer around his large body.

A woman traipsed out of the woods to the left of the trail and stopped at the edge of the vortex. The gossamer layers of her flowing gray dress obscured, but did not fully conceal, the curves of her body and the perky globes of her breasts. The leaves remaining on the trees softened the sunlight, making her alabaster skin glow in contrast with her rosy lips and fiery red hair.

A belt fashioned from silver links encircled her waist, hanging low in the front, weighed down by a green pendant. The slender, cylindrical pendant featured a flared top and tapered down to a point. A series of chevron marks decorated the flared cap, while horizontal lines wrapped around the cap's base. The shape seemed familiar, but I couldn't quite place where I'd seen it.

The woman's emerald green eyes glinted with specks of silver as she smiled—at Nevan.

I blinked rapidly, confused by the familiar way she smiled at him, like she knew him well and was quite fond of him. Like she *really* knew him. Like she'd...slept with him.

Nevan sprang to his feet, nearly bowling me off the bench. He left me to regain my balance on my own, since he was too busy striding toward the strange woman. Halting several feet away from her, with a stone bench between them, he gaped at her with a faint pallor under the bronze gilding of his skin. His eyes had gone wide, the swirling in them gone.

The woman stretched a pale, slender hand out to him. "I've found you at last, Tuathal my love."

She spoke with an Irish accent, like Nevan's but more pronounced.

"Ceara," Nevan whispered, stumbling backward a step. "You are...alive?"

Her laughter tinkled like tiny bells. "As I am here, clearly I live."

I hefted my body off the bench, inching closer to Nevan. When I touched his arm, he flinched, his gaze darting to me before zeroing in on the other woman once more.

"Nevan," I said, giving his bicep a gentle squeeze. "Who is this?"

The woman arched a single, elegant brow but did not glance at me for even a nanosecond. "Nevan? Is that what you call yourself in this life, Tuathal? I hadn't heard, but then, I've been indisposed for quite some time."

Nevan and the woman stared at each other, he with shock, she with amused interest. It was like I didn't exist anymore.

I shook Nevan's arm. "What's going on?"

He blinked slowly, as if emerging from a trance, and turned toward me. "This is Ceara. My wife."

Chapter Three

WIFE. THE WORD GOT WEDGED IN MY BRAIN, IN THE GAP BETWEEN hearing and comprehending. For the past six weeks, Nevan and I had shared more than hot sex. We'd shared the details of our lives, past and present. The future had been uncomfortable to discuss, given the uncertainty of his position as king and my newfound powers, the ones I still didn't understand and wasn't sure I wanted.

Nevan and I had agreed we needed to be totally honest with each other. I'd assumed he told me everything that mattered.

Until I'd been confronted with the ethereally beautiful woman he called his wife.

Nevan watched me with haunted eyes, the spinning colors of his irises duller and almost motionless, with only the faintest motion within them. His expression had gone stony. Though his shoulders slumped a little, a distinct tension made his body rigid.

I moved toward him, instinctively reaching up to lay my hands on his bare chest, needing the comfort of physical contact.

He backed away a single step.

A pang lanced through my heart. I was losing him, in the space of a few seconds. One minute, he was seducing me and the next...

Who the hell was this woman, this wife of his?

After everything we'd been through together, this was not how it ended. I'd almost died for him, he'd almost died for me, we'd fought an entire goddamn army of brainwashed sylphs together. He'd asked me to live with him, though I'd insisted I had to spend part of the time here in my world.

A sick feeling churned in the pit of my stomach. I'd never wondered why he didn't ask me to marry him. Hadn't known if elementals did that sort of thing. Maybe he hadn't asked because he knew his wife was still out there.

Christ. I could spin my brain in dizzying circles wondering and worrying, or I could make him talk to me.

Ignoring the eerily serene woman behind him, I closed the distance between us and raised onto my tiptoes. He held stone-still as I locked my hands behind his nape, forcing him to meet my gaze. Threads of bronze whorled in his irises, bright and alive, but only for a moment. My breaths reflected off his face, back onto mine.

"Tell me what's going on," I said.

When he spoke, his voice was a smidgen above a whisper, his words meant only for me. "Not here. Please."

His hands came around my waist, as if he needed to anchor himself to me.

"Tuathal," his wife said, "we must speak. Alone."

A knife-like edge sharpened the last word. I peeked over his shoulder at Ceara, who glared at me with eyes now transformed into twin disks of pure, shimmering silver. Something about the metallic color, the way it swallowed up the whites of her eyes, rushed cold through my veins. Her lips had flattened, her fingers had curled into her palms.

I sensed, on a level deeper than conscious thought, that she despised me with a seething intensity.

Nevan brushed a kiss on my lips, released me, and spun on his heels.

The instant he faced Ceara, the woman's eyes returned to brilliant green flecked with silver. She reverted to saccharine smiles and ethereal grace as she sashayed closer, stopping an arm's length from Nevan.

I clenched my fists and my jaw. This woman was married to my boyfriend. Didn't that make me his mistress? Oh great. In a heartbeat, I'd gone from girlfriend to adulterous lover.

Ceara deigned to shoot a haughty glance my way before she proffered one elegant, pale hand to Nevan. "Come with me, my love. We have much to discuss."

"Whatever you have to say," Nevan told her, "you will say in front of Lindsey."

Ceara lifted her perfect little nose and sniffed. "Very well, as you wish."

Nevan tensed, but he pulled in a deep breath and relaxed his posture. "Speak and be done with it."

"I've heard you became king of the sylphs. Congratulations."

Shoulders bunching, Nevan hissed out a breath.

Ceara's lips kinked into a smug smile. "Since you and I are still married, technically, this means I am your queen. I intend to claim my rightful place and rule by your side."

Nevan flinched as if she'd struck him but covered up his response in a heartbeat. "I choose my own mate. Lindsey will rule with me."

"Will she?" Ceara tapped her chin with one finger, then wagged it at Nevan. "Oh, but Tuathal, the council has not approved your selected mate. They have, in fact, resisted it. A mortal as queen, or even consort to the king, proves a bitter pill to swallow, does it not?"

"I am king." A muscle in his jaw ticked. "The council will accede to my will."

Ceara circled around Nevan, pushing between me and him, and trailed a finger down his bicep. When she crossed in front of him again, she tilted her face up to capture his attention. "Over all these thousands of years, have you spared a single thought for Daráine?"

Nevan swallowed visibly, his eyes darting away from Ceara and back to her again. "Of course I have. Her fate is unknown to me."

His wife leaned in, tipping her head back further to maintain eye contact. "Why did you never return to check on either of us? Once you achieved the forging, did your mortal life no longer matter? Did we no longer matter?"

"I—" He turned his head to the side. "The bargain I struck with Notus, to become immortal, forbade me from having contact with anyone from my mortal life or from looking in on my former life. I longed to make certain you and our daughter had survived the attack, but I could not."

Bargains wielded real power in the Unseen realm, power that could extend into the mortal world once the deal was struck. A nasty bargain had forced Nevan to search for the Janusite for a century and to do Skeiron's bidding.

Wait. Had he said daughter? I opened my mouth to speak, but words failed me. Nevan had neglected to mention both his wife and his daughter.

Ceara snapped her fingers in Nevan's face. "Look at me, Tuathal."

He turned his head toward her again, his face blank.

"You abandoned us," she said. "You ran away to fight the enemy and left me and our daughter unprotected."

"I instructed you to flee into the woods, to seek shelter far from the battle."

His voice sounded as dead as his expression.

"Ah yes," Ceara scoffed. "You told us. But we had no time to run, the enemy came too soon. When I saw them approaching, I distracted them so Daráine would have time to escape into the woods."

His gaze pinned to her, Nevan stood motionless, as if unable to tear free of her hold. "How did you—"

"Become an elemental?" She slashed her nails down his jaw, drawing a thin line of blood, then seized the back of his neck. "I sacrificed myself to gain Daráine time to flee. I had only a dirk, but I charged at the enemy screaming like a banshee and waving my dagger at strong men armed with swords. An enemy soldier cut me down within moments."

Nevan stumbled backward a half step. "Daráine?"

Ceara tipped her head, eyes narrowed, and studied him for a long moment. "She lived on. A family from another clan took her in and raised her as their own. She was, so far as I could tell, happy in her new life. Later, she wed and bore children of her own. Our line has survived the ages, Tuathal. Our descendants live today."

My brain, discombobulated by so many revelations, latched onto a crazy notion. What if I was one of Nevan's descendants? *Ew.* I couldn't think about that right now. Besides, Nevan had died five thousand years ago, which meant for all I knew, he could've been an ancient ancestor to ninety percent of the humans on earth.

Nevan lurched backward into the stone bench, his knees buckled, and he thumped down onto the hard seat. "You were permitted to watch over Daráine?"

Hands linked behind her back, Ceara rocked back on her heels with her nose held high. She kept her glacial gaze trained on Nevan, but he seemed to have retreated into the mire of his own memories.

I wanted to go to him but feared I'd be intruding. This was his wife, after all, and they were discussing their daughter. Their descendants. I couldn't fathom the span of time they'd both lived through, or the horrors they'd experienced.

Ceara sighed with exaggerated wistfulness. "The one who made me what I am was a master sorcerer, born of the fae but transmuted by his power into more than a solitary being. Shortly after my revival, when I was weak and confused and in terrible distress, he took pity on me and showed me Daráine. She never saw me or knew I had visited her."

I couldn't keep my mouth shut anymore. Nevan looked about to go catatonic, and I wanted some goddamn answers. Whatever Ceara wanted, it was more than to become queen of the sylphs. My gut told me everything about her indicated a calculating being who had plans. Big plans. For my honey.

Not on my watch, sister.

Stomping up to Nevan, I settled a hand on his shoulder. His usual heat had lessened into a warmth like that of a mortal body. Not good.

I cleared my throat, catching Ceara's attention. "What is it you want with us?"

She laughed softly, with no small measure of derision. "I want nothing from you, mortal. Tuathal is my husband. I hereby claim him and all rights inherent in our bond, sealed by handfasting."

"Five thousand years ago, when you were both mortals." I flapped a hand, as if might shoo her away. No such luck. "The forging changed you both. You can't hold him to a promise he made in another lifetime."

"Soul bonds are forever, child." She bared her teeth on the last word, a flash of white in the muted sunshine, then switched her focus to Nevan. "I will give you time to absorb all that I've told you. However, I shall not relinquish my claim. Not as long as I live, which will be for eternity."

Ceara vanished.

Chapter Four

Nevan and I faced each other—in silence, our gazes fused together—for a minute, maybe longer. Neither of us knew what to say. I sure as hell didn't, and based on his blank expression, he didn't either. He had a wife? From his mortal days?

And she'd come back for her husband.

Not quite right. She said she'd returned to take her "rightful" place as queen, which meant she'd come back for the power now bestowed on Nevan as king of the sylphs. But did she still love him? Had she ever loved him?

Did he love her?

"Talk to me," I said, my throat suddenly tight, my mouth parched. "Please, Nevan."

He covered his face with both hands, his muscular shoulders drooping.

The air around us grew colder and chilled the bare skin of my arms, exposed by my short-sleeve T-shirt. The cooling was distinctly unnatural. I had no idea if Nevan, as an air elemental, had the ability to alter the temperature in his vicinity, either by accident or on purpose. I did know he could create thunderstorms, so it seemed plausible he could affect the air temperature too.

Both of his hands swept up his face and through his longish hair, tousling the wavy, obsidian locks. Still slumped, he looked at me. "There is much to explain."

"No shit." Despite my harsh words, the bleakness in his eyes spurred me to take his face in my hands and feather my lips over his. "It's okay. Whatever it is, I can handle it."

What if he confesses his undying love for his eerie wife, can you handle it then?

My heart clenched, my chest ached. I'd have no choice but to deal with it. Though we'd known each other for six weeks, I couldn't imagine the rest of my life without Nevan.

"Not here," he said. "Never know when there may be prying eyes or ears about."

Yeah, like shapeshifting assassin-spies. Sure, Brennus the raven-man had become an uneasy ally in the wake of Skeiron's death, and the new guardian of the waterfall behind the shop, but I still preferred to steer clear of him. Brennus had slit my throat, though he'd done it because a bargain forced him to follow his master's orders. And his true master had been my ex-fiancé, Calder Blackwell, a newly forged elemental.

God, my life was so freaky these days.

Nevan gathered me into his arms and whisked us away. To the rest of the world, we would've appeared to vanish into thin air as we traversed a kind of interdimensional superhighway in the space of a millisecond. We emerged on the natural ledge of a red sandstone cliff some thirty feet high, alongside a waterfall that spilled down into a twenty-five-foot-deep pool. A wooden railing hemmed in the pool, with a quaint wooden bridge stretching across the far end of the little pond. My gaze wandered to the right, past the railing, to the small clearing where I'd first met Nevan. It felt like ages ago, so much had happened since that moment.

His arms still around me, Nevan leaped through the falls.

I gasped from the deluge of cold water that drenched us, soaking me to the skin and gluing my hair to my face. We whomped down inside the cave behind the cascade. Though the waterfall rumbled behind us, the magic invested within the cave muted the noise. The faint prickle of supernatural energy swept over my skin. I shivered from the mixture of cool, damp air in the cave and the cold water that had soaked me and my clothes.

Nevan released his hold on me, though he kept his body in contact with mine. He frisked his hands up and down the length of our bodies, his palms not quite touching me, and warm air rushed over us both. My clothes dried in an instant, my hair too. The droplets clinging to my skin evaporated. Nevan was dry as well, his hair restored to its perfect, wavy state with the locks kissing the shells of his ears.

I looped my arms around his neck and wound my fingers into the hair at his nape. "I appreciate the warm-up, honey."

He winced.

I'd started calling him honey a couple weeks ago, unconsciously at first, but his usual response was to smirk and kiss me senseless. Wincing seemed like a bad sign. If I'd said the dreaded T-word and thanked him, I might've understood his reaction. Though gratitude held no power in this world, he preferred I didn't say "please" or "thank you" at all. I needed to train myself to avoid incurring debts, he said.

Since I'd avoided the P – and T-words, why was he uncomfortable? Was he trying to figure out how to dump me graciously?

Ugh. I had to stop fixating on the worst-case scenarios. Nevan loved me, I knew it, he'd proved it to me over and over again. Still, I had good reasons for my angst about our relationship. My last boyfriend had turned into a monkey-man, framed me for murder twice, and sicked a raven-man on me to force me into accepting the forging. A girl had a right to some relationship paranoia after all that. The fact I'd met Nevan barely more than a month ago didn't soothe my innate tendency toward worrying. How much did I really know about the man whose bed I shared? The man to whom I'd gifted my heart and soul?

He'd told me everything about his past as an elemental. His mortal life remained a mystery, one he avoided talking about whenever I asked.

Nevan rotated us sideways to the falls and extended a hand toward the cave's back wall. With a flourish of his wrist, he accessed the veil between the worlds, between the land of mortals and the Unseen realm where elementals and gods reigned. The portal spun open to fill the rear of the cave. Its abyssal, inky blackness writhed with ribbons of red and purple.

Clutching me to him, Nevan leaped through the portal.

The instant we exited on the other side, he zipped us away. I had time only to glimpse the boulder that marked the portal on the Unseen side and the water burbling out of its top, tumbling down into a ten-foot-diameter pool. Next thing I knew, we stood at the base of a mountain sheathed in unnaturally green grass, surrounded by trees laden with moss instead of leaves. I bent my head back to gaze up at a swathe of the teal-colored sky. We were outside Nevan's home, his underground lair hidden inside the mountain and protected by magical wards that prevented anyone but him from entering.

No one else knew about his home. I could enter it only if he escorted me. He wanted me to live with him, but I couldn't get here without his assistance.

We poofed into his lair.

Nevan's arms fell away from me as he stepped back a few paces.

The air inside the chamber stayed a comfortable temperature for me, despite the fact his body temperature ran hotter than mine. I appreciated his thoughtful concession to my needs. Smooth walls carved out of the mountain's pale stone lightened the room, as did the gentle glow emanating from everywhere and nowhere. Chairs and tables sat here and there. At the far side of room, tucked into a cozy corner, hunkered the Nevan-size bed.

I'd spent countless hours in that bed, beneath the lush fur blanket, luxuriating in the afterglow of our love-making or simply relishing the serenity of lying in his arms. My body softened at the memories.

"You're smiling," he said, his brows crinkled.

"Am I?" Tearing my gaze away from the bed, I relinquished the memories and returned to the present. "Why didn't you tell me you had a wife?"

He ran a hand over his mouth, eyes averted. "It was a long time ago. I was, quite literally, a different person—a different being. The life I lived then became irrelevant the moment I underwent the forging, and I have spared no thought for it in many eons."

"But you had a wife and a daughter."

"They were lost to me after the forging." He began to pace, his posture tense, his focus somewhere else. "When the king, Notus, offered me immortality, he established a condition. I must never again have contact with my anyone from my old life, and I must never attempt to look in on them or visit the portion of the mortal realm where I had lived and died. The break must be clean, he said. I must commit to a new existence without looking back on my old one."

"But Ceara claims she was allowed to look back. She at least took a peek now and then, even if she didn't interact with anyone."

Nevan wheeled sideways in front of me. "Ceara was always stronger than I. She must have rejected the condition of no contact." He grimaced, fisting his hands. "I gave in to whatever requirements Notus demanded. Evading death was all that mattered to me."

"Stop it." I moved toward him and closed my hand around his bicep. Well, as much of his bicep as I could manage to grasp, given the extraordinary girth of his upper arm. "You were dying and Notus took advantage of that vulnerability. Besides, you have no idea what Ceara might've agreed to when somebody offered her the forging. You don't even know if what she's told you is true."

He shut his eyes. "Why would she deceive me? When I knew her, Ceara was a kind and loyal wife, a sweet girl."

"She's not a girl anymore. She's—" *An elemental bitch with a hidden agenda and designs on my man.* "She's different now. You told me the forging changes a person, and only someone with a strong will can survive it intact. That's why Calder came out wrong, because he wasn't as strong as you are. The weakness in his character meant the forging fractured him. Maybe the same thing has happened to Ceara."

"Perhaps." He sounded less than convinced.

Nevan had told me once the forging demanded a hefty price in blood and suffering. From what I'd gathered, the process of transforming a mortal into an elemental destroyed the human body at the molecular level and reshaped it into an altogether different form. Elementals considered pregnancy and childbirth to be unseemly. In Nevan's words, they connived to increase their numbers by preying on the fear of death to trick mortals into undergoing the forging.

But a weak human soul made for a twisted elemental being.

Case in point: My ex-honey, Calder Blackwell.

"Either way," I said, "Ceara's not the girl you knew."

He sighed, his entire body seeming to deflate. "But she is still my wife."

"Is she?" I crossed in front of him. "You both died thousands of years ago. The man and woman who married are long gone."

He still wouldn't look at me.

I cradled his face in my hands once again, hoisting up onto my toes to draw his attention to me. I spoke only when his eyes, swirling with hazy colors, zeroed in on mine.

"You said yourself everything from your first life is irrelevant. I heard what you didn't say, though. Your old life isn't irrelevant because it meant nothing to you, it's irrelevant because you are a different man." I locked my arms around his neck to lift myself higher, our lips a breath apart and our eyes level. "No one can hold you to a marriage vow you made in another life, because that man wasn't you."

Praying I was right and not merely desperate to eradicate the competition, I waited for his response. Seconds ticked by, counted on the metronome of my heart as he stared into my eyes, transfixed by thoughts I couldn't comprehend.

His arms came around me, tugging me tight against his firm body, the sizzling heat of his skin warming me.

"Lindsey, my love," he said in that rumbly, sexy tone he'd perfected, "you amaze me at every turn. Your strength and determination remind me of why I love you so deeply."

His words dissolved me and, eyes half closed, I inhaled the earthy scent of him. "I love you too. No matter what."

"You are a miracle." He flattened his palms on my back and crushed me to him, his mouth devouring mine, our tongues lashing and coiling around each other. The flavor of him, sweet and spicy and all Nevan, suffused my being like a magic spell, enchanting me like nothing else on earth could. The world spiraled away from us, as if we hovered inside our own bubble of reality. Pleasure rippled through me, hot and tempting, urging me to take more, give more, and never stop until we were naked and entwined in the fur blanket of his bed enjoying post-coital bliss.

Nevan severed the kiss, breathing hard. The vibrant colors of his eyes had flared to life again, a kaleidoscope of fire and molten metal.

Breathless, I could do nothing except gaze at him with shameless adoration. He had that effect on me every time he kissed me. What thrilled me most, though, was realizing I had the same effect on him.

I combed my fingers through his hair, loving the silky softness against my skin. "You know how much you mean to me, Nevan. I want to be with you and only you forever. But the only way this will work is if we're honest with each other, all the way. I've told you everything about my life, even the embarrassing stuff and the painful things I'd rather forget. I need the same from you."

He rested his forehead on mine, eyes closed. "You want to know about my mortal life."

"Yes." I let myself sink into the intimacy of the moment, the incredible bond I shared with him, one borne of love and passion and trust. "It's important because I want to understand you, but also because your former wife is butting into our lives. Do you think she can really make a claim? I mean, would the tribunal listen to her and—" I bit down on my bottom lip, raised my head, and dared to ask. "Do you think there's a chance they'll order you to take her as your queen?"

"I am king." He straightened, his jaw set. "They will not command me."

"You're king because they made you king after Skeiron was destroyed. What if they…I don't know, coerced you into a bargain with some kind of leverage as bait."

"Leverage?" He drew his head back, squinting at me. "You think they might use you as leverage to force me into a bargain, one in which I take Ceara as my queen."

"You can't tell me they aren't capable of doing something like that. The dirty bastards won't even let me into their powwows with you. They've refused to even meet me." I slid my hands down to his chest, my fingers crooking into his skin, and studied the lines of his muscles. "They'll never accept me, a puny mortal, as your…consort. I'm sure they'd jump at the chance to have an elemental woman on the throne."

He kissed the tip of my nose, his lips curving in a sweet smile. "You are many things, darlin', but puny is not one of them."

"Most folks in the Unseen think mortals are weak and useless."

Nevan crooked a finger under my chin and tipped my face up to his. "When I take a queen, it will be you. The tribunal will either accept you or suffer my wrath."

I'd witnessed firsthand what his wrath could do, but a simple fact remained. "You aren't as powerful as Notus or Skeiron. They ruthlessly pursued power at any cost and amassed enough to keep anyone from trying to oust them."

His mouth compressed into a line. "You believe me too ineffectual to rule."

"No, of course not." Groaning, I let my head fall onto his chest. "I'm saying this all wrong. What I mean is, they don't fear you the way they feared Skeiron, and Notus before him."

"If they try to keep me from you," he said, his voice tough as steel, "they will fear what I will rain down upon them. Heads will roll, in the most literal and graphic manner."

Craning my neck back, I rested my chin on his chest and smiled up at the man I adored. His threats of violence on my behalf never failed to give me a warm, fuzzy feeling. "Aw, honey, you always say the sweetest things."

"No one takes you from me. No one."

"Same goes for you. Any elemental hussy who tries to steal my man has a bloody fight on her hands."

A grin, slow and heated, spread across his face. "I do love your blood-thirsty side."

I laid my cheek on his chest, relishing the warmth and comfort of him even as an idea sparked in my mind. "Do you still glamour? I only saw you do it once, when we first met. It's still one of your powers, right?"

"It is. But I have no desire to utilize it. After a century of deceiving mortal women by disguising my appearance, I've had my fill of glamouring."

Yeah, I could understand that. Still, my curiosity about his past got the better of me. "Show me what you looked like as a mortal."

With a restraint that surprised even me, I kept from saying "please."

He cringed away from me, backing up a few paces, his gaze on the floor and his features slack. "You don't want to see it. I was not the man I am now, and the past matters nothing to our future."

"Beg to differ." I moved toward him but halted a couple feet away. "Total honesty, Nevan. I told you we both need that for this to work between us. Honesty means total trust too, and if you can't trust me to see the old, mortal you without judging—"

"I trust you." He cupped his hands around my upper arms, stroking up and down. "In every way, I trust you. But my human life—"

"Is a part of who you are today, whether you want to admit it or not. You're a different man since the forging, but your previous life influenced who you became after the transition. To have a future with you, I need to understand your past." I sidled up to him, snuggling into the hollow of his shoulder. "Don't make me say the P-word."

He groaned with resignation, his body slouching against me, then pushed away and adopted a regal, erect posture. His image shimmered and shifted, but I realized this was just a facade, not a genuine transmutation. Glamour allowed him to assume a different appearance without altering his actual form. I watched with amazement as his bronzed skin grew paler and his body adjusted to a new—or rather, old—version of him.

The mountainous muscles that made him an impressive and striking figure had shrunk to a more subdued kind of buffness, akin to an average Joe who earned his muscles through hard labor rather than gym workouts. He seemed shorter too, by maybe a few inches. His hair had become longer, dulling from its usual glistening onyx to a dark brown and losing most of its waviness.

And his eyes. The churning, metallic hues had vanished, replaced by a hazel shade that was striking but not as arresting as his normal colors.

I angled my head side to side, examining this alternate version of him. After a moment, I strolled up to him, hooked my arms around his neck, and kissed him thoroughly. Though he tried to remain stock-still and unaffected, he couldn't resist giving in to the demands of my lips and tongue. The kiss was slow and hot, charged with every emotion we harbored for each other and with the passionate devotion and scorching desire we shared.

When we uncoupled our lips, I gazed up at him with all the ardor he inspired in me, as entranced by the mortal Nevan as I was by the immortal sylph. "I love every version of you. I love what's inside you, your heart and your passion, and your determination to always do the right thing. I love your heroic side, your tender side, even your insecure side. The whole package. That's the real you, the rest is just wrapping paper."

Right there in my arms, he morphed back to his usual self.

"Wrapping paper?" he said with a smirk.

"You know what I mean."

"Indeed I do." He slanted his head closer to mine, his pupils large and his lips parted in disbelief. "No one has ever seen all of me and accepted it. But you accept me no matter what, and I love you all the more for that."

I placed my cheek on his chest. "You don't have to be afraid to share your past with me."

"I realize that now, and I cannot believe I ever doubted it." He caressed my hair, his thumb grazing my cheek. "You worry about the robed man and the girl he harmed, don't you?"

Unwilling to peel my cheek away from his skin, I splayed a hand over his chest "There's Ceara too. All of this is beginning to feel like a replay of six weeks ago, like somebody wants to drive me crazy again the way Calder tried to do."

"They may try, but you are far too strong to crumble."

"I'm scared, Nevan. This all feels much worse than what happened before, when Skeiron was hunting for the Janusite—for me. You're king, but the tribunal doesn't trust you. Somebody sent an abused girl to deliver a message I don't understand. Your dead wife shows up not dead but immortal and scheming to be your queen." I listened to his heart beating, the sound so close to my ear it felt like our bodies had melded. "I can tell you're more worried than you let on."

"There is reason for concern, but I will never let any harm come to you as long as I am alive and able to prevent it."

"I know." I pushed away from him, though his hands lingered on my waist. "But it's time, Nevan. I need to know about your past. Your human past."

He nodded grimly. "Perhaps I should start with end. The battle that altered my fate."

"Okay." I tromped over to the nearest chair, one fashioned from a honey-colored wood, and settled my behind onto the plush cushioning of the seat. The chair dwarfed me, since it was sized for Nevan. An odd anticipation zinged through me, along with an icy current of dread. He was about to reveal all to me and I wasn't positive I'd wanted to hear it. His reluctance to tell me made me wonder what awaited.

Nevan lowered his big body onto the chair beside mine. His arms went slack, his hands dropped onto his lap. "My people, the Partholonians, had lived in peace for many years, keeping to ourselves and away from other tribes. One day, a clan from far away landed on our shores and set to destroying us. The Fomorians cared for nothing but conquest. We stood no chance against them, with their overwhelming numbers, but we had no choice except to fight."

He leaned his head against the chair's back, his gaze directed at the ceiling. I wanted to take his hand in mine, to offer comfort, but understood this wasn't the time.

"When the alarm call was sounded," he continued, "the enemy had already breached the outer regions of our lands. All the men, including myself, rallied to defend our village. I believed my wife and daughter would be safest in our home, and so I left them there alone. Ceara is right, I abandoned my family."

I could keep silent no longer. Folding my hand over his on the arm of his chair, I leaned toward him and spoke with quiet determination. "I know you like to blame yourself for anything bad that happens, but sometimes bad things just are. We can't stop them no matter how hard we try. You did the best you could under the circumstances and if that b—" I caught myself before I called her a bitch. The woman gave me a serious case of the heebie-jeebies and I didn't trust her, but name-calling wouldn't help Nevan. All I cared about in this moment was protecting him. "If Ceara really cared about you, she wouldn't be packing your bags for a round-the-world guilt trip. Please don't see her again while you're feeling this way. It could be dangerous."

Without moving his head, he glanced my way. "You believe Ceara has ill intentions."

"Don't know. And neither do you." I squeezed his hand. "All I'm saying is be careful. When you do see her, make damn sure you don't get guilted into a bargain or debt."

He drummed the fingers of his other hand. "I have been dealing with magical bargains and debts since before your civilization existed. Never have I accidentally indebted myself or stumbled into a disadvantageous bargain."

"Except with Skeiron."

A dark look overtook his features. He glared straight ahead into empty space for a moment before he launched out of his chair. "That was different."

"Right." I rose too, moving in front of him. "Skeiron pushed you into a crummy deal by using your guilt over sleeping with his daughter against you. He threatened to murder her unless you did exactly what he wanted. How did that turn out for you?" I raised my eyebrows. "Oh yeah, you were enslaved for a century, forced to hunt down mortal women who had a 'touch' of the Unseen in them, and take them straight to Skeiron. You still have no clue what he did to those women before he sent them home, rejected because they didn't have the Janusite power."

Nevan scratched the back of his neck, his face pinched.

I was right, and he knew it. Being right failed to make me feel better, though, because it meant he was in danger if—when—he met with

Ceara. I realized I couldn't stop him from seeing her, but I wished to hell I could convince him of the risk.

Grasping his hands in mine, I held them to my chest. "I'm begging you, Nevan, be careful. Better yet, let me go with you when you see her."

To my surprise, he nodded. "Yes, you should accompany me. We share our lives, which means what affects me affects you as well."

"Yes, it does." I let go of his hands and draped my arms around his waist. "Nobody messes with my boyfriend."

Folding his arms around me, he teased my lips with his own. "Anyone who attempts to disunite us will pray for death."

"I love your bloodthirsty side too. It's oddly hot."

He took my bottom lip between both of his, releasing it little by little. "Remain here while I conduct an errand. I'll return swiftly, you have my word."

"Where are you going?"

"I've procured a surprise for you, but I must retrieve it." He glided his hands up and down my back, his fingers spread wide. "Two surprises, in fact."

"Mm, I love presents." I dragged my lips across the scar over his heart, flicking my tongue out to sample his skin. "But right now, I want something else more."

He slid his hands onto my ass, cupping both cheeks. "Wait for me in bed, love."

A sudden draft whispered over my skin from head to toe. I grinned, knowing without looking that he'd vanished my clothes. My bare nipples scraped on his chest and went rigid from the sensation of his velvety flesh on mine. His strong hands squeezed my behind. I almost moaned from the bliss of skin-on-skin contact.

His loincloth in place, he stepped back and went still, the precursor to his poofing away. Before he winked out, though, he hit me with his most sensual smile. "In bed, love."

The second he disappeared, I padded over to the bed. Slipping under the fur blanket, I imagined all the wonderful, erotic things we'd do together as soon as he returned. Visions blazed in my mind, of a nude Nevan on top of me, his hands everywhere, his mouth licking and nibbling wherever he could find a sensitive spot to tease.

Minutes ticked by. Lots of minutes.

The lovely state of arousal I'd reveled in began to wane, replaced by a gnawing pain in my gut. I climbed out of bed and found my clothes neatly folded and stacked in a corner, the same place Nevan always stashed my clothes when he blipped them away for me. Because I didn't have my purse with me, I couldn't check the time on its clock, so I had no way to gauge how much time had passed since he left. It felt like hours.

After dressing, I could do nothing more than pace the room, pop into the adjacent kitchen now and then, and wait. I paced until my legs ached and my eyes felt gritty, until my yawns became frequent and my eyelids grew heavy. Finally, I lay down on the bed on top of the blanket, with my clothes and boots on, too exhausted to stay awake any longer.

I spiraled down, down, down into a restless sleep.

CHAPTER FIVE

S OMETIME LATER, I WOKE TO A FLUTTERY SENSATION OF FEATHER-light kisses on my neck. Before I opened my eyes, I sensed Nevan's presence. Sure, he was the only being permitted through the lair's wards, but if we'd been at my apartment I would've recognized his approach all the same. From the day we met, I'd been able to sense him before he even appeared in front of me.

Driven by instinct, I thrust my hand into his hair and moaned my appreciation as he licked his way up my throat and over my chin. When he paused there, I made a disappointed noise.

"Soon, love," he murmured, his breaths tickling my lips. "But first, I have your surprises."

The haze of sleep evaporated as I recalled how long I'd waited for him to come back to me. I pushed up onto my elbows. "Where have you been? I was worried sick. Not to mention trapped in your lair."

"Our lair." Nevan straightened. His legs hung over the bed's edge with his hips alongside mine. He swept an errant lock of hair from my face. "I was unavoidably detained. I had no desire to cause you stress, please forgive me."

His use of the P-word zinged a magical current through me, faint but detectable, the unmistakable portent of a debt on the verge of being sealed.

I sat up, searching his face for some clue to his behavior. "You said the P-word. You never, ever say that. What's wrong?"

"Nothing." He hesitated, his expression unreadable, but then he smiled and chucked me under the chin. "The fae witch who helped me with your surprise took a bit longer than expected to finish the task."

"You said you had to retrieve my presents." The sharp tang of anxiety infiltrated my mouth, and I gripped the fur blanket. "Now you're saying you had to get them made. Why do I feel like you're hiding something? You never lie. Not to me."

"I am not lying. I believed your surprise would be ready when I met with the fae witch, but she informed me the magic involved was more complex than anticipated. Since I very much wanted to give you the gifts tonight, I decided to wait for her to finish."

His explanation made sense, and combined with his earnest expression, it eased my anxiety somewhat. Nevan would not lie to me, not willingly. He had disappeared for a long time, though. With Ceara out there, intent on becoming his queen, I had to wonder if she might've gotten to him. Tricked him. Guilted him into a bargain.

Nevan reached down to the floor, producing two wooden boxes, each fashioned from a rich, golden wood and engraved with ornate, decorative figures. He offered me the larger box.

I needed both hands to hold it. A small gold latch fastened the lid shut.

"This," he said, "should ease your worries about your safety."

My safety? I was freaked about *his* well-being. Still, I smiled and unhooked the latch, swinging the lid up to reveal…"Is this my gun? It looks like it."

Inside the box, nestled on a red velvet cushion, lay a Bond Arms Mini derringer. The tiny gun seemed even smaller in the large box, but the container also held two boxes of ammo.

"Not your gun," Nevan said, "but an identical weapon. I asked your mother where I might obtain such a firearm and she directed me to a website." He enunciated the word like a man who'd never seen a computer, much less visited a website. Which he was. "I asked if she might help me purchase the weapon. She did, and I had it endued."

"Endued?" I couldn't suppress the wonder that infused my voice. An endued weapon was imbued with powerful magic that enabled it to kill an immortal being. Nevan had acquired a new endued sword a few weeks ago, to replace the one he'd appropriated from Skeiron. Keeping the black sword of the man who'd enslaved him had been too weird for Nevan. He needed an endued weapon, though, to protect himself from whatever threats might crop up.

Now I had an endued handgun.

God, I loved this man.

Nevan picked up one of the ammo boxes. "I also had the witch endue the ammunition for your weapon, both the smaller ones and the large cartridges."

My mouth probably fell open as I ran my fingers over the box of shotgun shells. Nevan held a box of .357 rounds. The interchangeable barrels on the derringer allowed me to load either type of ammo.

And that's when I spotted the other barrel tucked behind the gun, the barrel sized for shotgun shells. I touched the metal. "Is this endued too?"

"Naturally."

I flung my arms around his neck and showered his face with kisses. "I love my present. I love it, I love it, I love it."

He chuckled softly. "I'm pleased you're pleased, darlin'. But I've got something even more important to give ye."

"Better than my very own endued weapon?" I sat back and rubbed my palms together. "Gimme, gimme."

"You are utterly adorable when you're excited this way." He handed me the other box, slanting toward me to murmur, "Though I look forward to exciting you in other ways."

Desire arced through me like electricity, triggering a dampness between my thighs, but nothing could distract me from my second present. I popped the little gold latch on the palm-size box and flipped it open. Inside, nestled on a crimson cushion identical to the one in the gun's box, lay a small, cream-colored stone.

"Pick it up," Nevan said, his voice deep and sultry. "You'll enjoy the sensation."

I plucked the stone from the box, cradling it in my palm. The stone warmed my skin, sending a pleasant tingle through my hand and out into my body. The tingling suffused me with a familiar, arousing sensation.

He cocked his head, his expression expectant. "Do you feel it yet?"

The warmth the stone conferred swelled into a rush of intoxicating heat.

Sucking in a shaky breath, I eyed Nevan. "It feels like...you."

"Because it is me." He surrounded my hand with his and eased my fingers closed around the stone, sealing it in my palm. "This is a soul stone."

"Which means?"

"Soul stones are indigenous to the Unseen realm. For one who knows how to tap into them, they absorb a piece of that individual's magical and spiritual essence—their soul—which may then be transferred into the recipient. It's considered a priceless gift."

I held a piece of his soul in my hand? The intimacy of his gift startled me. I must've looked it too, because he turned his face away.

"If you're offended by the stone," he said, "I will understand."

Offended? Hell, I had half a mind to sleep with the blasted thing ducttaped to my, um...chest. Yeah. My chest.

Not that I was going to do it.

Since his hand still enveloped mine, I laid my other hand atop his. "I love your gift."

"There is more to it." He gazed into my eyes, his aflame with brilliant colors. "I could have conferred my essence into the stone myself, but I required the help of a fae witch to bespell it with the appropriate magic."

"Appropriate for what?"

"To grant you access to our home. The soul stone also will open a hidden doorway so you may breach the wards and enter this place." He brushed the backs of his fingers up and down my cheek. "I want you to feel this is our home, not mine. With the stone, you may come and go as you please."

"It's a key to your place? I'd offer you a key to my place, but you zip in and out whenever you like."

"With your permission. And thanks to your powers, which let me cross boundaries as long you are in the mortal realm."

"Of course." I plucked at the hairs of the furry blanket. "Um, what happens if I accidentally misplace the soul stone? Could someone else take a piece of your soul?"

"You never do cease worrying, love." He pecked a kiss on my lips. "The stone is attuned to you. If anyone else should touch it, they would feel nothing."

I exhaled a relieved breath. "Good. Can I give you one of these soul stones?"

"I don't know if a mortal soul could interact with one of these stones. They are designed to work for elementals, not humans, and our souls are far more potent and rich with innate magic." He slipped an arm around my waist and pulled me into him, vanishing our clothes at the same instant. "Besides, I need no magic to feel the essence of you. Our souls merge every time we make love. I know you feel it, my sweet, mortal soul mate."

Oh yes, I felt it. The intense pleasure of our love-making generated more than mind-blowing orgasms, it also fueled a connection beyond anything I could've imagined might exist before we found each other.

His exact words finally hit me, and my breath hitched. "Did—did you call me your soul mate?"

"Naturally."

"You've never said that before. Do you mean it literally, or is that another endearment?" My heart began to race and my head grew light, as if the fate of universe depended on his answer.

His smile was tender and the tiniest bit sad. "I mean it, Lindsey. Why else would I gift you with a fragment of my soul? It's because you already possess all of mine."

I couldn't catch my breath. No one had ever expressed to me a sentiment anywhere near the depth of what he'd confessed. "My soul is yours too. A couple months ago, I didn't believe in soul mates or magic, but now I understand all of it exists. What we have, it's real and powerful and forever."

He scooped me up and lay me down on my back atop the blanket, covering my body with his. "At last you see, we belong to each other and no one may break the bond. Not the tribunal and not Ceara."

"I know you mean that." I chewed the inside of my cheek. "But something will come between us. I'm not immortal. You'll be forced to watch me slowly wither and die."

Lines etched across his forehead. "Why should I think of that? I will take whatever time I have with you."

"And then what? I'll be gone, but you'll live forever."

"What precisely are you trying to say?"

I shrugged, as much as I could with him on top of me. "Maybe the tribunal has good reason to disapprove of our relationship. I know how I felt when you almost died. Maybe it's selfish of me to hold onto you, knowing how devastated you'll be when I die. And I will die. That's kind of the defining trait of mortals."

He raised onto his elbows, gazing down at me with confusion. "Do you believe I will abandon you when you begin to age?"

"No, I'm positive you'll stick it out no matter what." My mind traveled back to the moment when he lay half dead before me, his chest punctured by Skeiron's endued sword, blood pouring from the wound. Tears pricked at the backs of my eyes. I blinked them away, a sudden ache burning in the back of my throat. "I'm not sure you should stay with me. Loving me will only cause you pain in the end, and I never want to be the source of your suffering."

"You could never be the source of pain for me." He bracketed my face with his hands, his thumbs resting on the corners of my mouth. "If losing you one day is the cost of loving you, then I will pay it gladly."

"It has to be tempting, though, what with your wife alive and immortal."

"What do you mean?"

"She can offer you something I can't. Eternity."

His expression hardened. "There is no temptation. I will take a lifetime—a mortal lifetime—with you over eternity with anyone else. You are my soul mate."

My heart swelled, even as my fingers went cold. In a small voice, I asked, "Did you love Ceara?"

"Until you, I had loved none but my mother and father, and they died so long ago I could scarcely recall the feeling." He his mouth twisted into a rueful smirk. "Some would've said I loved myself with unwavering commitment."

I made a rude noise. "You are not egotistical."

"Your faith in me is heartening, but I haven't answered your question yet." His focus drifted away from my face. "It was an arranged marriage, entered into according to the customs of my people. Ceara and I did not love each other, though we achieved a kind of awkward friendship."

"Obviously, you had sex with her."

"Three times only. As soon as she became with child, Ceara told me she would not engage in carnal relations again, that she did not enjoy the act the way a wife should, and she deeply regretted her shortfall. I assured her she owed me no further...interactions. I would not force my attentions on her."

"You were celibate after that, weren't you? I mean, you're not the type to screw around on your wife, even if you didn't love her."

A ghost of a smile curved his lips. "You truly do understand me."

"Well, we are soul mates." I walked my fingers down his naked chest, inch by inch, ever nearer to his groin. "After your forging, you didn't exactly abstain anymore, did you?"

"You already know this. I've told you I…dallied a great deal."

"Until you slept with Skeiron's daughter, and he found out. Yeah, I know the story. Thanks to the crazy king and his nasty bargain, you were enslaved for a century."

Nevan bent to rub his lips across mine once, twice, three times, before he murmured against my lips, "You freed me, my love, and I will never stop showing you how grateful I am."

"You freed me too, honey." I glided my hand down the length of his growing erection, curling my fingers around its rigid girth. "Let me express my gratitude."

I captured his lower lip between my teeth, sucking it into my mouth, while I pumped my hand up and down the sleek flesh of his cock. He hissed in a breath, his back arching. While I released his lip slowly, I grasped the nape of his neck to pull him in for a kiss. He devoured me with deep, lush strokes of his tongue and groaned into my mouth as I milked his erection.

He broke the kiss and locked his hand around my wrist to halt my intimate massage. "You first."

"Mm, I want you to pop your cork first this time."

With a gentleness that seemed incongruous with the heated tension in his body, he lifted one of my hands to entwine our fingers and press my hand into the plush blanket. "In my entire existence, I have loved only one woman and I intend to prove it to you every single time I thrust into your sweet body. That is why your pleasure always comes first."

I undulated my hips, grazing his swollen shaft. "When you put it that way…"

He showered my throat with light kisses, working his way down my chest toward my belly, his hands sliding down my arms with aching slowness. Every cell in my body tingled with anticipation. My back bowed up as he kissed and licked his way down my belly, inching ever closer to the hairs at the apex of my thighs.

"Oh Nevan," I moaned and rocked my hips toward his waiting mouth. "I've never loved anyone but you, and I never will. But God, right now all I want is you inside me."

"Easy, love." I felt his lips tighten against my skin, a sure sign he was smirking. "I see I still must teach you patience."

"Some other time. Right now, just—" I lost my voice, my breath stolen by the sensation of his lips edging nearer to where I most needed them.

Nevan froze. "Bloody hell."

He spat the curse, hoisting himself up on his arms, his face wrenched into a scowl.

"Oh no," I said, shaking my head, "don't tell me—"

"The tribunal is summoning me."

"Can't you ignore them?"

He rolled to the side, his legs swinging off the bed to touch down on the floor. With his back to me, shoulders slumped forward, he let out the most frustrated sigh I'd ever heard. "They won't stop calling until I go to them."

I elevated myself on my elbows. "Please tell me they can't see what we were doing."

Nevan rose to his feet, the loincloth materializing around his hips. "They cannot see where I am or what I am doing."

"Thank heaven for small mercies." I swung my legs off the bed, but they dangled several inches above the floor. "I really don't want elemental perverts getting their rocks off by peeping on us."

"I do love your colorful language." Nevan's smile, though closed mouth, brightened his face and carved out cute little divots in his cheeks. He bent over to kiss my forehead. "Wait here if you like, or return to your home and I will find you there once the meeting is over."

"What do you think they want? Considering your wife turned up today..."

"You believe the tribunal wants to speak with me about her." He scratched his head. "Perhaps they do, I have no idea."

"Take me with you."

"Lindsey."

I tilted my head back to meet his gaze and raised my eyebrows. "Don't *Lindsey* me. If your formerly dead wife is involved, I should be there."

"The tribunal will not admit you into their chambers, and I will not abandon you in the woods." He knelt in front of me and clasped my hands in his. "I will come back to you as soon as the meeting is over. Trust me to handle whatever matters might arise."

How could I say no to that? I trusted him with all my heart and soul, but I also understood the power of his guilt. It had gotten him enslaved once before. Still, I had to trust he wouldn't make the same mistake again. "Okay. Go to your meeting and come find me after. Think I'll head home and see what time it is in the mortal realm, in case I'm late to work or something."

Time could pass differently here in the Unseen, though I'd experienced the phenomenon only once. On that occasion, three hours had elapsed while I thought it had been half an hour.

"Before I go," he said, "let's make certain the soul stone works."

"Good idea."

He grasped me around the waist and hoisted me off the bed onto my feet. My clothes materialized around me, wrinkle free and perfectly positioned. I did note my T-shirt had wound up pulled lower in the front to expose more of my cleavage. Ah, my Nevan. He just couldn't help himself.

I extricated the soul stone from my jeans pocket. "What do I do?"

"Approach the outer wall." He gestured toward the smooth-hewn rock behind him. "Then simply instruct the stone to open a doorway."

"Instruct it?" Rolling the stone in my palm, I trudged to the wall. Instruct the stone. Sure, I could do that. I raised my hand, palm up, the stone cradled there. "Open a doorway, little soul stone."

Nothing happened.

He grinned and chuckled at my attempt. "Not like that, darlin'. Use magic to command the stone."

"Terrific." I let my head fall back and gave a piteous moan. "Magic hates me. It'll never work when I want it to."

"On the contrary." Nevan strode up behind me, encircling my waist with his arms, dipping his mouth close to my ear. "Magic adores you, and like me, it cannot resist your desires."

"Mm." I couldn't think of anything coherent to say, not with him teasing my senses with every whisper of his breath on my ear.

His fingers fanned out over my belly, tugging my backside into his front side. "You tap into the magic with so little effort, without intending to. It bends to your will, shifts and reshapes itself to ensure your happiness. When I was enslaved to Skeiron, you gave me the power to disobey him. Time itself loses its way around you, as enchanted by you as I have always been."

I covered his hands with my own, relishing the feel of his muscular form molded to my willing flesh. "If this is your plan, it's got a flaw."

"What is that?" he asked, licking at my earlobe.

"If I have to get turned on in order to use my powers, I'll be screwed when you're not around to get me hot."

"You've got it backward, darlin'." He fitted his mouth over the hollow my throat for a wet kiss. "The screwing happens when I'm here."

He stepped away, robbing me of his heat and tempting muscles.

I closed my hand around the soul stone and focused all my mental capacity on one command. "Open sesame."

Blue magic glittered in the air before the wall, spinning in iridescent whorls. The rock blurred and rippled, then poof, a me-size hole appeared. Beyond the opening, I spied the woods that surrounded the mountain.

I tossed the soul stone in the air and caught it in my palm, quite pleased with myself. I'd tapped into the magic at will—and not out of desperation because I was dying from a slit throat. Not this time, anyway.

Scrutinizing the opening, I said, "I thought we were deeper inside the mountain, but we're only a foot in."

"Have you not yet learned to take very little at face value?" Nevan pointed at the doorway, and in a patient tone said, "You compressed the distance."

"I did?" Tilting my head to the side, I eyed the doorway. "Cool."

We walked outside hand in hand, and the doorway telescoped shut behind us. Nevan hauled me into his arms, zipping us to the boulder that marked the portal. Nevan waved a hand to open the doorway to the other side.

"I will return to you," he said, "that is a p—it is the truth."

He'd almost promised it, a big no-no here in the Unseen, far too close to a debt. Though he had no qualms about indebting himself to me, he knew the idea made me uncomfortable. Once, he'd sealed a debt to me on purpose—but only to give me leverage to undermine Skeiron's hold over him.

"I'll be waiting for you," I said.

"And worrying, no doubt."

"Yeah, probably." I hunched my shoulders, feeling sheepish all of a sudden. "I can't help it. Worrying is my thing."

Nevan kissed each of my hands in turn, then let go of them and stepped away from me. "All will be well, my sweet love. Trust me on this. Now, through the portal with you."

I turned and crossed the veil between the worlds. Just as the portal began to telescope shut, I glanced back.

Nevan winked at me and vanished.

The portal spiraled shut.

I was left with a hollow ache in my chest and the niggling sensation I'd overlooked a vital clue somewhere in the course of this day. Nevan would be careful. But if Ceara played the guilt card, would he call her bluff or fold?

Please stay strong, Nevan.

Chapter Six

I DISCOVERED IT WAS THREE A.M. IN THE MORTAL WORLD, PROBABLY thanks to the way my powers screwed with time in the Unseen, making it move slower. The phenomenon hadn't happened in weeks, but the stress of today must've triggered a recurrence.

Since I had no idea when Nevan might return, I changed into my nightie and curled up under the sheets of my very ordinary bed in my very ordinary apartment. My next-door neighbor snored like a rusty chainsaw, the noise vibrating through the walls. But it wasn't the snoring that had me tossing and turning, getting tangled in the sheets in a totally non-sexy way. Anxieties about Nevan, the tribunal, the kidnapped girl, and everything else about my bizarre life bounced around in my brain pinball-style.

For hours, I struggled to sleep. The best I could manage was a fitful doze.

After an oh-so-refreshing forty-five minutes of naptime, I downed a bowl of cereal and drove to work, shambling into the rock shop while stifling a yawn. Stan, my boss, squinted at me but made no comment on my state. My clothes were clean and fresh, though I felt nothing close to cleansed or freshened. My new, endued derringer nestled against my hip, tucked in its waistband holster and loaded with my spiffy endued ammo. Today, I'd opted for .357 rounds.

The morning dragged by like pine sap in winter. Despite cradling the soul stone in my hand every fifteen minutes, the reassuring sensation of Nevan's peaceful essence failed to reassure me. I hadn't thought to ask if the stone offered a real-time glimpse of his well-being, or if it was a one-time snapshot. The thing was designed to get me into his home, not to connect us across time and space. Or that's what I thought. He hadn't mentioned any other capabilities of the stone. Next time I saw him, I'd ask.

If I saw him.

Dammit, I would. The tribunal could be real asses, as far as I could tell, demanding an enormous amount of Nevan's time. He was king, for crying out loud. They should bow down to him, not the other way around.

Nevan would give them a good dressing-down, for sure.

I skipped lunch, ignoring Stan's insistence that I needed to eat or I'd pass out—and then I'd be no good as an employee. These days, I understood his gruffness covered up the fondness he had for me, which he was too macho to admit. I'd grown rather fond of him too. Watching the guy battle immortal sylphs had given me a new perspective on Stan Lagorio.

Just past two in the afternoon, Travis showed up to update me on Megan's condition.

"She's okay," he said, leaning one hip against the checkout counter across from me. "Physically, anyhow. The bruises are old and pretty minor. She's got no internal injuries, but the docs can't say how she got so severely dehydrated. And the poor kid won't say a word about the bruises, panics if anyone asks."

"Is the hospital outside the boundaries?"

He screwed up his mouth, fidgeting. "As far as I can tell, the hospital's safe."

"Thank goodness for that."

"She wants to talk to you."

I paused in sorting through a stack of receipts. "Me specifically?"

"Ain't that what I said? Kid says she wants to talk to Lindsey Astrid Porter." He eyed me sideways. "You know this Megan girl?"

"No, of course not."

"Well," Travis said, gesturing toward the shop's entrance, "let's find out what she knows."

"Right now? I'm in the middle of my shift."

"I'll tell Stan it's official police business."

"Oh great." I let my head fall back, staring up at the bare rafters below the corrugated metal ceiling. "Just what I need, my boss thinking I'm a suspect in a crime—again."

"Relax, I'll make sure he knows it's nothing like that."

He marched straight to the door to Stan's office and, without knocking, strode inside. His presumptuous actions irritated me, but my brain had no room for it. I was too consumed with thoughts of what happened to Megan and who had sent her to me, not to mention why.

Travis traipsed out of Stan's office. "All fixed up. Let's go."

I snagged my purse and followed him out the door.

We had reached his vehicle, a Ford Expedition emblazoned with the logo of the sheriff's department, when Travis's phone warbled. He held up a finger in a silent request for me to wait, as he answered the call. His features shifted into stoic cop mode.

I leaned my back against the vehicle and rested my head on its hard metal. The morning sun unfurled streamers of pink and orange across the blue sky, igniting a smattering of puffy little clouds.

Something flickered on Travis's face, something like surprise mixed with anxiety. He resumed cop mode, though, and walked away from me to continue the conversation out of my earshot.

A moment later, he strode back to me. "Megan's gone."

I jerked upright, slammed with a wave of cold. "How?"

"You tell me." He pinched the bridge of his nose, eyes crimped shut. "I had a deputy posted outside her room, and the windows inside don't open. Another deputy was posted in the parking lot, in clear view of those windows. Nobody saw or heard a damn thing."

My blood seemed to have iced over, chilling me from my skin down to bones.

Travis flung hand up and then let it fall slack at his side. "She disappeared into thin air."

"We both know what this means."

"But there ain't no water near the hospital."

"Are you sure?" I stepped up to him, my head craned back to look him in the eye. "I thought my brother was safe, but Skeiron found a hidden spring that let him sneak into the mortal world and abduct Ash. The man in black must've found a similar opening. Any natural water feature, no matter how small, can serve as a portal between the worlds."

"Dammit!" He punched his fist into the Expedition's hood. Wincing, he cradled his hand. "I fucked it up again, didn't I?"

"Not your fault."

He scowled at the small dent he'd left in the vehicle's hood. "Doesn't matter whose fault it is. The girl's gone."

Taken by an unknown enemy, for unknown reasons. Yet Megan had told me herself this was all connected to me. She resembled me. She was forced to deliver a message to me.

I could think of only one reason for someone to target me. They knew I was the Janusite.

And I knew of only one way someone could learn that fact.

One of my allies had betrayed me.

Chapter Seven

I HEADED INTO THE WOODS A FEW MINUTES LATER, DETERMINED TO FIND
Nevan or…I didn't know what. Take action. Stop waiting for another
bad guy to hunt me down. Travis had rushed off the to the hospital to
examine the scene of the crime. I had zero expectations he'd find concrete
evidence. The man in black covered his tracks too well.

My boots made little sound as I marched past the vortex. I had no idea
what I'd do once I crossed the veil into the Unseen. Wing it, that's what
I'd do.

The sounds of the woods faded into a hush so unearthly it stopped me. I
turned my head left and right, listening to the absence of noise. In the moments before Megan staggered out of the woods to deliver her message, I'd
perceived the same kind of hush.

I held still, expecting…something. The stench of ammonia, akin to cat
urine, drifted on the barest of breezes. I crinkled my nose, but then I remembered smelling the same odor the last time the woods had gone quiet,
and goose bumps prickled my arms.

A crack and a whoosh pierced the preternatural silence.

My body tensed. My senses heightened, amped up by the adrenaline
coursing through my veins.

Crackling. Crunching.

The noises originated further down the trail.

Slipping the derringer out of its holster, I held the gun muzzle down
and trotted in the direction of the sounds. The source came into view
when I rounded a curve in the path, emerging into the clearing beside the
waterfall.

Fire had engulfed a bush.

The flames licked upward, stretching ever higher as if striving to reach
the sky. Before I could consider the reason for the fire, a shape on the

ground snared my attention. The bush partially concealed the object, so I sidled past it for a clearer view.

The gun tumbled from my hand, thumping onto the ground.

A girl lay prone beside the bush, her eyes wide and unseeing. A few feet away, behind the bush, another girl lay sprawled on her back with lifeless eyes aimed at the heavens.

I stumbled backward a step. No need to check for a vital signs, the truth was evident.

The girls were dead.

My skin crawled as I took in the totality of their appearance. Both girls had golden brown hair, blue eyes, and similar features. Not just similar to each other, but comparable to my hair and eyes and face.

Someone had murdered two young women who looked like me.

"Please, no."

A female voice whimpered the phrase from behind me.

I snagged my gun from the ground and whirled around.

A black-robed figure clutched a young woman, one arm around her waist and one pale, bony hand bolted around her throat.

Megan Kozlow whimpered again. "Please help me."

The man in black flicked one finger in my direction.

"There ye are, love," he said in a good approximation of Nevan's voice and accent, but without the indefinable element that made Nevan...Nevan. "I've been searching for ye."

I gripped my gun tighter. "If you're trying to convince me you are Nevan, you're doing a horrible job of it. Nevan is broad and muscular. You're skin and bones."

"A glamour, naturally."

His imitation of Nevan's voice came so close to the real thing that a weight of doubt settled in my gut. This was not Nevan. The creature before me must have no idea I could sense Nevan. I'd detected his approach right before Megan found me earlier, but I had not sensed Nevan this time. Yet the robed being wanted me to believe he was my lover.

Why?

He chuckled, nearly the way Nevan might, but with a thread of menace in the sound. "You've always worried you can't trust me, that I might be entrapped by another bargain. Now, you wonder if I'll choose Ceara instead of you."

Good guesses. He must've sent Ceara, and it didn't take a genius to figure out her rebirth would put stress on both me and Nevan. His assumption it weakened our relationship was dead wrong. This being had no clue about the depth of the connection Nevan and I shared.

Tears streamed down Megan's cheeks. She sniffled, whimpering again. "Don't punish me, please."

Bastard. He had to pay.

"What do you want?" I asked.

"To whittle away at your soul until nothing remains but fear and regret."

I hooked my finger over the derringer's trigger, poised to fire. "What's with the girls who look like me?"

He caressed Megan's neck with one finger, its sharp black nail grazing her skin. "Offerings to you, sweetness. To prove my devotion."

Megan sobbed.

I gritted my teeth but then forced myself to relax as much as possible under the circumstances. Getting this bastard to let the girl go had to be my priority.

"Listen," I said, edging a little closer, "you don't need another offering. I believe you're devoted to me. Let the girl go. You have me, you don't need her anymore."

"But you need the reminder."

He slashed his fingernail across Megan's neck, slitting her throat, and tossed her body to the ground. She gurgled and twitched.

I raced toward her.

And crashed into an invisible barrier.

Careening backward, I lost my grip on the derringer. It popped out of my hand and hit the ground with a thump.

I caught my balance, too late.

The robed being kicked Megan's body to flip her onto her back. Her eyes stared into eternity, her gaze as dead as her body.

I shut my eyes. Three girls dead because of me.

That was the point. This being wanted me to feel the guilt of their murders, as if I held some measure of culpability.

No, this was not my doing. It was all him.

And he would pay.

My trigger finger itched to fire an endued round straight into the robed bastard's head. But he'd erected a ward between the two of us, and I doubted even an endued bullet could penetrate it.

One way to find out.

I swung the gun up and pulled the trigger.

The shot boomed, reverberating off the trees and the sandstone cliff of the falls, but the .357 round ricocheted off the ward. It struck a tree, splintering bark off the trunk.

The robed being laughed.

Blood pounded in my ears. My body quivered with the rage building inside me, and I unleashed a guttural roar.

"What the hell do you want?" I demanded. "Murdering girls? For what? I know you're not Nevan. Who the fuck are you?"

"The one you love," he said. The Irish accent was gone, and his voice had lost the depth and vigor instilled in his imitation of Nevan. His voice took on a hoarse and brittle quality. "These three died the way you should have. Only when you've learned the lesson will you be ready for the truth."

His robes dragged on the ground as he crept toward the invisible wall between us. A single, sinuous finger stuck out of the robe's long sleeve to point at me.

"You," the being said, his voice disconcertingly calm and even, "are the key to everything. I feel no danger in telling you this because you cannot stop what is to come. When you realize the futility of fighting, you will join me."

The ward tumbled down with a flash of white energy.

I'd gone numb all over, from my skin down to my soul. "Who are you?"

"One who has waited eons for retribution." He raised his arm, stretching out his finger to touch my chin, sending a cold charge into me. "The girls, what I did to them. It was all for you, to prepare the way. Together, we will change the worlds."

The frigid touch of his finger shot a hard shudder through my body. I staggered backward. Even with shock muddling my thoughts, I latched onto a memory.

"Ceara called you a sorcerer," I said. "You're the one working with her."

"I am a sorcerer of sorts." He lowered his arm. "But you know nothing of my plans or intentions. Only when you enter the fold will I reveal my secrets to you."

"Never going to happen." I noticed a dark shape on the ground and marshaled enough wherewithal to grab the derringer and aim it at the sorcerer's head, smack between his eyes. "I won't let you hurt anyone else."

I fired the second, and last, round.

The bullet bounced off his forehead.

A personal ward around his body? *Shit.*

"You can't stop me," he said, and leaned forward. The hood still concealed his face, the sun too low in the sky to penetrate the shadows. "Unless you nourish your power and achieve the full potential of the Janusite. Then, you and will be equals."

"And then I will destroy you."

"No." He straightened, and his voice took on the bright lilt of half-suppressed laughter. "And then you will gladly join me."

"You're insane."

"If I am, you made me this way." He backed up to the edge of the clearing. "You don't belong in either world, Lindsey, and you never will. Nevan won't save you this time, because he won't choose you. Accept your fate or we will consume your power and your soul."

The sorcerer vanished.

I stood there, too numb to think or move, overwhelmed by the sensation nothing around me was real.

A raven squawked overhead and swooped down to land in front of me.

"Brennus?" I said. My solitary thought was that I'd imagined the bird. I still suffered the unsettling perception of unreality.

The raven rippled and shimmered, enlarging into a manlike outline. The shape resolved into a mountainous being, packed with muscles bigger than Nevan's and ebony skin tinted with a blue sheen.

Brennus fixed his coal-dark eyes on me. "My lady."

His voice was deep and resonant, and it always gave me the willies. He always gave me the willies. He'd started calling me "my lady" after Nevan became king, though no one else in the universe called me that.

The raven-man tilted his head in birdlike jerks. "You are unwell."

"No, I'm—" *Totally freaked out.* Willing myself to get a grip, I took a long breath and shook my entire body, like a dog after a bath. "I'm okay. What are you doing here?"

"I am guardian of the falls." He glanced at Megan's body, then nodded past my shoulder. "A shockwave in the magical fabric drew me here."

"A what?" I scuffled in a half circle, until I realized what he'd seen. The two bodies next to the bush. The flames had died out, but the branches smoldered.

"Who has done this?" Brennus asked.

"He calls himself a sorcerer." I swallowed, but my throat remained tight and dry. "Can the vortex resurrect them? We should find Tris and—"

"No, my lady." Brennus gave a single, sad shake of his head. "The magic that caused their deaths is poison. It cannot be reversed."

"How do you know? We have to try."

"I can taste the poison in it."

Though I had no reason to doubt his word, I couldn't shake the realization I'd had earlier. One of my allies had betrayed me. Was the traitor Brennus?

"You have powerful magics," he said. "If you try, you may taste the vile energy that has suffused their flesh."

When I'd asked Tris to heal Megan, he'd told me he could taste the dark magics in her. His words rang in my mind, harsh and final. *Ain't no coming back from this kinda sickness.*

I holstered the derringer and wrapped my arms around myself. "Do you know where Nevan is?"

"With the tribunal."

"Still?" I scrubbed my arms, uneasy at the thought of asking. "Could you check on him?"

Brennus blinked out, then blinked back a second later.

"I do not know," he said, "where the king is. I cannot detect him, but if he is with the tribunal that would be the case."

Dammit. I needed to talk to Nevan.

"It's okay," I said, waving a hand at Brennus. "You can leave. I'm fine. But if you see Nevan, tell him I'll be waiting for him at work or at my apartment."

His gaze flicked to the bodies and back to me, a question on his forbidding face.

"Don't worry," I said, "I'll call the sheriff and make sure these poor girls are taken care of."

The shapeshifter relaxed a bit, as if he'd been anxious about the fate of the deceased women.

Despite the fact he made me uneasy, thanks to our unfortunate past history, I'd come to realize of late that he had a softer side. His insistence on calling me "my lady" and his voluntary commitment to serving Nevan, those spoke to his innate honor. But his concern for the murdered girls told me he had compassion too.

"We'll find their families," I assured him, "and make sure they get home."

He didn't move, but glanced at the bodies again.

"Tell you what," I said, "why don't you stay here to watch over the bodies until the sheriff gets here. That way, nobody will stumble onto them by accident."

Brennus nodded once. "As you wish, my lady."

It continued to baffle me how a shapeshifting raven-man could project the aura of a medieval knight.

With a guard in place to protect the scene, I trudged back to the shop. Along the way, I called Travis to report the bodies in the woods.

How I made it through the rest of the day, I had no idea. Travis came and went without talking to me. An ambulance came and went, carrying away the remains of the young women who'd died because they resembled me. Images of the dead girls plagued me, and in between, worry for Nevan gnawed at my heart. Like a zombie, I ground through the day without any consciousness of what I was doing, performing tasks by rote until Stan told me he'd close up and I should go home.

I arrived at my apartment as the sun sank below the horizon—loosing fiery tendrils of pink, purple, and gold across the heavens—and made my way to my second-floor apartment.

A sorcerer whose name started with N claimed Nevan wouldn't choose me when some kind of battle began. The same anonymous sorcerer expected me to trust him with my powers after he murdered three young women who happened to look like me. He claimed I'd willingly join forces with him.

Yeah, right. I was *that* gullible.

Inside my apartment, I sank onto the sofa, letting my head fall back against the thick cushions. The air conditioning hummed in the background. The lamp on the endtable bathed the sofa and me in warm, pinkish light. The hum and the soothing glow lulled me into a dreamless sleep, and when I woke, for a minute I couldn't remember where I was. Oh right, my apartment. Alone.

Where was Nevan?

Sitting up, I yawned and rolled my head left and right to iron out the kinks in my neck. The clock on the wall read 11:03. I'd slept for about three hours. And still no Nevan? He'd said he'd find me right after his three a.m. meeting with the tribunal. An entire day had gone by without a hint of him anywhere around.

The sorcerer must've known Nevan would be detained, and he would be free to impersonate my lover in his attempt to freak me out. Much as I loathed admitting it, the sorcerer's tactics had worked. I was balanced on the head of a pin, teetering on the verge of tumbling off into an abyss of fear and doubt.

Stay strong, don't give him what he wants.

I pulled the soul stone out of my pocket, turning it over and over between my thumb and forefinger. Energy zinged over my skin, faint yet distinctive. It was the unmistakable essence of Nevan. Unfortunately, the bit of his soul infused into the stone gave me no clue to his whereabouts or his well-being, so I stuffed it back into my jeans pocket.

The hairs on my arms and the back of my neck lifted, as awareness sizzled over my skin. *Nevan.* I jumped to my feet in the instant he poofed into the room right in front of me, with no more than a couple inches separating our bodies. His heat radiated over my skin, and the tension inside me unwound at the sight of him. I threw my arms around his neck and hugged him tight.

"Where have you been?" I asked, unwilling to relinquish my hold yet. "I was afraid something went wrong at your meeting."

"I am unharmed."

The weariness in his voice made me pull back enough to see his face, though I kept my arms around his neck. His hair looked messy, tangled. Dark circles bruised the skin under his eyes, which themselves seemed duller, more like the slow swirl of cream in a coffee cup than the blazing whirlpool of his supernatural irises.

I cupped his face in my hands. "You may be uninjured, but you're not okay."

The only other time I'd witnessed him appearing so exhausted had been right after Skeiron almost killed him. Then, a gaping sword wound in his chest had bled the life out of him. Tonight, I had no explanation for his state of utter exhaustion.

But I felt it. Inside me. A cold undercurrent trickling through the radiant heat of his body into my flesh, my heart, my soul.

Nevan shut his eyes, leaning into my touch, and exhaled a long sigh. "I'm in need of sleep, love. That's all."

"We can go back to your place."

He cracked his lids open and gave a weak shake of his head. "It will have to be here. No energy left for…traveling."

No energy? Nevan? He was a living nuclear reactor, pumping out a life force more vital and alive than anyone I'd ever known. Now he couldn't zip back to the Unseen?

I clasped his hand and ushered him into the bedroom, pulling back the covers when we reached the bed. He collapsed onto the mattress, and it bounced under his sudden weight. His eyes slid shut. His breathing grew shallower.

He was asleep. Just like that.

This was bad. Very bad.

Without bothering to undress, I crawled into bed with him and tucked my body close against his, with my back against his front. Though he remained asleep, he unconsciously slipped an arm around my waist. His breaths fluttered my hair, tickling my ear. I drew the covers up over us, disturbed by a deep, though nebulous, unease. Twice he had gone off to meet the tribunal and not returned for an unnaturally long time. His long absence when he retrieved my endued gun and ammo seemed explained, but now I had to wonder. This time, he'd been MIA for twenty hours, his longest absence yet.

I shouldn't have slept, not with a maelstrom of worries whipping around in my brain. But the warmth and solidity of his body cocooning mine soothed me into slumber. I dreamed of a dark, faceless figure haunting the woods, snatching away innocent girls no matter how hard I tried to stop it. The girls were whisked away into the abyssal blackness of the forest, their tortured screams echoing after them. The sorcerer's demonic voice rasped in my ear.

Accept your fate or we will consume your power and your soul.

Coming awake with a jerk, my heart racing, I held still until I felt sure no one had sneaked into the room. Nevan hadn't moved even a millimeter. The burnished glow of sunrise filtered through the lacy curtains that hung closed over the window. I slipped out of Nevan's arms, out of the bed, and he never stirred. His face seemed peaceful in sleep, no longer shadowed by dark circles and fatigue.

I brushed a wisp of hair from his eyes, then bent to feather a kiss over his forehead. I couldn't lose him. I wouldn't allow it.

Megan had said forces were allying against me. The sorcerer had said "we." Did he mean Ceara was on his side? Or did he have more evil masterminds as his allies?

No matter who rallied against us, Nevan and I would fight them together.

He won't choose you.

Screw what a damn anonymous sorcerer claimed. Nevan would always choose me, like I would always choose him. We'd been through too much together to let anyone jam a wedge between us. They'd separate us only one way—by prying my dead body away from his.

Realization shivered through me, warm instead of frigid, exciting rather than unsettling. I knew what I wanted. What I'd always wanted. What I'd been afraid of because my last serious relationship ended so horribly. No more would I let fears rooted in the past taint my relationship with Nevan.

I sprinted out of the apartment, set on a mission.

I LAY ON THE BED, ON MY BACK, FULLY CLOTHED AND WITH MY TOES TAP-ping a drum tattoo in the air while I waited for Nevan to wake up. Given his exhaustion last night, I hadn't wanted to disturb his sleep. But I needed to know he was okay and to talk to him about my encounter with the sorcerer, as well as the murdered girls.

And to share my news with him. Maybe my decision should've seemed unimportant in light of recent events, but instead it seemed even more im-portant than ever. With imminent death once again looming, I needed him to understand the depth of my commitment to him.

Sighing, I drummed my fingers on my belly.

"Impatient as always," Nevan murmured, snaking an arm over my waist, beneath my hands. He wriggled closer and nuzzled my neck. "What vexes you this morning?"

"Are you serious? What vexes me?" I flipped onto my side to face him. "You disappear for twenty hours, then you come back looking like a vampire sucked the life out of you and literally fall into bed—but not to ravish me, to lapse into a coma."

He caressed my cheek with his fingertips, a gentle smile on his lips. "I apologize, Lindsey, I had no intention of causing you distress. But you're mistaken, I could not have been away for such an extended time. It was only a few hours at most."

"Like hell it was. I can tell time, Nevan." I studied his face, hunting for a clue to whatever was going on with him. "Maybe you're the one having trouble counting the hours."

He pushed up onto one straight arm, frowning. "Time can move differ-ently in the Unseen."

"Only when funky magic interferes with it. You told me that." I sat up too and fixed my attention on him, willing him to recognize the truth. "Why would your magic be funky? I've only noticed time passing differently over there when I'm the one crossing the veil."

"Perhaps your magic…" He scratched his head, his features cinched up in confusion.

"You can't seriously be claiming my Janusite magic traveled all the way from here into the Unseen to screw up time for you."

"I've no idea what caused it."

I ran a hand over his forehead, trying to smooth out the lines. "We'll figure it out together."

He relaxed a bit, nodding.

"But first," I said, skimming my fingertips over his lips, "I need to tell you what happened while you were gone."

I relayed the entire sequence of events, from Lilia's disappearance from the hospital to the sorcerer's final words to me. Nevan listened without comment, without expression save for the lines etching into his forehead once again.

"What do you think?" I asked.

"I don't know." His mouth twisted into a frown, then relaxed as he pressed his lips to mine. "We will figure this out together as well. I should speak with Brennus. Perhaps he and I can—"

"You are not leaving me again, not after the coma incident."

He fell silent, his fingers absently tracing the curve of my collarbone.

I debated whether to tell him my good news, but if I'd learned one thing since meeting him, it was that I shouldn't waste any opportunity for happiness. Besides, solving our problems required plenty of thought and plenty of dangerous endeavors, no doubt.

"We could both use a bit of good news," I said. "Don't you think? I mean, before we traipse off to get poisoned by death magic or whatever."

"You have happy news to share, I gather."

Hopping off the bed to stand beside it, I straightened my clothes. "I have a surprise for you."

His dark brows hiked up, as did the corners of his mouth. "What is it?"

"Me."

"You?" He slid off the bed with feline grace, rising up before me, taking my upper arms in his muscular hands. "I already have ye, darlin'."

"True," I said, skating my palms up his chest. "But not the way you really want."

His eyes narrowed.

I swept my hands over his pecs, drawing invisible circles on his flesh, delighting in the firmness of his muscles contrasted with the silky smoothness of his skin. "I want to move in with you. I've already told my landlord he should look for a new tenant and I started packing—"

Nevan sealed my lips with two fingers. He didn't blink, but his lips seemed to tremble the tiniest bit. "Did you say…"

"I'm moving in with you."

He scooped me up and twirled us both around and around, whooping and laughing. I couldn't keep from giggling and kicking my feet out, letting them fly through the air as the floor receded from us. Nevan had levitated us halfway to the ceiling before he ceased spinning and just grinned at me, his face lit up with pure joy. He was stunning this way, glowing from within, from a wonderful melee of emotions. The same joy rushed through me as well, and I peppered his face with kisses between my giggles.

My boots dangled several feet above the floor.

I glanced down, at last catching my breath. "You can come in for a landing anytime now."

"Why?" He claimed my mouth with his own, thrusting his tongue deep, pausing only to say, "Shall we head for a cloud?"

My body flashed back to a full-sensory memory of the one and only time he'd whisked me away to a cloud, to make love to me in the stratosphere. No experience on earth could compare with Nevan's aerial prowess.

I tore my lips from his but had to shove a hand between our mouths to keep him from diving in once more—and to keep myself from letting him. "On the floor, please. I'm still not used to this flying stuff."

In the blink of an eye, we went from floating in midair to lying on the floor with me flat on my back and him on top. And we were naked.

"Nevan," I chastised halfheartedly, "this isn't what I meant."

"You should be more specific in your requests."

Oh yeah, I should've learned that lesson by now. "Wouldn't you rather get me moved into your place first?"

We winked out and winked back in, both of us on our feet and fully clothed. Well, he was as clothed as he ever got, the loincloth in position around his hips.

Nevan flicked his wrist, gave a decisive nod, and said, "There. You are moved in."

"Huh?" I glanced around and realized my belongings had vanished. Shaking my head, I tried to suppress a smile, but failed. "Did you poof my stuff into your underground lair?"

"I did."

"Thank you." I hooked my arms around his waist, my chin on his chest, and gazed up at him with unabashed adoration. "You sure are convenient to have around."

"Convenient?" Amusement glittered in his eyes, like golden stars plucked from the sky. "Perhaps I should demonstrate precisely how *convenient* sharing a home with me will be."

"Oh yes, please do." I snuggled into him, inhaling his unique and delicious scent.

"We should discuss—"

"After." I wriggled my hips and raked my tongue across the scar over his heart, earning a sharp intake of breath from him. "Take me home and make love to me."

He whisked us to the ledge beside the waterfall, launched us through the cascade, and before I had time to gasp at the sudden onslaught of cold water, he threw open the portal and flew through it. We emerged into the Unseen realm dry—well, I was dry on the outside. Another part of me had grown very wet from the way he spirited me away. So masculine. So authoritative. So damn bossy and yet totally hot.

After a brief few seconds of adjustment, he transported us straight into our home. The underground lair glowed with a mellow light from the mysterious source that emanated from everywhere and nowhere. The air, attuned to my temperature, caressed my suddenly naked skin. He'd popped us in on the bed, me on my back and him on top. The weight of him pressed me into the fur blanket. His rigid shaft stretched across my belly, pinned there by our joined bodies.

"It's been days," he rumbled against my lips, "since I felt your heat around me."

"Promise me one thing." I spread my legs, bending my knees to bracket him. "If the damn tribunal summons you, ignore it."

"Fuck the tribunal."

I'd never heard him use the F-word before. Oddly, hearing him say it now gave me a warm, glowy feeling. He meant it.

Nevan collected my hands, securing them above my head with one of his hands around my wrists. His other hand drifted down my side, skimming my flesh, making my pulse accelerate and my breaths quicken. He slid his hand between our bodies, into the cleft where I was drenched and aching for him. Strong, sure fingers worked my nub and rubbed my folds until I arched into him and gasped from the sheer bliss of his touch.

I struggled to free my hands, desperate to grope him everywhere I could reach, but he held my wrists fast. "Please, Nevan, please."

"Shouldn't speak that word here."

"Don't care, I want you inside me." When he mercilessly ground his thumb into my nub, a sweet arc of pleasure shot through me and I writhed beneath him. It felt so good, but I still hadn't reached the climax, though I strained to get there, driven ever nearer little by little while his fingers tortured me. "Oh God, Nevan, I'll do anything you want if you take me *now.*"

He chuckled, low and husky. "I need no magic to entice you to do anything I want."

It was true, and maybe I should've been embarrassed by that fact, but with his body on top of mine I couldn't feel anything but so damn good.

"Thunder and hail," he cursed, his voice an erotic rasp, "you are so wet for me."

"Always," I moaned. "Hurry it up, I—"

My voice choked off on a cry of pleasure when he surged downward and latched his mouth onto my nub, lapping at it and scraping his teeth over the tender flesh. My release exploded through me, scorching me from the inside out with a stunning ecstasy.

Nevan raised his head to gaze at me over my mound. His lips tightened in a smile of pure masculine satisfaction, with a hefty dose of carnal hunger. Those dazzling irises flared in bright, molten shades of red, purple, and bronze. The colors of his passion.

He dragged his tongue across his glistening lips, sampling my wet-ness.

Speechless, my sex throbbing with a new and far more intense need, I could nothing except gaze, enraptured, at the man I loved.

Rising onto his knees, he towered above me with his erection waving in the air.

A drop of moisture beaded on the rosy tip. Any inhibitions I might've had left crumbled away at the sight of his gloriously nude body. I pushed up into a sitting position, my face in front of his cock, and daubed the liquid from its tip with my tongue.

He hissed in a breath, his chest heaving.

I fell back onto the bed and hit him with my sauciest grin. "You're right. Without any magical compulsion, I will do anything to satisfy you."

Letting out a long groan that resonated in his chest, he dropped onto all fours, his hands at either side of my shoulders, one knee between my thighs. He urged my legs wider apart and filled me in one powerful thrust. The sensation of his hard shaft inside me, stretching my body, never failed to thrill me. Goose bumps tingled over my skin, activating every fine hair. I craved him with a lust like none I'd ever known before Nevan—and like I'd never experience with any other man. I recognized this fact without an ounce of fear or doubt. I belonged to him, and he belonged to me.

Nevan began to move inside me, gliding in and out, his rhythm slow and steady, stoking the fire in me with deliberate tenderness. He let his elbows buckle, his head lowering until his lips touched my forehead. I grasped his upper arms and held on tight for the ride, rocking my hips into his gentle strokes, moaning and gasping. He shifted position, bowing his back to bring our mouths into alignment, and then he crushed his lips to mine, plunging his tongue deep and demanding my response. I wrapped my legs around him, flung my arms around his shoulders and clung to him, answered his kiss with frenzied lashes of my tongue, starved for the flavor of him.

The connection between us, the bond engendered by love and passion and commitment, flared inside me, bright and warm and unquenchable. Pleasure and magic swirled together, coalesced into a power beyond comprehension, rising within me and expanding to suffuse my entire being and spread into Nevan. His eyes flew wide, his focus snapping to me, but his movements stayed smooth and fluid, his shaft gliding out and diving back inside me as if our bodies had merged. A wave of glittering magic, ice blue and heartbreak-ingly beautiful, flowed out of me to envelop us both. It tingled through our bodies, enhancing the physical pleasure, infusing it with a depth derived from more than lust, from a bond no one and nothing could sever.

Nevan's pace quickened, his thrusts harder and deeper. An expression of shocked joy overtook his features, fueled by the spectacular blue magic that shimmered all around us.

Tears streamed down my cheeks, tears of completeness and a kind of happiness I'd never dreamed possible. Oh God, this connection, it was... eternal.

I buried my face in his neck, desperate noises bursting from my lips. A new excitement, sexual and emotional, propelled me through the atmosphere and rocketed me higher and higher toward the weightless bliss of release. Nevan's thrusts grew frantic, his grunts and groans as desperate as my noises. Higher. Higher. Couldn't breathe, couldn't move except to cling to him.

My orgasm convulsed through me and hurled me into outer space, spinning, flying, screaming from the earth-shattering ecstasy. Nevan froze for a heartbeat, his breaths ragged and hoarse, then his release pulsated inside me. He threw his head back and roared his pleasure, as I floated back down to earth.

The glittering magic fizzled out, tiny blue sparks the only remnant. They faded too, leaving no sign of the incredible event.

Nevan collapsed beside me, drawing me in to tuck me close against his sweat-slicked body. I enjoyed the afterglow for a moment, while my heartbeat and my breathing returned to normal. Sex with Nevan was like a wickedly naughty ride in an adults-only theme park, and I didn't even have to worry about birth control. The first time we'd made love, he'd assured me he couldn't get me pregnant without a conscious effort to make it happen.

With my power of speech restored, I shimmied away from him far enough to see his face. "Did you see that? Did you feel it?"

"Yes." He touched my face with his fingertips, his eyes shining with... tears. "I saw and felt it."

"What was that?"

"Lindsey, my love, you know what it was." He kissed the tip of my nose. "That was your magic."

Nevan hadn't witnessed the only other time I'd tapped into my Janusite powers on purpose. When Brennus had abducted me and was about to cut out my heart, I'd summoned the same kind of glittering blue energy. "Yeah, I know it was me doing it. But I don't understand why it happened. I wasn't trying to use magic."

"You agreed to share a home with me, to share a life with me. I know you wrestled with the decision for weeks." He took my hand and laid it over his heart. "Perhaps the heightened emotions of finally reaching a decision activated your powers."

"How did it feel to you? I mean, did I hurt you?"

Shaking his head, he laughed. "No, darlin', I felt nothing close to pain. Only the ecstasy of worshiping you, intensified by whatever unconscious magic you employed. It was as if our souls had merged, for a few moments."

"That's what I felt too. But I have no control over my powers, don't understand them at all, so I want to make sure you don't feel any side effects."

He pulled me snug against him, roving his hands up and down my back. "I have noticed one aftereffect. I feel energized, fully free of whatever had robbed me of energy last night."

Energized? Free? Wow, I'd done that. And I had no clue how.

I wiggled to get a small distance between us while staying on my side. "We need to talk about your prolonged absences."

"I was with the tribunal."

"For twenty hours?"

He shrugged one shoulder. "I must have been."

"You're not sure?" I sat up, braced with one arm, my palm flat on the bed. "Tell me everything you remember about visiting the tribunal last night."

Nevan rolled onto his back, one arm bent above his head, and frowned as he struggled to recall the event. "I remember taking you to the portal. I waited until you had crossed the veil, then I went to the tribunal's chambers and I was admitted inside. They had many complaints. I listened to their irritating demands for as long as I could stand—a length of seconds that could likely have been counted on one hand—and then I informed them I am king. They may bring their grievances to me, but I will do as I see fit, not as they desire."

"What happened next?"

"I—" He gazed at the ceiling, his face blank, for long enough I began to wonder if he'd gone catatonic. At last, he swiveled his head toward me and blinked slowly. "I've no idea. At that precise point, things grow…hazy. The next thing I recall is appearing in your apartment, feeling drained and confused."

"Hazy? Drained? That's not good, Nevan."

"No, it is not."

I folded my legs under me, hands on my thighs. "Have you, um, seen Ceara again?"

He shook his head. "Not that I recall."

Not that he recalled. Hardly comforting. "We need to find out what happened during your missing time incidents."

"You speak as if it's occurred more than once."

"It has." I shifted to sit cross-legged, turned to the side so I could look at his face. "Two days ago, when you moved me to my apartment while I was asleep, you were gone until afternoon, but you said you only met with the tribunal. Then you left for hours when you supposedly visited the fae witch and nothing else. Then there's the last time." I bit down on my lower lip, remembering the entire day of waiting, worrying, not knowing. "You were gone for twenty hours and you don't know why. I count three incidents, but the last one was the worst by far. Your missing time has to be related to the sorcerer."

Not because he is the sorcerer, I assured myself.

Unless somebody bamboozled him into a bargain that gave them total control over him.

My instincts told me that wasn't the case, and I'd learned to trust my intuition.

Nevan swung his legs off the bed, rising, now seated on the mattress's edge, with his back to me. "I had not realized…You are right, Lindsey. I have no explanation for why each of those absences took so long. However, I was not exhausted after the first two."

"Something was different this time." I slid to the bed's edge and let my feet dangle off it. Taking Nevan's hand, I folded both of mine around it. "We need to retrace your steps. Start with the fae witch and work forward from there. Are you sure the witch didn't curse you or whatever?"

"I cannot believe Ennea would do anything of the sort."

"One way to find out." I jumped off the bed. "Let's go interrogate the witch."

"Ah…" Nevan rubbed the back of his neck, wincing, avoiding my gaze. "I'm not certain you want to meet her."

"Why?" Hands on hips, I waited for him to answer. When he didn't, but simply kept grimacing and looking everywhere but at me, I cleared my throat in the most obvious way. "Nevan."

"She is Tris's sister." He made a face, somewhere between annoyance and embarrassment. "The one I, ah…became involved with."

"Oh, I get it. This Ennea chick is the sister you slept with, and when Tris found out, he stopped talking to you."

"Yes."

I marched up to Nevan, grasped his chin, and angled his face up so he had no choice but to meet my gaze. "Do you really think I'm so sensitive I can't handle meeting one of your ex-lovers? Hell, I just met your dead wife who isn't dead and wants you back. I think I'll survive an introduction to Tris's sister."

He shut his eyes, his shoulders slumping. "Perhaps it's I who cannot handle you meeting another of my former lovers."

"You're embarrassed?"

One massive shoulder hunched in a half shrug, and still he would not look at me. "I've endeavored to keep my past away from our present. Whatever came before you matters not one bit. However, if you're confronted with the reality of my previous behavior…"

Now I got it, and I was mildly offended that he thought I might disapprove. But then I realized with a heady rush why he worried about it. He loved me so much he couldn't stand to risk alienating me with a parade of his ex-bedmates. When we first met, I had been jealous of the women he kissed in the commission of his duty, hunting for the Janusite. A lot had changed since then—me, in particular.

I knelt before him, pushing between his thighs to fold my arms around his waist and hug him close. His face was still averted, but I felt his body stirring from my proximity, the way my body inevitably awakened when he pulled me close.

"Listen," I said in a gentle voice, "I'm not jealous, not anymore. What we have is real and powerful and forever. I don't care how many women from your past flounce up to throw me haughty looks and announce you belong to them. I know the truth."

His eyes moved only his eyes to consider me.

"You're mine," I said, sliding my arms up to encircle his neck. "Nobody's taking you away from me because you want me and only me, just like I want you and only you. There's no need for jealousy or insecurity. And that goes for you too, my scorching-hot sylph king. Got it?"

At last, he turned his face to me and his expression softened. "Yes, I've got it."

He smirked when he spoke the last two words. His arms came around me, crushing me to him as he mashed his mouth to mine, thrusting his tongue inside to tease the roof of my mouth. I opened to him fully, surrendering to the demands of his lips and tongue, loving every second of the kiss.

Before I knew what had happened, we were on our feet and no longer kissing.

"Let's talk with Ennea," he said, "and try to discover what occurred during my missing hours. It may well hold clues to the sorcerer's identity."

With my arms around his neck and his around my waist, I held on for the journey ahead.

And for whatever might come next.

Chapter Eight

Inside the gloomily lit cavern, the flames from several oil lanterns flittered their light across the coarse rock walls and floor, but my eyes needed time to adjust to the new environment. The space housed tables of various sizes, and on each table sat sundry tools and bowls that looked straight out of a movie about witches, complete with a small cauldron bubbling and steaming atop the nearest table.

Behind the waist-high table, a young woman bent over the cauldron with a slight smile on her lips, her gaze directed at the cauldron's contents. She stirred the boiling liquid with a large ladle as she hummed a lovely yet eerie tune. Though she appeared young, I'd learned better over the past weeks than to assume she was young. Her red hair and creamy, freckled face mirrored her brother's coloring, but she had an elven cuteness to her that the other leprechaun lacked.

Nevan led me toward the table and the woman.

"Ennea," he said, inclining his head in greeting.

The witch glanced up at him and a knowing smile spread across her face, making her eyes glint with what I could describe only as amused knowledge. Ennea set her ladle down on the wooden tabletop, placed her hands on the surface, and swept her gaze from Nevan to me and back again. Her brows hopped up and down twice.

"Well, lookie here," she said in an accent much like her brother's, somewhere between Chicago and the Bronx. "It's the king of the sylphs, gracing a lowly witch with his presence."

Her tone conveyed teasing rather than disdain. This woman had slept with Nevan, who knew how many times, and I was getting the impression she still held a certain fondness for him. It seemed more like friendly familiarity than sexual desire or romantic attachment.

Ennea turned her sly gaze on me again. "And you must be the king's mortal plaything."

I bristled at the mention of my unwanted moniker. Tried not to, but I couldn't help it. "My name is Lindsey."

"Easy, girl." The fae witch grinned. "I like anybody who ticks off the sylph tribunal, seeing as they're a bunch of stick-up-the-ass know-it-alls. The fae council isn't much better. Why do you think I live in a cave? To get away from all those arrogant cheese-heads who think the universe revolves around their egos."

I flashed a grin at Nevan. "I like her."

He rolled his eyes and tilted his head back in a melodramatic gesture of resignation. "Spare me from female bonding."

Ennea tapped her long, black nails on the tabletop. "You guys didn't come here to gab about the elitist asses who run the worlds. What's up?"

"We need your help," Nevan said, his hand tightening around mine. "I seem to have, ah…a sort of problem with, uh…"

Oh for heaven's sake. We'd never get anywhere if he kept hemming and hawing.

I barged right into the conversation. "Nevan has missing time. He was gone for twenty hours, but he only remembers coming here, then coming home to me, and a little while later going to meet the tribunal. We think something happened to him during or right after the tribunal meeting, because his memory goes hazy at that point. He came home totally exhausted."

Ennea's brows knit together over her button nose. The humor vacated her features. "That is a conundrum."

"Can you help us find out what happened to him?" I asked. "Unless, of course, you're the one who did it to him. Are you?"

She folded her arms over her chest and eyed me with appreciative respect. "Nevan's got himself a feisty one, huh? But to answer your question, no, I didn't do a frigging thing to him except endue that weapon he brought me. Took awhile, and he got grumpy about the wait, but I wouldn't screw with his memory just because he annoyed me."

To Nevan, I said, "I believe her."

"As do I," he confirmed. He asked Ennea, "Can you help?"

"Sure can do." The witch leaned her hip against the table, pulling in a deep breath of the steam wafting out of the cauldron, and smiled with blissful contentment. Focusing on us, she tapped a finger on her chin. "If I'm going to cast a spell for you, Nevan, I need to know if there's anything I need to know first. Magic's a delicate and dangerous craft, the slightest unknown variable might throw the whole thing off. And next thing you know, you're a toad hopping around at my feet. I think you catch my drift, Your Majesty."

"I do," Nevan said. He angled toward me and I looked into his eyes, struck by the gravity of his expression. "She needs to know."

He was right, of course, but I didn't relish exposing my secret to someone I'd met a minute ago. One of my allies might've betrayed my secret to the enemy, but I had to trust somebody sometime. Her brother, Tris, knew I was the Janusite. If I trusted him, surely I could trust Ennea. Besides, my powers did have a tendency to muck up magic. The spell might be for Nevan, but we were connected in ways I didn't understand one hundred percent. My Janusite powers had affected his magic before.

I nodded. "Tell her."

Nevan faced Ennea again, though he maintained his hold on my hand, his fingers intertwined with mine, his thumb rubbing my skin. "Lindsey is the Janusite."

Ennea gave a low whistle. "Leave it to you to hook up with the prophesied gatekeeper of the worlds. Does the tribunal know?"

"Of course not," he snapped, then took a breath and regained his composure. "You mustn't tell anyone. Lindsey will be in grave danger if the truth is revealed."

The witch raised her hands. "This bird won't sing."

"Good."

"You think Lindsey's powers might knock my spell out of whack?"

"They have interacted with my magic on previous occasions," he said, "as well as affecting other types of magic. The first time I brought her to the Unseen, her powers caused time to pass more slowly on this side of the veil."

"Good to know. I'll need to work a little something-something into the spell to account for it."

I stepped into the discussion when Nevan fell silent. "How will this spell work?"

"This kind of memory spell taps into the Oversoul to bypass whatever mojo your unknown baddie worked on Nevan." Ennea rubbed her chin with her thumb and forefinger. "It'll rewind his recollection to the last moment he remembers clearly and let him relive it from there, in his mind."

Nevan fidgeted beside me, his fingers flexing and curling around mine.

I must've looked baffled, which I absolutely was, because Ennea gave me a patient smile. "See, it's kind of like retroactive astral projection. Your mind experiences the event as it happens, and you feel like you're actually there, but you're invisible to the participants and can't interact with the environment."

Sure, that made perfect sense.

Nevan grasped my other hand and turned us toward each other. He stared down at me with a tension-darkened expression, his full mouth squashed into a slash. "Without knowing what was done to me, the magics involved may cause a severe reaction with the spell implanted within me. I need you to do this for me, love. Will you?"

"Experience your memories?" I glanced at Ennea. "Is that possible? Can I do it for him?"

"You can," she said. "If your bond with him is strong enough, you can act as his proxy during the spell."

"It's strong enough," Nevan said. "Will you do this?"

The silent "please" at the end of his question tugged at my heart. He was asking me because he worried about magical interactions, yes, but also because he was afraid of what he might see.

As if he'd read my mind, he said, "We need an objective party to witness whatever occurred. I trust you to handle this."

"You could handle it too." I extricated one of my hands from his to caress his cheek. "You're the strongest man I've ever known. But if you need me to do stand in for you, I'll do it."

He nodded, his gratitude evident on his face.

"But for the record," I said, "where you're concerned, I am in no way objective."

Ennea smiled and shook her head at us. "New love is so adorable. But if we're going to do this thing, I need a magical assist."

"From whom?" Nevan asked.

She held up one finger in the universal gesture for patient silence. Then she opened her mouth and hollered, "Triskaideka!"

Ennea canted her head as if listening.

Nevan screwed up one corner of his mouth. "Perhaps he doesn't care to respond, since you are helping me."

My gaze flicked back and forth between him and the witch. "He who?"

Ennea rolled back her shoulders. "Oh, you bet your rock-hard ass he'll respond. Triskaideka, get your sorry butt in here before I call Ma and tell her what you did last night!"

A figure blipped into view alongside Ennea. Tris rolled his bright blue eyes at his sister, who narrowed her bright green eyes at him.

"Ya don't gotta scream," Tris said. "I heard you the first time, but I was trying to have a piss in the woods."

I couldn't help asking. "What did he do last night?"

Ennea smirked. "Went drinking with a busty little undine. Our ma hates those slippery water sprites. She wants Tris to settle down with a nice fae girl, preferably a copper fae."

"Copper fae?" I repeated, lost in this conversation. "Undine?"

Tris aimed his most condescending look at me. "Don't Nev teach you nothing about our world? Undines are water elementals. Copper fae is what leprechauns are, on account of we're tied to the element copper."

"I thought elemental referred to air, water, earth, and fire."

"You think that's all there is? Sure, we got the basal elemental beings— sylphs for air, undines for water, salamanders for fire, gnomes for earth. But the fae are tied to more specific chemical elements."

I stood mute as comprehension dawned little by little. "You mean chemical as in the periodic table of elements?"

"Yep." He scratched his head. "Though we ain't got no charts or tables. That's a mortal thing."

"How many kinds of fae are there?"

"As many as there are elements." He puffed out his chest, his chin raised. "The fae are the largest race of elementals in the Unseen, comprised of one hundred and eighteen tribes."

Nevan groaned. "Enough. Lindsey doesn't need the unabridged history of the magnificent fae."

"He's right," I said. "We have a mystery to solve."

Ennea led me behind a deck of shelves to a wooden chaise upholstered with dark fabric and plenty of cushioning. She waved a hand toward it. "Lie down, get comfy."

I settled onto the chaise, fidgeting until I found a comfortable position, my legs stretched out along the length of the backless sofa. The elevated end held my head and torso at an angle.

Nevan perched on the chaise's edge, concern dulling his eyes.

"Don't worry," I said, "everything'll be fine."

He gave a weak nod, but seemed less than convinced. Hell, I would've been freaked out too, if somebody was messing with my brain, so I couldn't blame him.

Ennea took a position at the foot of the chaise, her back straight and shoulders square. "Nevan, you'll need to hold her hand to keep her grounded to you. Lindsey, remember you can't interact with anyone or anything, and no one can see or hear you. Tris, let's get ready."

I heard rustling behind me, followed by the noises of Tris knocking around in search of whatever they needed for the spell.

"Careful with that," Ennea chastised in the kind of tone used only by mothers and bossy sisters. "That's all the potion I've got. You know how long it takes to chant up another batch?"

Tris grumbled. A moment later, he emerged from behind me to approach his sister. With one hand, he offered her a gilded ceramic mug.

Ennea nodded toward me. "Give it to the one who's drinking it."

"Drinking what?" I asked, levering up into a sitting position. Tris held the mug out to me. I studied it with trepidation, my stomach churning at the thought of imbibing an unknown magical substance. "What is it?"

Nevan's eyes crinkled at the corners with restrained laughter. "Relax, my suspicious love. It's not poison."

"How do you know?" I said with a touch of sarcasm in my voice and a teasing lift of my brows.

Tris bristled, but Ennea looked amused. "It's a potion to ease you into the memory spell. I could explain the magical mechanics of it—"

"Unnecessary," Nevan said. He enfolded my hands in his, rubbing his palm across the back of my hand. "Trust me."

I understood what he was asking. He trusted Ennea, and I trusted him, so therefore I should trust her.

Accepting the mug from Tris, my other hand still enclosed in both of

Nevan's, I swigged the contents. Tart and viscous liquid rushed over my tongue, making me splutter as it washed down my throat. I coughed a few times, waving a dismissive hand when Nevan leaned toward me with wide, worried eyes.

"Nothing wrong," I said. "Take it easy, honey."

Tris smirked at that, barely choking back a derisive snort. "Honey? Man, you are domesticated."

"Shush," Ennea hissed, her expression going stern. "It's our turn, Triskaideka."

He made a face. "Stop calling me that."

I started to smile, but froze as a bizarre sensation spread through my body, sprouting in my chest and expanding outward into every nook and cranny of my being. It began as a cool tingling behind my breastbone, then mushroomed into a hard, hot tingle that scorched through me. I gasped, my eyes flew wide, my back bowed and my head was thrown back into the cushion.

Nevan gripped my hand, while with his other palm he grasped my face.

"Stop fighting," Ennea said, and though her tone was forceful, it was tempered with an underlying calmness. Her face exhibited the determined serenity of one used to toying with unnatural forces. She bent close to my face, as I struggled to drag in breaths. "Listen to me, Lindsey. The magic will try to push you out. This kind of memory spell fights back, so you need to fight even harder. Focus on Nevan. Let your bond with him soothe and guide you. *Focus.*"

When she straightened and took Tris's hand, moving out of my direct line of sight, my gaze shot to Nevan. The tightness and anxiety smoothed out of his features. He held my hand between his again, and I let myself spiral down into the vortex of his eyes, carrying me ever downward toward the depths of his soul. I felt him, like a warm and sultry breeze caressing my skin, delving beneath the surface of my being to embrace me in a way no one else could.

Peace. Completion. Belonging.

My eyes drifted shut. My body relaxed into the upholstery, its softness cradling my limbs. An odd lightness overcame me as my mind disconnected from my body, and yet the heat and solidity of Nevan's hands tethered me to him. A sweet, wonderful binding. The safety of our connection quieted my nerves.

I floated through an abyss, nowhere and everywhere at once.

"Hear me," Ennea intoned. "Empty your thoughts. Hold to the bond and let it take you where you need to go."

An energy tugged at me. I resisted the urge to struggle against it. My mind moved through nothingness toward a destination I could neither see nor sense.

The tingling erupted in my chest again. Hot. Hard. Hungry. This time, the nasty thing came with tiny, razor-sharp teeth that clawed at me from the inside, tearing, shredding, devouring.

A strong and soothing wave crested over me, sweeping away the pain.

Nevan. I clung to him in the darkness, shoving the evil thing out of me with all the strength in my soul. But another power intensified mine—the essential strength of Nevan's soul fused with mine.

Blinding whiteness exploded around me.

I burst out into an underground chamber lit by a fire burning within a single, large, metallic bowl situated atop a wide dais. It must've been four feet in diameter, with flames leaping up from its confines to lick at the air. Five beings, cloaked in flowing robes of gold with hoods shielding their faces, had assembled in a semicircle around the fire on the dais.

Nevan stood before the group, with the fire between them. He wore a white, toga-style garment that hooked over one shoulder, held in place with a bronze clasp.

His expression was thunderous.

I edged closer, tiptoeing despite the fact I knew none of them could see or hear me. Somehow, sneaking just seemed prudent. I stopped alongside Nevan, angled so I could see both him and the tribunal.

"My answer remains the same," he said, grating the words through his clenched teeth. "I am king, you will accept my decree."

"Decree?" said one of the cloaked figures, the voice male and raspy. "We are the oversight for the king. If we determine your actions are against the welfare of the sylph kingdom—"

"Shut up." Nevan barked the command, his shoulders bunched so tightly he seemed ready to explode. "I have told you. There is no discussion, and my decision has no bearing on the welfare of my people, which I have worked diligently to assure. Only the five of you seem to have a grievance with my ruling techniques."

"Your Majesty," said another of the beings, raising a placating hand. "You cannot truly mean to install a mortal as queen."

Ohhhh, of course they were talking about me. The mortal plaything.

Nevan clenched his fists, his jaw tight as steel, and he seemed to grow taller and larger, his eyes glinting with bright red fire. "Lindsey is my mate. She will rule at my side, and you will accept and obey her—and swear your fealty to your new queen."

Obey me? Swear fealty to me? Aw, he really did say the sweetest things.

"You leave us no choice, then," the tribunal member said, lowering his hand.

Nevan narrowed his eyes to slits. "You have no say in this."

He assumed the position I'd come to recognize as his pre-vanishing posture. He flinched the tiniest bit, his eyes darting.

"You may not leave," the raspy-voiced being said. "We have activated the wards and tuned them to prevent your departure."

The tribunal chamber had wards protecting it. I should've guessed. But holding their own king hostage? Unease slithered through me. This could not be good.

Nevan's nostrils flared. "How dare you attempt to—"

Feminine laughter echoed through the chamber, light and mocking. Ceara emerged from the shadows behind the tribunal, the epitome of ethereal beauty, her gray dress swishing as she sashayed across the chamber. The pendant suspended from her belt swayed with every motion of her hips.

Her silvery eyes took in Nevan, and her lips curled in an arrogant smile.

The raspy-voiced being, who seemed to be in charge, stepped forward and spread his arms wide. "We have chosen your queen."

"No one," Nevan growled, "chooses my queen for me."

"She is your wife. And she is of the Unseen."

"Do you know what she is? Of what elemental race?" Nevan squinted at Ceara, his gaze assessing and austere. "What are you, wife?"

He spat the last word.

She sashayed toward him, halting alongside the fire. "I am your wife, Tuathal. The rest is immaterial."

"Why," Nevan said, "have I not seen or heard of you for five thousand years?"

Ceara shrugged one elegant shoulder. "Perhaps you were too busy fornicating with every female you encountered. This mortal child is merely the last in a line of meaningless flings, and you will come to realize that once you cease resisting me."

Nevan ground his teeth hard enough for me to hear the noise. He scanned his furious gaze over each of the tribunal members in turn. "Never will I accept this creature as my wife, much less my queen. Never."

Mr. Raspy clapped his hands together and the fire flared high and blindingly bright for a heartbeat. As the flames settled down again, he jabbed an accusing finger at Nevan. "So be it. If the king refuses to concede, we must take dire action against you."

I glanced at Nevan's face, my pulse racing, but he'd gone stony. Was I about to discover what they'd done to him? Did I want to know?

Yes. I did. I had no choice, because no way in hell would I stand by while they manipulated him.

The air in the chamber quivered. The walls groaned and rippled, like a living thing awakening.

Ceara's eyes were wild, her hair fluttered on a phantom breeze. An eerie glow surrounded her, silvery and sparkling. When she spoke, her voice became imbued with an echo-like quality. "Let my master's will be done."

Nevan spluttered, gasped, his eyes bulging.

I jerked, stopping myself from running to him at the last second. I couldn't do anything about this. Couldn't stop whatever was happening. *Powerless.*

He froze for an instant, then his entire body slackened, though he remained on his feet. His eyes had gone flat, his gaze distant. My vibrant, vital sylph had been transformed into a zombie.

"This will require much time," Ceara told the tribunal as she strolled up to Nevan. "I must take him to my master, but I can begin the process here."

I watched, helpless to intervene, while she bracketed his face with her pale hands.

"Tuathal," she cooed, bringing her lips near to his. "You may not have loved me before, but soon I will become the center of your existence. Without me, you will be an empty shell devoid of purpose. Only I possess the power to enliven you."

She pressed her mouth to his.

Tendrils of silver energy snaked out from her fingertips and her lips to burrow under his skin, pulsating as they entered him.

Bile leeched into my mouth, searing and sour.

Nevan began to kiss Ceara. Claiming her mouth. Plunging his tongue inside. His arms crushed her slender body to him, and their kissing escalated into a more heated and frantic encounter, as if they couldn't get enough of each other.

My gorge surged high in my throat. Cold sweat broke out on my brow, and I gulped down the nausea. He couldn't really want her. He couldn't really be enjoying her as much as it seemed like he was. She'd done something to him, I saw it.

Nevan loved me. She might force him to respond to her touch, but she could never—never in all eternity, never in any world—make him love her.

But could she coerce him into leaving me? Or...killing me?

Ceara separated from Nevan, taking a step back, her smile rife with disdain. Nevan seemed paralyzed, his expression vacant.

The evil bitch rotated her gaze toward me.

My heart thudded. No, it couldn't be. She couldn't—

"Little mortal," she said, her lips twisting into a nasty grin, "you see how he wants me. How I can make him want me. Nothing will prevent me from taking my place at his side, as queen of the sylph kingdom. Nothing—not even your pathetic love."

A bolt of soul-shattering power slammed into me. Agony ripped through my astral body, wrenching a scream from me.

I was yanked back through the abyss, through the frigid cold of emptiness, and hurled into my physical form. A gasp exploded out of me as my eyes flew open, and violent shudders racked my body. Sweat streamed down my face, mingling with hot tears that flowed like salty rivers down my cheeks.

Nevan hauled me into his arms. He rocked me and stroked my hair, murmuring soothing sounds.

The agony and terror seeped out of me gradually. I went limp in his embrace, my head on his shoulder, exhausted beyond anything I'd experienced in my life.

Drained.

After several minutes, I managed to lift my head and look at Nevan. The grief on his face stabbed a pang into my chest.

I raised a trembling hand to his cheek. "I'm okay."

"You don't look it." He brushed a hand over my forehead, then down my face, and swept his palm over my shoulder and down my back. "You seem… drained."

I couldn't deny it, and besides, I 'd vowed to keep no secrets from him. "Yeah, but I'll get over it."

Ennea peeked at me over Nevan's shoulder. "Did you see?"

"Oh-ho yeah. Did I ever see."

"We can discuss this later, when you're well again."

"There's no time," I said. "It was Ceara."

Surprise flickered on his face. "Why?"

"Not sure yet, but she's turning you into some kind of zombie." I pulled in a deep breath and let it out slowly. "Her sorcerer friend is helping her. She took you to him, and they did God knows what to you."

"You didn't follow?" Ennea asked.

"Couldn't." I looked straight at her. "Ceara saw me."

Chapter Nine

"THAT IS IMPOSSIBLE," ENNEA SAID, HER VOICE AND HER FACE TAINTED with a potent mixture of shock and wonder. She shook her head weakly. "The spell is like a recording, not a live event."

"I don't know much about magic," I said, "but I know Ceara saw me. She looked right at me. Spoke to me. Told me my pathetic love couldn't save Nevan from her evil plan to become queen of the sylphs. And yeah, I'm paraphrasing. Not about the pathetic love part, though."

"What else went down?" Tris asked. He scuffled closer, a pained look on his face, seeming for all the worlds to care about the answer to his question.

I glanced at my proud sylph, who kept his arms around me. "Maybe I should tell Nevan in private first."

"Your discretion is appreciated," he said, "but unnecessary. It's clear you and I alone cannot defeat this unidentified enemy. Ennea and Tris are powerful elementals, ones we can trust."

Had he admitted to trusting Tris? Next, he'd confess to liking the leprechaun. They had been friends once, but for as long as I'd known the two of them they'd been less than friendly to each other. A lot had changed since then, though. Like Tris helping me save Nevan's life when Skeiron drove an endued sword through Nevan's chest.

And somehow, that event had begun to pale in comparison with the threat we now faced. This was different, worse, more insidious. I had no evidence to support my assertions. Nothing more than a deep, icy wriggling in my gut.

I related everything I'd seen and heard during my astral journey into Nevan's memories, concluding with Ceara's zombie-fication of him, their super creepy kiss, and the way she'd ejected me from the spell.

"Kicked me to the curb," I said, swinging my legs around Nevan's body to clamber off the chaise. He rose as well, twining his fingers with mine, and I looked to the leprechaun on the other side of the chaise. "If that was really the past, a recorded memory, then how on earth could Ceara interact with me?"

Ennea scrunched her lips and her brows. Her delicate nose crinkled, and her striking emerald eyes sharpened on me. "This is far outside the scope of my powers and knowledge. Seems like Ceara's nothing but a minion. The sorcerer must've installed some kind of alarm in Nevan's memories, to alert him if anyone tried a spell like we did. I'm good, but this is insanely advanced magic."

Nevan's fingers tightened around mine. "What are you saying?"

"You need somebody way more powerful than me."

Tris nodded, his expression grave. "Yeah, you need an oracle."

"Exactly," Ennea said.

Back when we'd first learned I might be the Janusite, Nevan had planned on taking me to the oracle who issued the prophecy about me, but we'd never made it to his hideaway. Skeiron had ambushed us.

"Where do we find an oracle?" I asked.

"Tris can take you," Ennea offered. "He knows where to find one."

I turned my attention to Tris, who'd lost all his snarky attitude since the spell-casting.

"Yeah," he said, "I'll take you to one. Never talked to this oracle myself, but I went to his pad a few times to request an audience. He turned me down."

Ennea snorted. "Because you wanted the oracle's help in finding a wife. That's not in his job description."

My exhausted mind couldn't quite wrap itself around the concept of Tris volunteering to help Nevan. I probably gaped at him when I asked, "You're going to take us to the oracle? No griping or bargaining?"

Tris rolled his eyes. "I know you think I'm an obnoxious little twerp, but I ain't a villain."

He was quoting the words I'd screeched in order to summon him when I needed his aid in healing Nevan. I would've screamed anything to get the leprechaun's attention. "I don't think that anymore. But you are prickly at times."

"Yeah, Ennie's always telling me that."

"Off to the oracle, then?"

Nevan rubbed his neck. "Perhaps you should stay behind, Lindsey."

"Why?"

"You are the Janusite," he said, "and I'd be more comfortable keeping that secret amongst a small, select group of allies."

"Then we won't tell the oracle."

Ennea cleared her throat. "It won't be so simple. Oracles can sense what you are, even if you try to hide it with a glamour or another type of spell. They have the power of foresight, yes, but also insight. As soon as he looks at you, the oracle will know."

Terrific.

I tugged Nevan's hand, and he followed me to a corner of the room out of earshot of our hostess and her brother.

"Take me with you," I said. "I can wait outside the oracle's underground lair."

"What makes you believe he has an underground lair?"

"Don't all of you live inside mountains or hills or whatever?" I raised one finger, swirling it in the air to indicate our surroundings. "This is underground, right?"

He almost smiled. "Indeed it is. But you cannot come with us to the oracle's abode. I will not risk anyone else discovering what you are. The Janusite's power has been coveted for over a century, and there are those who would go to any lengths to possess you." He bent to stare into my eyes. "You may recall Skeiron."

Yeah, I had a vague memory of that bastard. "Vague" as in completely clear and as vivid as the day it all went down.

I stared right back at Nevan. "Told you before, I am not leaving you alone. Ceara might find you, or worse, her sorcerer pal."

"Tris will be there to—" He grimaced. "Protect me."

"I thought he ate copper and fueled the healing vortex."

"As you've seen tonight, he has great power. He does far more than manage the vortex, he also oversees and guards the portal."

"I thought Brennus was the guardian of the portal, since you quit to become king."

"He is guardian of the falls, protecting the portal from the mortal side. Tris handles the Unseen side."

Every new fact I learned about the supernatural made me realize how many more I had yet to discover. No wonder elementals were immortal. They needed eternity to comprehend the full scope of their own world.

"Guess that explains," I said, "how Tris pulled a little of the Unseen into the mortal world when he healed you."

"It does," Nevan said. "I will take you home and return here so Tris and I might travel to the oracle."

"No." I all but snarled the word, overcome by a stab of panic. "I mean, I don't want you to be alone at any time, not with a brain-sucking sorcerer after you. Tris can come with us to our place."

"As you wish."

I wasn't getting what I wished because I wished his previously dead wife hadn't teamed up with a sorcerer to scour out my lover's brain and murder three women. Oh if wishes were candy, I'd be on a major sugar high right about now.

"Wait," I said. "Take me to the portal, not home. I have to tell Stan I need some time off, and I need to talk to Travis."

About the dead girls. Nevan understood that without asking, and he also realized I didn't want to talk about it in front of Tris and Ennea.

"One more thing," I said, guiding Nevan back to the leprechauns. "Ceara wears a green pendant around her waist. It looks like a round sword with a dull point and a flared top. There are chevron lines on the cap. Anybody know what that is? It feels important, but I can't explain why."

Three elementals exchanged thoughtful glances.

And then they all shrugged.

"Without seeing it," Ennea said, "it's hard to say."

"Do you have a pen and paper?" I asked.

Nevan lifted his open hand, and poof, a pen and paper appeared in his palm.

I took the items and quickly sketched the pendant, then held up the drawing for all to see. I was no artist, but my rather crude depiction illustrated the basics.

Nevan took hold of the paper's edge, his gaze trained on the image. "I cannot say for certain, but this appears ancient Egyptian. A symbol I can't quite recall."

Egyptian. That gave me a starting point for uncovering more about the symbol.

"I'll check it out later," I said, and folded up the paper to stuff it into my back pocket. I hopped up on my toes to kiss Nevan's cheek. "What would I do without you?"

"Get into a great deal of trouble."

I pinched his arm. "Smart-aleck sylph."

Tris made an irritated noise. "We going to the oracle's pad or what?"

"We are," Nevan said, and waved to Tris. "Come. We will stop off at the portal to deposit Lindsey there and then journey on to the oracle."

The icy wriggling started up again in my gut. The tiny, slippery worms of doubt and dread coiled around my soul. If the oracle couldn't help us...

God save us all.

———

NEVAN CLEAVED ME TO HIS BODY FOR THE TRIP TO THE PORTAL. HE dropped me off there, kissed me goodbye, and vanished without speaking one syllable. I'd felt the tension in his body and seen it in the tight lines of his expression, as well as in the roiling, cool colors of his eyes. The sorcerer, and his apparent hold over Nevan, bothered my honey more than he cared to admit.

Men, even immortal ones, disliked feeling powerless. Hell, they hated it with a burning intensity. They'd resort to almost anything to avoid it.

I got myself through the portal and back to the rock shop without incident. When I informed Stan I needed a few days off, he responded by saying, "Sure, fine. Do what you gotta do."

Once a grumpy, confirmed skeptic of the paranormal, my boss had seen his illusions shattered on that day six weeks ago when the sylph army invaded the mortal realm. These days, Stan Lagorio adopted a "don't look, don't ask" attitude. He'd listen if I told him about the supernatural among us, but he never asked about it and worked really, really hard to avoid seeing anything unusual. Steering clear of the vortex and the waterfall kept him safely ensconced in his comfort bubble—most of the time.

Before I had the chance to call Travis, he walked through the shop's open front doors.

I hurried out from behind the counter to meet him halfway. Though he was in full cop mode, stoic and erect, the look in his eyes betrayed his true mood. Something was up.

"What is it?" I asked.

He blew out a breath and scratched the back of his hand. "It's about Megan."

I fiddled with the neckline of my shirt, trying to pull it a little higher.

"The doctors got the final test results," he said. "They'd been giving her tons of fluids, but it's like her body was rejecting it. They couldn't get her rehydrated."

"What does that matter? The sorcerer cut her throat."

"Lindsey, it wasn't your fault." He reached out to grasp my hand. "Even if you'd saved her from him, she would've died anyway."

Dark magics made her sick, that's what Tris had said. Brennus told me he smelled the poisonous magic on all the dead girls. Nothing, not even a vortex, had the power to bring them back. Slitting Megan's throat in front of me had been, what? A show of power?

No. The sorcerer had meant to torment me. Drive a searing blade of guilt into my heart. Make me doubt myself. Make me doubt everything and everyone.

"Dammit," I hissed. "He got exactly what he wanted."

Travis squeezed my hand. "Who?"

I'd forgotten he was holding my hand. Maybe I should've pulled away, but in this moment I needed human contact. He was my friend, after all.

"The sorcerer," I said. When I called to report the deaths, I'd given Travis a summary of my encounter with the man in the black robe, so he'd understand the context of the murders. Not that he could do anything about it. Arrest a sorcerer? No cop received training in how to handle a supernatural perpetrator.

"How'd he get what he wanted?" Travis asked, his fingers warm around my cold hand.

"I let him unsettle me. Let him get inside my head and make me suspicious of everyone. But worst of all, I let him convince me I can't stop him."

"You can do it, Lindsey." He gave my hand another squeeze. "But you don't have to do it alone. Me, Nevan, Stan, even that weird Tris kid, we're all here for you."

"I know." Wriggling my hand out of his, I stuffed my hands in my pockets. "What about the other girls? Have you identified them?"

"Not yet." He hesitated, shuffling his feet. "Seems like they had the same severe dehydration as Megan, though, which means they would've died even without being murdered."

"They were murdered either way. The sorcerer used dark magics to poison them."

His face went slack. "Uh-huh."

I patted his arm. "Don't worry, you'll get used to this stuff eventually."

We said goodbye, and Travis headed back to the sheriff's department.

I trudged down the path to the falls, intent on examining the crime scene. Travis had done so earlier, but I needed to investigate on my own. At the wooden railing, I paused to study the gushing water that careened over the cliff and pummeled the pool below. Sometimes when I studied the falls, I got an odd feeling of…discontinuity. I couldn't describe it any other way. This was where the mortal world collided with the elemental realm, like a breach in the space-time continuum. I could almost feel the energies of both worlds merging and dividing like solar systems crashing into each other.

Who controlled the collisions between the mortal and elemental worlds? Elementals would say they did, for sure. Humans were not slaves to the desires of immortals, though. We could fight them. We had fought them. If the worlds ever went to war, for real, could we win? Was this why the boundaries existed? To keep the Unseen realm at bay and prevent an apocalypse?

A sensation of awareness prickled over my skin, as if another presence hovered nearby.

I stepped away from the railing and turned in a circle, scrutinizing every shadow, every tree, every bush and blade of grass. Nothing. I was alone.

My intuition warned me otherwise.

The breeze delivered a familiar odor to my nostrils. The stench of ammonia faded away within seconds.

I froze, touching my fingers to my lips. That smell, I recognized it. Yes, I'd smelled it two days ago when Megan staggered out of the woods and again today just before the sorcerer appeared. That wasn't the reason for my déjà vu. I recognized the ammonia-like stench from six weeks ago. Back then, a shapeshifter had produced the odor, thanks to the monkey-like traits he inherited from the curse that spawned the kerkopes.

That shapeshifter had been Calder Blackwell.

But he had been destroyed. Nevan snapped his neck and drove an endued sword through his heart. No coming back from that, right?

Anything is possible, Nevan had said.

I swung my head left and right but saw nothing.

"Calder?" I shouted. "Are you there?"

Silence.

This was crazy, right? But hadn't I commented to Nevan how recent events reminded me of Calder's campaign to push me over the edge?

A black-robed figure separated from the shadows, shuffling out into the sunlight filtering down through the trees. That preternatural hush had come over the earth again. It seemed to surround him like a bubble, spreading outward wherever he moved. The sorcerer halted halfway across the clearing from me.

"Why do you call for a dead man?" he asked.

"Are you Calder Blackwell?"

His head tipped left and then right. "We are many things."

My hands wanted to wring each other, but I flattened them on my thighs, wiping away the clamminess. "What does that mean?"

"We can be whatever, whomever, you most desire."

His image quivered, the colors morphing as his shape altered.

The sorcerer assumed the likeness of Nevan, complete with the loincloth and the face of the sylph king.

I laid a hand on my chest, pressing it flat. This was not Nevan. The glamour was excellent—perfect, in fact—but the being facing me was not my lover.

"Nice try," I said. "I didn't fall for it the first time, and I'm not falling for it this go-round. You are not Nevan."

The sorcerer ambled closer, hips undulating with each step, the loincloth tightening and loosening as muscles worked. "Are ye certain of that?"

His Irish brogue hit the bull's eye, even better than his first attempt.

My throat went thick, my blood chilled. He lingered an arm's length away, too close for my comfort, but I refused to give this being the satisfaction of making me retreat. I lifted a hand to my hip, reassured by the hard outline of my holstered derringer.

"Don't I look like Nevan?" the sorcerer asked in a casual, slightly amused tone. "Don't I sound like him? Don't I smell like him?"

He inched forward, so close I could scent him. He smelled of earth and thunderstorms, like Nevan, but underneath another odor gave away the game. The stench of something acrid and sour, almost sulfurous. Like spoiled meat or...death.

I slipped my hand inside my waistband, taking hold of the gun's grip. "Oh, you've done a bang-up job of impersonating Nevan. The scent was a nice touch, but you can't cover up what you really are. You stink of rotten things."

He chuckled, grinning, and his eyes crinkled the way Nevan's did. The colors inside his eyes, however, had a sickly green undertone. "You are as clever as I'd hoped. Perhaps you prefer this?"

The image of Nevan went fuzzy, morphing into the likeness of Travis in his sheriff's uniform.

I took one step backward. "Since you glamoured right in front of me both times, why would believe I'd fall for this trick? What's the point?"

He shrugged, and in Travis's Texas drawl, he said, "Don't listen, do ya? We can be whatever you want. Once you've reached the pinnacle of your powers, and you accept you can't defeat us, all you gotta do is say the word. Sweet thing, we can replace what you're going to lose."

More head games. *Just like Calder.* Except Calder hadn't glamoured to impersonate people I knew. He'd lurked in the shadows until the moment he had me at my weakest, when he was positive I'd give in to his plan to make me his monkey-mate.

The sorcerer was doing the same thing, except he coveted my Janusite powers. Calder hadn't cared about that.

Fake Travis smiled. "You'll see."

He vanished.

I'd see what? Maybe I didn't want to know, but I realized I had to know the answers to every question raised by my encounters with the sorcerer.

Travis, the real one, had been right. I needed my allies with me in this battle.

I climbed over the railing and up onto the rock ledge alongside the falls, sidling up to the thundering cascade. Dozens of times, I'd leaped through the curtain of water, going to or coming from the portal within the cave behind the falls. My encounter with the not-Nevan and not-Travis glamours seemed to have infected me with a lingering uncertainty about everything. What if I stumbled when I jumped through the waterfall? What I hit my head and tumbled into the pool below to drown in its depths?

Oh for heaven's sake. What kind of wuss had I turned into if one measly old supernatural encounter with a creepy sorcerer had me quaking in my hiking boots?

"May I be of assistance, my lady?"

I squawked at the sudden appearance of Brennus right in front of me, his bare feet planted on the rock ledge.

Suddenly breathing hard, I slapped a palm on the red sandstone of the cliff. "You scared the bejesus out of me."

He bowed his head in apology, then offered me his hand. "May I?"

"Sure, why not."

Brennus grasped me around the waist, hefted me off the ledge, and spun toward the falls. His long arms pushed me through the water into the cave, where he set me down on the solid, if pockmarked, stone floor without the shapeshifter ever stepping off the ledge outside.

"Thank you," I hollered through the waterfall.

I hadn't expected him to respond, since he probably couldn't hear me, but my innate politeness compelled me to say it anyway. Nevan would've winced at my expression of gratitude, but I was still on the mortal side of the veil.

Water drenched me and streamed off my body onto the floor. My dripping hair hung limp around my face, locks of it pasted to my skin. I swiped them away.

The wall to my left caught my eye, and a memory barreled through my mind. Nevan backing me up to that wall, both of us naked. The slap of my back meeting the rock. Nevan hitching my legs over his shoulders as he set his mouth to my sex and pleasured me. His voice echoed in my mind, his words as fresh as that night, when he'd stripped away the last threads of my inhibitions with two syllables—*trust me.*

In that moment, I'd relinquished all my trust to him. My faith in him had only increased since that night, because of everything we'd survived together. No goddamn sorcerer or formerly dead shrew of a wife would destroy my trust in Nevan.

Squeezing my eyes shut, squeezing my fingers into my palms, I sent out a silent invocation. *I believe in you, Nevan.*

I opened my eyes, shook off the remnants of fear and uncertainty, and willed the portal to admit me. The swirling, inky blackness telescoped open in front of me, the tendrils of purple and blue thrashing within it. I marched through the portal and out into the Unseen.

Chapter Ten

I TRAVERSED THE LITTLE CLEARING THE PORTAL OPENED INTO, HEADING for the dirt path through the trees. At the edge of the woods, I stopped. Where was I going?

Glancing around, I realized I had no idea. Nevan had always accompanied me and whisked me straight from the portal to his—our—home. On my own, I'd have to take the long way there. I had no idea which way to go. Nevan hadn't given me directions or a map, and I hadn't thought to ask. At least he had the excuse of someone screwing with his brain. I should've remembered to ask the question. *So, honey, how do I get home?*

Of course, I'd been distracted by his predicament. And by the weirdness of the Nevan impostor and the murders of three innocent women. Still, how could I have been so stupid? I got myself stranded.

Letting out a little growl of frustration, I turned to stomp back to the portal and go back to the mortal world until I figured out a solution.

Something tiny and red leaped out of the grass to land at my feet.

I yelped. My heart thudded and my hand flew to my chest.

The little lizard gazed up at me with shiny black eyes, its fiery red skin glistening in the sunlight. Glints of iridescent orange flashed on its flesh as the breeze rustled the moss-like foliage of the trees, causing the sun to glint brighter and flash darker with each flap of the branches. The creature—with its long and slender body, stubby legs, and tapering tail—resembled lizards I'd seen in the mortal realm.

Listing its head to the side, the creature blinked once.

I crouched to get closer to the little guy—for some reason, I thought of it as male—and reached a finger out to touch it.

Flames erupted around the lizard in a miniature conflagration, only to snuff out a split second later.

The lizard was gone.

I stared at the spot where it had been. A red critter that vanished in a puff of flames. This world kept getting weirder and weirder.

A burst of itty-bitty fire caught my eye peripherally. Leaping up, I spun toward the flash.

The tiny creature squatted there, no longer aflame, its dark eyes gazing at me with what I swore was curiosity. It tilted its head to the side again, blinked, and scuttled toward me.

I scuttled away from it, not at all certain I wanted to attract this little guy, no matter how cute he was. Things in the Unseen could appear innocuous, then spin around to bite you in the ass in the most literal way. But this was the first animal life I'd encountered here, and I couldn't help feeling as curious about the alien lizard as it seemed to be about me.

The creature halted, blinking up at me with wide, gleaming eyes. Its little mouth opened and closed.

I had the oddest sensation the lizard was trying to communicate. My intuition assured me this creature meant me no harm. I bit my lip, studying the tiny beastie. What harm could come from interacting with a teeny-weeny thing like this lizard?

Kneeling, I lowered my hand to ground level and turned my palm up.

The lizard toddled to me and climbed onto my palm.

Its miniature feet felt strangely warm. Its tail flicked, tickling my skin. Thanks to its tail that measured longer than its body, the creature occupied the entire length of my hand from the heel to the tip of my middle finger. I touched a fingertip to the top of its head. The skin was warmer there, almost hot, with a slick, smooth texture. Giving in to an inexplicable impulse, I began to pet the lizard's tiny head.

The creature purred softly, and I swore its almost nonexistent lips curled into a smile.

I couldn't keep from smiling too. This had to be the most adorable denizen of the ooky and dangerous Unseen realm I'd met so far.

The lizard pushed his head up into my finger as I petted him, like a cat would've done. Filaments of flame, red and orange and yellow, flitted through his black eyes. His skin grew hotter, almost too hot.

What was I doing? Petting a lizard? Nevan was in trouble, and I paused to befriend a cute critter I came upon in the woods? *Cut it out, Lindsey. Get back on task.*

I set the lizard on the grass, gave him one more pat with my finger, and said, "Nice meeting you, little guy, but I have to go."

Rising, I wheeled toward the portal.

The lizard chirped.

I half turned, eying the creature.

He sat back on his hind feet, lifting his front legs in the air like a dog sitting up to beg for treats. His throat quivered on another chirp.

"I really have to leave," I said. "Go on home, little guy."

The lizard slowly blinked his big, dark eyes.

Crouching, I spoke to the beastie. "Look, my boyfriend is in a load of trouble and I need to get back to our house, but I can't find my way. It's a long story, okay? I have to go back to my world and…Hell, I don't know what I'm going to do. You're really cute, and I'd love to hang out with you, but I just can't. Understand?"

No idea why I told the lizard all of this, but in normal life I'd talked to dogs and cats and even cows. Why not an otherworldly lizard?

The flame-colored creature raced to me, skittered up my leg, and grabbed onto the pocket of my jeans with his tiny front feet. He tugged on the fabric, looking up at me with unblinking eyes.

"What are you doing?" I asked, as if a lizard could respond. But he did seem to be…I don't know, trying to tell me something.

Like what?

The lizard tugged at my pocket again.

What in my pocket could attract the interest of a creature like this one?

A chill shimmied down my spine, raising the hairs all over my body as I realized the answer. The pocket where the salamander perched held the soul stone.

I took the little red guy in my hand, holding him gently, and rose. I dug the soul stone out of my pocket. Taking it between my thumb and forefinger, I lifted it to the eye level of the lizard.

"This what you wanted?" I asked.

The salamander nodded. Swear to God, it nodded.

"Why?"

His onyx eyes blinked.

No idea what that meant. I didn't speak salamander.

Groaning out a sigh, I bent to deposit the lizard on the ground and patted his head. "I don't know what you're trying to tell me, and I don't have time to figure it out. I'm going home. Bye-bye, little cutie-pie."

I took one step toward the portal.

The salamander chirped and raced toward the dirt path that led into the woods. There, he stopped to gaze back at me. The creature jerked its head, beckoning me to follow the way a person might.

My mouth open but unable to speak, I gaped at the beastie. Could a lizard know how to find Nevan's underground lair? The salamander had drawn my attention to the soul stone right before he scampered over to the woods trail. Maybe he meant the stone would guide me.

I rolled the stone in my palm, the awareness of Nevan it engendered rippling through me in warm, calming waves. If I followed the salamander's advice, such as it was, I might wander in the woods for days, lost and alone. But if I went back to the mortal world, I might never come up with a better plan.

Better than taking advice from a lizard? *Ugh.* My life had become totally surreal.

Closing my hand around the stone, I marched to the salamander.

He skittered up my leg, hopped onto my arm, and scampered up to my shoulder. Stationed there, he nodded toward the stone in my hand.

"Got any idea how I make this work?" I asked.

The lizard sat up on his hind legs and shrugged his little shoulders.

Ohhh-kay. Guess I was doing this. Taking advice from a red lizard.

I shut my eyes and focused on the sensations from the soul stone. Warmth tingled through me, emanating from my hand and spreading throughout my entire body. The familiar, arousing energy of Nevan infused my being, as if he'd wrapped his arms around my very essence. The thrilling intimacy of it triggered sense memories of making love with Nevan, of our magics twirling around each other while our bodies merged and the pleasure mounted.

Nevan. I needed to help him. Needed to find our home. Right now.

My eyes flew open in the instant the world shifted. I zipped through the dark tunnel that had once clawed at my flesh, before I'd come to terms with my Janusite-ness, but that now whisked me away in a fraction of a heartbeat. I barely glimpsed the void around me before I popped out at the base of the mountain that concealed our home.

And the salamander still sat on my shoulder, on all fours, his tiny fingers clutching at me. His eyes had gone wide and I could've sworn his red skin had paled a shade.

"Wow," I said, swaying the tiniest bit. "That was a rush."

My new friend grinned, exposing tiny little teeth lined up in rows on his upper and lower gums.

I stroked his head. "Guess you liked it too, eh? I had no idea I could do that. Thanks for pointing me to the soul stone. Hell of a lot easier than tromping through the woods for who knows how long hoping to stumble onto this place."

The salamander closed his mouth and banked his head to the side.

"I live here," I said. "So I'm afraid this is where we say goodbye."

He made a soft, whimpery noise and scampered up my neck to perch atop the shell of my ear. My hair fell over his tiny body, even as his tail tickled the skin behind my ear.

Laughing, I plucked him off my ear to hold him in my palm. "Ah, little guy, I can't take you with me."

Well, since I'd brought him along on my interdimensional journey here, I supposed I probably could take him inside the house with me. But should I? Nevan and Tris might return at any moment or they might be gone for hours and hours. I had no idea how long it might take to track down an oracle, or what kinds of hoops that oracle might force them to jump through to gain his help. That left me alone with nothing much to do.

My new friend had assisted me. Maybe I could find a way to communicate with him better and learn something from this odd little critter.

Some individuals, not all of them human, would've called me an odd little critter.

What the heck.

Cradling the salamander in one hand, I raised the soul stone in the other and commanded the entrance to open. The solid rock wall, with its overhanging weeds and moss, telescoped out until a large, oval hole appeared in the mountain. The doorway extended from the ground up to about eight feet in height, just the right size for my tall and hunky significant other.

A sliver of worry wormed its way into my heart. Nevan was in danger, and I had to do something—anything—to help him. Trouble was, I had no idea what I could do.

I crossed the threshold with my red friend. The door telescoped shut behind us. I stood in the vacant living room, bathed in the omnipresent golden light, inside the home I shared with the only man, of any world, I'd ever loved. My gaze wandered to the bed, the mussed sheets, and my brain conjured a memory of the musky scent of sex permeating the room as Nevan and I expressed our passion and devotion to each other in the most carnal and intimate ways.

The salamander danced in my hand.

"Oh no," I said, glancing down at him, "am I squishing you? Let me set you down."

I dropped to my knees, lowered my hand to the floor, and opened my fingers.

My new friend dashed away, darting this way and that, his tiny head bobbing as he examined his surroundings. How odd that I called a lizard my friend. How sad that I did. Of course, I had other friends of the bipedal variety, but they were all busy. Travis had murders to investigate. Stan had a business to run. Tris was off babysitting Nevan on his oracle quest.

At the very least, I had a pet to keep me company.

I sat back on my butt, my legs outstretched, hands limp on my thighs.

The salamander halted at the bed, his little neck craned to stare up at it. He rose onto his hind legs and grimaced.

No, I must've imagined that.

Then again, he'd grinned at me earlier. Why couldn't he grimace as well?

"What's the matter?" I asked, leaning forward a bit. "You want up on the bed?"

My new pet spun around, raced toward me, and stopped a few feet from my boots. He went stone-still, eyes unblinking.

A gigantic mass of flames shot up from him to lick at the ceiling.

The heat roasted me, and I scrambled backward on my ass using hands and feet like a crab.

The flames snuffed out.

In their place lounged a man as tall as Nevan, with a physique as broad and muscular as the sylph's. The stranger's skin, tanned and tinged with a coppery sheen, glimmered with tiny gold flecks as if dusted with glitter. His dark brown hair, shot through with maroon streaks, cascaded down to his shoulders in wavy locks. But the aspect of him that captured my focus resided lower than his shoulders, much lower.

The guy was stark naked. And his long, thick penis hung slack between his massive thighs.

With a long-suffering sigh, he stretched his enormous body and said, "My, it's good to be in human form again."

"I—wha—" My legs splayed before me, still flat on my ass, I gaped at him. "Who are you?"

"Max." He said it as if I should've known this fact.

Sitting forward, I surveyed the being in front of me. "What are you?"

He grinned and chuckled. "I've been assigned to you. I'm your new familiar, which means I'll lend a hand in your efforts to understand and control your newfound magics."

This creature, Max, spoke with an English accent.

"Uh-huh, sure." I pushed up onto my knees, staring up his naked body to his face. "What kind of elemental are you?"

"An incubus, naturally."

CHAPTER ELEVEN

"AN INCUBUS?" I SCRAMBLED TO MY FEET, BACKING AWAY FROM him. "You say 'naturally' like I should've expected an incubus to show up and announce he's my familiar. And I thought witches had familiars. I'm not a witch."

He laid a hand on his abdomen, his lips pursed but curled upward at the corners and his eyes crinkled with amusement. "Familiars are for any magical beings in need of a helping hand."

"Hmph. Isn't an incubus a sex demon?"

"Not a demon." He tsked. "Mortal mythology can be bloody annoying and inaccurate. An incubus feeds off sexual energy, but I don't steal into women's bedrooms at night to ravage them."

"If you say so."

He looked to the ceiling, perhaps hoping for divine intervention, and then his shoulders wilted. "I'd heard you were quite difficult. The rumors are spot on."

"Seriously? I'm the bad one? You tricked me." I stabbed a finger in the air in his direction. "Pretended to be a cute little salamander so I'd bring you into my home."

"I am a salamander." He roved his gaze up and down my body, and one corner of his mouth ticked up. "Glad to hear you think I'm cute, though. Means you're up for it."

"Up for what?"

"Getting a leg over."

Maybe I was dense, but only then did I realize he was talking about sex. And only because I'd watched a lot of British TV.

"Oh please," I said. "Calling a tiny lizard cute does not mean I'm going to sleep with you. And you're avoiding the real issue here, which is that you tricked me."

"Tosh," he said with a dismissive toss of his head, then strode closer to tower over me. "Since you clearly weren't listening the first time, let me repeat it. I am a salamander."

I threw my hands in the air. "Salamanders are little lizards. Not giant, manlike whatevers."

"Whatevers?" He stared at me like a mushroom had sprouted from my ear. "I am not a whatever. I am a salamander." When I started to protest, he held up a hand. "Wait. Salamanders are incubi. The term incubus is more of a general description, since we're shapeshifters who can take human form whenever we like. In fact, we spend more time as humanoids than as salamanders."

"Of course. I should've known."

"Yes, you should have." He gave me a closed-mouth smile, his dark eyes lit up with unwinding ribbons of bright red and yellow. "Has your lover taught you nothing about this world? The various species of elementals? How we interact? What a bloody familiar is?"

"Nevan's been kind of busy lately."

Max's smile deepened, dimpling his cheeks. "I'll teach you. As your familiar, it's my duty."

"I don't recall ordering a familiar. Afraid I'll have to return you to the magic shop."

His brow scrunched, wrinkling his forehead. "I am not returnable. I was sent to help you."

"Sent?" I clasped my hands in front of me. "Who sent you?"

"Can't say."

"Naturally," I said, mocking the way he'd spoken the word earlier. I walked around Max in a circle, surveying him from head to toe and front to back. Though he had a hot body and a gorgeous face—were there any ugly people in this realm?—his good looks did nothing for me. Since I'd met Nevan, no other male of any realm could compete. I wanted him and no one else.

"Do you mean," I said, stopping in front of him again, "you feel it's your duty to help me, or that someone magically compelled you to be my familiar?"

"Ahhh," he said with appreciation. "I see you've learned about debts and bargains. That's a relief. You're much less likely to get yourself in trouble when you understand the stakes."

"You haven't answered my question."

"Because I can't."

I lodged my hands in my pockets. "I get it. You're stuck in a bad bargain that prevents you from speaking the words. Was it the sorcerer who did this to you?"

"That," Max said, "I can tell you. The sorcerer wants you to know I'm his gift to the Janusite. Use me as you see fit."

"Hmm." I rocked back on my heels, tapping my tongue on my front teeth. "Why should I trust you? I mean, you're the sorcerer's puppet. No offense."

"None taken. You're right, I am his puppet."

"Which means anything I tell you, anything you see me do, you'll go back and tattle to your master."

"No." He turned away, ambling toward the bed, then turned around again and stopped. His face was pinched as he threw a sidelong glance at the bed. "The sorcerer wants me to help you, and he knows you won't accept my help unless it's confidential. I'm forbidden to share with him anything I learn, see, hear, smell, or whatnot while I'm with you."

"And I'm supposed to take your word for that."

Max shrugged. "I have nothing else to offer. This is a show of good faith on his part."

Show of good faith, my ass. This was all part of the sorcerer's plans, though I couldn't puzzle out the purpose yet. He wanted me at full power so he could steal my magic. But giving me Max and ordering him to respect my privacy? Weird.

"Okay, fine." I moved to one of the chairs and settled onto it, hands on my knees. The Nevan-size chair all but swallowed me. "Don't suppose you can tell me who the sorcerer is. Or what his plans are."

"Afraid not."

"Or if Calder Blackwell is involved."

He shook his head.

"Maybe you can answer one question." I hesitated, part of me balking at the idea of asking, but I squared my shoulders and did it anyway. "When an elemental is destroyed, can they be resurrected?"

His brows lowered as he gazed down at the floor as if considering his answer. His tone uncertain, he said, "I haven't heard of it happening, but then, if someone did pull off the feat they might not want to spread the news. The threat of destruction is the best deterrent for bad behavior."

"What happens to the soul when somebody's destroyed?"

"It moves on, I guess. Unfortunately, I can't be more informative."

"Don't worry about it. I'll ask Nevan later."

Max glanced at the bed again and grimaced.

I leaned back in the chair. "What's your problem with the bed?"

He sauntered to the other chair, situated alongside mine but separated from it by a little table, and sat down. The chair fit him just right. He relaxed into it, his arms on the chair's arms. "The bed smells of sex, a fragrance I'd normally fancy. But it also smells of…him."

"Him?" I tucked my legs under me, angling slightly toward Max. "You mean Nevan."

"Yes." Max's mouth twisted into a partial frown. "I don't fancy smelling him, knowing you've shagged a sylph."

I laughed, but it came out as a snort. "You're prejudiced against sylphs?"

"They prance around like they own the forest. In fact, they're air elementals." He lifted his chin, puffing out his chest. "The tossers have no claim on the ground. They sniff their haughty noses at salamanders, but we have domain over the true power—fire."

Oh great. I'd not only acquired a familiar who was some kind of sex demon, but I'd also been dropped smack in the middle of the Unseen realm's socio-political shenanigans. I hated mortal politics and snobbery. Sure as hell didn't need the immortal variety.

"I love Nevan," I told Max in a firm tone. "I live here with him. If that bothers you, then toddle on back to the salamander cave."

He harrumphed.

"Besides," I continued, "sylphs are made of air and earth. They have as much right to walk on the ground as you do."

"You would defend the sylph king. He protects you. Though I can't fathom why a beautiful woman like you would fall for a—"

"Before you finish that sentence," I said, nailing him with a hard look, "you should think carefully about what you want to happen here. We could be friends, maybe, if you stop dissing my boyfriend. Or I could destroy you."

He barked out a laugh. "You? Destroy me?"

"Don't scoff. I took out Skeiron."

"Did you now?" He ginned, slapping his hands on the chair's arms. "Brilliant! That wanker deserved to be shredded into atomic bits 'n bobs."

"You're very strange, Max."

"Same to you, Lindsey."

As I considered my new familiar, my thoughts gravitated back to Nevan and the fact he'd been forged rather than born an elemental. I asked Max, "Were you a mortal once upon time?"

"Yes, during the heyday of the Roman empire."

"Did you ever forge anybody?"

He moved his hands onto his lap, staring down at his restless fingers. "Once. I will never repeat the mistake."

My curiosity pestered me to question him about it, but his limp posture and his gloomy expression dissuaded me. I didn't know him well enough to press him for details.

I settled into my chair, chewing on the larger situation for a moment. "You mentioned you're not returnable, but I could kick you out of my house anytime. Right?"

"Why do you call this your house? It belongs to the sylph, doesn't it?"

Of course he would assume that. I hadn't gotten around to adding my feminine flair to the place. "I live here too. That's my girlie stuff over there."

I jabbed a finger toward the boxes of my still-not-unpacked possessions stowed against the wall. One box was open, and a flowery scarf dangled half out of it. Some of the boxes contained books, most of them related to mythology and ancient history.

"Ah yes," Max said in a condescendingly patient tone. "How could I have overlooked it."

"What is your problem? You've been Mr. Prickly Pear ever since you smelled the bed."

He arched one brunet brow. "Prickly pear?"

"Missing the point, Sherlock."

The incubus stared at me for a moment before leaning back in his chair again. "I can't help it. I am an incubus, and the urge to mate with fertile females is both innate and virtually irresistible. To be in the presence of a sensual woman and then to scent that another bloke has mated with her, it's maddening. Your passion rolls off you in enticing waves, so much so I can almost taste you."

"Get this through your innately urged head. Only one male is allowed to taste me or mate with me or any other dirty things you're thinking of."

A lazy grin spiced up his demeanor. "I can think of well over a thousand things to do to you. And that's what I've dreamed up in the past few minutes."

"Forget it all. Not interested." And I wasn't. If Nevan had spoken the exact same words to me, I would've melted into a puddle of lust at his feet. Max's statement left me unaffected.

Well, mildly annoyed. But unaffected in any sexual way.

He scrutinized me with narrowed eyes, his gaze drifting down to my breasts. But then he sighed and faced forward. "I can see you aren't in the least aroused by me. It's bloody humiliating. The incubus power of seduction is legendary, but you look at me like I'm a genuine lizard."

"Sor—" *Crap.* I'd almost apologized, something I couldn't risk in the Unseen. I jiggled in my seat, wishing to hell Nevan would come home. "Don't take it as an affront to your mojo. Nevan and I have a connection even I don't understand, but it is unbreakable."

"I'm beginning to understand that."

I slumped back against my chair. "There's also the weirdness of me to consider. Magic tends to go wonky around me."

He leaned forward to squint at me. "Wonky?"

"Means it messes up other magic." I drummed my fingers on the chair's arm. "You never answered my question. Why do you think I can't send you packing?"

"I'm bound to serve you until one of us dies."

"Can't I zip away and leave you in my magical dust?"

His brows furrowed as his eyes glazed over. He shook his head, as if shaking off the confusion. "Now that we've met, and I've declared my intention to serve as your familiar, I can't leave you or be left. Should you 'zip away,' as you put it, I'd pop in wherever you landed."

Just what I needed. A salamander-slash-incubus I couldn't shake off my tail.

I cringed inwardly. Nevan would freak when he found out I'd brought home a pet sex demon.

Where was Nevan? How long did a trip to the oracle take?

"I'm going to trust you," I said, "and accept your help. If you promise to stop insulting Nevan."

"No promises. Not in this world."

"Right. Almost forgot."

He slouched in his chair. "I will voluntarily refrain from disparaging him. Though I still can't understand the appeal of King Nevan of the Air Fairies."

Max was soooo lucky Nevan wasn't around to hear him insult sylphs. Nevan had once tossed Travis into tree for calling him a jungle fairy.

I fidgeted in my too-big chair but couldn't quite get comfy. "Man, I wish this place had a sofa."

Max waved a hand, and a sofa appeared in the corner adjacent to the doorway to the kitchen. No, not a sofa. A red velvet chaise lounge, of the sort a decadent queen might sprawl herself across to entice a lover.

I glanced at Max. "Thought you were supposed to help me with magic, not indulge my every whim."

"Can't I do both?"

"Rather you didn't. Just because I say I wish for this or that doesn't mean I actually want it. I have a bad habit of voicing my passing thoughts out loud."

"I'll take that into consideration."

"How about you ask me if I really want something before you make it appear?"

The incubus screwed up one side of his mouth. "If you insist."

"I really do."

Max let his head fall back onto the chair, his gaze unfocused though his eyes pointed at the ceiling. His face went slack, as if he were lost in thought.

"Lindsey."

The stern voice from behind us made my pet incubus jerk forward and twist around to peer over the back of his chair. His eyes widened briefly, but he regained his cavalier bearing as he unfurled his body from the chair.

I stayed curled up in my chair, gazing at the sexy hunk of sylph standing behind Max's chair. The two men stared at each other—Max with a neutral expression, Nevan with flinty eyes and squared jaw.

"Hi, honey," I said brightly. "You're home."

Nevan swiveled his gaze to me. "Who, may I ask, is our visitor?"

"Oh, this is Max. My familiar."

"Your what?" His entire body bolted straight and taut. He tucked his chin, his eyes locked on me. Those swirling pools of brilliant color shimmered and sparked with white, a sign of anxiety. Nodding toward Max, Nevan said, "He is an incubus."

"I know, Max told me." I clambered out of the chair. "Maybe we should talk privately, huh?"

Max smiled with territorial glee. "Yes, I'd love to have a private discussion with my mistress."

"Not you," I told the incubus. I pointed a finger at Nevan. "You."

The white still shimmering in his eyes made my stomach knot up and an invisible hand clamp around my heart. It wasn't my new friend unsettling him. It had to be what he'd learned from his visit to the oracle.

"You," I said to Max, "over there."

I gestured toward the chaise lounge.

Grumbling, shoulders slumped, he shuffled toward the backless sofa and flung his body onto it lengthwise. With one arm draped down his thigh, he propped his head up with the other arm.

Nevan came up behind me, curving a hand over each of my upper arms. "Where did that thing come from?"

"The incubus or the sofa?"

"Both."

"Well, you see, I kind of wished out loud for a sofa and Max sort of poofed one into the room for me."

He laid a hand on his forehead, head down. "Lindsey, you must be more careful around magical beings."

"I didn't know he'd do that."

Nevan caught my hand and led me toward the bed on the opposite side of the room from the nude incubus, who had begun to smirk. Nevan gestured for me to sit on the bed. I perched on its edge, my feet suspended several inches above the floor, and Nevan lowered his big body onto the fur blanket beside me.

"Tell me," he said quietly, "how you acquired a familiar. An incubus, no less."

"Well..." I hunched my shoulders and peeked up at him through my lashes. "You see, I wanted to come home, but you forgot to tell me how to get here...I should start at the beginning."

I relayed the whole story to him, from the revelation about the dehydrated girls to my latest encounter with the sorcerer, and finally to my befriending of the harmless little salamander and Max's big reveal in the living room. Nevan listened without expression, his gaze on me, his eyes calming to a bronze-and-gold whirlpool that spun in gentle circles. By the time I finished explaining, he'd slipped his hand into mine and laced our fingers.

"So that's it," I said. "Totally unintentional acquisition of a familiar. If I'd known what Max is, I wouldn't have brought him into our home."

"Mm." Nevan raised our joined hands to fold his other hand around them. "Lindsey, my love, you are far too intelligent and suspicious to do such a thing. Whatever possessed you?"

Yeah, I'd wondered that too. I gave him the best explanation I could offer. "I was worried about you, and I wanted to do something to help, but I couldn't think of anything. I was feeling, um..."

"Powerless."

"Kind of."

"And uneasy, because you fear the sorcerer is Calder."

"That too." I hadn't stated my fear in explicit terms, but as usual, Nevan had no trouble reading between my lines.

He released my hand, pulling me into his arms. With my cheek to his chest, he combed his fingers through my hair. "Neglecting to tell you how to find your way home was inexcusable. Did you truly employ the soul stone to get here?"

"Uh-huh." I snuggled into him, grateful to have him here again, alive and well. But his skin felt a touch cool again, almost clammy. "Are you feeling okay?"

He sighed, his chest deflating. "Quite tired, to be honest."

Beneath the bronzed surface, his skin evidenced a faint pallor. I noted shadows under his eyes too.

Placing a hand on his cheek, I searched those beautiful eyes, now dulled by a deep exhaustion. "How did the meeting with the oracle go?"

His face blanked. "The oracle?"

"Yeah, the—" I glanced around, suddenly aware of one fact. "Where's Tris?"

"Tris?"

I grasped Nevan's face in both hands. "Your friend, the leprechaun. Snarky redheaded kid in ripped jeans."

He scowled. "I know who Tris is."

"Then where is he? Tris promised he'd stay with you every second until he brought you back to me."

Nevan opened his mouth, then shut it. His eyes went cloudy, his gaze distant.

He had no idea what I was talking about.

With my hands still bracketing his face, I gave his head a little shake. "Wake up, Nevan. What's the last thing you remember?"

His focus reeled back to me. "Our visit with Ennea."

"But not our discussion about the oracle, or visiting the oracle with Tris."

"No." He shut his eyes. "It's happened again."

"Looks like. But where the hell is Tris?" I jumped up and snagged Nevan's hand. "Come on, we have to find him. I need to know the sorcerer hasn't gotten his mitts on Tris."

Nevan heaved his body off the bed, seeming more wiped out with every passing moment. He trudged toward the wall that concealed the doorway. I trailed behind him, suffering an ever-increasing sense of impending doom.

He flourished his hand. The doorway telescoped open.

There, inches beyond the opening, hunched one very irritated leprechaun. Tris had his hands on his hips, one foot tapping the ground. His mouth was compressed into a tight line.

"About damn time," Tris said. "Where have you been?"

"Get him inside," I told Nevan, who plodded over the threshold to grasp Tris's shoulder and usher him through the doorway, then shut it again.

Tris held up his hands to me, palms out. "Don't blame me, sister. I was sticking right beside him, like you told me to, but then—" He snapped his fingers. "Just like that, the dude was gone."

"Did you try to find him?"

"Searched everywhere I could think, but found zilch." The leprechaun rubbed his jaw. "Even went to Ennea, but she couldn't catch the tiniest magical whiff of him. Like the sylph just ceased to exist."

"Ceased to exist?"

"For a while, yeah," he said, his tone uncertain. "Ennea finally got a hit on her locater spell, and I hightailed it over here." Tris swept his gaze over Nevan. "Man, you look like roadkill."

I could think of a solitary explanation for Nevan's disappearance. The sorcerer had summoned him.

"We need to talk to an oracle," I said. "But we can't let Nevan out of this house. So far, he's been taken only when he's out in the world. Right?"

"It would seem so," Nevan said. He squinted at me. "I know what you're thinking, and the answer is no."

I marched up to him, bent my head back, and fixed my hardest stare on him. "The answer is no? Since when are you the boss of me?"

He ran a hand over his eyes. "Never have I succeeded at reining you in."

"Exactly." I rose onto my tiptoes, spreading my palms over his bare chest. "Here's my plan. Uh-uh, stop right there. Before you get all snooty on me, remember I came up with the plan that got rid of Skeiron."

"Indeed you did." He laid his palms on my back, over my shoulder blades. "Let us hear your grand plan, my clever love."

Couldn't keep from smiling. Every time he complimented me, I went all gooey inside, even in the face of unknown peril.

He hugged me to him, his hands holding me up on my toes.

"Tris will stay here with you," I said, "while Max and I track down the oracle."

"No," barked Nevan, Tris, and Max.

The one time all three men could agree was when they wanted to thwart my plan. Figured.

Max piped up first. "I have no idea how to find an oracle."

"I do," Tris offered, "which means it's me who needs to go with Lindsey, not the man-whore over there."

He threw a derisive look at Max, whose self-satisfied smile deepened.

Nevan touched his nose to mine. "I still have considerable reservations about letting you out in the world when an unidentified sorcerer is after you.

One who has, it seems, contacted you directly and sent you—" He scowled at Max. "—a gift incubus."

"I prefer salamander," Max said, still sprawled across the sofa. He let one foot hang off the chaise, his toes swishing, and I got the impression he argued about designations strictly for the sake of being contrary.

Nevan scowled harder, but his features softened when he focused on me. "I must go with you."

"Every time you venture outside," I said, "you vanish and come back exhausted, like somebody vacuumed the life out of you. The part of my plan where you stay here is nonnegotiable. I love you too much to risk it happening again."

Out the corner of my eye, I noticed Max rolling his eyes. Tris simply stared at the floor, hands in his jeans pockets.

Nevan kissed the tip of my nose. "I love you equally as much. Which is why I cannot let you leave here with only an inc—a salamander for protection. Tris would suffice."

"Suffice?" Tris said, insult evident in his tone.

Ignoring him, I slid a hand up to Nevan's cheek. "And I'm not leaving you alone."

"Then we are at an impasse."

"Maybe not." I chewed on my lip, chewing on the problem in a physical way. The answer came to me, and I smiled. "Tris will go through the falls and bring Travis here. Then, Max and Tris and I will find the oracle."

Max sat up, suddenly attentive. "Who is Travis?"

"The sheriff," Nevan said, "of the region on the mortal side of the falls. He despises me."

I patted Nevan's cheek. "Not anymore. Travis puts up with you these days, like you put up with him. And he knows how important you are to me, which means he will guard your life for my sake."

"Because he's smitten with you," Nevan muttered under his breath.

Winding my arms around his neck, I molded my lips to his, rewarded by the rush of heat along his skin that spread into me, kindling a matching warmth. The heat didn't last, though, snuffed out by the clammy coolness of his body.

A hard pit congealed in my gut. I couldn't do nothing while his very life force seemed to be trickling out of him. I knew of a single technique that might work, because it had worked once before.

My mouth to his ear, I whispered, "Maybe we should have sex. It reinvigorated you before."

"Not with an audience," he murmured in my ear. "Besides, I have a feeling I would be unable to, ah…perform."

I dropped down onto my soles. "Really? It's that bad?"

He nodded slowly.

"Then we have to go with my plan."

"I suppose we do." He bent to rest his forehead on mine. "I'll be relying on you to save me—again."

"You've saved me plenty." I twisted my head around to speak to Tris, who was watching us. "Go get Travis. He'll be at the sheriff station, which is outside the boundary. Stan will let you use the shop phone to call him. Be sure to tell Travis this is an emergency and a favor to me."

"Will do."

Nevan opened the doorway and escorted Tris outside. The leprechaun blinked away. Nevan strode back inside, shutting the door.

He glanced at Max, and his lip curled for a brief moment. "Darlin', would ye mind instructing your servant to cover himself?"

I poked a finger into his chest. "You walk around naked, or almost naked, all the time."

"This is different."

"Are you jealous?" I fanned my hand over his chest, moving it in a slow circle. "You know I don't want anyone but you."

"He is an incubus. They possess powers of seduction."

"There's nothing to worry about." I glided my hand up to his shoulder, massaging with my fingertips. "I've spent awhile with Max today, and I haven't felt the slightest inkling of and inclination to ravish him. But the second you got home, I was ready to jump you."

His lips stretched into a gratified smile.

I dragged a finger down his bicep. "I'm yours and only yours."

"And I am yours." His hands drifted down to my buttocks. "But…"

"If it'll make you feel better." I craned my neck to see around Nevan's big arm. "Max, put some clothes on, hey?"

"How much clothing?" he asked, sounding a tad petulant.

I looked at Nevan, whose smile had turned down. "A shirt and pants. Shoes, if you want."

When I glanced at Max again, he'd donned a pair of gray slacks and a black, skintight T-shirt. His feet remained bare.

"Good enough?" I asked Nevan.

"I suppose it will do."

"You don't like him, I get it, but Max has already helped me. I didn't know the soul stone could bring me home." A thought occurred to me and I asked, "How will we know when Tris comes back with Travis?"

Nevan stepped back. "I hadn't thought of that."

"Why not leave the door open? It couldn't take that long."

He opened the doorway with his usual hand gesture.

The three of us stood there in silence, the awkward variety, for several minutes. I swung my hands, clapping them together in front of me on each pass, while Nevan leaned one hand on the wall beside the doorway. Max paced the width of the living room.

At last, Tris and Travis popped up outside the doorway.

"Little help?" Tris said, waving at the invisible barrier of the wards.

Nevan shambled outside, clapped a hand on each man's shoulder, and ushered them inside. He left the door open.

Travis caught sight of Max, and his brows shot up. "Who the blazes is that?"

"My pet incubus," I said. "Travis, meet Max. He's my familiar. Max, this is Travis Blackwell."

Max halted his pacing, eying the newcomer with strange interest.

"Let me get this straight," Travis said. "You're asking me to babysit your boyfriend?"

"Yep. Nevan, give him your endued sword."

Nevan opened his mouth, then clapped it shut. After brief pause, he asked, "Why?"

"To guard you with. If anybody shows up to nab you, at least Travis will have a shot at stopping them."

"I suppose," he said cautiously.

"Come on, honey, give it to him."

Nevan conjured his sword and handed it to Travis. The sheriff accepted the weapon, but his arm wavered a little under its considerable weight.

"Can you handle it?" I asked.

Travis hefted the sword, giving it a cautious swipe through the air. "You bet your ass I can."

Nevan pinched the bridge of his nose with his thumb and forefinger.

I kissed him on the cheek. "Be nice. He's doing us a favor."

My honey grunted, but he escorted me, Max, and Tris outside before retreating back into our lair. Neither I nor Nevan moved, our gazes glued to each other, as the doorway telescoped shut and severed us from each other.

I pulled in a shaky breath, exhaled it with more confidence, and faced my companions. "Let's go find us an oracle."

Chapter Twelve

W E MEANDERED THROUGH THE NIGHT-SHROUDED FOREST, THE ALIEN stars above concealed by a canopy of stringy foliage and vines. Despite the fact it was daylight beyond the confines of this precinct, we'd plunged into full night on crossing into the woods. Max assured me this was part of the safeguards established to protect the oracle. *Creepy magic at work here,* my paranoid subconscious warned.

The girths of the tree trunks measured in yards, most far too big for me to wrap my arms around, if I'd been so inclined. I wasn't. The bark, even masked in gloom, looked gnarled and slippery with a dark, viscous liquid. The scent of ammonia crept over me, faint yet distinct.

Calder? The sorcerer? Both?

Max and Tris, my ersatz guardians, had taken up positions at either side of me. They meant well, and I appreciated their support, but I would've felt much safer with Nevan.

"What is this place?" I asked.

"The dark woods," Max said.

"Of course. And why does it smell like disinfectant, and why do the trees look like they're oozing something I don't want to touch under any circumstances?"

"This place is connected to the source of all magic. It looks forbidding on purpose, to deter passersby from trespassing here."

"Well, it's working. I feel plenty deterred."

I let my arms drop to my sides but then snaked one hand into my pocket to feel the soul stone. The warmth of Nevan's essence surrounded my skin, as if he'd wound both his hands around mine in my pocket. I swore I could hear his voice rumbling in my ear, assuring me, "You are far too obstinate to let the oracle's theatrics stop you."

And I was. For Nevan, I had to be.

I withdrew my hand from my pocket with reluctance, and said, "Shouldn't we go faster? We need to find this oracle guy—person, creature, whatever—in a hurry. Nevan's getting weaker by the minute. Can't we blip there?"

"Blip?" Max asked.

"She talks funny," Tris said. "You'll get used to it. And no, lady, we can't travel that way through this forest. The whole place is warded to prevent it."

I slung an irritated glance his way. "But we can walk faster."

"Yeah-yeah."

Tris sped up his pace, forcing me and Max to hurry to catch up with him. The leprechaun led us down a narrow trail partly overgrown with grass and weeds that, if there'd been more light, I was pretty sure would've still looked black and glossy. The moons must've glowed in the false night sky, but their light filtered down through the forest ceiling to trickle over us and the ground in a wan, greenish glow. In the odd lighting, Max's elegant face took on an otherworldly quality. In daylight, he resembled a human in many ways. In the gloom of the forest, he exemplified this world. Strange, powerful, beyond my comprehension.

Tris looked pretty much the same in the eerie glow of the dark forest.

I kept scratching my arms, infected with an itch I couldn't dispel. The creepy forest was affecting me, that was all. A distraction might make this never-ending journey more bearable, I decided, and opted for my usual backup plan. When in doubt, or when creeped out, ask annoying questions.

"Since we have nothing else to do at the moment," I said, "maybe one of you will answer a question for me."

The leprechaun and the salamander both groaned.

"I'll take that as a yes." Jamming my hands in my pockets, the fingers of my right hand brushing the soul stone, I waited out the wave of Nevan-flavored energy and then asked my question. "Are there boundaries on this side of the falls? Like the ones in the mortal world, I mean."

"Nah," Tris said. "We don't need 'em over here."

"Why not?"

Max replied this time. "The Great Bargain made provisions for barriers only in the mortal realm. Some wanted boundaries here as well, but to convince all elemental species to sign on to the Bargain, the elders had to make concessions."

"Great Bargain?" I glanced at him, but he kept his focus squarely ahead of us. "I don't understand."

Tris grumbled. "Humans don't know crap, do ya? The Great Bargain was a deal hammered out a way long time ago by the elders of all the elemental races. It's kinda our code of laws, but with magic to enforce it."

"But why—"

"The Bargain," Max said, "came about for practical reasons. Eons ago, elementals used magic whenever and however they pleased. The bad among us perverted white magics into black magics, manipulating and controlling anyone who stood against them. The mortal realm became a playground for denizens of the Unseen. A wicked playground I very much doubt mortals enjoyed."

"Okay. So this Great Bargain cleaned things up."

"Yes." He tipped his head left and right, his lips scrunched. "For the most part."

"And the boundaries?"

"It was a concession. To stop evil magic from spreading and consuming both worlds, the elders had to give up the notion of closing the portals." Max ducked as we passed under a low-hanging branch. "The boundaries were a compromise. Elementals can visit the other side, but they can't go more than one mile from a portal. The Bargain also created the healing vortexes as an extra layer of protection for mortals. That's why there are no vortexes in the Unseen."

"Does this world have one leader? A king or something?"

"Each elemental kingdom has a ruler, but there is no ruler of the world." He eyed me sideways. "Would you want that? I seem to recall humans fight against a single ruler having so much control."

"Yeah, we don't like dictators."

"Neither do we. That's why Skeiron had to die, isn't it? At any rate, the only being with omnipotence is the Oversoul."

"The what now?"

He gave me a patient smile. "An ethereal, unknowable, and benevolent presence that governs all of existence, in all worlds."

"You mean a god."

"Oh no. We have gods, not all of them benevolent."

Through the trees up ahead, a gurgling sound emanated from a small stream. We halted about a dozen feet from it. The waters flowed and burbled, skipping over stones embedded in the glistening earth, and steam wafted up from the water. The odor of sulfur choked my nose, making me gag.

Max waved a white cloth in front of my face. Cool, fresh air seemed to emerge from the cloth, and I gulped it in, cleansing my lungs and my sense of smell. He held his hand there, keeping up the flow of sweet, clean air from the strange fabric.

"What is that?" I asked.

"A little something I conjured. Cloth made of air, which I stole from a sylph."

I snatched the cloth from his hand. "Did you steal this from Nevan?"

"He won't miss it."

Holding the fabric over my mouth and nose, I shook a finger at him. "No more stealing from my boyfriend. Got it?"

"Fine. I won't take from him again."

"We gotta cross the stream," Tris said. "No 'blipping' over it."

The hint of trepidation in his tone awakened butterflies in my stomach. Butterflies with steel-tipped, razor-sharp wings.

I glanced at the steaming water, which began to churn and spit. The stream was too wide to jump over, at least twenty feet across. "You mean we have to wade through it?"

"Absolutely not," Max declared, straightening and squaring his shoulders. "I can jump it. You'll need to lock your legs around my waist and tightly hold your arms around my neck. Otherwise, you'll risk falling into the waters. It's pure acid."

Of course it was.

I had to cling to an incubus? Good thing Nevan wasn't here to see this.

My chest ached. If Nevan were here, I would've clung to him for the ride.

"You can't let go of me, Lindsey, no matter what happens." Max glanced at the stream. A glint of cold, white fear sliced through the red-hot lava in his eyes. "There are things in the trees, things that wait for a weak moment and pounce on it."

Of course there were. "I assume leaping over this obstacle counts as a weak moment."

"It does. We will be vulnerable." Max turned toward me, his expression grave. "You can still give up and go back."

"No way. I need to do this, and I trust you and Tris to keep me safe."

"Are you sure about that? I'm enslaved to your enemy."

"But you're my familiar. You serve me, right?" When he gave a curt nod, I stuffed the air cloth in my pocket. "I trust you. Take me over the stream."

Max averted his eyes for heartbeat, then met my gaze. "You do realize getting the truth from the oracle might cost you more than you want to give."

"Oh, I figured as much. But I've got no other options."

Circumstances left me a single path. Charge ahead, or Nevan would die.

Max moved closer, but stopped a couple feet away. He gestured at me with one finger. "I'll need to take hold of you."

"Go ahead."

He sidled up to me, lowered his hands to grasp my buttocks, and hefted me off my feet. I locked my legs around him, ankles tight as a padlock, horrible visions flashing in my mind of being incinerated by acid water. As he shifted his arms to my back, firming up his grip, I hooked my arms around his neck.

My cheek flush with his, I said, "Ready."

In a blur of motion, he spun toward the stream and launched us into the air. Tree branches whizzed past. Air buffeted my face and arms, brittle and cold as the vacuum of space. My eyes burned. I held my breath, unable to summon the courage to inhale whatever those bizarre trees exuded. Our momentum shifted downward, the gale instigated by our flight gusting up at me instead of down.

A clawed hand latched onto my leg. The sharp talons dug into me through my jeans, and without thinking, I kicked out at the attacker.

"Stop!" Max's voice hollered in my ear.

The talons dug in deeper. One pierced my jeans, and the razor edge sliced my flesh with searing agony that overwhelmed reason. I knew I shouldn't move, but my body had taken control of itself, shutting out my brain. I flailed my leg. The thing attached to the talons lost its grip, freeing my leg.

I glimpsed a dark, monkey-like shape sailing downward away from us.

An inhuman shriek rang out below us.

We veered sideways. I padlocked my legs around Max again, but it was too late. The momentum of my battle with the monkey-thing had thrown us off balance. We spun out into a wild tumble, aimed straight toward the ground. I held onto Max, helpless to do anything to spare us from a bone-crushing impact with the ground.

He lurched. The movement flipped us over and halted our free-fall with his back to the ground. He shoved me away, hurling me up instead of down while he slammed into the earth with a sickening thud.

I sailed down, about to strike him.

He reached up to pluck me from the air and curb my descent. My body balanced on his palms, he lowered me to the ground beside him, easy as a leaf. My body met slippery earth. I sprang to my knees, scrubbing at my face and arms and chest, desperate to cleanse myself of the greasy, foul-smelling mud.

Max lay motionless beside me.

I scrambled to my knees. He'd smacked into the ground at full speed. I threw a hand out, intent on jabbing my finger into his neck to check for a pulse.

His strong fingers clinched my wrist.

"You're alive," I gasped.

Max sat up, letting go of my wrist. "Didn't I explain, in explicit terms, you shouldn't let go of me under any circumstances?"

His anger hit me like a slap. I deserved it, yeah, but his warning had been a tad vague. "If you'd said watch out for the crazy monkey-things with razor claws, I might've suggested we find another way around the acid river. Hey, why is my familiar getting testy with me? I'm your mistress."

"There's no other way across the bloody river. And yes, you are my mistress. But I'm allowed to point out when you bollocks up the plan and nearly kill yourself." He flung his arms around my waist and leaped to his feet, hoisting me up with him, then ripped his hands away and stumbled backward a step. He stared at the ground for several seconds before his head slowly lifted. "Did you say a creature attacked you?"

"Uh-huh. Looked like one of those damn kerkopes things." I gave an exaggerated shudder. "I had to shake the monster off. I know you said not to let go, but what else could I do? Its claws—"

"Are you hurt?" His unblinking gaze searched my body.

"It scratched my leg a little, but I'm okay."

Max dropped to a crouch. With one hand he seized my ankle, while with the other he yanked up the leg of my torn jeans. He muttered in another language, different from Nevan's sylph tongue, but I was pretty sure it was a curse. With a swish of his hand, he conjured a bandage. After securing the adhesive bandage over my wound, he uncoiled his body before me and ducked his head to fix me with a chastising glare.

"Don't give me that look," I said. "If Nevan can't cow me with it, you sure can't. What did you expect me to do? Let the monkey-beast shred my leg?"

He growled out a sigh, his tension easing a bit. "I realize you acted on instinct, but you could've told me one of the kerkopes was attacking you."

"What would you have done about it?"

"I don't know. Shot flames at it, for a start." He rubbed his neck. "How do you know about kerkopes? You seem ignorant of most everything about this world."

"Way to brown nose with your mistress, lizard boy." I rubbed my arms, not cold but still itchy from the weirdness around me. "I met one. He was my ex-fiancé, forged into a monkey-man monster."

"I see."

"Didn't think, and I caused a problem that got you—" *Slammed into the ground like a meteorite.* If he'd been hurt, it would've been my fault. "You hit the ground so hard. Are you okay?"

"Yes." He whirled around to confront the path that led away from the acid river. "We should go."

We marched onward through the forest, as its bows thickened into an impenetrable roof. No light leaked in from above, yet the pale green glow suffused the environment. It seemed to originate from nowhere and everywhere, its light enough to guide us but too faint to reveal any details. We trudged through a landscape of shadows and silhouettes, Max and Tris at my sides, Max's bare feet slapping on the greasy earth. My boots squished into the ground, the earth giving just enough to slither unease through me.

My stupid imagination kicked into overdrive, assailing me with vile visions. Me stepping into a hidden sinkhole, the slimy dirt gobbling me up whole. Monkey-things plummeting out of the trees to slash me to ribbons. A hooded figure popping out of the blackness to abduct me and suck my brain.

The sorcerer. He couldn't know where we were, could he?

I stopped dead and grabbed Max's arm to halt him.

He gave me a questioning look.

"The sorcerer." I glanced up at the sky, or where the sky should've been. "Can he find us here? Do the kerkopes work for him?"

Max's jaw clenched, a muscle jumped there.

I threw my head back and moaned. "You can't tell me."

"Try rephrasing your question."

I contemplated the options. How to phrase it so he could answer without violating his deal with the sorcerer? "Will the wards in this forest keep anyone and everyone from whisking in? Does everybody have to travel the old-fashioned way?"

"Yes and yes."

I gazed up into the darkness. "What about the monkey-things?"

"They guard the river," Max said. "I doubt they'll hunt us anymore."

"If you say so."

Setting out again, we followed Tris down a narrowing trail. No more monkey-things leaped out at us. I wondered whether the kerkopes attack had anything to do with Calder. He might've been the beast that assaulted me, but since I'd never seen him in his monkey form, I had no way to figure that out.

After a time, the length of which I couldn't gauge, the forest spread its arms out to reveal a small clearing and a gigantic boulder seated at its center. The rock was taller than Max, though not by much. He escorted me to the giant rock and knocked on it. A portion of the stone rippled, thinned into a semi-transparent barrier, and dissolved. Its absence exposed a doorway and a pitch-dark passage beyond it.

Tris entered first, and Max shepherded me inside. The passage was narrow, so I walked behind Tris with Max behind me. I clenched the soul stone in my pocket, grateful for the connection to Nevan as we penetrated deeper into the blackness.

The passage curved left. When we rounded the corner, a faint yellow glow became visible in the distance. Max moved in front of me, and I peeked around his massive shoulder to spy the source of the light. Up ahead, the passage dead-ended at a doorway shorter than the corridor ceiling, shorter than Max but taller than Tris. Inside the doorway, a fire burned within some kind of large container.

Tris entered the room.

Max stepped sideways, blocking my view, then hunched over to cross the threshold.

Inside the room, he stopped. I hurried up beside him, suddenly aware of the surroundings. We'd entered a chamber hewn from solid rock, but the dark walls were gilded with a semi-translucent coating of pale gold.

A solitary object occupied the space. The fire I'd glimpsed burned inside a metal bowl about five feet wide, perched atop curving legs that terminated in cat-like feet. The bronze bowl had a rough texture to it, catching and releasing the light in glimmers and glints. The flames stretched upward several feet, their amber color intensely beautiful.

The fire reminded me of Nevan's eyes.

I sidled closer to Max, though not so close we touched. "Is the oracle some kind of elemental?"

"No," a strange voice replied, echoing from elsewhere. "Not anymore."

A figure traipsed out of the shadows at the room's periphery.

The oracle was a man. His tailored, navy-blue suit conformed to his slender body as he moseyed up to the fire, a few yards away from us. The flickering light shimmered on his short, slicked-back gray hair.

The oracle smiled, his copious wrinkles deepening. "Not that I've got anything against elemental kind, mind you." He wandered closer, stopping a few yards away. His voice bore a strange accent, unlike any I'd heard before. "I've got nothing against anybody. I've moved beyond those designations is all. Understand?"

His bright green eyes fixed on me and sparkled—not from the firelight, but with an internal brilliance. His irises exuded a light so similar to the eerie illumination in the woods that I knew the two must be connected. I sensed it on a visceral level.

"Do you understand?" the oracle demanded.

"Yes, I get it." Didn't really, but telling this being I was confused seemed like a bad idea.

"No need to apologize, dearie." He ambled to the fire, waving a hand into the oily flames, fluttering his fingers with indolent interest. "You came to ask a question. Get to it, then. I'm a busy man."

"Are you really the oracle?" I think my mouth flapped a couple times, as I took in his appearance one more time. "You look like you might negotiate a corporate merger, not foretell the future."

"Were you expecting flowing white robes?"

Yeah, I had been. Another preconception dashed on the invincible rocks of reality.

"Guess I was," I said.

A soft laugh accompanied his brief smile. He shook his head and let out a melodramatic sigh. "You humans and your mythology." All business again, he fixed me with a stare so laser-sharp it cut down to my soul. "Your question, please."

"I, uh, well—"

"Spit it out, mortal."

His tone sharpened the word mortal into a threat and an insult.

Max's shoulders arched in high tension, and the air around him buzzed with it. I settled a hand on his arm, amazed by the granite hardness of his muscles, and grumbled under my breath, "Take a chill pill. I'll handle this."

His mouth opened, a protest on the verge of erupting, but he heeded my command.

The oracle shoved one hand inside his waistband, one hip cocked. The fingers of his other hand curled and uncurled within the flames. His eyes drilled into mine, the power of his attention searing. "This matter concerns the sylph king, yet you bring a leprechaun and a salamander instead."

"Nevan isn't feeling well. Besides, somebody's after him and he has to stay inside our warded home for his own safety."

"You speak for the king, Janusite?"

Everything inside me went ice cold, freezing me in place. Ennea's warning that the oracle recognize my true nature had done nothing to cushion the impact of his statement.

"Relax," the oracle said. "I'm a seer. Did you really think I wouldn't know what you are? But rest assured, I have no interest in spreading the news. Only those who make it here receive my counsel, and I don't share with anyone who has an evil heart." He gaze flicked to Max, but his expression did not change. "The fact this one was admitted to my sanctum should tell you something."

"Are you saying Max won't betray me?"

Wrinkles deepened on the oracle's face as he smiled with genial fatherliness. "You know the answer. You feel it in your heart. And you, dearie, have the truest heart and strongest soul of any I've met."

Two forbidden words rose in my throat. I gulped them down. Thanking this man—or whatever he was—seemed even more ill-advised than my gratitude to Tris had been all those weeks ago. "Mr. Oracle—um, your highness—er…"

"Call me Bob."

"Seriously?"

He chuckled, sounding very much like Santa Claus. The unsettling green glow of his eyes dimmed to a twinkling emerald. "You could invoke my full name, Bobanzhistilanovitz, but most people find it easier to call me Bob."

"I can see why." I took three halting steps toward him and proffered my unsteady hand. "I'm Lindsey Porter, puny and inconsequential mortal from the other side of the falls."

"And I thought my appellation was a mouthful."

Bob clasped my hand, his cool against my palm, the grip firm and powered by taut sinews. As he bent toward me, his pecs flexed against the thin fabric of his dress shirt.

No Santa Claus after all.

He slid his other hand beneath mine, pancaking my palm between both of his. "Pleasure to meet you, Lindsey. But you should know one thing before we continue."

"What's that?"

"The sylph will be your undoing."

Chapter Thirteen

"WHICH SYLPH?" I ASKED, THOUGH THE SICK FEELING IN MY STOMACH told me I knew the answer. It had to be a load of crap. Someone was messing with Nevan's head, though, and I had to wonder whether the oracle's claim held any truth.

"You know the answer," Bob said. "The sylph king, Nevan. Your lover."

"Nevan wouldn't hurt me."

"That's true. And yet, he will destroy you. Leave him now, before—"

"No." I barred my arms over my chest. "I'm not abandoning Nevan because a weirdo in a cave claims to have mystical insight."

"Listen to me, mortal." Bob's voice resounded through the cavern, loud and clear and tinged with empathy. "You are the most important being ever to be born in any realm. The power of the Janusite must not fall into the wrong hands. If you stay with the sylph king, he will lead you to your destruction."

I squinted at Bob, desperate to debunk his claims. Really, how did I know he was an oracle and not an impostor? The sorcerer had impersonated Nevan, after all.

"Your turn to listen, bucko," I said. "I need some proof you are who you say you are. All the immortals I've met have the ability to glamour into any disguise they want. You're the oracle, huh? Prove it."

His lips formed a tiny smile, without mirth. "You're a canny one, aren't you? And rightly suspicious. Someone has been impersonating your lover, someone with immense power and a grudge to settle."

Okay, so he knew about something I'd told no one but Nevan. If Bob was the sorcerer, he would know about the fake Nevan because he was the one inside the black robes.

"I need more proof than that," I told the oracle. "For all I know, you are the one who's been pretending to be Nevan."

"There is something else I could reveal," Bob said, "but you might not want your friends to hear it."

Max glanced at me sideways, a question in his eyes. Tris shuffled forward to stand at my other side.

"Your decision," Tris said. "But we won't tattle. Will we, salamander?"

"Never," Max agreed.

Did I trust these two? Tris had been through an apocalyptic battle with me, besides performing the magics that saved Nevan's life. Max I'd just met, but my instincts assured me I could trust him. He was my familiar, after all.

Oh hell, it wasn't like I had a choice.

"It's okay," I told Bob. "You can say it in front of them, whatever it is."

"If that's what you want." He strolled around the fiery cauldron to stand directly in front of me. "The last time you had sexual relations with Nevan, you invoked your magic to restore his vigor. Blue energy surrounded you both." He smiled with his lips closed, yet it wrinkled his eyes and dimpled his cheeks. "And it was the best sex either of you has ever had. Nevan theorized your magic was activated by the heightened emotions that came from your decision to move in with him."

I opened my mouth but couldn't form words. Bob had quoted Nevan almost verbatim. No one but Nevan and I knew what had gone on in our home this morning.

Tris snickered. "Feeling a little tired myself. Can I get some of that magic?"

Max glared at him. "Show respect to the Janusite."

"Zip it, both of you," I said. "My magic is for Nevan and nobody else."

Bob tilted his head left and right, as if sizing me up. "Now that you know I'm the real deal, maybe you'll take my words to heart. You are the most powerful—"

"Yeah-yeah, I get it." I yearned for Nevan's arms around, for his presence filling me with a depth of solace the soul stone couldn't replicate. "How does being a supernatural taxi service make me so damn important, anyway?"

"Has anyone told you the whole prophecy?"

"No."

"You should hear it." Bob scratched his chin, then squared his shoulders and lifted his chin. In a resonant and powerful voice worthy of a deity, he said, "In the twentieth era of the mortal calendar, a girl child shall be born into an enlightened clan. She will possess the power of Janus, god of the doorways and of transitions, and like him she will face both ways, belonging to neither but bound to everything. Boundaries fall in her presence. The veil shall open to her, she who holds the power to converge the worlds, she whose power is beyond any seen before in any realm. She is the bearer of the key and the staff, the child of the god, she is the Janusite."

I tried to speak, but managed only a squeak too soft for anyone to hear.

Max spoke to the oracle. "You told this to Skeiron."

Bob made a raspberry and flapped a dismissive hand. "I'm not dumb. I told Skeiron the Janusite would be born in the twentieth century of the mortal calendar, and she will have the power to escort immortals across the portal boundaries."

"That's it?" I demanded. "You didn't slip up and tell him I'm the most important thing ever to be born?"

His eyes locked onto mine, sending a faint shiver through me, pure cold and certainty transmitted from him into me. I hated the way he could do that. My connection with Nevan seemed rooted in our sensual bond, and thus, it gave me a pleasurable shiver. But the oracle's gaze made the hairs at my nape quiver.

"I don't slip up," he said. "Skeiron wanted you because he was dead-set on taking over the mortal realm."

"What about the sorcerer? I'm assuming you know about him. You said he has a grudge to settle."

"I know of him, but I haven't had the displeasure of meeting him." Bob jammed his thumbs inside the waistband of his slacks. "I imagine he wants you for the same reason Skeiron did."

"Dominating one world isn't good enough for these creeps? They have to trample my world too?" Before he could respond to my rhetorical questions, I charged ahead with a real one. "Who is the sorcerer? What's his grudge? And does it have anything to do with what you said about me being the bearer of the key and the staff?"

Bob rocked back on the heels of his shiny leather loafers. "The sorcerer's grudge is hard to pinpoint, though I can sense the seething nature of it. I can't see his identity, which is odd. Whatever magic he's tapped into is blocking my foresight, but I can sniff the odor of stolen power on it. The girls he killed, they all had a touch of the Unseen in them. He depleted them of whatever magic was inside them and extracted the innate magic of their souls."

That explained so much, more than I could comprehend at the moment. "Can't you give me any information about the sorcerer himself?"

"What I can tell you is—"

A *thwack* reverberated through the small space.

Bob twitched, his eyes bulging.

The blade of a sword burst out of his chest, blood dripping from its tip.

He tumbled to the floor. His eyes remained wide, the vitality leeching out of them as his body crumpled into a heap on the stone floor.

The oracle was dead.

Paralyzed, I couldn't move so much as my eyes—and for a moment, I couldn't process the sight before me. At the back of the cavern, behind where Bob lay lifeless on the floor, the sorcerer's minion wielded a blood-soaked black sword.

Skeiron's sword.

Ceara smiled, like a snake opening her jaws to consume her prey.

"You lose again," she said. "Stop fighting and come to the sorcerer. Only then might your friends and loved ones be spared a horrific death."

A rage burning with a cold fire erupted inside me. I yanked out my endued derringer, aimed it straight at her head, and fired.

She vanished.

The bullet slammed into the rock wall.

Max laid a hand on my arm, the one still raised to brandish my gun. "She's gone."

I whirled on my so-called familiar, shoving my gun into his chest. "Did you lead her here? You both work for the sorcerer."

"I haven't knowingly led his consort here. A familiar serves his mistress above all others and cannot knowingly endanger her safety or betray her confidence."

"You said knowingly twice. I'm guessing that means you're not sure you didn't accidentally lead Ceara here."

Max made a pained face but did not look away from me. "I can't be sure. I wish I could, because I don't want to betray you, even without my knowledge."

Damn if I didn't believe him. A matter of weeks ago, I'd scoffed at the idea of intuition—until I met Nevan and had no choice but to trust my gut about him. That instinct had proved right. Today, my intuition whispered I could trust Max. Once again, I had no choice but to rely on my inner voice.

"I believe you," I told Max. "But these woods are supposed to be protected. I'm guessing this chamber is too. How did Ceara get inside?"

Tris, who'd been stiff and immobile since the villainess attacked, turned his haunted gaze toward me. "Bob said the sorcerer has immense power, and he's somehow able to cloak himself. If even an oracle can't divine the creep's identity…"

"We're in deep shit." I curled my fingers into my palms. "The sorcerer and his minions can break through the forest wards, which means we can't get away from them."

My pulse accelerated, my mouth went dry, and the room seemed to tilt around me. I must've swayed, because Max grasped my upper arms to steady me.

"What is it?" he asked.

"Nevan. The wards." I wrenched free of Max's grip, shoved the gun into its holster, and sprinted for the doorway. "I have to get home. *Now.*"

Tris and Max raced up behind me, the narrowness of the passage keeping them from coming up beside me. Our footfalls thudded on the dusty rock floor, echoing down the passage.

"Lindsey," Max began.

I cut him off with a flap of my hand. "No time."

Bursting out of the passage into the coal-dark woods, I exploded into a dead run.

Max leaped in front of me, forcing me to halt.

"Out of my way," I spat. "I have to get home."

"Why? You said something about Nevan."

Through clenched teeth, I said, "Our home is protected by wards. The sorcerer can get through wards. You do the math, genius."

His eyes widened, his lips parted.

Tris sidled around me to stand beside Max. "There's the river and a gang of kerkopes in our way."

I shoved my hand in my pocket to stroke the soul stone. It sizzled with Nevan's energy, with his life force, and tears stung my eyes at the sensation of it pouring through me. *Hold on, Nevan, fight it. For me. For us.*

"We have to hurry," I said, and dashed down the trail through the murky woods with an incubus and a leprechaun hot on my heels.

Running. Running. Shoes slapping on slimy earth. Lungs burning. Muscles cramping. On and on and on I ran without any thought for my companions, my mind consumed with visions of Nevan being abducted, or worse, all because I hadn't considered the sorcerer's incredible power and that he might be able to infiltrate the wards. If anything happened to Nevan, it would be my fault.

I barreled onward, heedless of my surroundings.

Max's arms locked around my midsection, and he snatched up me mid-step as he hopped backward away from the river. My heart thumped against my ribs. I hadn't noticed the acid-spitting flow in front of me. Max didn't have to tell me what to do this time. I spun around, flung my arms around his neck, and locked my legs around him. He clenched me tightly, on the verge of cutting off my air, as he bounded up and over the river.

We struck the ground with a jarring thud. Tris landed right beside us, already breathing hard, his cheeks flushed.

Max released me, and I took off.

Chattering broke out overhead, in the treetops.

Recognition zinged through me. I glanced back to see Max and Tris sprinting after me, edging closer with each stride but still a good fifteen feet behind.

"That noise," I called to them. "What is it?"

"Kerkopes," Max shouted. "Stop and I'll—"

A black shape hurtled down from the treetops. It smacked into Max, bowling him over, and he whumped onto the ground face-down. Another monkey-thing collided with Tris and sent him careening into a glistening black bush.

A weight smashed into me from above and behind my head. I stumbled forward. Lost my footing. Tumbled toward the ground. Talons snagged the back of my shirt, jerking me back but then shoving me forward. Fabric ripped. I crashed into the ground face-first, oily mud thrust into my nostrils and open mouth, gagging me with its acrid stench and revolting taste. Those talons latched onto my waist at either side, sinking into my flesh.

The monkey-monster hefted me up and propelled us into the treetops.

I screamed Nevan's name.

Somewhere in the back of my crazed mind, I realized he wasn't here. And down there, in the murk far below, I spied two limp figures.

My captor let out a gleeful cackle. We rocketed straight out of the trees into the vacant, blinding sky.

CHAPTER FOURTEEN

MY LEGS DANGLED FREE, FLAILED BY THE WILD CURRENT OF OUR MOtion. I held my arms up to shield my face from the gale. The monkey-thing soared so high over the forest, I knew if I shook free of the beast I'd plummet to my death, crushed by my own velocity. The beast's talons pierced my skin. The pain stung, but not as hotly as the knowledge I was being flown Air Sorcerer, right into the clutches of the one being I did not want to meet again.

Max excelled at jumping, but he couldn't jump into the stratosphere. If he could have, he'd be killing this flying monster right now. So what, I'd just wait to be dumped in the sorcerer's lap?

Like hell. I'd rather die.

I wrestled with the talons, but the monkey-thing gripped them harder, puncturing deeper. A warm liquid trickled over my skin, and pain shot out across my back and abdomen. A wave of nausea pushed my gorge high in my throat. I choked it back and swung my fists up to pummel the beast in the face. My fist connected with a crack.

My captor cackled.

Dammit. I couldn't get a good position to attack while restrained by black talons. I felt my flesh ripping within the wounds, those talons shredding deep.

Darkness speckled my vision.

I could not go down like this, no way. I struggled, but succeeded only in unleashing a torrent of agony that racked my whole body. My ears rang. The darkness encroached more and more into my vision. The wind of our travel lashed my arm into my body, and my hand slapped into the holster hidden beneath my shirt.

The gun. Of course, the gun.

I floundered for the holster and missed it, my body thrown side to side by the flapping of the beast's wings and its zigzagging flight path. At last, my fingers latched onto the gun's grip. I closed my hand around it, tearing the weapon free. I'd fired one shot at Ceara, which meant I had one round left in the chamber. One shot to save myself.

My finger poised over the trigger, I jammed the muzzle into the monkey-thing's chest and fired.

Its body convulsed. We swooped lower, my feet grazing the treetops. Pitch-black leaves erupted up around us. We flew onward, even as crimson blood streamed from the wound in the creature's chest, spraying over my head, into my hair and onto my face.

I flipped the derringer over to pound the butt into the creature's wound.

The monkey-thing wobbled. Its talons popped open.

I sailed downward, straight into the trees. Branches scraped my skin and thwacked into me. I grunted with each blow. The gun slipped out of my hand, and I shielded my head with both arms.

The ground. It was coming. Fast.

I would die. It would be more agony than I could imagine but at least, I prayed, it would be quick.

Something caught me.

Arms cinched me tight against a hard body. I kicked at my new captor.

"Stop, it's me. It's Max."

I stopped struggling and cracked my lids open to peek at the being holding me in his arms. It looked like Max, but that was no comfort anymore.

As if sensing my paranoia, he set me down on my feet.

Tris galloped up behind him, doubled over and fighting for breath. "Jeez Louise, I didn't know salamanders could run like that."

"Powered by fire, we can."

That was when I noticed it. Tiny, flickering flames of yellow and white. They flowed over his skin, dying out here only to pop up there, like a second skin made of fire.

And then I noticed his hand, the one he cradled in the opposite palm.

I grabbed at his wrist. "Are you hurt?"

"Take it easy," he said, dropping his uninjured hand to show me the damaged one. "It will grow back."

His middle finger was gone. Snapped off. No blood poured from the wound, because there was no wound. The skin had sealed shut over the stump.

"Grow back?" I asked.

"Yes," he said, eying me with concern. "Salamanders can regrow many of our body parts."

I remembered reading that once, long ago, in a magazine article or something. The mundane salamanders in the mortal world could regrow limbs.

Max scanned his gaze up and down my body, assessing me without even the tiniest hint of sexual interest. Instead, he seemed…worried. Very, very worried.

"You're injured," he said, his tone gruff. "Let me see the wounds."

"Most of the blood isn't mine."

"I can tell. It's kerkopes blood." He gently lifted the hem of my shirt, exposing my side, and swallowed a gasp. "These wounds…"

Blackness licked at the edges of my vision. The pain in my sides had dulled, overtaken by a growing chill. Part of me recognized this was bad news, but my mind was clouded, my body energized by a burst of adrenaline I knew wouldn't last long.

Max's brow furrowed as he studied my wounds. He lifted my shirt higher to expose the other side of my abdomen.

"Lindsey." The shock in his voice barely penetrated my brain, as numbness swept through me. He shifted his hands to my upper back, his gaze zeroed in on mine. "You're seriously wounded."

"Duh." It came out as a frail murmur.

I swayed against him. The world gyrated around me, but I was sinking ever downward. "I'm going to pass out. Promise you'll get to Nevan first, worry about me later."

Max scooped me into his arms. "I have to obey, but my friend doesn't."

He passed me to Tris.

The last thing I saw was Max's face, darkened by grim determination, right before he blazed into the woods moving faster than any being I'd seen and dragging a wake of fire behind him.

My eyelids, too heavy to stay open, drifted shut and the world slipped away.

———

I WOKE WITH A JOLT, MY HEART POUNDING. LIGHT ENVELOPED ME, COMING from nowhere and everywhere. Blinking rapidly, I tried to sort out what my eyes revealed to me. I was lying on the red velvet chaise, cushioned by its plushness, with my head elevated. Pushing up into a sitting position, my legs splayed before me, I rotated my head left and right to take in the scene around me.

This was home. Mine and Nevan's.

Tris hunched several yards away near the doorway to the kitchen fiddling with his fingers. He nodded as if listening to something or someone. Gradually, the sounds penetrated the fog around my mind and I recognized Max's voice. I couldn't understand his words, though, because he spoke in a hushed tone.

The open doorway caught my attention. The door to the outside. The sun shined out there, and despite knowing the oracle's forest had existed in a false night, my brain tripped up in its efforts to comprehend the presence of daylight.

Out the corner of my eye, I spied a shape on the bed maybe ten feet from where I huddled on the floor. I glanced at the bed—and the breath caught in my throat.

Scrambling to my feet, I rushed to the bed and perched on its edge.

Nevan lay limp atop the fur blanket, eyes shut, face ashen. His chest seemed not to move, and even when I settled a palm on his torso, I couldn't feel his lungs inflating. I mashed my ear to his chest, my arms going weak when I heard the steady, if slow, beating of his heart. I held my ear to his face and felt the faintest whisper of his breaths on my skin.

With my hands at either side of his head, I bowed mine in silent thanks to whatever power kept him alive. *Thank God. Thank the Oversoul. Thank every divine being in the heavens.*

"You're awake," announced a male voice tinged with a Texas twang.

I startled, lurching upright, and half turned toward the man who'd slunk to the head of the bed a few feet away from me.

Travis looked sick, like he might throw up any second, but he kept his posture straight and taut. "You okay?"

"Yeah." I knew without checking my wounds had healed. "Tris fixed me up?"

"He did. Couldn't heal Nevan, though. Something about putrid magic." Travis ducked his head, bunching his shoulders. "I fucked it up big time."

I slipped my hand around one of Nevan's, grateful for the contact but disturbed by the chill of his skin. "The sorcerer was here."

"No, his girlfriend."

"Ceara." I shut my eyes for a moment, struggling to hold back the anger and terror swelling inside me. Time to rein it all in and make this right, somehow. "She must've zipped over here right after she killed the oracle."

"Seems like. Max filled me in on your little adventure."

I ran my hand up to Nevan's cheek. Cold, so cold.

"Tell me," I said, "what happened here."

"She came, she attacked, I tried to fight her off." Though my focus remained on Nevan's pallid face, the way Travis cleared his throat told me he dreaded sharing the rest. "I tried to use the sword, swear to God I did, but she was so freaking fast. And he was helping her."

My gaze shot to Travis. "Nevan? He helped Ceara fight you off?"

"Yeah." His attention shot to something past my shoulder, and I glanced there to see Nevan's sword leaning against the wall. A long, thin, dark-red splotch stained its blade. Travis gripped the back of his neck. "I got in one good poke, but all I did was wing her. Nevan threw me into the wall, and I was too stunned to think for a minute. That's when she, uh…"

One hand on Nevan's chest, I fixed Travis with my hardest glare. "She what?"

He cleared his throat again, shoving his hands in the pants pockets of his sheriff's uniform. To his credit, he met my gaze head-on. "She kissed him. A full-on, all-tongues-in kiss. And he stood there, not moving, like he was—"

"In a trance." I smoothed my fingers over Nevan's forehead. "I've seen it before."

"After that, she skedaddled." Travis sighed and crouched beside me. "I let you down, Lindsey, big time. You left me here to protect him and I—"

"Did the best you could." I clutched my hands on my lap, feeling my lower lip tremble as I said, "This was my fault. I should never have left him here, should've guessed the sorcerer would have a way to get past the wards. He's got loads of power, and I'm—" I held my breath for a moment, refusing to cry. "I am nothing compared to him. What chance have I got to stop this and save Nevan?"

Travis settled a hand on mine, the touch tentative. "You can't blame yourself. This ain't nobody's fault but that bitch and her boyfriend."

Boyfriend. The word rang in my mind, stirring a memory of what Max had said about Ceara. *I have not knowingly led his consort here.* At the time, I'd focused on the "knowingly" part of his statement. Another fragment of it became so much more important right now.

I stalked across the room to where Max and Tris loitered. "Max, you called Ceara the sorcerer's consort. Are you saying she's his lover? His mate?"

"Lover, yes," he answered, bracing his body against the kitchen doorway. "Mate? Can't say for sure. The term implies a bond, and I can't speak to that. He does impart some of his power into her when they join."

"You mean when they screw."

He gave a bitter laugh. "Yes, I do mean that. An apt description for the bloody disturbing things they do to each other."

"You've watched?"

Max averted his gaze, his head bent downward. "They would order me to revert to salamander form, then lock me in a cage. It was kept near their bed."

Yech. I couldn't imagine being forced to witness whatever depraved acts two evil sickos performed on each other.

Tris made a disgusted face. "How does knowing they do the nasty help us?"

"Not sure yet," I said, "but every scrap of information we can get has to be of use sooner or later. If they're lovers then maybe, just maybe, one or both of them has gotten attached to the other. We may be able to use that."

Travis had joined our little confab, coming up beside me. "What now?"

"Nevan doesn't look so good," Tris said. "Anybody got an idea what they're doing to him?"

Travis raised his hand, like a kid in a classroom. "Almost forgot, Ceara said to give you a message."

"What message?"

"Said when she's done with him, Nevan will be as hollow as a the trunk of a dead tree, the perfect vessel, and you will have surrendered willingly."

"Hollow..." I struggled to comprehend the meaning, but couldn't. "No idea what that means. I failed Nevan. I can't save him, can't save anyone, can't do a damn thing to stop the sorcerer."

"Bullshit," Travis said, with a conviction that gave his voice a raspy edge. "You're the Janusite."

"Which means I can ferry immortals across the boundaries in the mortal world. I can open portals on my own. Big fucking whoop. When I'm confronted with real power, I crumble. Being the Janusite means diddly-squat."

Max grabbed my shoulders and shook me. "Stop this, Lindsey. You are not powerless, not against this Ceara and not against the sorcerer. You heard what the oracle said. You are the most powerful being ever to be born in either world."

His eyes glowed with swirling torrents of flame. Red, white, blue, orange, yellow. All the colors of fire whipped through his irises while feathery, translucent flames licked upward from his skin.

"I am your familiar," he said, with a forcefulness that captured my attention, "to use as you see fit. I can help you harness and strengthen your magics, to understand where your power stems from." He pulled me a smidgen closer, near enough the scorching heat of him seared my skin. "So use me, Lindsey."

Travis edged away from us, studying the Janusite and her familiar with furtive glances.

Alongside Max, Tris leaned back against the wall. "Can I watch?"

Max threw him an annoyed glance. "There will be no sex involved, perverse little leprechaun."

"I wasn't talking about that. Never seen a familiar and his mistress at work, though. Might be kinda cool."

Max stared into my eyes. "Use me."

"Okay, fine." I wrestled out his grasp, turning to look at Nevan's unconscious form. "But I need Tris and Travis to do something else in the meantime. And I will not leave this house."

Max inclined his head. "Of course."

"The wards are down, I assume. Since you and Tris got inside."

"Yes, they're gone." Max gave me a considering look. "Maybe you and I can get them up again—and give them a power boost."

"Think we could sorcerer-proof the wards?"

"Worth a try." He arched a brow at me. "If you're willing to fully embrace your magics."

I glanced at Nevan again, and my heart constricted. "I'm ready. Time to use my familiar."

Which didn't sound at all weird. These days, weirdness had become my new normal.

"Tris," I said, "go to Ennea and see if there's anything she can offer."

"Like what?" he asked.

"Anything," I repeated, over-enunciating each syllable. Then I looked to Travis. "You go home and find out everything you can about the murders. I know they're connected. I'm counting on your cop skills to ferret out as much information as possible."

"You got it," Travis said.

He and Tris headed out the still-open doorway.

I pointed at the door. "Was that open when we got here?"

"Yes," Max said. "Your friend the sheriff told me Ceara blasted it open. Apparently, the whole mountain shook."

"Terrific. That doesn't sound at all impossible to stop."

"Not impossible," a weak voice said from behind us.

Max and I both swung our gazes toward the bed, where Nevan slouched in a semi-upright position with his legs hanging over the edge, his feet on the floor. He pushed up with both arms, clearly trying to stand, but his limbs gave out. He dropped back onto the bed, still half sitting.

I hurried to him, kneeling in front of him with my hands on his knees. He looked so exhausted, so tapped out. I lifted a hand to his cheek. "You shouldn't get up. Lie back down and rest."

Despite the pallor of his skin and the redness of his eyes, he gazed at me with the same certainty and determination as always. "Not until I convince you all is not lost. Not for you."

"I'm not worried about myself. I'm worried about you."

"You can defeat the sorcerer, I know this with every fiber of my immortal being." He laid his cool hand over mine on his cheek. "Listen to the incubus. Let him assist you in harnessing your magics. You are the only one who can stop the sorcerer from enacting whatever plan he has in mind, and you can be certain it's nothing benign."

"Kill all mortals, probably." I sat on the bed next to him, considering everything I'd learned so far. "Then again, the oracle said the sorcerer has a grudge to settle. Maybe he wants to punish other elementals."

"Perhaps," Nevan said, his eyes half closed, shoulders slumped.

I took his hand and guided his arm to rest across my shoulders, supporting him with my own body.

"What else did the oracle say?" Nevan asked.

As I recounted my talk with Bob, Max retreated into the kitchen. Giving us privacy. Had to admit my familiar had shown nothing but respect for me. Good to know, since I was about to let him teach me how to use magic.

I told Nevan what he himself had done when Ceara arrived, since once again he had no memory of his fugue state. Finished with my tale, I let my head rest on Nevan's shoulder.

He kissed my forehead, his lips cool and dry. "There's no time to waste. You must stay here with Max, reestablish the wards, and practice your powers."

"You mean we have to stay here with Max."

Nevan said nothing, his breaths soft but unsteady against my forehead. "I mean you, Lindsey. I must leave this place, go far from you and make certain no one can employ me as a weapon again."

"Make certain how?"

Ice crystallized around my heart as the things he'd said replayed in my mind. He'd said all was not lost—for me. I was the only one who could stop the sorcerer. I must stay here with Max, while Nevan made certain no one could…

"No," I said, shrugging off his arm so I could face him. "Nevan, you are not killing yourself to save the world."

"For the world? No." He straightened with an effort that made his face warp with pain. "I will do this for you."

"Absolutely not. I forbid it."

"Lindsey."

I jumped up to stand in front of him, determined to dissuade him by any means necessary.

He managed to lift one eyebrow, though just a little.

My hands on my hips, I declared, "You're way too weak to leave here without help, and I will not help you. In fact, I'll order my familiar to hold you down until you pass out from exhaustion. Give up on this stupid idea right this instant."

Nevan sighed, sounding wearier than I'd imagined anyone could. "Lindsey…"

"Uh-uh." I grasped his face in both hands. "I would never force you into a bargain to make you stay here, but I need you to do it voluntarily. For me. Please don't give up, Nevan."

He grumbled, making a face. "You've said that word again. I thought you'd given up saying it with gleeful abandon."

"I'm serious, Nevan. I will get Max to restrain you if necessary." When he maintained his mulish expression, I turned my head to shout, "Max, get in here—"

"Fine," Nevan growled. "I will refrain from ending my existence."

His self-sacrificing side had shown itself before, when he tried to make me stay home in the mortal realm while he confronted Skeiron. This time was different, though, and it terrified me. I could not let him commit suicide to protect me. We would find another way, we had to.

Looking miserable, he slumped even further.

I turned his face toward me and pressed my mouth to his, unsettled by the coldness of his skin, and lingered there a moment with our lips barely touching. We gazed into each other's eyes, like two souls bound by a silent and unbreakable promise. He'd given me his word, and he would never renege on it.

Brushing my fingers over his temple, I murmured, "You know what I want to say."

Thank you. But I couldn't say it. Nevan would hate to have me indebted to him, even an itty-bitty bit.

"I do know," he said. "It's unnecessary."

Max ambled out of the kitchen then, munching on what looked like an oddly shaped apple. "Were you summoning me, mistress?"

Yep, I detected a bit of sarcasm in the question.

And he'd shed his clothes.

"Clothing, Max," I said. "And give me a minute."

His outfit materialized on his body.

I took a seat beside Nevan again, our shoulders nudging each other. "Killing yourself was a dumb-ass idea. There's another way, and we will find it."

"A moment ago you believed you're powerless to change our fates."

"I realized I have to do it." I covered his hand with mine. "You know I'll do anything to save you. Anything. If that means fighting Ceara and her master, I will do whatever it takes."

"Even if it's the death of you."

"No one on my team is dying."

His mouth formed the barest of smiles. "Your team?"

"All my allies. Travis, Max, Tris, Ennea." I pecked a kiss on his cheek. "And you, my soul mate."

Max approached us. "This is terribly touching, but we need to start your training. The situation is somewhat dire, wouldn't you say?"

"Yes." I stroked my palm over Nevan's cheek. "Rest, honey. Max and I have work to do."

I rose, and Nevan stretched out on the bed with his hand over his abdomen. Yesterday, I would've fantasized about those sculpted muscles. Today, the sight of his gorgeous bod couldn't stir any desire in me. Things had gotten so much worse and so much more pressing since this morning, when Nevan had made love to me in this very bed.

"Okay, Max," I said. "Let's crack open my magic."

Chapter Fifteen

Face to face, the incubus and I raised our hands between us. Max held his hands palms up, while I hovered mine palms down above his with a space of millimeters between our skin. Within the gap, currents of magic crackled and pulsed over my flesh. They seeped under my skin to permeate my flesh, radiating out from my hands into the whole of my body. The magic burned strongest in my palms, instigating a stinging sensation that was both frightening and exhilarating.

Magic suffused me. Infused me. Charged me like a high-voltage cable plugged straight into my soul. My pulse raced, my mouth went dry, and I had trouble drawing in enough oxygen. The tingling that swept over my scalp and face had nothing to do with the supernatural energy coursing through me. It was a sign of hyperventilation.

I recognized this, and yet I couldn't force my lungs to work.

The incubus stationed immobile and impassive before me coughed. "Breathe, Lindsey. Or you'll pass out and this will all be for naught."

We'd have to start again. Max had warned me about this heady and disconcerting sensation, and that I'd need to call on my strength of will to control the power. It was difficult, though, when so much energy coursed through my nerves, my blood, down to the core of my being.

Maybe a mortal wasn't supposed to carry this kind of power. Maybe I couldn't handle it, but I had to try. Marshal every iota of willpower I had in me and make this work.

I inhaled, my breaths ragged at first, dragging in as much air as I could in spite of my muscles resisting the effort. My breathing grew steadier, stronger. I exhaled and hauled in another long, deep breath. Sweet, clean air flooded into my lungs and energized my mind and body for the battle ahead.

The battle for my own power.

"It's your magic," Max said, his tone even and assuring. "Do not let it control you. The Janusite owns her power and molds it to her needs. Take the reins, Lindsey."

Once upon a time, in another age that had been six weeks ago, I'd admonished myself to "rein it in." Then, I'd meant my emotions and especially my passions—anger, joy, lust, anything that put me at risk of getting hurt. Nevan had shown me holding back had kept me from experiencing the full spectrum of life and that embracing strong emotions and sexual desires could set me free, make me stronger.

I closed my eyes, let the magic rush through me for a moment, and reveled in the sheer power and intensity of it. My magic. My power. *Serve me, you wild energy, serve the Janusite.*

The magic balked at my command with a tiny jolt. I gritted my teeth, envisioning the power as an unruly stallion and imagining a bridle in my hands. First, I had to calm the magics. I summoned the memory of my most placid moments, all of which had taken place in Nevan's arms. When he held me after we made love. When he consoled me during tough times. When he gaze gazed at me with pure love.

My magic calmed enough I could slip my imaginary bridle over it, jump onto its back, and rein in the power.

An intoxicating sense of victory surged through me, but I resisted the impulse to celebrate. I hadn't gotten what I needed yet. The tingling had dissipated, and the energy coursing down my nerves had quieted into a gentle current, but I still couldn't direct the power. *Use the reins*, I reminded myself, and gave them a light tug in the direction I wanted.

I aimed the magic at the wards—or where the wards had been.

Tendrils of power spiraled out in visible blue streams that twirled and whipped in the air in every direction as they crept toward the walls of the underground lair. The tendrils diverted around Max, curling around his body as if tasting him. They flowed over Nevan, where he lay on the bed with his eyes closed and his body slack. I fed more fuel into the magic, commanding it with my thoughts instead of spoken words.

My magic, my desires, they melded into a swirling mass of glowing, sparkling streams emitted from my skin. The feel of energy unleashing from within me was empowering, exciting...arousing.

The vacuum left behind by the shattered wards began to fill in, as I crafted a web of magic to protect my new home. The web in turn filled in with more solid, stronger power. The wards became a blue wall of shimmering power erected like a second skin over the earthen walls, the body of the mountain. When I sensed the completion of the barrier, like a lock thunking into place, I reeled my power back inside myself.

The walls became solid earth again, the wards once more invisible.

I understood, in a way I couldn't explain, that the barrier was stronger than before and impenetrable even to the sorcerer's efforts. I had become connected to the wards, and they in turn had become an extension of me.

"Well?" Max asked, his arms hanging loose at his sides.

"It worked." I listened to the soft buzzing of the wards as the sound faded away. "Didn't you feel it? When the wards clicked into place?"

"A familiar can't experience his mistress's magic. He provides an anchor, not a conduit for power."

"I'm still kind of confused about the familiar thing, but it doesn't really matter. I control my own magic now." Glancing toward the bed, I squared my shoulders and lifted my chin. "Which means I can recharge Nevan. All the way this time."

Max touched my arm. "Is that wise? The sorcerer might bleed him dry again, and you can't keep recharging his magic indefinitely."

"Won't have to. We're going to stop this damn sorcerer coward."

"How?"

"Not sure yet, but I know we can do it. With my power under better control, I can do a lot more than shoot the bastard with my endued gun."

I hurried to the bed and settled on the blanket beside Nevan. My heart hurt when I took in his appearance, his skin so pale it was nearing white, his lips almost blue and his breaths deathly shallow. At least I could energize him, for a time, and alleviate his suffering. He would be virile enough to fight at my side.

The aftereffects of harnessing my power rippled sexual desire through me, a warm and stimulating energy. My body hummed with it, and my nipples grew hard.

Over my shoulder, I called out to Max. "Maybe you should go in the kitchen again. I need to recharge Nevan the only way I know how."

Not sex. Nevan was too weak for that. But I needed physical contact and a connection fueled by passion. A bone-melting kiss ought to do the trick.

And I didn't particularly want an incubus watching.

Without a word, Max retreated into the kitchen.

I smoothed hair from Nevan's forehead, running my fingers over his temples and down his jawline. His skin was cold and clammy.

Not for long.

Leaning over him, I set my hands at either side of his head and invited the magic to vibrate through me again, hot and electric. The hairs on the back of my neck lifted, then the hairs on my arms. Goose bumps pebbled my skin beginning at my wrists and sweeping up my arms. My breaths grew labored, my breasts tightened, my lips burned for what was to come.

I laid a thumb on his chin, easing his mouth open.

He stirred, mumbling wordlessly, his eyes still shut.

My head seemed to float above my body, weightless and disconnected. But the second I crushed my mouth to his, everything inside me reconnected and awakened. I licked at his lips, relishing the distinctive flavor of him, even as my lips imparted magic into him. *Not enough.* I delved my tongue into his mouth, coiling it around his again and again, desperate for a response, thrilled by the way his flesh heated up and his breaths grew heavier. I plastered my chest to his, my breasts mounded against his firm muscles.

The magic whirled around us, penetrated into us, swelled and spread and enlivened every inch of our bodies as if we were one being.

His arms came around me, his hands groping my back.

I braced my forearms at either side of his head, thrusting my fingers into his hair in the same instant I thrust my tongue deeper into his mouth. He groaned, his hands shifting to my ass, and plunged his tongue into my waiting mouth. Our tongues tangled and danced, wound around each other and separated, while the heat of our kiss saturated his entire body.

My scorching sylph was back.

Without severing our lip-lock, he flipped us over so I lay trapped beneath his massive body, a willing prisoner. I hooked one leg around his, arched my hips into him, tunneled my fingers through his hair to hold him against me and prolong the kiss. I moaned into his mouth, and he grasped my hip in one big hand to pull me snugly into him.

His erection began to blossom between us.

Nevan tore his lips away from mine. Panting, eyes glossy and lips swollen, he gazed down at me with his familiar sexy smirk. "We must stop, for the moment. Though I have to admit, darlin', I do love the way you save me."

"Wish we could do the hot sex kind of saving." I nodded toward the kitchen doorway. "But my familiar is waiting."

His lips kinked downward, though only for a second. "He has helped you, then."

"Max is an invaluable assistant."

"Glad to hear it." Nevan rocked his hips, grinding his rigid shaft into me. "Your magic has grown powerful—and powerfully arousing."

I scrunched up my face. "Hope I don't have to use sex to defeat the sorcerer. I might let the worlds be annihilated if that's the price for saving them."

"Have faith. You control your power, which means you may channel it however you wish."

"Mm, I wish to channel it into a steamy kiss with you."

A grin lit up his face, making him seem younger and less burdened by current circumstances. "As long as it's only with me, I have no objection to your method."

"Probably need to come up with an alternate method, though."

He rolled off the bed and sprang to his feet, then grasped me around the waist and lifted me onto my feet.

I flattened my palms on his chest. "Sure are spry for a man who was almost a goner a few minutes ago."

"You must have used a great deal of magic to reinvigorate me." He scowled, though I knew he was frightened rather than angry. "Don't do it again, Lindsey. I will not have you depleting your magics in an effort to keep me alive. It's far too dangerous for you."

"A minute ago, you said you loved the way I save you. All of a sudden it's dangerous?"

He laid his hands over mine on his chest. "I do love your method, but I fear for your health if you continue to resurrect me after each attack by Ceara and the sorcerer."

"I won't stand by and let you wither away into nothing."

"You must, for your own sake." He crushed my palms to his chest. "Please consider the consequences. This may be the sorcerer's plan, to siphon away your power using me as a sort of battery to store the energy of your magics. He then has Ceara retrieve the energy from me."

"Nevan, you said the P-word."

"Your bad verbal habits are infecting me. And I am desperate to keep you from harm."

His theory almost made sense, except for one thing. "If the sorcerer can siphon anyone's power, why wouldn't he kidnap me and suck me dry? Why use you as a go-between?"

I watched him struggling to compose an answer, his lips contorting and his eyes flashing.

After a moment, he said, "I cannot explain it."

"Care to hear my theory?"

"I'm listening."

"The oracle said the sorcerer has a grudge to settle." I wrested my hands free of his, leaning in to garner his full attention. "He's teamed up with your formerly dead wife. He keeps having her suck the life out of you. The answer seems pretty obvious to me. You're part of his grudge."

"But he covets your magic."

"Sure, but he's definitely punishing you for something. He sent Max to me, to get my powers in tiptop shape before he does whatever he plans to do to me." I rose onto my toes, leveling our gazes. "He won't take my magical energy until I've increased it as much as possible. Until it's worth stealing. But you…This guy has a serious jones for torturing you, destroying you bit by bit. That's not using you as a tool. That's revenge, Nevan."

His mouth opened, but he said nothing.

"I'm right, and you know it." Dropping back onto my heels, I let my hands rest on his shoulders. "So tell me, sweetie. Who hates you with an eternal, blistering vengeance?"

"Besides Skeiron, who is gone, only one individual meets your criteria." He scrubbed a hand over his mouth. "Notus. The one who forged me."

Chapter Sixteen

"Notus?" I felt my brows crinkle at the mention of the former king of the sylphs, the one who'd ruled before Skeiron, the one Skeiron had defeated to become king. "You told me once Skeiron beat Notus in a long and bloody war for the kingship. What exactly did Skeiron do to stop Notus? I thought elementals destroyed each other, like I destroyed Skeiron."

Nevan pursed his lips, his gaze going distant as if he were peering into the past. "I've also explained that immortals, such as the elemental races, cannot die in any conventional sense."

"It takes something supernatural, like an endued weapon or an enchanted poison."

He focused on me again, his eyes simmering with molten shades of bronze and silver. "A dark spell can also achieve the desired result. That is what Skeiron employed."

"Dark spell?" I moved my hands to his chest, relieved to feel his hot skin, obliged to whatever power had allowed me to restore his natural heat. My power had done it. The magic I'd somehow acquired from a long-gone god, Janus. "Is that how Janus was taken out too?"

"Not precisely the same. The gods, not elementals, destroyed Janus."

"Right, I remember you said they combined their magics to get rid of him because they feared how much power he'd amassed." I let my hands fall to my sides and rocked back on my heels. "I don't understand. The gods aren't elementals? They live in the elemental realm."

"They exist in the Unseen realm."

"Which is different how?"

"Ah…" Nevan scratched his head. "It's difficult to explain. The gods are not strictly elemental in nature, but neither are they not elemental. They exist apart from all other beings in the Unseen and might be viewed as one level below the Oversoul."

"You mean God."

"I mean the unknowable force that created the universe."

The same vague thing Max had said. The first pang of a headache sprouted behind my eyes, and I rubbed my forehead. Understanding the big picture of the Unseen realm seemed out of my grasp and, for now, unimportant. "Let's forget the philosophical stuff for the moment and get back to Skeiron and Notus. Tell me what Skeiron did to get rid of his competition."

Nevan exhaled a long and weary sigh. "I was not present when Skeiron annihilated Notus. I know only what Skeiron told his followers after the battle. He claimed he had undergone an arcane and arduous ritual to acquire greater power, darker power, with the intention of using it to end Notus's existence. The magics he gained allowed him to destroy the one-time king and scatter his essence to the Four Winds."

"The same way the gods scattered Janus to the Four Winds."

"Yes, though by a different method."

Just when my headache had waned, it threatened to return. "What's the difference between an essence and a soul, or an essence and powers?"

"None that I'm aware of. They might be the same, or they might be different, depending on the circumstances."

"In other words, you don't know." I threw my head back on a gusty sigh. "Does this mean I might have Janus's soul inside me?"

"Doubtful. His essence was scattered, but the Four Winds captured his powers and held them until you were born. Then, they imbued them into you."

"Hmm." I rocked forward on the balls of my feet, considering what he'd told me, but I didn't have time to wonder about Janus's essence. "Let me see if I get this. The gods scattered Janus to the Four Winds, Skeiron scattered Notus to the Four Winds, I scattered Skeiron to the Four Winds, and Brennus planned on scattering my power to the Four Winds—at the command of my ex-fiancé. There's kind of an epidemic of scattering, hey?"

Nevan hooked a finger under my chin, lifting my face to him. "You killed Skeiron in self-defense. Skeiron acted out of a lust for power."

"My point, which I admittedly am not making too well, is that I have magical abilities because I inherited Janus's powers after they were scattered." I walked around Nevan, stuffing my hands in my jeans pockets, absorbed with the thoughts bouncing around in my mind. Making sense of all this craziness could tax a human brain. "Scattering doesn't eradicate a being's power—or the soul?"

"No, it eradicates the being's physical form. The soul generally moves on, but the power is redistributed to the Four Winds."

"Which are avatars and guardians of energy and magic," I said, quoting what Nevan had told me six weeks ago. "I still don't quite get that. What do they do with the powers they receive?"

"Guard them," Nevan replied, turning to watch me pace the length of the room. "They protect the orphaned magic so it will not fall into the wrong hands, and in the right circumstances, they might gift another being with all or a portion of the magical energy."

"Could someone steal the power of a destroyed elemental from the Four Winds?"

"Perhaps, though I've never heard of such a feat being accomplished."

I stared down at the floor as I paced back and forth, my shoulders caving in toward my chest. An inkling of an idea had formed in my mind, but I couldn't quite express it in words yet.

Nevan stepped in front of me, halting my nervous movement, and took my upper arms in his hands. When I looked up at him, he gave me a patient, if small, smile. "What are you thinking?"

We gazed into each other's eyes for a moment, comfortable in the silence between us, until I at last formulated a coherent idea.

"If a being's power survives," I said, "could someone steal that power from the Four Winds and use it to resurrect the destroyed elemental?"

He studied me, his brow furrowed and his eyes squinted. "I don't know. With enough magic, nearly anything is possible. But a being is made of more than power, and what is re-created may not be the same as the original being."

"Is there any way to resurrect the physical body of an elemental?"

Nevan opened his mouth, but quickly closed it again.

"I believe there is a way," said a voice from the kitchen.

Max emerged from the kitchen in human form, dressed in his conjured clothing, and strode up to me and Nevan.

"How do you know this?" Nevan asked.

The incubus shrugged. "Because of Ceara's pet name for the sorcerer."

I turned to Max. "Which is?"

"My undead inamorata."

"Undead? Please don't tell me he's a vampire."

Sylph and incubus alike scoffed. They exchanged a look that implied I was being ridiculous, but really, zombies didn't seem any more outrageous than shapeshifters—at least, to a mortal like me. Nevan had said ghosts were real, so how should I know if other supposedly mythical creatures existed? *No vampires, check.*

I believed that for about three seconds, until Nevan wrecked my limited peace of mind.

He shook his head, still making a huffy scoffing sound. "Vampires have only the most limited of magics."

"Weaklings," Max concurred.

My shoulders caved in a little further. I pulled my hands out of my pockets to clamp them around my head. "Oh dear lord. Vampires are real? What about zombies?"

"Those can exist," Max said, "only if a powerful mage creates them from scratch."

Head. About to explode. My brains, all over the floor.

Nevan wrapped an arm around my shoulders and hugged me to him. "Take it easy, love. You still have much to learn about this world."

"No kidding." I leaned my head against him, in need of his solid and comforting presence. To Max, I said, "I know you can't tell me who the sorcerer is, but you must've seen his face."

"I have, but I don't know what Notus looks like. I was born and forged long after the former king's demise."

"Can't confirm or deny, then."

"With or without a bargain restricting me, I'm afraid I can't identify the sorcerer."

"Not your fault." A portion of what he'd said rang a bell in my mind. He'd mentioned earlier today that he was born during the age of the Roman empire. Interesting, but not relevant at the moment.

Wait a second. Maybe it was relevant.

Extricating a piece of paper from the back pocket of my jeans, I unfolded it and offered the sheet to Max.

He took the paper and squinted at my drawing of Ceara's pendant. "What is this?"

"A pendant Ceara wears around her waist. Nevan thinks it might be Egyptian, and I was hoping you might recognize it. The Romans conquered Egypt, after all."

"That they did, and I spent some time in Alexandria." He pursed his lips, his eyes darting as he studied the image. "I didn't notice the pendant when I saw Ceara, but it was rather a kerfuffle then."

"Do you recognize the symbol?"

"It looks like a papyrus column." He turned the paper left and then right. "Can't recall what it means."

I blew out a breath between my lips. "Back to square one, eh?"

"Not quite," Nevan said. "Thanks to your wonderful mind and your bravery in seeking out the oracle, we now have reason to suspect Notus has been resurrected. Or, at the least, his powers have been transferred into another being determined to enact vengeance for the king's destruction."

"What does that have to do with you?"

"I was Skeiron's right hand during the war for control of the sylph kingdom." He tucked me against him, seeming to need the soothing contact while he revisited the past. "I believed Notus had strayed too far into the darkness, and Skeiron would be our salvation. When Skeiron bade me to lead our army against Notus's as a distraction, so he might confront the king alone, I agreed without hesitation. I had believed, until recently, Skeiron became depraved because of the power he inherited from Notus. Only after Skeiron's death did I learn he'd employed the darkest of magics to win the war with Notus, and it set in motion his own descent into madness."

I propped my chin on his chest. "How did you find that out?"

"When I became king, the tribunal told me. They presented the information in the form of a warning that I should not attempt to use dark magics, else they would depose me by any means necessary."

"But they're working with Ceara and the sorcerer. I doubt those two are using sweet, fluffy spells."

Nevan smiled with an affection that sparkled in his eyes. "You do say the most bizarrely charming things. To address your concern, I suspect the tribunal thinks the sorcerer is their only hope of dethroning me."

"Or controlling you. But why would they want to do either? You're way better than that skeezy bastard Skeiron."

Max chuckled softly behind me. "Skeezy bastard? His Highness is right. My mistress says the most unusual things."

Had my familiar called Nevan by a kingly appellation for the first time since they'd met? Why yes, he had. *Interesting.*

"You should talk," I said to Max. "I bet you've never been to England, but you spout all the Brit-speak."

"Can't argue with that," said the incubus. "It's instinct, though, picking up modern language from my descendants."

"Whatever you say." I addressed Nevan next. "Any more thoughts on why the tribunal hates you?"

Nevan threaded his fingers through my hair. "I have no idea why the tribunal despises me. Within days of crowning me king, they became wary of me—and they've become decidedly hostile."

"And I'd bet all my Janusite power the sorcerer convinced them you're a threat."

"I do wish you'd refrain from betting. Far too close to bargaining for my liking."

"Yeah, I know." I gave him a sheepish smile. "My mouth tends to run off on its own when I'm distracted and totally freaked out."

"I am well aware of that."

My gaze bounced around the room, while thoughts bounced around in my brain. I saw the chairs, the bed, the boxes of my stuff pushed up against the wall.

I snapped my gaze back to the boxes. My stuff. I had books about ancient mythology, a topic I'd become a bit obsessed with since learning I was the Janusite. Max had identified Ceara's pendant as a papyrus column, an ancient Egyptian symbol.

Racing to the boxes, I rifled through them one by one, tossing unbreakable items aside in my hunt for the right book.

"What are you doing?" Max asked.

"Gimme a sec." I found it at last, and flipped the book open to a section about ancient Egyptian symbols. Skimming my finger down the list of symbols, I located the papyrus column. "Ah-ha. Ceara's amulet, the papyrus column, was believed to grant the wearer vitality and the power of regeneration."

The clanging of an alarm bell resounded through the underground house.

Max flinched, his gaze swerving back and forth. "What the bloody hell is that?"

"Whoops, I did that," I said. "When you helped me reestablish the wards, I installed a security system so we'd know when somebody's out there."

"Do we have any way of knowing," Nevan said, "who it is out there?"

"Open the door and see. The wards will stay up, so there's no risk." I hesitated, then added, "Well, very minimal risk."

Nevan pulled away from me to approach the section of rock wall where the door was hidden and activate it with a swift motion of his hand.

Travis waited outside in his uniform, one hip cocked, his hand on the Sig Sauer holstered on his belt.

"Gonna let me in or what?" he said.

Nevan glanced back at me with a questioning look.

I waved my hand toward the open door. "The wards should work like before, letting you and me bring people inside."

He still seemed uncertain, but he walked out the doorway in spite of his less-than-complete trust in my magical aptitude.

I couldn't blame him. Until today, I'd done little more than ferry him over the boundary in the mortal realm and open the portal to the Unseen. Well, that and destroy Skeiron. But the boundary had done all the work for me there.

Having survived crossing through my new wards, Nevan clapped a hand on Travis's shoulder and gestured for him to proceed into the house. The two men strode inside, and Nevan closed the door.

Neither of them burst into flames or started screaming in agony. *Nonlethal magical wards, check.*

"You got the whatchamacallits back up and running," Travis said as he came toward me. "Nice job, Lindsey."

"Th—" *Oops.* Almost thanked him. "I appreciate the vote of confidence. What did you find out about the dead women?"

"Found out who they are, for starters." He adjusted his belt, his lips twisting into an odd expression. "The bodies may have been dumped in Mandan County, but only the last girl was in the area at the time of her disappearance. One was from Israel, the other from Australia. Megan was a tourist, but the other two had never been to America. All three somehow wound up on the outskirts of Lutin Falls, in the woods behind the rock shop."

Three young women had died near the town where I'd lived for the past three years, in the woods behind the shop where I worked.

"All of them have got two things in common," Travis said. "First, they've got a resemblance to you. Not like you're twins, but enough similarity to be suspicious."

"We knew that already. What's the other thing?"

"They were all born on the same day. Your birthday."

CHAPTER SEVENTEEN

Everything inside me froze, as if I'd been injected with liquid nitrogen that penetrated every single cell of my body. All the dead women shared my birthday. I'd suspected the women had some connection to me, besides our resemblance to each other, but this confirmation hit me hard. I couldn't speak or move, and even breathing became difficult. A phantom weight bore down on my chest, making it hard to pull in enough air.

My birthday.

One of my allies had betrayed me. That's what I'd thought yesterday, because the sorcerer knew about my powers—and my birth date, it seemed. The more time I spent with my allies, including the newcomers Max and Ennea, the less I could believe any of them might betray me.

Who else could have done it?

Nevan took my face in his hands, the heat of him chasing away the chill in my cheeks but failing to eradicate the coldness in the rest of my body. I let his mesmeric eyes capture my focus, but for once, their swirling couldn't distract me from the fear seizing control of me.

No. I would not give in to the fear. Not this time.

The old me would have, but I'd changed in the past six weeks. I wasn't a coward repressing my feelings anymore.

I placed my hands over Nevan's. "It's okay. I'm okay."

He searched my face—for a sign I was reining it in like I used to, no doubt—but then nodded and lowered his hands to my shoulders. "The connection to you is no longer a hypothesis. The sorcerer killed these women because they resemble you. Perhaps in an attempt to find you, based on appearance and birth date."

"But he knew who I was when he killed Megan. He said the girls were an offering to prove his devotion to me."

The sorcerer had vowed to "whittle away" at me until I had nothing left but fear and regret. He swore I'd want to go with him in the end. Why did he want me? It was more than my powers, of that I was certain. The sorcerer had told me he could become whomever I wanted, offering to glamour into Nevan or Travis. Nevan, I could understand, but why did he choose to glamour into Travis?

He'd called me "sweetness" and "sweet thing." Only one person had ever called me either of those things.

"The sorcerer is Calder Blackwell," I said. "He has to be, it's the only way this makes any sense."

Everyone looked dubious, so I laid out the evidence supporting my claim.

Nevan spoke first. "It does make a certain sense, though your theory fails to account for the sorcerer's vendetta against me. Calder wanted me out of the way, so he could have you."

"And the sorcerer is spending a ton of time and energy on torturing you," I said. "That seems more Notus-ish. But murdering girls as an offering, and trying to wear me down so I'll join him, that seems more Calder-ish. I still don't understand the burning bush thing either."

Max coughed, garnering everyone's attention. "That would be me."

"You set the bush on fire?" I asked. "And the sorcerer doesn't mind you telling me?"

"Apparently not."

"What was the burning bush supposed to mean?"

"Nothing. I was supposed to get your attention by igniting the bush, to lure you to the bodies."

"Well, at least we solved one mystery," I said. "But I still think the sorcerer is Calder, somehow brought back to life. He would know I'm the Janusite, and he'd know my birthday. Notus couldn't know any of that."

"He could," Nevan said, "if someone told him. The entire sylph army witnessed you destroying Skeiron. I erased their memories of the battle, but the sorcerer might have restored their recollections using his dark magics."

Travis cleared his throat, making a pained face. "You're ignoring the obvious, Lindsey. There's somebody who could've told them and might not even remember doing it."

Cold sluiced through me anew, and every hair on my body stiffened.

No, it couldn't be true. I refused to believe it.

And the sorcerer might be counting on exactly that reaction.

I looked steadily into Nevan's eyes. "It could've been you."

The alarm clanged.

Nevan and I kept our gazes glued to each other, each of us praying it wasn't true but unable to refute the idea. I knew him well enough to realize he was thinking the same thing I was. And I knew what he'd believe he needed to do to protect me.

He wanted to sacrifice himself—and somehow, some way, take out the sorcerer at the same time.

The alarm clanged again.

Nevan stalked to the doorway, commanding it to open.

Tris and Ennea smiled at us from the other side of the wards. Well, Ennea smiled. Her brother had his mouth contorted into a hybrid of a frown and a smirk.

Passing through the invisible wards, Nevan guided the leprechauns into our home. He moved his wrist as if to shut the door, then dropped his hand. "I will leave it open for the moment. I suspect we will be leaving soon, on separate missions."

"Fine," I said. "Come back over here, though. We're having our little mission briefing on this side of the room."

He returned to my side, his expression unreadable.

My intuition shivered a warning through me. Nevan had promised not to take his own life, but that left so many other options open to him if he resolved to act on my behalf. He knew how I felt about such recklessness, but his damn honor might override his promise if he decided I was in too much danger and only he could rectify the situation.

I slipped my hand into his, twining our fingers. His hand closed around mine, warm and strong, but the comfort of his touch failed to melt the icy spike lodged in my heart.

Travis spoke first. "What do we do? If Nevan can be controlled, any of us could be under the sorcerer's....whatever you call it."

"His thrall," Max offered.

"Under his thrall, then," Travis said, looking miserable at the idea. "How do we handle this? We can't have the bad guys finding out our plans."

"We got plans?" Tris said. "Nobody told me."

Max raised his hand. "Don't forget about me. I'm already influenced by the sorcerer, thanks to our bargain. I might've exposed Lindsey's identity and had my memory wiped clean."

"I appreciate your honesty," I said, "but this game of 'who's the traitor' will get us nowhere. We need one person we can trust, someone who has the means to figure out which, if any, of us is enthralled by the sorcerer."

The six of us lapsed into silence, our expressions running the gamut from extreme unease to befuddlement. The problem seemed insurmountable, but I had to believe we could find a solution.

"Come on," I said. "Look at us. A sylph, a salamander, a law enforcement professional, two leprechauns—one of whom is a fae witch—and the Janusite. We're like a team of superheroes, and we can't figure it out? Baloney. We can do this."

Travis arched his eyebrows. "I'm not a superhero, Lindsey. Just a cop. A mortal one. I'm the one who doesn't belong in this group."

"You're smart and tough as nails. You belong here."

"He can be our Batman," Tris said. "You know, the guy with no super-powers who fights evil."

"You read comic books?" I asked.

"Uh, no. I watch TV sometimes." He hooked a thumb at his sister. "Ennea created a spell to catch satellite signals from the mortal realm. She's addicted to home improvement shows."

Maybe it was a nervous response, but I couldn't keep from laughing. An image had flashed in my mind, of Ennea and Tris gathered around a TV in a cave somewhere eating popcorn and heckling the shows for their inaccurate portrayals of the fae.

"The point is," I said, having gotten my inappropriate laughter under control, "we can find a way to do this. To determine if any of us is being used by our enemies."

Ennea's face brightened, as if a proverbial light bulb had powered up in her brain. "You, Lindsey. You're the one who can do it. Of all of us, you are the only one we can be sure isn't under the sorcerer's influence."

"How do you figure that?" I asked.

"Girl, you told me yourself the first time we met. Magic goes a little woo-woo in your presence."

"Yeah, but I don't know for sure that means I'm immune to the sorcerer's control."

"Think about it," she said. "If he could exert any power over you, he'd have you already. Instead, he's torturing Nevan and sending his nasty girl-friend to wreak havoc."

"Someone told him my birthday."

Max's gaze ping-ponged around the room, like he was trying really hard not to meet anyone's eyes.

I squinted at him. "You know something, but you can't tell me."

He coughed into his fist.

"I'll take that as a yes." Hands on my hips, I drummed my fingers and ran-sacked my brain for a way around his restrictions. He'd managed to convey the fact he knew something without violating his bargain with the sorcerer. Maybe grunts and coughs didn't count as telling me. Worth a shot. "Maybe the sor-cerer mentioned how he found out my birthday."

Max coughed.

"Okay." *Eureka.* I'd found a chink in the armor of Max's deal with the sorcerer. "Maybe he talked to another elemental, or some other being who lives in the Unseen, and they told him."

Another cough.

Nevan curled his hand around my forearm. "An oracle."

Silence.

Time for the life-altering question. "Was it Calder?"

Max shrugged.

"Notus?" Nevan asked.

Another shrug. The incubus didn't know the answer.

I thought for a moment, then said, "The tribunal must be working with the sorcerer. He must have a hold on them."

Max coughed twice.

"They're forced to do it against their will."

Silence.

I canted my head at Max. "They allowed the sorcerer to enchant them or whatever, because he offered them something they want."

A short cough.

Nevan huffed. "They want to dethrone me, because they fear I'll lose my mind as the previous kings did. The sorcerer convinced them of this."

Max cleared his throat.

"But they don't know," I said, "I'm the Janusite. The sorcerer's keeping that to himself."

One loud, harsh throat clearing.

"Ceara killed the oracle because he was going to give us vital information about the sorcerer."

Max cleared his throat so forcefully he almost choked.

Tris waved toward Max. "That's all super cool to know, but how do we know we can trust the incubus?"

"Lindsey needs to do a spell," Ennea said. "One that will show her who's lying, even if they don't realize they're lying."

"Me?" I pointed at myself. "I don't know how to work a spell."

Nevan clasped my hand. "Of course you do. The spell you crafted to reestablish the wards is stronger even than the one Ennea created for me."

"Ennea created the original wards? You didn't mention that before, only that a fae made them."

"It didn't occur to me to tell you her name."

"Have your tiff later," Ennea said. "Lindsey needs to do a spell now."

The fae witch took my arm and guided me away from the group, motioning for Max to accompany us. When Nevan moved to follow, Ennea shook her head. He gritted his teeth, a muscle in his jaw ticking, but stayed put. Ennea led Max and me across the living room, to a doorway on the opposite side from the kitchen.

She leaned across the threshold, craning her neck to peer inside the room beyond. With a decisive nod, she motioned for us to trail her into the room.

"What is this?" she asked, turning in a circle to admire the surroundings.

"The bathroom," I said, though the word fell short of describing the amazing space Nevan had created.

A cascade splashed out of a crevice high on the eight-foot walls, raining down in a perpetual shower. The water flowed into an ankle-deep pool that spilled out a hole in the floor opposite the miniature waterfall. Green plants and colorful flowers sprouted out of cracks in the rock walls, their long limbs tumbling down toward the water.

"Amazing," Ennea said. "I've never seen a bathroom like this one, and I've been to a lot of elemental homes."

Most sylphs, Nevan had told me, leaped into the nearest natural pool or lake to cleanse their bodies. He, however, enjoyed having his own private waterfall. When I'd asked him how many women he'd bathed with under the cascade, he'd declared, "I have brought only one woman to my home."

A delicious glow warmed me at the memory of those words. No one else had reveled in the sensual delight of showering with Nevan in the privacy of this beautiful space.

"Wake up, Lindsey."

Ennea's voice yanked me back to the here and now. I must've zoned out, lost in the memory of happy times. It felt like an eternity had elapsed since the last time I'd showered with Nevan in this room, but only a few days had gone by.

"How do I do this?" I asked.

"Have to figure that out on your own," the witch said.

"But you're the expert on spells."

"I'm not the Janusite, I'm a witch. Your magic is clearly different." She closed her eyes, rubbing her finger up and down the bridge of her nose. When she looked at me again, she said, "You created a security system for the house, as part of the wards. How did you do it?"

"Commanded it, and it happened."

"Will-based magic. Interesting." She studied me with a thoughtful expression. "Do that again. Access your power and command it to show you who's honest and who's lying."

No, it couldn't be that easy. But I had no better ideas.

I held my hands out to Max with my palms down, and he hovered his hands below mine with his palms up. The small gap between our hands crackled with unseen energy as my magic reflected off him, strengthened and enhanced by the presence of my familiar. It felt different this time, because I no longer worried about what might happen when I accessed my power. I knew what it would feel like.

The first time, magic had flooded through me and overpowered my intentions. With experience under my belt, I could funnel and direct the flow of power so it enlivened my magic without steamrolling me. Blue energy glittered on the surface of my skin, and my scalp tingled as the same energy lifted my hair like static electricity.

I focused all my will on one task. *Show me truth versus lies.*

Nothing happened.

Squeezing my eyes shut, I gritted my teeth and commanded the magic to obey. A wave of stronger energy rushed through my body, hot and crackling with power, stunning a gasp from me.

Click. The spell powered on.

At least I thought it powered on. Time for a test.

I opened my eyes and, with my hands still hovering above Max's, I said, "Tell me a lie. Need to test the spell."

He hesitated, then told me, "I am a mortal man."

A red ball of light flashed once on his forehead, then vanished.

"The truth now," I said.

"I'm an immortal incubus."

A white ball flashed on his forehead this time, then winked out.

I clapped my hands together. "Seems to work."

Ennea took my shoulders and turned me toward her. She squinted, scrutinizing me with her lips compressed and her hands grasping me stiffly. After several seconds she let go of me, and the tension smoothed out of her features. "You seem fine. Time for the big test."

She gestured for us to exit the bathroom.

As we crossed the threshold, I murmured to Ennea, "Did you see the balls of light?"

"What lights?"

"The ones my supernatural lie detector made. A red one for lie, a white one for truth."

"Only you saw them," she said, making a beeline for the three males awaiting our return in the center of the living room. "Makes sense, though. You wouldn't want a traitor to know you know they're lying."

"Do you think it'll work if the person doesn't realize they're lying?"

"Beats me." She cast me a thoughtful sideways glance. "But remember, it's magic. You control it, and it has no limits. Elementals can control their physiological responses, but they can't stop a spell from sniffing out the truth. If you make proper use of your spell, that is."

Not the comforting answer I was hoping for, but I'd have to accept it. Whether this worked depended on the strength of my will and my belief in my own magic.

When we reached the others, Ennea instructed all of them to line up for me to assess their honesty. She took her place at the end of the line, beside Tris.

I wedged my clasped hands under my chin as I pondered what I must do. Determine who betrayed me. Could I deal with the answer?

What if I learned Nevan was the traitor?

I scanned the row of potential traitors—my friends, my cohorts, and my lover. Ennea wore a pleasant expression, and when she saw me looking at her, she smiled and nodded her encouragement. Tris had his thumbs hooked in the pockets of his ratty jeans and a rueful half smile on his lips. Next to him, Travis stood tall and straight with his arms at his sides and a stoic look on his face. Max came next in line, his posture relaxed but his eyes a duller red than usual and his mouth tight at the corners.

And then there was Nevan. He resembled a bronze statue in a museum, unmoving, giving away nothing in his expression.

I longed to run to him, fling my arms around his neck, and kiss him until we both forgot about the current circumstances and the world outside our little underground haven. I couldn't do it. Despite dreading what I'd learn, I had to test each and every one of them.

Starting with Ennea, I asked each of my friends the same question. "Did you tell the sorcerer details about me, including my birth date and that I'm the Janusite?"

Ennea answered, "No."

The white light flashed.

Tris answered, "No way."

A white light flashed.

Travis met my gaze head-on when he answered, "No, never."

Another white light. Another honest ally.

Nodding, I moved to Max. He lifted his chin slightly and said, "I have not."

The white light flashed.

Nevan was next. The only one left to test.

I couldn't move, my feet seemed cemented to the floor in front of Max.

Nevan aimed a sad smile in my direction. "It's all right. Do what you must."

Taking a deep breath, I stepped in front of Nevan. Our eyes met, the connection between us as strong as ever, a warm current of love and commitment and trust. Yet my pulse thundered in my ears, and ice trickled down my veins.

"Ask," he said.

"Did you tell the sorcerer details about me, including my birth date and that I'm the Janusite?"

"No."

A white light pulsed on his forehead.

Relief gushed through me, weakening my knees. I locked my knees to stay upright. "It's not you either. None of my allies is the traitor."

"It makes no difference," Nevan said, finality in his tone. "I may not have exposed your secrets to the sorcerer, but I remain susceptible to his control. As long as the sorcerer lives, as long as I live, I pose a grave threat to you. You know what must be done."

Dammit, he was right. I recognized the truth of it in my soul, but I couldn't condemn the only man I'd ever loved without even trying to save him. I wouldn't do that to any of my allies.

Skeiron had tried to take Nevan away from me. I'd scattered that scumbag to the Four Winds. The sorcerer had somehow gotten a hold over Nevan, without his knowledge, and would use my lover in his plot to steal my powers.

Like hell he would.

Nevan eyes widened the tiniest bit. "No, Lindsey."

I stalked up to him, grasped his face in both hands, and kissed him hard. "Stop telling me to give up on you." When he opened his mouth to speak, I cut him off. "Not. Going. To. Happen."

He closed his eyes, exhaling a sigh that deflated his shoulders.

Backing up a few steps, I addressed my friends. "We need to figure out how the sorcerer is controlling Nevan, how he's draining the life out of him. Any ideas?"

Ennea, Tris, Max, and Travis gathered around me to hash out ideas, but none of us could think of anything feasible. There had to be a way. I was too new to magic to know how to handle a situation like this.

Nevan lingered several feet away from the group, his head still bowed.

I stared at the top of his head, at the wavy locks falling over his forehead, and I longed to brush them away and murmur comforting words to him.

His head lifted, his eyes locked onto me.

Not giving up on you. I prayed my silent vow showed on my face, prayed he would give up his self-sacrifice plan.

His lips curved up in a small, melancholy smile.

An odd sensation wriggled in my gut, a kind of unease I couldn't decipher.

Tris tapped my arm to regain my attention. I turned back to the group, listening as Ennea explained the difficulties with attempting to free Nevan from the sorcerer. We had no conception of what type of spell bound Nevan, no clue how much magic would be required to break it, no frigging idea about much of anything, and on and on.

"If the tribunal's involved," Ennea said, "maybe we can get them to talk."

"Good luck with that," Tris said.

"Squeeze them hard enough and maybe they'll pop."

"I'd love a crack at 'em," Travis said, his hand resting on his Sig.

The conversation prattled on, but words began to smear into noise in my brain. Meaningless, incomprehensible noise.

An awareness rattled through me, sharp and unforgiving.

Max's lips moved as he focused his worried gaze on me, though I heard nothing he said. My gaze swung past my friends, beyond their shoulders, to the front door still wide open.

Nevan was marching toward it, shoulders back, head held high, every bit the strong and decisive king of the sylphs. In one hand, he grasped the endued sword.

Determined. Armed. *Enacting his plan.*

"No!"

My cry reverberated off the stone walls as I bolted for Nevan, shoving my friends aside on my way to him.

He strode across the threshold and through the wards, glanced back at me, and vanished.

Chapter Eighteen

I BROKE THROUGH THE WARDS, SPINNING IN A CIRCLE WITH MY HEAD thrown back, as if I might glimpse Nevan flying away. A patch of empty, eerily blue sky glared down at me, and the moss dripping from the trees swayed in a light breeze.

He'd abandoned me—in the name of protecting me.

"Lindsey?" Ennea's voice called to me from inside the wards. "Where's Nevan?"

I tilted my head down and found Ennea watching me, her eyes large as saucers.

"Gone," I said. "Grabbed his sword and took off. He still thinks he needs to sacrifice himself to save me."

Cursing, I kicked the ground but only managed to send a sharp pain shooting up my ankle.

Travis appeared in doorway, inches from the wards. "What do we do?"

I shoved my hands in my pockets, shoulders hunched. The fingers of my left hand contacted the smooth, warm surface of the soul stone, and a delicious energy rushed up my arm. A piece of Nevan, with me always.

The soul stone had brought me to our home.

Yanking the stone out of my pocket, I held it between my thumb and forefinger. The sunlight shimmered on the disk-shaped chunk of cream-colored rock. I swept the pad of my thumb over the surface, and a taste of Nevan whispered through me, the taste of strength and power and determination.

Something else rippled beneath the surface emotions. Something far more powerful than any magic. The unending strength of our love.

The soul stone had empowered me to whisk from the portal straight to my new home. Could it take me to Nevan?

I closed my hand around the stone. "I'm going after him."

"How?" Ennea asked. "You have no idea where he went."

"Don't need to know." I clamped my hand tighter around the little rock. "Nevan gave me a soul stone. Max showed me I could use it to transport myself here. I'm sure I can get it to take me to Nevan, wherever he is."

"You're sure?" She toyed with her ear, her expression hesitant, but then seemed to shrug off her doubts. "You are the Janusite, so who am I to question what you can do."

Max stepped into view behind Travis and Ennea. "Take me with you, mistress."

No sarcasm in his voice this time when he called me his mistress.

"You can't come with me this time," I told Max. "Have to do this on my own."

"I'm meant to stay at your side and—"

"Not this time." I held up the soul stone for everyone to see. "I'm sorry, Max, I need you to stay here with the others and brainstorm plans."

I could tell he wasn't happy about my orders, but he nodded his agreement.

The worrier in me reared her head, compelling me to ask, "Max, would you ever tell the sorcerer or any of his cohorts what you, me, and the rest of my gang talk about? Would you ever share our plans?"

"No. Absolutely not."

A white light flared on his forehead.

One less thing for me to worry about, assuming my lie detector spell was accurate. I had to believe it was. I needed to believe in my powers, in myself, or I'd never get through this ordeal.

Nevan had always believed in me, even when we had no idea I was the Janusite. I would not let him down.

"Hold down the fort," I told my friends. "This might take awhile."

"Good luck," Travis said.

I faced the woods. Faced the sky. Head thrown back, eyes closed, absorbing the fiery power of the Unseen realm's twin suns. Nevan had been forged from the earth and the sky, from the elemental power of the air and everything contained within it—particles of water and dirt, even fire in the form of electricity. I clutched the soul stone between both of my hands, and the distinctive scent of Nevan enveloped me.

Male spiciness. Damp, virgin earth. And the sweetness of ozone, evocative of thunderstorms.

Energy hummed through the soul stone and spread outward into the whole of my body, and deeper into core of my being. I concentrated all my willpower on Nevan, on reaching him, saving him. The world shifted, faster than the first time I'd done this, and the momentum pushed against my back.

I peeled my eyelids apart, squinting into the gloom around me. Though I'd emerged inside a shadowy corridor carved out of solid rock, up ahead I glimpsed the inconstant light of a fire. It lay beyond a doorway, out of my direct line of sight.

No Nevan.

Without knowing where I'd wound up, I couldn't risk calling out his name. I sensed him near, in a visceral way I couldn't describe. The way I always sensed his approach. My bond with him remained intact, for now.

No, not for now. Forever.

I tiptoed down the rough-hewn corridor toward the doorway, sidling up to the wall so I could peek around the threshold into the chamber beyond.

A fire burned within a single, large metallic bowl perched atop a wide dais. Flames lashed upward from the depths of the bowl, striving to reach the ceiling. This was the tribunal's chamber. I'd seen it when Ennea's spell let me tap into Nevan's memory of the last time he'd come to this place.

The five members of the tribunal gathered in a semicircle around the fire, atop the dais, like they had in Nevan's memory. The hoods of their flowing gold robes masked their faces.

Nevan stood before the tribunal, tall and stiff, the sword in his grip with the point aimed at the earthen floor.

"Why have you summoned us?" one of the tribunal asked in a raspy voice.

Oh yeah, I remembered this jackass from before. Mr. Raspy, the one who'd ordered Nevan to take Ceara as his queen.

"I am king," Nevan said, his voice sure and authoritative. "I summon you at my pleasure."

"We are not your subjects."

My lover sneered at Mr. Raspy. "Every citizen of the sylph kingdom is my subject. I serve their interests and welfare, but I also must know when to take decisive action against those who would endanger my kingdom."

"The tribunal no longer recognizes your authority." Mr. Raspy raised a long, skinny finger at Nevan. "You will serve our master, or you will be destroyed."

Nevan adjusted his grip on the sword, probably itching to plunge it into Mr. Raspy. I would've loved to do it myself.

"I serve no one," Nevan said. "And my subjects do not serve me. I am their leader, not their master. Anyone who volunteers to become a slave to another's whims is a fool at best and a traitor at worst."

"You threaten us?" another tribunal member said.

"Only if you threaten my kingdom."

Mr. Raspy took a shuffling step forward. "By your kingdom, you mean your mortal whore."

The muscles in Nevan's shoulders bunched, and he growled his words through gritted teeth. "I mean every innocent being under my aegis."

"This is your last chance," Mr. Raspy said. "Take a proper queen or suffer the consequences."

"Ceara will never be my queen."

Nevan raised his sword, widening his stance. The firelight glanced off the blade.

I pulled the derringer out of my waist holster, flicked the safety off, and stepped through the doorway.

An invisible force flung me backward.

Flat on my back, I slammed into the solid rock floor of the corridor, the thin covering of dirt no cushion against the bone-rattling force of the impact. My head smacked down last, and bright white lights exploded in my vision. Pain erupted in my head, my shoulders, my hips, scorching through my entire body.

The derringer skittered across the rock floor.

I must've screamed, because some kind of horrible keening reverberated off the stone walls and ceiling.

Dazed, I lay there for what seemed like an eternity but had probably been a matter of seconds. As the pains in my body ebbed to a dull ache in more places than I could count, my mind recovered from the shock. The world around me came back into focus, ushering in an awareness of what had happened. An awareness of two facts.

One, a ward had deflected my attempt to enter the tribunal's chamber.

Two, the keening hadn't been me. It had been Nevan.

He towered in the doorway, breathing hard and flirting with the ward that must've been millimeters from his skin. The sword he held at his side, tip down. He bared his teeth, his eyes wide and aflame with shades of crimson fury.

I pushed up into a sitting position. My head swam for a couple seconds but then settled down. "I'm okay."

"You should not be here."

"Neither should you." I tried not to wince as I scrambled to my feet, but the pains in my body overrode my wishes. "You promised."

"I will not harm myself." He narrowed his eyes to slits, the breath blustering out his flaring nostrils. "I will harm them."

"Nevan, please calm down before you do something—"

He whirled toward the tribunal, and Mr. Raspy stumbled backward.

Nevan swung his sword up and, roaring so loud it hurt my ears, stormed at the tribunal.

Dammit, I had to get through the ward.

A few feet from Mr. Raspy, Nevan froze. Sword raised. Mouth open on a bellow that died on his lips. He seemed to be bound in place by an invisible force.

Ceara winked into view right in front of him.

The fucking wards. My heart pounded, my head throbbed, but I summoned all the will I had inside me to harness my power. Blue energy shimmered in my palms. The power grew inside me, wild and hot, surging in my veins and waiting for my command.

I hurled it at the ward.

And the magic ricocheted off it, slamming into me.

Wham. I hit the floor on my backside, lights bursting in my vision, pain coruscating through my bones. Dizziness rocked my senses, but I scrambled to my feet and confronted the ward, my body swaying.

Inside the chamber, Nevan was paralyzed. Only his eyes moved to glimpse me, and in them I spied a miserable desperation. He couldn't protect me, and it tore at his heart the way my inability to reach him tore at mine.

Ceara smiled at me, the kind of smile that oozed menace and wicked glee. She ran her hands up Nevan's bare chest, fondling and stroking him as if she owned his body.

Maybe she did, for the moment. Fueled by the sorcerer's magic, the power he'd stolen from others, she controlled Nevan's movements but could never control his mind or his heart.

"It is time, Tuathal," she said to Nevan, but with her silvery eyes fixed on me. "Time to complete your humiliation and destroy your soul."

Her dress billowed around her legs, and her long hair fluttered around her face. The papyrus column amulet hung from the chain around her waist, its shiny, bluish green surface reflecting the flickering firelight. The same eerie glow I'd seen in Nevan's memory glittered like shards of silver around Ceara, and even her voice had taken on an eerie quality.

I pounded my fists on the ward. It hurled me backward, but I twisted to the left and struck the floor on my side. The impact reverberated through my hip and shoulder, though I'd spared my skull. I could do nothing but watch as Ceara enacted her master's plan.

Powerless again.

The evil shrew grasped his face in her hands, and with a triumphant glance at me, she mashed her mouth to his. He didn't move or react, his eyes open and haunted. Then his whole body slackened, his gaze turned remote and lifeless. Thin, silvery threads of magic snaked out from her fingertips, whipping and coiling around Nevan's face, slithering over his shoulders and down his arms.

Heaving my body off the ground, I kept my arms down and rotated my hands to direct my palms at the doorway. My magic had failed before. Not this time. Fear had ruled my heart when I lashed out at the ward the first time. For this go-round, I summoned every iota of searing hatred within me.

In the chamber, the serpents of Ceara's energy squirmed their way down Nevan's chest and back, converging around his hips to bleed down both legs. Soon, the visible evidence of the spell sheathed his body in its tentacles.

My hands grew hot, burning with the power I'd marshaled.

Ceara's magic pierced Nevan's skin, the tentacles burrowing in one by one with startling swiftness.

Blue energy exploded from my hands and rammed into the ward.

Nevan's body jerked. White sparked in his eyes, then sputtered out.

The magic shielding the doorway shattered with a boom that echoed in the corridor and the tribunal chamber.

Shaking all over, my head pounding as hard as my heart, I snatched my derringer from the floor and stormed into the chamber, straight to Ceara and Nevan.

Every member of the sylph tribunal backed away, retreating into a shadowed corner of the room.

Ceara curled her lips in a victorious smile.

"Tuathal," she said, and gestured toward me with a sweep of her arm, "show the Janusite the true nature of what you feel for her."

Nevan swiveled toward me, stretched out one thickly muscled arm, and clamped his hand around my throat. His long and powerful fingers encircled my neck, squeezing just enough to make me fight for breath. He lifted me off my feet as if I weighed no more than a feather, my feet suspended a foot off the floor. I lost my hold on the derringer, and it clattered to the ground.

Clutching at his wrist with both hands, I peered into those dead eyes but recognized nothing in them, no fragment of the man I knew and loved. Not the sweet and passionate lover or the fierce and noble warrior, not the former mortal afflicted with guilt from his past or the sylph liberated from magical enslavement. Nothing of Nevan remained in the body that gripped me with steel-reinforced efficiency.

I couldn't feel him either. The warm and vital connection between us had disintegrated. This was not Nevan anymore, but a hollow shell bearing his likeness.

He was hollowed out, exactly how Ceara had predicted.

Tears stung my eyes, threatening to flow, but if I let them come I might never be able to stem the tide. I'd been too late to save Nevan.

"Ahhhh," Ceara purred, moving closer to brush the back of one hand down my cheek, "you begin to understand. Would you like to know what I've done to him?"

I couldn't respond, what with Nevan's hand around my throat. No, not Nevan. I had to think of this shell as separate from him, or else I'd never have the resolve to do what must be done. This wasn't Tuathal either, because Nevan had carried a piece of his former, mortal self within him. This creature was the Anti-Nevan.

"Oh, you poor thing," Ceara cooed, stroking my cheek again. "Can't speak, can you? I shall assume you want me to tell you what I did to your beloved."

I gathered enough saliva in my mouth to spit in her face.

Chuckling, she wiped away the saliva. "My master was right, you are a feisty little mortal. It won't save you, though. Not your or your friends. You are powerless to stop what is coming." She pressed her lips to the Anti-Nevan's, then patted my cheek. "You see, pitiful human, I have stolen his power and channeled it into my master. Nevan's magic will add to that which the sorcerer has already amassed, making him more powerful than any other being in the universe—excepting the sorcerer, of course."

I kicked out with one foot and punted the bitch in her knee.

She winced but then sneered at me.

"That's not all I've done to him," Ceara said, backing away. "Release her, Tuathal."

The Anti-Nevan opened his fist, and I tumbled to the floor.

In a heap on the cold stone, I levered up into a sitting position and massaged my throat. "Tell me what the hell you did and get it over with. All your dramatic pauses make me want to rip your shriveled, slimy heart out. Oh wait, I already wanted to do that."

Ceara squatted before me, her silver eyes glowing. "I've stripped out his soul. It's gone, forever, lost in the abyss of time and space."

"Bullshit." I knew she'd turned him into a hollow shell, but to annihilate his soul…No, I refused to believe it. His essence was out there, somewhere, and I would find it.

"It's true," Ceara said. "And now Tuathal—or rather, his vacant body—will become the weapon of your destruction. You and every other mortal."

A shape moved among the shadows in the farthest corner of the room.

The damn tribunal. While Ceara had carved out Nevan's soul and tormented me, the spineless tribunal had cowered in a dark corner. They'd allowed this vile woman to destroy their king. They had betrayed him.

My Nevan. Lost. Adrift in an eternal abyss.

I would get him back, whatever the cost.

The Anti-Nevan stood motionless and vacant, its eyes unfocused.

My derringer lay near the Anti-Nevan's feet. I snagged the gun and leaped up, swerving my arm to target the derringer on Ceara's forehead.

She wagged a finger at me as she clucked her tongue. "Silly mortal, your weapon cannot harm me."

"Never heard of an endued firearm, eh?" I curled my finger over the trigger. "Let me enlighten you."

I fired the gun. The blast reverberated inside the chamber.

Ceara blipped out.

The noise of the gunfire should have been deafening, but something in this chamber dampened it. The cave behind the waterfall, the one concealing a portal between worlds, featured a similar noise-dampening spell. The waterfall where Nevan had taken me after Skeiron almost killed him. The place where he'd taught me how to let go of my fears.

Do this for Nevan. No fear, no doubt.

The shot had missed Ceara's head, but a robed figured stumbled out of the darkness pawing at his chest. Blood spread across the fabric of his robe, bright red against the gold. The sylph staggered another two steps, then collapsed to the cold, hard floor.

Ceara reappeared beside the fallen tribunal member. She touched a slender finger to the blood pooling around the sylph's body and sniggered.

I fired the gun straight at her.

With her attention on the fallen sylph, Ceara responded to the shot too slowly. The .357 round slammed into her side in the instant before she ducked out again.

Fortified by a determination I'd never known before, I glared at the spot where she had been. Had I killed her? Doubtful. She could run back to her master-slash-lover and, most likely, get patched up by his pilfered magic.

I dug two more rounds of .357 ammo out of my pocket and fumbled to get them into the derringer's barrels. My fingers trembled as I dumped out the spent cartridges. I dropped the new rounds, snatched them up, and stuffed them into the barrels.

Ceara winked back into view inches in front of me. Sweat beaded on her brow. Her chest heaved with each breath, her pale face had gone a shade whiter, and red blood poured from the wound on her side, dribbling out between the fingers of the hand she'd pressed to the wound.

"You," she snarled, teeth bared, spittle flying from her lips. "You will pay for this. The storm-bringer shall consume your powers and lay waste to your world. No mortal will survive his wrath, for it is the apocalypse."

"I've heard this spiel before," I said. "Didn't go well for the last creep who threatened to raze the mortal world. He's in the wind these days, as in annihilated."

"That is what you think?"

My nemesis pitched her head back and cackled. When her wicked laughter subsided, she angled her head up to peer down at me over her nose upturned. "Silly child, you think you know so much and yet know nothing at all."

I clacked the derringer's barrel shut. "I know I'm going to kill you."

Ceara disappeared.

Shit. I knew better than to chat before shooting.

The other woman's voice resounded in the chamber. "I would kill you now, but my master requires you alive, for the moment. Come, Tuathal, we have much to do."

The Anti-Nevan disappeared.

Alone in the hollow silence of the chamber, I trembled not from fear or anguish. I trembled with a deep, dark fury unlike anything I'd experienced in my life. I hated Ceara. *Hated* her. This was no mere dislike. I burned to tear the heart out of her chest and ditch her body into a well of acid. The rage had fueled my powers, letting me crack the ward around this chamber. I sensed it could fuel anything I wanted to do, any dark spell I wished for, any evil deed I could imagine. Was this what I had to become to defeat my enemies? A heartless monster willing to use any magic, no matter how evil, to achieve my goal?

I stuffed the derringer into its holster. No, dammit, this wasn't me. I was not a monster.

A warmth burgeoned inside the left pocket of my jeans. It seeped into me, sweet and gentle, infused with an inherent goodness beyond explanation. I shoved a hand into the pocket, and my skin slid over the stone disk hidden there.

The soul stone.

I shut my eyes, inviting the stone's essence into me. A piece of Nevan's soul lived on within the simple chunk of smooth, round rock.

Awareness rushed over my skin, penetrating beneath it to suffuse me with the wonderful, unmistakable essence of the only man I'd ever loved. He wasn't dead. His soul persisted, if only in the smallest way.

Nevan wouldn't want me to give in to darkness. It would've been a betrayal of everything he'd shown me and taught me and inspired in me. And I had a sick feeling it was exactly what the sorcerer—the stormbringer, as Ceara had called him—wanted from me. If he pushed me into staining my soul with darkness, that might make it all the easier for him to gobble up my power.

I pulled the soul stone out of my pocket and touched my lips to the warm and oddly soft rock. Something pulsed through me, spreading from my lips throughout the rest of my body. Tender, sweet, passionate, resolute, and strong.

Nevan. Dear God, he'd kissed me back.

Which made no sense whatsoever, and yet I knew with total conviction he had touched me. He was out there, waiting for me to bring him back.

I felt enlivened, awakened, and...purified. His soul had cleansed mine.

Shutting my eyes, I closed my fingers around the stone. *Thank you, Nevan.*

Footsteps shuffled.

I slipped the soul stone back in my pocket and leveled my gaze at the tribunal. The four surviving members had gathered before me in a loose grouping, their postures slumped and their wary eyes on me.

"You are the Janusite," Mr. Raspy said, his tone cautious and almost fearful. "This is why the king defended you with such passion. He has been protecting the Janusite. You."

"Nevan defended me because he loves me, and I love him."

Mr. Raspy pushed his hood back, and it settled around his shoulders to reveal the face of an elderly man with gold-sheened skin. "You speak as if he lives. The sorcerer's consort has taken him, body and soul."

"He's alive and I'm going to bring him back."

"What of us?" He nearly cringed, as if he expected me to lash out with my power.

I'd done just that moments ago, so I couldn't blame him for fearing me.

"Listen," I said, "I didn't mean to shoot your friend. I was aiming for Ceara."

"We know," Mr. Raspy said. "Understand we had no knowledge of what the sorcerer intended for the king. Stripping his soul…If we had known, we would never have dealt with the sorcerer. We wish we could aid you, but our bargain with him prevents it."

My lie detector spell seemed to have fizzled out after the enormous amount of magic I'd expended to shatter the ward around this chamber. I didn't need a spell this time. My instincts told me the man was telling the truth, and my instincts had never led me astray.

"I believe you," I said, "and I'm not going to hurt you. Even though you tried to force Nevan to dump me and take the sorcerer's evil slut as his queen. Even though you let Ceara hollow him out like a discarded Halloween pumpkin. Even though you betrayed your own king."

Mr. Raspy had the decency to look ashamed.

I sighed, weary of wasting time on these worms. "Can you at least tell me what the sorcerer promised you in exchange for your help?"

"He promised to ensure Nevan would no longer be king, and that we would rule over the sylph kingdom in his stead."

"You accepted the deal without bothering to ask how Nevan would be dethroned."

Another tribunal member plodded forward and flipped back his hood. His copper-tinged face was youthful and fringed with red hair. "We could not have guessed the sorcerer meant to destroy Nevan's soul."

"What you mean is, you didn't give a shit how it was done as long as you got the power you've been lusting for." I shook my head, eying each tribunal member in turn, even the ones who still hid inside their hoods. "A bunch of cowards, that's what you are. The lot of you should be grateful for the chance to kiss Nevan's feet. He's a thousand times the man any of you could hope to be."

The other two tribunal members lowered their heads, and as one the entire group fell to their knees.

"Forgive us," Mr. Raspy said. "If we had known the king wished to make the Janusite his queen—"

"You would've sucked up to us both because you're afraid of my power." Oh, I really didn't have time for their sniveling. I waved my hands in a get-up-off-your-sorry-asses gesture. "Stop genuflecting. I'm not going to hurt you unless you hurt me or the people I care about. By the way, that includes every single person in the mortal realm."

The tribunal rose but kept their heads down.

"You slimy little toadies," I said, "aren't worth my time. I am going to stop the sorcerer and save you gutless backstabbers, even though you don't deserve it. You can thank me later."

I yanked the soul stone out of my pocket and tapped into its energies, whisking myself out of the chamber and straight home.

CHAPTER NINETEEN

MY RAGTAG BAND OF ALLIES HAD GATHERED AROUND ME IN THE LIVING room to listen as I recounted the events in the tribunal chamber. Max had sprawled over the red sofa, but the tension on his face belied his nonchalant posture. Ennea and Tris occupied the two chairs, while Travis leaned against the wall in the threshold to the kitchen.

I slouched on the bed, my back against the wall, with my legs stretched across the bed's width and my feet barely reaching past the other side. I kept petting the fur blanket without any conscious intention, as if I might draw strength from the silky feel of it or from the memory of being with Nevan in this bed. In our bed. In our home.

Travis cleared his throat. "I know you want to save Nevan, but should that really be our priority?"

"He's my priority, not yours." I yawned for the umpteenth time, exhausted from the expenditure of magic required to break into the tribunal chamber. "I asked you guys to brainstorm ideas for a plan. Haven't you got anything?"

Four sets of eyes zeroed in on me, surprise evident in them.

Okay, maybe I had sounded a tad bitchy. Finding out your boyfriend had his soul ripped out of him and his formerly dead wife had control of his body did not ease a girl's anxiety. And this girl needed some serious easing.

I sneaked my hand into my pocket, sighing as the soul stone imparted a fragment of Nevan to me, but then withdrew my hand. As much as I needed the connection, the reminder he wasn't completely lost to me, I could not keep relying on the soul stone for comfort. What I needed was a plan for rescuing Nevan, but I shouldered the responsibility for that task, not my friends. Stopping an apocalypse had to be their number one priority.

Even if we saved the world, living in it without Nevan…That was unacceptable.

"We do have an idea," Ennea said.

Tris snorted. "A crap-ass one."

"You got a better one, big mouth?"

"Nothing's better than something that'll get us all shredded into confetti."

Ennea slapped her hands on her chair's arms. "Nothing is what we've been doing, and in case you haven't noticed, the bad guys are winning. They got Nevan."

All gazes veered toward me, rife with apology and sympathy. I didn't want them to feel bad for me. I wanted us to do something.

"It's okay," I said. "You can mention his name. I won't fall into a heap on the floor, weeping and wailing over my lost love. He's not gone forever, and I will get him back."

The only word to describe their expressions was doubtful.

My friends believed I couldn't get Nevan back.

Let them believe what they wanted, I knew I'd find him. No force in the universe, not even a sorcerer and his whackjob consort, would stop me from rescuing Nevan.

Everyone else in the room continued to look at me like I'd morphed into a pathetic little abused puppy.

I clambered off the bed to stand straight and resolute before them. "Everyone stop looking at me like I'll fall apart if you breathe in my direction. I'm not hopeless or helpless. But I do need my team to stand with me in defeating the sorcerer."

"Team?" Travis said, his brows hiking up.

"Yes. We are a team." I surveyed my allies, once again struck by the strangeness of this group. We were all so different and yet united in a cause. United by friendship. "We can do this, guys, I know we can. I need you to believe it too."

As for that twinge of uncertainty in my gut, they didn't need to hear about it. My team needed bolstering, and apparently, I had become the de facto leader. If Nevan were here, he'd know what to say. He wasn't here, so I had to do this on my own.

I'd never led anything. Not so much as an online chat.

The sylph will be your undoing, the oracle had warned.

Bob had told me his foresight was hindered by the sorcerer's magic. Since Bob hadn't foreseen his own death at Ceara's hands, I wondered how accurate his predictions were. Maybe I prayed they were faulty. I could've gotten mired in denial, refusing to see the potential consequences of attempting to save Nevan. I'd given in to my darkest impulses back in the tribunal chamber. Would I succumb to it again in my desperate attempt to get Nevan back? Would the sorcerer win because I darkened my own soul?

A figure moved in front of me.

I struggled to focus on the world me around again after getting mired in my thoughts.

Travis watched me from a couple feet away, concern tightening his features.

"What's going on?" he asked in a hushed voice. "I can tell you're freaking out on the inside, but you're trying to hide it from the rest of us."

Sometimes I forgot how well Travis knew me. Not as well as Nevan did, but pretty damn well. Travis and I had been friends for years before I met his brother and everything went to hell. No point in lying to him.

"I…" My voice trailed off as I struggled to find a way to explain. "I had a weird experience in the tribunal chamber."

He examined me for a moment, then faced the rest of the group. "Lindsey and me need to have a private talk. You guys hash out your plan or come up with a new one. We'll be back in a minute."

Our friends said nothing, though they looked uncomfortable.

Travis took hold of my elbow and guided me across the living room toward the bathroom doorway. The soothing rush and patter of water cascading into the pool emanated from the space beyond. As we entered the bathroom, I glanced back to find our friends staring after us. When they noticed me looking at them, they quickly averted their gazes.

Inside the bathroom, Travis led me to the farthest corner from the doorway. The pool frothed beside us, and the wall behind penned me between its smooth stone and Travis's bulk.

He grasped my shoulders, bending down to peer into my eyes. "Tell me what's going on, Lindsey."

I sagged into the wall, my arms crossed over my belly. "Ceara was about to rip the soul of Nevan. I couldn't get to him because the tribunal chamber has a ward protecting it. To get past the ward, I had to summon a hell of a lot of magical energy."

"You've done that before."

"This was different." I hugged myself, rubbing my arms, chilled despite the temperate weather inside this little sanctuary. "I had to channel a lot of rage in order to power up my magic enough to blast through the ward. A lot of rage. It was…disturbing."

"Getting mad is understandable."

I shook my head. "You don't get it. This wasn't normal anger, it was pure hatred. I gave in to the darkness and let it feed my power. What if I'm evil?"

He sighed, laying his hands over mine on my upper arms. "Lindsey, you are not evil."

"But—"

"I know a thing or two about evil." One corner of his mouth kinked in a sardonic expression. "My brother turned into a monster—an actual monster, straight outta Greek mythology. You're nothing like him. Even when Calder was trying to turn you into a kerko-whatsit like him, you would've rather died than give in to it. You're one tough chick, Lindsey Porter."

Travis hadn't been there when his brother tried to kill me in hopes of making me into a monkey-thing. Nevan had told him about it while I lay unconscious after Tris healed my wounds. The story had impressed Travis, who had begun calling me a tough chick—his way of showing respect for my fortitude, I guessed.

"Listen to me," Travis said. "You went through hell to get over your troubles. Don't let one wacko sorcerer and his hag of a girlfriend make you doubt yourself again."

He was right, of course. I'd almost died multiple times on my journey to realizing my true potential, not only as the Janusite but as a mere mortal too. The sorcerer wanted my powers at full strength, yes. But he also wanted me weak, wanted me doubting everything, so he could steal my power. If I cowered in a corner worrying about turning evil, I would give him exactly what he wanted.

"You're getting it, aren't ya?" Travis said, his warped mouth smoothing out into a closed-lip smile.

Pushing away from the wall, I opened my mouth to speak. The words "thank you" wanted to come out, but I cut them off. Could I indebt myself to another human? Travis wouldn't abuse the debt, but I preferred not to test the boundaries of our resurrected friendship.

"I appreciate the pep talk," I said. "You're right. I let myself wallow in self-pity for a while, but that's over."

"You would've gotten out of the funk on your own, but I was glad to lend a hand." He patted my arm. "That's what friends do, ain't it?"

I smiled, amazed I could under the circumstances. "Yeah, I think it is."

Someone whistled from the other room.

"We got a half-assed plan," Tris hollered. "Come and hear it, ya mooks, or we'll sign you up for the crummiest jobs."

Travis rolled his eyes. "Never thought I'd be teaming up with a snotty leprechaun."

I slapped his arm. "Welcome to my world, sheriff."

He sighed with dramatic heaviness. "Better get out there. Team Lindsey is having a mission briefing."

———

I LOITERED IN THE CENTER OF THE ROOM, SURROUNDED BY MY ALLIES, digesting the plan they'd laid out for me. The name Team Lindsey sounded ridiculous to me. When I'd voiced my objection to the team being named after me, Max had replied, "You are the fearless leader of this micro-army. Of course, it bears your name."

"Fearless?" I'd said. "I'm not a superheroine."

"You confront your fears and break through them to achieve great things." Max had sat up on his sofa then, elbows on his knees. "You're the bravest of us, and not because you're the Janusite."

To my total shock, Tris had piped up to add, "Yeah, you could've gotten massacred when you gutted Skeiron with a sword. And you almost drowned coming to get me so we could heal Nevan." He'd looked at me with genuine admiration. "You're a rock star, lady."

At that point, I'd grown uncomfortable with the "Lindsey is awesome" festival and steered the conversation back to their plan. Ten minutes later, I remained skeptical.

"I want this to work," I said, sneaking my hand into my pocket. The soul stone feathered a trace of Nevan over my skin. The sensation was beautiful, but very distracting. I hooked my thumbs inside the waistband of my jeans. "I'm still not clear on how we pull this off."

Ennea, slouched in one of the chairs, propped her head up with one hand. "We capture Ceara, that's how."

"Uh-huh, I got the what part of the plan. It's the how part I'm fuzzy on."

Max heaved his body off the red sofa and traversed the room to me. "You lure her, mistress."

"I'd really appreciate if you could stop calling me mistress. Makes me sound like a brothel-keeper. Lindsey will do."

"If you insist—Lindsey."

"Much better." I tapped the toe of one boot on the floor. "Nobody has explained how I'm going to lure Ceara anywhere."

"She despises you," Max said. "You shot her, and she wants vengeance. Anger can be a powerful tool, but it can also lead a person astray. Play on her hatred of you."

"How, exactly?"

"That's up to you, our courageous leader."

"Flattery will not make me love this plan."

Their plan, as outlined to me over the past twenty minutes, involved using Ceara as bait to draw out the sorcerer. I'd once mentioned we might be able to use his feelings for Ceara against him, if he had feelings for her. Max had told me the sorcerer and Ceara were lovers, which might indicate a bond deeper than lust. "Might" was the keyword.

"Your whole cockamamie scheme," I said, "revolves around the assumption the sorcerer gives a damn about Ceara. They might be sleeping together, but we have no idea if he cares about her as anything but a tool for achieving his goals." When Tris started to speak, I silenced him with a raised hand. "And may I point out, we still don't know our enemy's endgame."

"The crazy broad told you," Tris said. "Apocalypse."

"A bit vague for my comfort." I scratched the top of my head, mussing my hair with random movements of my fingers. Combing my hands through my hair to smooth it out, I began to pace the length of the room. Pacing had become my go-to action when I needed to think, particularly pacing inside this house. My new home.

If I didn't iron out the mountain-size kinks in this plan, I'd wind up living alone in the home Nevan had built, with nothing but the soul stone to keep me warm at night.

"Even if we capture Ceara," I said, halting near the bed and turning to face everyone, "the sorcerer still has the Anti-Nevan, and the Anti-Nevan still has sylph powers."

"Anti-Nevan?" Travis said.

"What they have is not Nevan, it's a shell that used to be his body. I will not think of that thing as Nevan, so I call it the Anti-Nevan. It's the opposite of everything he is."

"Kind of like the Antichrist?"

Was that a smirk he was trying to quash?

"Get snarky with me if you want," I said, "but pay attention to the important point I made. Even if we get Ceara, the sorcerer still has a powerful weapon in the Anti-Nevan."

Tris levered his body out of the chair where he'd reclined throughout our discussion. He moseyed up to me, shoulders hunched, hands in his pockets. Despite his discomfited posture, he met my gaze with a sharp clarity in his bright blue eyes. "That's where your plan comes in. It's up to you to restore Nevan's soul and take away the sorcerer's new toy."

Max touched my upper arm. "Are you sure you can do it?"

"Yes."

"Then I'm with you, Lindsey. Until the end."

"We all are," Tris said. He glanced over his shoulder at Travis and Ennea. "Aren't we?"

"Absolutely," Ennea said.

"Damn straight," Travis added. "Though I'd like to know how you're planning to get to Nev—the Anti-Nevan."

"How else?" I smiled. "Magic."

"All right, but you gotta find Nevan's soul first."

"Don't need to find it." I dug the soul stone out of my pocket and held it up for everyone to see. "I have it right here."

Max's mouth slid into a knowing smile. "The soul stone. That's brilliant."

Travis frowned at the stone. "A soul what?"

"Nevan gave me this," I said, tossing the stone and catching it in my palm. "It's a soul stone, a special rock from the Unseen realm that can hold a piece of someone's soul. He intended it to help me get through the wards around our house, since they were attuned to him. Max showed me I can use the stone to access Nevan's poofing ability."

"Poofing?" Travis looked so flummoxed, I had the urge to give him a hug.

"Yes," I said. "Poofing, or whisking, is what I call teleportation. The point is, I have Nevan's soul right here in my hand."

"A piece of his soul," Ennea said. "Where's the rest of it?"

"Still connected to the soul stone, I can feel it." At the skeptical looks I received, I reminded them, "I have a connection with Nevan. Anyone doubt that?"

Four people muttered, "No."

"I believe his soul couldn't be scattered or destroyed or whatever," I told them, "because of our connection. Because of the soul stone. I'm going to use it to return his soul to his body."

Travis grasped the back of his neck. "The shell you call the Anti-Nevan."

"Yep."

"Sounds good, but you have to get him here."

"Not here. I need a secluded place to do this." The rest of my plan I'd kept to myself, because I had no proof of what I believed. The Anti-Nevan may have been a shell, but magic gave it life. The shell being was alive. Its hot skin and audible breaths told me as much. If it lived, even without a soul, it must have some kind of emotions. I planned on tapping into them to get him riled up, get him incensed. No one knew better than I did the destructive power of out-of-control emotions.

Yep, that was my plan. Crazy, for sure. But our physical connection had provided a fertile conduit for my magic and allowed me to restore Nevan's vitality, which I theorized had meant reinvigorating his soul. Getting the Anti-Nevan worked up, without risking my safety, should provide a suitable conduit for me to use the soul stone to get Nevan back into his body.

I might have gone insane. Totally, irreversibly insane.

Didn't care, as long as I got Nevan back.

Boom.

The mountain shook from a massive concussion. Another boom made the furniture jump and my friends stagger to stay upright. Bits of rock sheared off the walls, crumbling to the floor.

"What the—" Travis cut off his question as another boom rocked the house.

"Is it Ceara again?" Tris asked.

"No," I said, overcome by a grim certainty of what was assaulting my home. "It's not her this time."

"Then who?"

I approached the hidden doorway and willed it to open. The stone wall shimmered and telescoped open to reveal the being standing just beyond the wards.

The Anti-Nevan's gaze snapped to mine.

A horrible dread coiled around my heart, cinching tight until my chest felt as if it might implode from the pressure.

The Anti-Nevan held out his hand to me and smiled. "Come, love, and I will spare your friends."

He'd called me love. He sounded like Nevan, looked like Nevan, but he was not Nevan. This was a new ploy from the sorcerer, one I should've expected. Use the shell that once contained my lover to confuse me. Something was different this time. Back in the tribunal chamber, the Anti-Nevan had acted like an empty shell, devoid of feeling or awareness. Now, he seemed like a real, living being—though not like the real Nevan.

What had Travis said Ceara told him? Nevan would become a hollowed-out shell. But there had been more. A corollary to the hollowed-out statement. She'd said...

The perfect vessel.

Ah, of course. A vacant statue wouldn't make me throw down my derringer and surrender. The sorcerer had filled in the shell with something else, something dark and bound to his will, something that looked and sounded like Nevan. The sorcerer hoped to confuse me, make me reticent to harm the Anti-Nevan. He thought Nevan was my weakness, but he was wrong. Nevan gave me strength.

I had the soul stone in my palm, protected by my fingers closed over it. The real Nevan was with me.

A hand on one hip, forcing my body to relax, I cast a haughty gaze on the Anti-Nevan. "Nice try, but no. I'm comfy here."

"Your wards are puny." He leaned forward, looming over me despite the five feet of space between us. "I will breach them and take you anyway. But that is what you like, is it not? For me to take you."

I resisted the urge to back away, unwilling to expose the fact I was disconcerted. Did this creature know what I'd told Nevan the night we first made love? *Take me, Nevan*, I'd said. But this thing couldn't know about that.

Unless he retained some or all of Nevan's memories. A cheap photocopy of our life together.

A weapon I could use.

"You?" I scoffed. "I enjoy sex with Nevan, but I don't screw hollow shells being controlled by an evil scumbag. The nasty crud he filled you with would leave a bad taste in my mouth."

"Nevertheless, I will take you from here." Lips parted, he darted his tongue out to moisten them. "He has promised me your body, after he strips away your powers. As a powerless mortal, you will be helpless to stop me from enjoying you. Whether or not you enjoy me."

Oh, that sneaky sorcerer. He had no intention of handing me over to anyone else, but he lied to the Anti-Nevan to gain his loyalty. Maybe the sorcerer sensed what I did, that the Anti-Nevan suffered from uncontrollable passions. Either way, I decided to keep the truth to myself for now. Might come in handy later.

As for me being powerless...The Anti-Nevan would learn a hard lesson about that too.

I let my arms fall slack at my sides and shrugged one shoulder. "Go ahead. Bang your head against the wards as long as you like. You'll get a migraine, but you will never breach my magic."

The Anti-Nevan slammed his fist into the wards. The recoil sent him flying backward into a tree. He struck it with a *thwack*, slumping down onto the grassy earth.

I folded my arms under my breasts, producing the unintended effect of pushing them up so they mounded against the V-neck of my shirt. "See? I'm stronger than you, puny shell-man."

His face twisted into a mask of raw fury, redness blooming beneath his bronzed skin. He sprang to his feet and rushed at the wards, moving so fast he became a blur. A hair's breadth from the wards, he stopped.

"You," he spat. "Soon, you will need to leave this place. I will be waiting for you."

Anti-Nevan vanished.

I glanced back at my friends. "That's how I'll get to him."

Travis glared out the doorway. "I don't get it. How does what just happened give you a way to get to this Anti-Nevan? He's waiting for you to go out there so he can grab you."

"He has Nevan's memories, or at least some of them." I leaned against the wall beside the doorway. "And he wants me. I can use all of that against him and get close enough to put my plan into action."

Four people stared at me, confused, but it was Travis who asked, "What plan?"

"Saving the real Nevan."

"But that thing out there will come and get you the second you leave the wards."

My gaze wandered back to the view beyond the wards. The Anti-Nevan was out there, somewhere. When I left this house, he would find me. "I'm counting on it."

Travis shook his head once, his brows lowered. "This is nuts."

Ennea waved a hand to get my attention. "How can you be sure the soul stone will work?"

"It's simple." I tossed the stone in the air and caught it in my palm. "Intuition."

"If you're wrong," Max said, "you might die in the effort."

"A risk I'm willing to take." I pushed away from the wall, looking through the doorway into the darkening woods beyond. Sunset had arrived in the Unseen realm. I couldn't see the Anti-Nevan, but I knew he waited for me out there.

I faced my friends, rolling my shoulders back. "I'm getting Nevan back tonight. And once that's done, we are going to destroy the sorcerer."

Chapter Twenty

S O THAT'S OUR PLAN?" TRIS ASKED, SEEMING EVEN MORE DUBIOUS than he had when I explained my idea for getting Nevan back. "Don't you think it's way too simple?"

My allies had collected in a haphazard grouping in front of me. Ennea lingered near her brother, while Max had sidled closer to me, and Travis hung back behind the others. He kept his gaze trained on me, like a cop monitoring a suspect. Actually, it was more like a cop protecting an endangered witness.

I planted a hand on the edge of the open doorway to the outside. "Complexity is a recipe for disaster. If we each do our part, this will work."

"You're awful confident about that," Travis said. "Overconfident, maybe."

"Believe me," I said, "I am fully aware of how this could turn into a cataclysmic disaster. We have no other choice, though, do we? Unless somebody thought up a new plan in the last ten minutes."

No one spoke up.

I gazed out into the deceptively still night. "Then we go with what we've got. But may I remind you negative thinking could get us all killed. If you walk out there screaming 'oh shit, we're all gonna die,' then we all will die."

Tris quirked a brow. "We should be thinking sunshine and rainbows?"

"Be smart. Be strong. Think positive, but be vigilant."

Travis saluted me. "Yes, ma'am."

"We're ready," Ennea said.

Max nodded. "We are."

An army of misfits. That seemed the best description of us. But we were all that stood between two worlds and total devastation. What else could an apocalypse mean?

It wouldn't happen on our watch.

"Everyone gather 'round," I said, waving them closer. "Once I get us through the wards, all hell might break loose. Remember, the Anti-Nevan is out there waiting for us—for me. Don't get distracted by whatever happens, stick to your assigned tasks."

My allies, my friends, gathered close around me. Each of them offered a single hand to me, and I took two in one of my hands and two in the other. Thus linked, we were ready to exit the wards.

I glanced at Tris and Ennea. "The second we're outside, you two hightail it out of here. Max, you get Travis to the designated rendezvous point."

Travis had taken up a position right next to me, his shoulder and arm pressed to mine and his free hand on his Sig. Since his weapon wasn't endued, and we had no time for Ennea to undertake the long and arduous spell to endue it, he would have to aim for the head and hope any attackers were stunned by a .40-caliber slug to the brain. It might give him enough time to escape.

My derringer rested snugly in its holster, inside my waistband. I'd reloaded it and stuffed additional rounds in my pocket. If it came to a choice between the Anti-Nevan and me—or Travis or Max—I would do what Nevan would want.

I'd shoot him straight between the eyes.

My chest ached at the idea of killing his body. I could do it. I would do it.

But only if I had no other recourse.

I surveyed my friends. "On three. One, two—"

We stepped over the threshold, through the wards, to halt inches past it.

Nothing chirped or croaked or howled. No breeze stirred the leaves. Stars glimmered in the oval of sky we could glimpse above us, but trees penned us and blotted out the rest of heavens. The only light came from inside the underground lair and from the full moon overhead. I recognized it as the smaller of this world's two moons. The larger one must've been in its new moon phase. The smaller one bathed the world in a glow slightly brighter than a full moon in the mortal realm.

"Go," I whispered.

Ennea and Tris blinked out.

Travis threw me a worried look as Max zipped him away.

Rather than pulling out my derringer, I withdrew the six-inch knife Max had conjured for me. Mystical symbols decorated the wooden hilt and curled down the center of its curved, double-edged blade. The knife was not endued, as I had requested. I needed a nonlethal weapon this time. Besides, I had the derringer in case of emergency.

With the knife gripped in my hand, I walked into the center of the clearing, scanning the darkness for some sign of the Anti-Nevan. A sign of anything. The world seemed to have frozen, as if time had stopped. Though time could move slower in the presence of my magics, I doubted time had actually stopped for me. The sensation of unnatural stillness disconcerted me nonetheless.

A pair of iron-hard arms seized me around my waist, dragging me backward and belting me to an equally hard body.

I flinched at the hot skin mashed into my backside, searing me through my clothes. Hotter than Nevan. Filling his body up with evil crud must've overheated it.

The Anti-Nevan bent his head to growl in my ear, "I have you."

I'd figured there was a fifty-fifty chance he'd pop up behind me, but I'd hoped for the other option. It was the hard way, then.

"You sure about that?" I said.

His arms strapped me tighter to him. "I am certain."

"Arrogance is a nasty habit. Might get you killed."

Though I held the knife in front of my thigh, he clearly hadn't noticed it. Adrenaline electrified my body, heightening my senses, and I realized I had one shot at this. No room for screw-ups. No room for doubt. All in or nothing.

I swung the knife up and drove it into his leg.

He bellowed and staggered backward, releasing me so he could use his hands to staunch the flow of blood from his thigh wound. Blood streamed from the wound anyway, dribbling out between his fingers. His lips peeled back from his clenched teeth. "You will suffer for this."

I brandished my knife in the air, twirling it to let the ambient light glint off its silvery blade and glisten on the streaks of blood there. "Why don't you bad guys ever get a new line? Just one. I mean, 'you will suffer' and 'I will decimate the world' are getting pretty stale."

Crouching, I drove the blade into the soft earth and withdrew it. The dirt had cleansed the knife, leaving behind only scraps of earth. I wiped them off on my jeans, then rose to watch the Anti-Nevan struggle to stand up straight.

The agony on his face crumbled away.

I hadn't expected the wound to stop him for good. A few seconds had been all I needed.

"Since you like tired phrases," I said. "Here's one for you. Catch me if you can. I'm headed for the spot where Nevan and I steamed for each other."

A spark of something in his eyes gave me hope he retained that memory too.

Shoving my hand into my pocket, I touched the soul stone and teleported out of the clearing. I caught a glimpse of the Anti-Nevan's face contorting with rage but then the abyssal tunnel swept me away toward my destination.

I materialized at the portal, in front of the boulder that housed it. With a Nevan-like flick of my wrist, I spun the portal open and leaped through it into the cave behind the waterfall on the mortal side. The rock shop was not far from here, but I had a different destination in mind. Leaving the portal open—wouldn't want to make it too hard for the Anti-Nevan to follow me—I marched through the falls onto the ledge outside and whisked myself to the predetermined location.

Woods surrounded me. The branches of the trees—aspen, maple, pine, and fir—curved over the small clearing, almost forming a canopy overhead. Through the small, circular opening above, the bright light of Earth's full moon shined down on me.

I turned in a circle to canvas the area. A smile pulled at my lips, a smile tainted with heartache but underpinned by the sweetest memories of the night my entire life had transformed. I'd been here once before, six weeks ago, on the night Nevan had enticed me to let go of my iron grip on my desires by asking me to steam for him. The night we became lovers. The night he'd come far too close to dying. I'd risked my life to find Tris and get him to heal Nevan via the unmarked healing vortex in this clearing. This location held great significance for me and for Nevan, and I needed to give Nevan a powerful anchor to draw him back to his rightful place in the universe. What held more meaning for either us than the night a metaphor about pots and kettles had become an erotic reality?

Yes, I'd once been a pot who locked up her strong emotions under a tight lid. Nevan had coaxed me into becoming a kettle and releasing all that pent-up steam. Right here, in this clearing.

Tris had provided invaluable aid the last time I'd come here, but he couldn't help me tonight. No one could. The sole burden of saving Nevan weighed on my shoulders, a massive boulder of responsibility and risk.

Nevan had told me vortexes could enhance our bond and our pleasure. Tonight, I was counting on this vortex to strengthen our connection.

I advanced toward the trees at the clearing's edge. "You guys there?"

Two figures separated from the shadows of the forest, moving toward me. The moonlight glinted off the badge on Travis's chest as he and Tris halted an arm's length from me, sneaking out from behind a screen of bushes and saplings.

"The creepy dude ain't here yet," Tris said. "Started a magical trail at the portal's edge, like we planned, but you're the only one who's come through."

"Yeah, he might need a few minutes," I said. "The gaping knife wound will slow him down a little, but it's probably healing as we speak."

"The trail should lead the shell guy right to you."

"Your trip go according to plan?"

"We hopped around so much," Tris said, "the tough guy here almost hurled. The overlapping boundaries got us here, though. Eventually."

Travis watched me, stoic as ever. "Are you sure about this, Lindsey? Your plan is pretty damn dangerous."

"I know. But we need Nevan if we're going to beat our enemies." I needed him, but that was rather irrelevant to anyone else.

Travis took another step toward me, the intensity of his stare making me uneasy. "I don't want anything to happen to you."

"Neither do I." My tone came out a bit too breezy, like I was trying too hard to minimize the danger. In a more sober tone, I added, "I'm counting on you and Tris to barge in if things go pear-shaped."

Tris lifted his right hand, wielding a wickedly sharp and curved sword. "Got me an awesome weapon. Take him awhile to get over being stuck with this bad boy."

"I got one too," Travis said, hefting a bigger, badder sword reminiscent of Viking weapons I'd seen on TV. The lowly human sheriff held it as if the massive thing weighed next to nothing, his biceps bulging and straining the fabric of his uniform. Yet his arm was steady, he seemed comfortable with the weapon. "One of us'll get him if he lays a finger on you."

"Uh-uh," I said, shaking my head. "He has to lay a finger on me for this plan to work, and I'll have to let him. You don't attack unless I'm in imminent danger of death. Understand?"

He ground his teeth. "Yeah. I get it."

The leprechaun raised his free hand. "Question. How are we gonna know if you get Nevan's soul back where it belongs?"

"You'll know, trust me." I glanced back at the clearing, then to my allies. "I don't know exactly what will happen, but I'm positive it will be unmistakable. At that point, you two will want to leave."

"Hell no," Travis said. "Ain't leaving without you."

"You don't want to see the rest. When I use my magic on Nevan, it has… um…unusual side effects."

"Unusual? Like what?"

"Well…" Oh hell, what was the point in being coy about this? They'd figure it out once things got moving. "We'll both be highly aroused."

Travis scrunched up his entire face in disgust, diverting his attention to the ground. When he looked at me again, I swore I noticed a faint blush on his cheeks. "Yeah, I get the picture."

"Maybe Tris should keep watch, and you should turn your back."

"No." Travis shot ramrod straight, shoulders back and chin lifted. "I'm a goddamn officer of the law. I've seen worse than you and him getting it on."

"Fine, watch if you want." I waved them away. "But for now, shoo. I need stealth guards, not obvious targets for the Anti-Nevan to mow down with a flick of his finger."

Travis winced, and I suspected he was remembering when Nevan had tossed him into a tree. Of course, Travis had been threatening to arrest me at the time. *Bygones.*

Tris's eyes flared wide. "He's through the portal."

"Good," I said. "Let's hope he understood my hint."

"Be careful," Travis said, his voice low and intense.

"You too." I gave Tris's arm a quick squeeze. "Both of you."

Generating almost no noise, the two men retreated behind the screening vegetation.

Everything depended on the fact Nevan could cross the boundaries as long as I was somewhere in the mortal world. If the trick didn't work on Anti-Nevan, I'd lose the real Nevan forever.

One deep breath. I exhaled it slowly, turned, and walked to the exact spot where everything had begun the last time I'd visited this place. My gaze fell on the patch of grassy earth where, mere weeks ago, Nevan lay dying from a wound inflicted by an endued sword. The fingers of my right hand crooked into my palm, my throat went tight and dry. *I can do this, I will do this.*

With the knife in my left hand, I slipped the derringer out of its holster with my right hand. Shooting was my last resort.

A chilly breeze rustled the leaves in the trees. Goose bumps cropped up on my arms, not solely from the cool air whispering over my skin.

The Anti-Nevan materialized in the center of the clearing, a dozen feet from where I waited. We faced each other, his hand brandishing Nevan's endued sword, my hands gripping the knife and my endued derringer.

He sneered at me. "I caught you."

Overconfidence. Excellent, my plan was on track.

He sauntered toward me with long, leisurely strides. His hips swayed, his muscles flexed and slackened with each step, the loincloth stretched taut over his groin. That unearthly gaze locked onto me, a glowing, sizzling whirlpool of molten metal. Bronze, gold, silver—and an undercurrent of bright, hot red.

I couldn't hide the shiver that rippled through me. No going back now.

He stopped an arm's length away, dipping his head to the side to examine me with detached interest. "Why did you permit me through the boundary?"

"Figured it was time we meet and discuss the situation."

"The situation is simple." He crept closer, silhouetted by the full moon behind him. "I have you, Janusite. Attempt to run, and I will seize you. Attempt to stab me again, and I will strike you down. You will remain alive, though you may wish you were not."

Raising the knife, I turned it side to side so the moonlight gleamed on its blade.

He bristled the tiniest bit, his jaw tensing.

"Try to leave," I said, "and the boundary will disintegrate you."

Anti-Nevan growled through clenched teeth. "I can kill you where you stand."

"But your boss wouldn't like that, would he? You have to deliver me alive and well enough to keep my powers at full strength. Correct?"

The way a muscle jumped in his jaw answered my question.

"I thought so." A lump hardened in my throat at the realization of what I must do next. The biggest gamble of all. I resisted the urge to glance into the trees, to where Tris and Travis hid, and instead focused on Anti-Nevan. "The sorcerer lied to you."

He moved closer, forcing me to bend my head back to keep our gazes aligned. "You are the one lying—to yourself."

"The sorcerer promised you could have me after he steals my powers." Pulse racing. Skin prickling. No way but forward, plunging into the unknown, bolstered by faith. "He's never going to give me to you. He wants me for himself. Told me as much, when he murdered an innocent girl right in front of me."

Anti-Nevan gave a derisive little laugh.

Before he could speak, I said, "The sorcerer offered to become whomever I want him to be. You, Travis—"

"Not him." Spittle sprayed from Anti-Nevan's lips, while his face flushed crimson.

Jealousy. I could work with that.

"Why not?" I said. "Travis is a big, strong man. And hot? Whoa, mama, is he ever."

Anti-Nevan pitched toward me, narrowing the gap between our bodies to scant inches. Menace rolled off him in waves of psychic energy that gnashed at the edges of my magic.

We both occupied the precise spot where not so long ago Nevan had sprawled in a pool of his own blood. The potency of the memory, of the location, shivered through all my senses and roused the Janusite within me.

"Maybe," I said, "I'd rather be with a human male, not a freak from another dimension."

Anti-Nevan glowered at me for a long moment, so long I feared I'd pushed him too far in the direction of anger. His physical strength alone gave him the power to smite me. I could've tried to craft a personal ward around me, but he'd sense the energy of my spell for sure.

His gaze wandered down to my cleavage. His features softened, his lips parting and his breaths quickening. He touched a finger to the neckline of my shirt, skating the tip down to the slope of my breast. "No mortal can bring you to climax as swiftly or as powerfully as I can."

The empty shell chock-full of evil was trying to seduce me. *Ick.*

Anti-Nevan licked his lips as his hooded eyes blazed with the scorching colors of fire.

He reached out to touch me.

I whipped the knife out, slicing it across the back of his hand.

Fury blackened his expression and seethed in his eyes. His nostrils flared on a blistering exhalation.

He grabbed for me.

I slashed his arm, drawing a thin line of blood. "No touchy, no feely. I'm not that kind of a girl."

Shouting through his gritted teeth, he swung the sword up as if to strike me down with it. His arm froze in mid swing. Frustration warped his features. He bellowed, mouth open wide, and hurled the sword to ground. It landed point down, wedged into the earth with only the hilt and a few inches of the blade protruding.

Score one for the puny mortal.

He flung his hands up, bellowing again, his face crimson and his eyes wild.

I started to shuffle backward, the instinct to flee an efficient motivator, but I stayed my movement with my heel elevated off the ground. Setting it back on the earth, I steadied myself for the most terrifying part. I'd known I might need to adjust my plan midway, and the time had come for a new tactic. To restore Nevan's soul, I would risk everything.

Raising the knife, I flipped it tip down and let it fall to the ground.

Anti-Nevan's gaze tracked the knife's nosedive, then veered up to my face. His brows knit together and his mouth fell open a crack.

I dumped my gun. The derringer hit the grass with a soft thud.

He angled his head to the left and then to the right.

Back when we first met, I'd confounded Nevan quite often. I could still confound him one in a while. And clearly, my talent for befuddling elemental males extended to this magically created entity.

Score two for the puny mortal.

"What," he said, his confusion tinging his voice, "are you attempting to accomplish? I could have you whenever I wish."

"Go on, then. Try it." I summoned an eensy bit of magic, just enough to make my palms glow a faint, shimmering blue. "I've got more in my arsenal than mortal weapons."

"As do I."

Squelching the magic, I slipped my hands into my jeans pockets. My left hand found the soul stone, and the essence of Nevan heated my skin. "Bet you can't take me."

Anti-Nevan rushed at me.

I forced myself to hold still, to accept his hands clamping around my upper arms and yanking me into him. When he crushed his mouth to mine, I nearly choked on the vile, ice-cold energy that roiled out of him. I refused to open my mouth, though, and he snarled deep in his throat, like a wild and deranged animal.

Clutching the soul stone, I wrenched my left arm free of his grasp. Before he could react, I slammed my palm onto his, the stone trapped between our flesh, and locked my fingers around his hand to bind us.

Energy pulsated through me, a crackling power that surged along my nerves and veins, shooting straight down my arm and into the soul stone.

Anti-Nevan flailed his head back, gasping for breath.

I seized his head with my other hand.

His eyes bulged, the whites shining in the moonlight.

The magic had hit a barrier where our hands met, exerting pressure against my palm. I bore down on the barrier with everything inside me, every scintilla of Janusite power, every ounce of my love for Nevan, shaping it all into a magical battering ram.

I bludgeoned the barrier.

It fractured with explosive force, bucking us both.

Anti-Nevan gurgled and choked.

Energy poured through our hands into the body possessed by the invading force of the Anti-Nevan. A black, sticky energy assaulted me in response, encasing me with its tendrils. The dark power writhed beneath Anti-Nevan's skin as a visible force, caught in a desperate battle to fend off the strength of my magic, magnified by the soul stone. I propelled the energy deeper and deeper into the vacant region where Nevan's soul belonged.

The darkness shattered.

A black cloud whooshed out of Nevan's body, dissipating as a wave of blue magic sparkled all around him and a bolt of pure goodness rocketed through us both.

We gaped at each other, breathing hard, our hands still coupled.

My other hand skidded down his neck to his shoulder.

I gazed into the eyes of the man I loved. The swirling, burning eyes of Nevan.

Blue energy pulsed inside us, rushing into him only to rush back into me in a never-ending loop that united our bodies, our hearts, our souls. The power grew warm, liquid, a sensuous flow of magic that shivered over my skin and awakened every fine hair on my body. Desire throbbed within me, setting off a heated torrent of wetness between my thighs.

A flash of movement diverted my attention for heartbeat, just long enough for me to spy Tris and Travis hustling away. Tris slapped a hand on Travis's shoulder, and the pair vanished.

"Lindsey?"

Nevan's voice, rough and yet bewildered, pulled me back to him.

"You're here," I said, between panting breaths. "I did it."

He peeled his palm away from mine, took hold of the soul stone, and stared blankly at it. "This…"

"I saved you with the soul stone. Brought you back from…wherever."

Nevan ran a finger over the stone. "I recall darkness, emptiness, nothingness. And then a bright, warm light embraced me. I felt it was you." The inferno of lust in his eyes stole my breath. "You saved my life, my indomitable love. Thank you."

His gratitude lashed a magical tether between us, cementing a life debt, the strongest kind.

Neither of his gave a damn about that. We couldn't sever our gazes. His loincloth had grown tighter, with a distinct lump swelling beneath it. My nipples shot rigid, my breasts ached for his touch, all of me ached for him. The intensity of the hunger swept everything else aside, encasing us in a bubble of our own making, molded out of love and passion and all-consuming need.

Nevan dragged me into his arms, devouring me with his kiss. I hooked my arms around his neck and sagged into his hard, hot body. He thrust his tongue deep inside my mouth, spurring me to plunder his slick and velvety flesh with my tongue. He tasted sweet and spicy, earthy and unearthly, so good I moaned and plunged deeper into his mouth. His hands raked down my back to grasp my ass and hoist me up.

I flung my legs around him. He groaned, growled, shoved my groin against his engorged shaft. The pressure of it rubbing against my sex through my clothes impelled me to nip at his tongue, at the inside of his lips, frantic for more of him.

Just like the first time, here on this spot, when passion had overtaken us both. We couldn't resist it now any more than we had then.

He staggered forward with me wrapped around him, until my back slapped into a tree. His tongue rolled around mine once more, a possessive stroke that made me whimper into his mouth.

Nevan broke away, his nose brushing mine, our eyes riveted to each other.

"I need you," he said, his voice hoarse and hungry.

"Yes." I rocked my hips into him, loving the feel of his hardness against my soft and wet core. "Get rid of our clothes."

"Lindsey, I—" He snared my bottom lip with his teeth, scraped his tongue across it, and let it slide out of his mouth. "Can't be gentle, barely in control as it is. If I take you—"

"I can handle it."

His mouth dropped open, his sultry breaths blustered over my face.

"Nevan, please." I dove my hands into his hair, hauling him closer until our lips grazed each other as I spoke. "I trust you with my life, with my soul. I need you inside me *now*."

Our clothes vanished.

And he whisked us away.

Chapter Twenty-One

OOL NIGHT AIR FLOODED OVER US THE SECOND WE MATERIALIZED, AND goose bumps prickled my naked skin. The heat scorching me from the inside, the searing and desperate need for Nevan, erased my awareness of everything except him. His mouth claimed mine while his fiercely aroused body shackled me to a wall of cold rock. A delicate curtain of water spilled down the rock, trickling over my shoulders and down to my breasts, hardening my nipples, dribbling down between our bodies and exciting every inch of my skin. With our bodies plastered together, the water dribbled off my skin and onto his. The gentle cascade murmured a soft sound behind our passionate moans and cries.

To experience the satiny texture of his skin, the silken glide of his tongue, the firm nudging of his erection…These things reminded me of what we'd nearly lost today. His soul might've been extinguished, the glorious light of Nevan gone forever. We might still die, if the plan I'd hashed out with my friends failed us. We should've stopped this and hurried to meet our friends, to finish the battle tonight.

I couldn't make myself pull away from this ravishing kiss and forsake the bliss of making love with Nevan. Passion propelled us like a runaway train barreling toward a cliff.

His tongue toyed with mine, and his fingers kneaded my ass as he rocked my hips forward, angling my body for penetration.

If this was our last night together, I'd hurtle over the edge with him one more time.

Frantic with lust, I bucked my hips into his erection, chafing my swollen flesh along the length of his cock, up and down, up and down. I shoved a hand between our bodies to fasten my fingers around the base of his shaft.

He tore his lips from mine, gasping for air, then sealed his mouth over the pulse point on my throat. With one hand on my lower back, he urged me to arch my spine, boosting my breasts up. With a feral noise, he latched onto my right nipple with his open mouth.

I threw my head back on a loud, throaty moan and tunneled my fingers into his hair. His tongue teased my nipple with light licks until I ground my sex into his erection and cried out for more, then he nipped my taut peak and began to suckle it with a fervor that shot arcs of pleasure straight down to my core.

"Please, yes," I begged, scraping my nails on his scalp.

He froze, his mouth still covering my nipple.

"Nevan," I gasped, "don't stop."

The air chilled my damp nipple as he unhooked my legs from around him and set me on my feet, leaving me confused and thrumming with need. Struggling to catch my breath, I couldn't summon my voice to complain. The spill-over from the delicate waterfall lapped around my feet, just deep enough to tease my sensitive arches and tickle my toes. The gentle streams of water rolled down my body, tormenting my rigid nipples and drizzling over the hairs at the juncture of my thighs.

Nevan backed away a couple steps. His shaft bobbed in front of his body, but he either didn't notice or didn't care. His voice came out rough and strained. "We must talk."

"Huh?" My body burned, my sex throbbed. A haze of lust clouded my thoughts, and all I could focus on was his rock-hard arousal and its glistening, red tip.

"Lindsey."

His stern tone should've snapped me out of it, but I'd completely lost my hold on reality. I craved. My body felt empty and starved, and I knew only one thing could satisfy this want.

Nevan let out a sharp groan. "You said pl—that word. Far too close to gratitude for this side of the falls."

Dazed, I gaped at him for a moment before my brain powered up again and my thoughts cleared. "You can't seriously be upset I said the P-word. After you thanked me and triggered a life debt."

"I shouldn't have."

Though my legs trembled, I pushed away from the wall to lay my palms on his chest, where droplets of water still beaded on his hot skin. "What's really bothering you?"

"You shouldn't have done this."

"Done what? You kissed me, which means you started this."

"Not…that." He shrugged away from my touch. "Restoring my soul. You wasted precious time bringing me back, when you should have been searching for a way to stop the sorcerer."

"I—" A tightness gripped my chest as I flashed back to the moment when Ceara had banished his soul from his body. "Wasted time? Nevan, I could not leave you stranded in limbo, or wherever you went. If the situation had been reversed, you would've done the exact same thing for me."

"Lindsey."

"Don't." I stabbed a finger in the air at him. "You know you can't *Lindsey* me into shutting up. I don't regret what I did, and I'd do it again. Rescuing the soul of the only man I've ever loved is not a waste of time." When he started to protest, I slapped a hand over his mouth. "Shut up. I need you with me if we're going to defeat the sorcerer. I need you, period, so quit telling me I made a mistake. We're stronger together."

I lowered my hand.

His entire body had gone as rigid as his waving penis. He fisted his hands at his sides, his jaw tight enough to pulverize diamonds to powder.

Christ, if he got any more tense, he'd snap in two. I couldn't watch him suffer like this. His anxiety I could deal with later, but his physical needs I could handle right here, right now.

I splayed my hands on his smooth chest and let my breasts brush against him. The lines etched across his forehead softened the tiniest bit. I caught his earlobe between my teeth, nibbling and licking it. The tension drained out of him little by little, and his hands drifted up to span the small of my back.

"We can't have a reasonable conversation," I whispered into his ear, "when we're both high on lust and desperate to have each other."

"There's no time for it. We must talk about the sor—"

I snared one of his hands and shoved it between my thighs, mashing his fingers into my drenched cleft. "Talk later. Take me now, you stubborn sylph."

He yanked his hand away. I fastened my hand around his shaft, pumping his length in long, firm strokes. He made a strangled noise and hoisted me off my feet with both his hands on my ass. A thrill of anticipation raced through me. He hauled me into him as I strapped my legs around his hips.

"Yes," I moaned, mindlessly writhing against him.

"This is a terrible idea," he hissed, even as he backed us up to the rock wall, my backside flush with the cool, wet stone and pinioned there by his body.

"You need this," I said. "I need this. Forget the rest of the world and give us both what we want."

"Indulging our desires is a luxury we do not have at the moment. Our enemies are hunting for us as we speak."

"So what's new? We're always being stalked by evil bastards."

Maybe the mention of imminent danger and probable death should've doused my passion, but my thirst for Nevan obliterated everything else. I sank my teeth into his shoulder, earning a deep groan from him that resonated in his chest.

"We'll face the danger together," I said. "But first, let's come together."

He collared both my wrists in one big hand, effectively handcuffing me to the rock wall and stunning a gasp from me. "You have no idea what you're asking."

"Yes I do." I struggled with halfhearted effort, more on principle than anything else. I had no desire to be free of him. His grip was unyielding, though not painful. He seemed to know the exact amount of pressure to exert to keep me bound without hurting me.

He slanted his head down, and with his free hand cupped my chin and tipped my face up to his. Those luscious lips swept across mine. His entire body quivered with a need so contained it threatened to erupt out of him.

"You convinced me to let go," I reminded him, "and embrace my passions. It's your turn. Quit holding back and show me how you feel, all of it, no holds barred."

"I can't, don't make me—" He squeezed his eyes shut, lips flattened. "I am in no state to make love to you. Not the way you deserve."

"You're scared of letting me see all of you, I get it. But I can handle it, Nevan. I can handle you. Any way you need me, I'm yours."

He switched his hand to my behind and kneaded it with fierce ardor, his strong fingers branding me even as he rested his forehead on mine. "Careful, darlin', or I'll take ye up on that offer. And it won't be like anything I've shown ye before."

No, with so much dark tension coiled up tight inside him, it wouldn't be like any other time with him. My need for him deluged me, sultry and thick, like heated oil poured over my skin. I was dying to know how he'd take me this time, with fear and lust warring inside him, his need a living thing clawing to get out.

"I will not risk hurting you," he said, "no matter how great my need for you."

"Honestly, Nevan." I rolled my eyes to the heavens, letting out a frustrated growl. "I love you, but sometimes you are such an overprotective idiot. I trust you. I know you will never hurt me, I don't care how racked with lust you are. I'm not afraid of you, and I never will be."

"A mistake. You have yet to experience the full force of my passion."

"Suddenly I'm a wilting flower?" I leaned back against the wall, hissing in a breath at the sensation of water cascading over me. "What are you really afraid of?"

"You risked your life for me, again." He braced his forehead on the wet stone beside my ear. "I should walk away from you, to spare you from the necessity of saving me in the future. But I lack the will to leave you. I've developed a crushing need to both protect you and bury myself inside you as often as possible."

A crushing need. I experienced the same passion every time he touched me, and the need to protect him, to save him, had overwhelmed me after Ceara stole his body and expelled his soul. "I get it, I really do. But avoiding me, avoiding having sex with me, won't fix a damn thing."

"If I cannot protect you from the sorcerer," he said, "at least I might protect you from me. You have no conception of what it will be like if I unleash all of my desire for you. In my current state, I would lose every last fragment of control."

"Good."

He raised his head, the fiery shades in his eyes a spellbinding spectacle.

With his body restraining me against the cliff and his hand shackling me there, I found my breaths quickening and my heart pounding.

Nevan dipped his head to sniff my hair, my neck, my cheek. The moonlight glistened on his damp skin, accentuating his straining muscles, transforming him into the embodiment of unstoppable hunger.

"You smell of honeysuckle and sunshine," he purred. "And sex."

My skin tightened from his proximity, from the delicious heat radiating off him and soaking into me. Since the day I'd met him, the heat of his body had taken on an erotic significance, no simple fact of his biology but a means to stoke me into higher arousal. I reveled in the intensity of it, in the nearness of him, in the response from my body as it readied for him.

With a low growl, he freed my hands only to reposition them and cuff my wrists to the wall with both of his hands, gliding them up to my palms to interlace our fingers. "Are ye certain?"

The gruffness of his tone belied the tenderness of his hold on my hands, but the combination of his command and his body molding every inch of me into the wall left me breathless and lightheaded. Latched around him, I couldn't move except to nuzzle my face into his neck and absorb the exotic, heady scent of him.

"Do it, Nevan. I want you to."

He rasped his tongue up my throat, then nipped at the hollow where jaw met neck.

I shuddered, every inch of me sensitized to his touch.

A ragged breath escaped him. He rolled his hips back, nailed his gaze to mine, and plowed into me so deep he filled me to the hilt. I cried out, clenching my fingers around his hand. His hips thrust in a relentless rhythm, driving his length impossibly deep, exciting every nerve and hitting sensitive spots I'd never known I had.

With a primal roar, he punched his fist into the rock wall. Bits of stone showered the pool, and the cliff trembled.

His cock throbbed, scorching me with each thrust, and his body scraped against my clit, pushing my arousal higher and higher, so high my head spun. Robbed of breath, of sense, of the ability to feel or hear or smell anything except him, I clutched him tighter with my legs and hoisted my hips up as he lunged into me again and again, harder and faster, until the pace became frantic and almost violent.

"Nevan!" I screamed, my spine arching, my head falling back.

The orgasm wrenched my entire body, my sex pulsating around him, gripping and releasing his shaft, as out of control as we were. He kept on pumping into me, even as my screams echoed off the trees and the rock wall until I went hoarse with the last spasms of my climax.

Nevan plowed into me again, roaring, ramming my body into the wall hard enough to force an explosive gasp from me. A hot jet exploded through my womb, penetrating me further than his body could, claiming the deepest and most secret parts of me. It must've been an extension of his magic, the way the rush of it consumed me with its power. Another punishing thrust shot more of his searing energy into me, and with a third and final plunge, he collapsed against me and let his head drop to my shoulder. His hands slid down my arms, across the coarse and wet rock, to fall slack at his sides.

With him still buried inside me, his magic warming me from the inside, I cradled his head in my arms. The waterfall washed away the sweat of our passion and pasted my hair to my cheeks.

"Wow," I said. "When you let go, it's a genuine earth-shattering experience."

His face in my hair, he released a miserable groan. "I shouldn't have done that."

"No complaints here." I rubbed my cheek against his head, his hair silky soft and damp on my skin. "It was even better than this morning."

"But I—" He raised his head to stare at me, wide eyed, his expression almost panicked. "I've taken away your choice."

"My choice?" I searched his gaze but found no answers there. "I don't understand."

He urged my legs away from his hips, depositing me on my feet.

My body felt empty without him inside me, and the vestiges of my monumental orgasm still buzzed through me. Sex with Nevan was always spectacular, but this...I had no words to describe it.

He shuffled backward a couple steps, into the shadows of the trees. "Do you recall what I told you about birth control?"

"Sure. You can't get me pregnant unless you consciously decide to."

"That's how it has always been." He swiped a hand over his mouth. "Never before I have lost control completely."

"What are you trying to tell me?"

"You must've felt it. At the end, when I—Did you not feel it?"

He lifted his head to aim those beautiful, otherworldly eyes at me. They glowed with cool colors, white and pale blue, the shades I knew represented fear.

I walked up to him and took his hands in mine. "I felt it. Your magic, right?"

"No." He shut his eyes briefly. "I released my seed into your womb."

My hand flew to my belly, right over the womb in question. "Are you saying..."

He fisted his hands at his sides. "I may have impregnated you."

"Would that be so horrible?" My mind still reeled from his revelation and what it might mean for us—for me. A half-sylph baby? How would I raise a supernatural child? The kid would part human, but also part Janusite. What did that mean for our baby? I wasn't sure I wanted to burden a child with my powers and their associated problems.

On the other hand, our child would be half Nevan. Half wonderful, strong, compassionate, loving, protective Nevan.

"It would not be horrible," he said, "in terms of having a child with you. I would love nothing more than to start a new family with the woman I adore. But a hybrid pregnancy can be perilous for a human mother."

"Perilous? How?"

My clothes reappeared on my body amid a blast of heated air that dried my skin. He'd dried himself as well and regained his loincloth. "The human body is not designed to contain the magics inherent in a part-elemental child. I've witnessed the trauma such a pregnancy can bring about."

I squinted up at him. "You're being awfully vague about it. Exactly what might happen to me?"

"Of the fourteen hybrid pregnancies I know of…" He swerved his gaze to the sky. "The human mothers perished in every instance, within the first three months."

Cold poured over me, as if someone had dumped a bucket of ice water on my head. All of them died? Jesus. But the deed was already done, and neither of us could change it.

"I'm the Janusite," I said, knowing it was probably a lame response. "Maybe I can handle the pregnancy magics. I mean, I've handled my Janusite powers pretty well."

"Perhaps you would be different." He fingered a lock of my hair, admiring it much the way he'd done the first time we met, as if he'd never seen such a thing before. "I cannot lose you."

"I don't want to lose me either." I smiled but received no reciprocation from him. "Look, the odds are I'm not pregnant anyway. Don't know how it is with elementals, but mortal women don't automatically get knocked up whenever a guy, um, releases his seed. We might be worrying about nothing."

"You are not angry? For what I've done to you?"

"Oh, you mean for rudely unleashing your sperm?" I rose onto my tiptoes to peck a kiss on his nose. "Relax, honey. I ordered you to lose control, so I can't possibly be mad that you did. Besides, it was the most incredible experience of my life."

I secured my arms around his neck and kissed him full on the mouth. He folded his arms around me, and his lips yielded little by little, softening and opening to welcome me inside his mouth. We explored each other with slow, tender strokes of our tongues, savoring the intimacy of this moment—not simply the kiss, but the realization we might've created a baby.

When we separated our lips, I brushed a lock of hair from his face. "Whatever happens, with our potential baby or with our enemies, we'll deal with it together. Agreed?"

"Agreed."

"No more running off either, no matter how noble you think your mission is."

"I will never abandon you again. I vow it." He feathered a kiss over my lips while tracing a line down my jaw with one fingertip. "In my entire existence, I have loved but one woman."

"Who might that be?"

He tapped my chin, the old twinkle in his eyes again. "A maiden I met in Peru."

"Well, maybe I've got a hottie on the side too."

"You don't." Both his hands rushed down my body to grasp my behind. "You belong with me, and I belong with you. We need no one else."

Feeling suddenly weak, in a good way, I leaned into him. "You're the only man I've ever loved. Can't imagine ever feeling this way about anyone else. We do belong together, but more than that, we gain strength from being together."

"We do."

"And it's more than magical strength."

"It is." He slid his hands up my back. "We have other, more urgent matters to deal with. Ceara and the sorcerer—"

"Oh, we've got a plan for that." I smiled at his obvious disbelief. "Chill out, Nevan. Team Lindsey's got it covered."

"How?"

"While you were in limbo, we came up with a plan to trap Ceara. Then we'll use her to draw out the sorcerer." I bit my lip, considering another dilemma. "I wish we could go into this knowing for sure who the sorcerer is and what he wants."

Nevan let go of me and stripped my arms away from his neck. "He must be Notus. Only the former king would want to punish me in this manner."

"Yeah, but something's hinky about the whole thing." I glanced around absently, taking in the entirety of my surroundings for the first time. The rock wall behind us scaled up about ten feet, half the height of the falls behind the rock shop. The trees seemed different. The waterfall had scoured out a flat, shallow pool on the ground composed of rock that matched the short cliff. Though the moonlight provided good illumination, it couldn't dispel the shadows that concealed the top of the cliff.

"Are we in the mortal realm?" I asked.

"We are."

"You sure? We didn't go through a waterfall, but this clearly isn't the Keweenaw and—"

Nevan sealed my lips with his fingers. "Chill out, Lindsey."

He over-enunciated the words, clearly pleased he'd gotten the chance to tease me with my own slang.

I smacked his chest with the back of my hand. "Explain, please. This does not look like Michigan."

"Because it is not." His expression changed, becoming softer and rather wistful. "This is Ireland. Five thousand years ago, I was born and lived in this region, and I frequented these woods. When the Fomorians attacked, I fell for the last time here."

I couldn't speak, too stunned by the revelation to have any idea what to say. The mortal version of him, Tuathal, had died right here on this spot.

He nodded at the waterfall. "This is where I was forged."

Chapter Twenty-Two

"I N THIS PUDDLE?" POSITIONED INCHES AWAY FROM THE SMALL AND SHAL-low pool, I couldn't mesh the sight before me with what I'd envisioned as the site of Nevan's forging. "The way you described it before, I was picturing something more like the waterfall behind the rock shop."

He wandered closer to the pool, his pensive gaze gravitating to its waters. "This was larger thousands of years ago, and the precipice was taller. Time wears away the mightiest structures."

I longed to pull him into my arms, because he looked so sad, but I had the feeling he needed to keep a distance while we talked about this moment from his remote past, from another lifetime.

Lifetime. Life. I froze. Life debt. We were in the mortal realm, though.

"How did you seal a life debt to me," I asked, "when we're in the mortal world?"

"We are standing atop a portal," Nevan said without glancing at me. "Perhaps your Janusite powers allowed you to pull in a bit of the Unseen, as the fae do if they need to utilize a healing vortex from this side of the veil. Remember, debts incurred in the Unseen hold sway here."

Pulled in the Unseen. Like Tris had done back when he healed Nevan after his battle with Skeiron. This was interesting, but I cared more about other matters at the moment.

"Why did you bring me here?" I asked.

He knelt by the pool, swishing his fingers in its cool waters. "I did not bring us here intentionally. My need to get you away, to a secluded place far from our friends and our enemies, drove me to transport us."

"Your subconscious led you here." When he nodded, I said, "Why do you think that is?"

He withdrew his fingers from the water and shook them dry. "I do not know. Perhaps because I believe Notus is the sorcerer."

"Yeah, I know you think so, but something doesn't add up here."

He swiveled his head to look at me. "You believe he is Calder."

"Not sure. I can see Notus wanting to punish you." Kneeling beside him, I laid a hand on his arm. "But the sorcerer wants more. He banished your soul, then filled up your body with evil muck and tried to use it to torment me. My powers are super strong, I've embraced them completely, so why not grab me and suck me dry? From everything he's said to me, and based on his actions, his plans are similar to what Calder had intended to do. Push me to the breaking point and make me wish for death, so I'd volunteer to be forged. But you're right, parts of this point to Notus…"

My voice trailed off as an impossible realization occurred to me. *Totally impossible.*

Nothing was impossible. I'd learned that lesson weeks ago.

"What is it?" Nevan asked.

I looked into his eyes, baffled by what seemed to be. "I'd swear we're dealing with two or three different bad guys. The sorcerer wants to punish you, like Notus would want to do. He also wants to steal my powers, like Skeiron planned on doing. And he's tormenting me, seemingly in hopes of making me want to die."

Nevan's muscles tensed under my hand. "You've seen but one sorcerer. Though we've all seen Ceara, no other associates have shown themselves."

"The sorcerer often refers to himself in the third person. 'We' will consume your powers. 'We' can do this or that. Only when he was glamouring to look like you and Travis did he speak in the first person."

"He is insane. Nothing he says can be taken at face value."

"Maybe—I don't know." I let the spinning waters of the pool take hold of my focus, easing me into a semi-trance that freed my mind to explore the possibilities. "Ceara said something to me, something I didn't understand at the time. She told me 'you think you know so much and yet know nothing at all.' I had just mentioned Skeiron being gone, scattered into the wind. I've also smelled that weird monkey-man smell, like I did back when Calder was stalking me. And the kerkopes attacked me. I assumed the sorcerer sent them, but it's a weird thing to do when he has Ceara to do his bidding. Though he might use the kerkopes if he's one of them."

Nevan rose and urged me up with him. "What are you suggesting?"

"Think about it. Ceara represents a past you'd rather forget, and Calder does the same for me." I took in the falls and the pool, the place he had died and been reborn all those eons ago. "Our pasts are being used to torment us, to weaken us. We talked about someone possibly having resurrected Notus. What if that person resurrected Skeiron and Calder too?"

Nevan's gaze bored into me with such penetrating intensity it seemed to pierce straight into my soul. "I killed Calder. Ran him through with Skeiron's endued sword after I severed his spine."

"Okay, but if Notus could be brought back…"

Nevan cursed under his breath. "So could the others."

"We should assume they're all back." I frowned at the ground, because so much still made no sense. "It's weird, though. I've only seen the sorcerer and Ceara. Even if one of our previously knocked-off baddies is the sorcerer, why haven't the other two shown themselves? I guess the better to torment us, but it feels off somehow."

"We have no time to determine the answers to these questions."

"I know, we have to take out Ceara and her boyfriend." I bracketed his head with my hands and compelled him to look down at me. "Ceara has power over you only if you let her. Whatever might've happened to her is not your fault. I need you in warrior mode, not wallowing in guilt over things that happened in the Stone Age. Got it?"

His lips tightened, ticking up at the corners. "You're quite fetching when you issue commands."

"Right back atcha, sweetie." I skimmed my hands down to his neck. "And you're wicked hot when you smite the bad guys with your big, manly sword."

"Am I now." He laid his hands over mine, removing them from his throat to clasp them to his chest, right over the scar that slashed across his heart. "Best be on our way, before we forget the hammer of imminent death hovering over our heads and forgo our mission in favor of tearing each other's clothes off."

"Oh, we wouldn't do that." I smiled brightly. "You'd make our clothes disappear."

"Nevertheless…" He enfolded me in his arms, hugging me to his body. "We should be going. You can tell me our final destination en route."

Chapter Twenty-Three

THE SIX OF US GATHERED INSIDE A CLEARING, SURROUNDED BY THE MOSS-laden trees with their black bark, beneath a sky lit by a moon three times the size of Earth's companion. The milky glow of the moon illuminated the area with an eerie pseudo-daylight. A thick carpet of grass silenced our footsteps.

Ennea and Tris loitered near the periphery of the clearing, while Travis had taken up a position to my left with the Sig in his grip. Both he and Tris had given up their swords for the sake of mobility, since they weren't used to handling the hefty weapons.

On my right, Nevan grasped his endued sword, legs spread to strengthen his stance, shoulders back and his face a mask of absolute resolve. I would've preferred he conjure his armor, but he'd rightly pointed out Ceara would become suspicious the instant she saw him dressed for battle. He'd offered to conjure armor for me, but I declined for a similar reason. Ceara would realize Nevan must've whipped up the protection for me. He groused about my refusal of armor because, according to him, I had a tendency to get in trouble.

Nah, not me.

Well…maybe.

Nevan's gaze rotated in my direction, as if he'd sensed me studying him.

"Perhaps you should leave," he said. "You seem distracted, and distractions herald danger to come."

"You know better than to tell me to go away." I nudged his upper arm with my shoulder. "Stubborn, annoying mortal here, remember?"

"Stubborn, yes. Never annoying." His mouth twitched in a half smirk he struggled to repress. "I've grown rather fond of your relentless determination. In all facets of our shared life."

"You don't complain about my stubborn streak when it benefits you."

His lips curved into his trademark devastating smile, the one that melted me in the most intimate and wonderful ways. "I don't mind at all, darlin', in certain contexts."

We both knew what he meant. In bed, he loved my determination to give him as much pleasure as he gave me.

Apparently grasping our meaning, Travis let out an irritated sigh. "Can we focus on the mission?"

"Absolutely," I said. "We're good to go, right?"

Four heads nodded, with Nevan abstaining.

I touched his arm. "This will work."

He flung an arm around me and hauled me in for quick, hard kiss. "I love you, Lindsey."

"I love you too."

Releasing me, he stood tall and strong and ready for a fight. "Let us begin."

I glanced at Travis.

He gave a sharp nod and retreated to the clearing's edge, behind a thick tree.

Tris and Ennea linked their hands and ducked behind a large bush.

Each of us had our jobs to do in this crazy plan. Crazy had worked for me, for all of us, before. If Team Lindsey could defeat a sylph army, we could sure as hell capture one evil shrew.

Please, God, let this work.

"You're up," I said to Nevan.

He threw his head back and bellowed, "Ceara!"

The roar of his voice thundered in the clearing, resounded off the trees, and left the rest of us wincing at the unbelievable power of his voice. I'd heard Skeiron bellow, but Nevan's call boomed like nothing else.

"Better manhandle me," I said.

Nevan grasped my upper arm.

I gave him my best exasperated look. "Be more convincing, honey."

He gave me *his* best exasperated look, huffed out a breath, and dragged me backward into his body. One of his arms clamped around my midsection, leaving his other hand free to wield the sword. He raised its tip to my throat, careful not to nick me.

My derringer was holstered inside my waistband, concealed by my shirt. Ceara wouldn't notice, with any luck.

Squashed against Nevan, I muttered out the corner of my mouth, "Much better."

He grumbled his displeasure.

"You're not hurting me," I assured him. "Did you do your thing?"

"The confusion spell is active," he said.

When we'd first met, he'd used the spell—one he acquired from a fae, though not from Ennea—to confuse Travis and his deputies when they sought me, believing I'd killed a man. The spell made them think I'd gone in the opposite direction from where I'd actually ended up. The confusion wouldn't last long, but it ought to give us enough time to nab Ceara.

The minion in question materialized in front of us.

"Tuathal," she said, her silver eyes luminous in the moonglow. "What are you doing? You were to bring her to us, not hold her here."

She surveyed the clearing with a suspicious gaze and blinked as if trying to clear her vision.

Nevan stiffened. "Her magic interferes with mine. She has cast a spell of some sort to prevent me from taking her with me."

"Hmm." Ceara sauntered closer, her gaze wary even as she turned her nose up to gaze down it at me. "The little mortal is resilient. I must admit to a certain admiration for her."

"Do not admire her," he hissed, his act awfully convincing as he prodded me with the sword's blade. The sharp tip pressed in enough to put pressure on my skin without hurting me. "The filthy human stabbed me with her pathetic little blade."

My turn. I struggled against Nevan's grip, but he held firm. "This filthy human is right here, you know, listening to your stupid conversation. Maybe you should address me directly."

Ceara sniffed, waving a dismissive hand in the air. "I have no further to need to speak with you, the chattel of my master."

I barked out a laugh. "Oh man, you are so in for it."

The other woman lifted one slender brow. "You are mistaken. My master will—"

"Torture me endlessly, bend me to his will, make me wish I was dead. Blah, blah, blah, I've heard it all before." I jammed my elbow into Nevan and, understanding my request, he moved the blade to lay it across my throat. The sharp edge didn't pierce my skin, but I couldn't help the frisson of anxiety that whispered through me like the chill breath of a ghost. "Listen up, evil assholes. If you don't release me, I will unleash my wrath on you."

Ceara laughed, the brittle melody of it echoing off the trees. "You puny—"

Unseen energy electrified the air as the wards slammed down around us, sealing off the clearing inside a dome of magic.

Ceara whipped her head left and right, her eyes large.

"How's it feel to be caught?" I said. "Like a puny animal snookered by a hunter's trap."

Her face flushing crimson, Ceara screamed her frustration. She jabbed a finger toward Nevan. "Kill her!"

Nevan dropped his sword arm and hugged me with the other arm in an embrace no one would mistake for hostility. "Why would I murder the only woman I have ever loved to save the pale shadow of my deceased wife?"

Ceara, her eyes so wide the whites shone in the moonlight, thrust out one hand with her palm to the sky. She screamed again, swatting the air with her hand as if some foul substance had become glued to her skin.

"You cannot conjure," Nevan said, stepping sideways to stand alongside me. "The wards block any attempt to use magic within their confines."

"Except by me," I said, "and Nevan and our friends."

Ceara hurled her entire body at mine, tackling me amid a flurry of scratching nails and gnashing teeth, spittle flying from her lips with every enraged cry. Her hands seized my throat to throttle me.

I kicked her, punched her, bit her—but the woman held on like a demon.

Until she was ripped off of me.

Ceara shrieked. Though she thrashed and scratched at him, Nevan gripped her by the back of her neck with one of his hands.

He pitched her to the ground.

She smacked down with a thud and a crack, flat on her face. Stunned, she lay there panting and shaking.

Nevan took my hands and helped me to my feet. He touched his fingertips to my throat.

"I'm fine," I said. "She's damn strong, but I'm damn stubborn."

Ennea and Tris hurried to us, while Travis jogged to the dazed woman on the ground. Ceara blinked up at him, her silver eyes bleary, as the sheriff pulled her hands behind her back and slapped cuffs around them. The shiny gray metal of the handcuffs glimmered with a faint blue sheen, thanks to the spell Ennea, Tris, and I had cast on them. Our collaboration imbued the cuffs with enough power to hold back a god, according to Ennea.

The fae witch fixed her blue eyes on me, and I sensed the question there. She wasn't worried about the cuffs. Though Ceara struggled against them, the metal bound her with solid magic. Ennea worried, I knew, about the wards. I had helped with that spell too. Since the wards I'd constructed around the underground lair had repelled the Anti-Nevan, we figured a dash of my magic would prevent Ceara or the sorcerer from penetrating the wards around the clearing. Nothing was for certain, though.

Not with a sorcerer who'd acquired immense power.

Travis bent over Ceara with one foot on her back, confining her to the ground. He glanced at me and mouthed, "Too easy?"

I shrugged. Maybe it had been, maybe not. We'd expended a lot of magic on setting the scene and confusing Ceara long enough to trap her. The toughest part lay ahead of us, though, and we all knew it.

Pulling the derringer out of its holster, I squared my shoulders. "Time to get the sorcerer. Nevan, will he feel her distress?"

"If he has true feelings for her, yes. He should."

I turned toward Travis and his prisoner. "Let's get her up."

Travis moved his foot off Ceara's back, rolled her over, and gestured for her to get up. She thrashed a bit, hampered by the cuffs, but clambered to her feet. Her long hair fell wild over her face.

She blew a blustery breath out the side of her mouth to disperse the hair away from her face. "You will be destroyed, every last one of you. In the most pain—"

"Zip it," I said, shooting a pointed look at her bound hands. "Nobody wants to hear the sorcerer's little puppet mouthing off."

The puppet's eyes narrowed to slits and she hissed a breath out her nose.

I glanced at Nevan, but didn't need to tell him what to do.

He jammed the tip of his sword into Ceara's chest, right over her breastbone, pushing until he drew a bead of blood. It trickled down her alabaster skin.

"If I pierce your chest," he said, his voice low and menacing, "you will not die immediately, but you will suffer excruciating pain. Call for your lover, and I will slice your head from your body for a clean and relatively painless death."

She spat at him.

"As you wish." He grasped the sword's hilt in both hands, as if preparing to drive it into her chest with painstaking slowness.

Ceara's mouth dropped open on a gasp, her eyes went wide and pure white. Only two small disks of black indicated her pupils. Whatever kind of elemental she was, her eyes were like nothing I'd ever seen.

Was she an elemental? The pendant she wore around her waist signified vitality and regeneration. Might the sorcerer have rejuvenated her body with a spell, not the forging?

Nevan hesitated, his features tense and rife with a dark anger. "This your final chance, Ceara. Call your lover."

"I cannot," she said, her lips quivering despite her haughty stance. "He forbade me to do so, to dissuade our enemies from attempting what you are."

Nevan glanced at me, a grim resignation on his face.

We had no choice but to test the theory her lover would sense her fear and come running to her aid.

"Step away," Nevan told Travis.

The other man hustled backward away from Ceara, and away from Nevan and me. I backed up a few steps too. Nevan and I had discussed the options, and I realized what he must do.

With the sword held to Ceara's chest, Nevan did not look away from her fear-whitened eyes. He made no motion at all, giving no hint of what he was attempting.

A wind whipped to life inside the dome of the wards, whirling around and around all of us, concentrating itself until it narrowed into a dervish that revolved around Ceara's body. Her hair lashed her face and shoulders. Grass and bits of earth spun up from the ground, caught within the whirlwind, and the kinetic energy of it ripped clumps of mossy stuff off the trees, incorporating the debris into the chaotic mini-tornado that imprisoned Ceara.

She thrashed, desperate to escape the whirlwind, but it formed a gale-force wall around her. Dirt and grass stained her skin. She ducked to avoid debris and, finally, squatted inside the tempest with her head between her knees.

The mini-tornado howled, its racket bouncing off the wards in a frenetic feedback loop.

I covered my ears, and the others did the same—everyone except Nevan. He'd retracted his sword, focused on the tempest with a deadly intensity.

Ceara screamed. Her voice conveyed not anger or frustration, as before, but a wrenching terror.

We had succeeded in terrifying her. How long would the sorcerer take to respond? Would he respond? Getting naked with Ceara didn't necessarily mean he cared about her. Max had thought the sorcerer did care, though he admitted he couldn't be sure.

Nevan gripped the sword in one hand, and with the other he crooked his fingers into his palm. The whirlwind answered his command, constricting around Ceara. Not much, an inch or two at most. Enough to make her scream and wail and curl up in the fetal position.

A pained look squinted Nevan's face.

I laid a hand on his arm, squeezing gently. He hated this, I knew. Hated tormenting anyone this way, even if she had purged his soul from his body. Nevan had not one ounce of cruelty within him, and I loved him all the more for it.

Our friends had averted their eyes, their faces displaying varying levels of discomfort. Despite the impulse to shut my eyes, I had to bear witness to Ceara's suffering. I would not leave Nevan to watch it alone.

An explosion rocked the earth with a deafening boom.

The wards flashed blue, undulating from the force of the blast. The epicenter of it mutated a circular section of the ward, perhaps four feet wide, into a blood-red splash. Power as black and frigid as the depths of space walloped into me and rebounded away. I choked on a gasp, doubling over as if someone had slugged me.

Nevan's attention swerved to me, and the whirlwind around Ceara faltered.

I gave him a tight smile.

He reinforced the spinning gale that bound Ceara.

Another explosion rocked the wards, the earth, and ricocheted off me. I glimpsed Ennea and Tris, but the attack seemed not to have affected them. My blue magic formed the foundation of the wards. I was connected to the spell far more than either of them.

Or they were more accustomed to this kind of assault.

I braced myself against the onslaught of dark magic, weaving my blue energies into a kind of suit around me. And then I prayed the protection would work.

Another deafening boom. Another flash of blue as the wards quavered and the center of the attack spilled blood-red over the dome's side. The darkness pummeled my suit of magical armor, but it couldn't breach my protections.

"Let her go," I told Nevan. "He's here."

The tempest evaporated. Bits of dirt and grass rained onto the ground, some of it landing on Ceara. Panting and whimpering, she lay motionless for a few seconds before she opened her eyes and realized the tornado had gone away.

Another blast crashed into the wards.

I waved for Travis to come closer.

He took up his position beside Ceara.

Nevan and I approached the epicenter of the assaults on the wards. The moonlight petered out within the forest, the darkness there deep enough to shelter anyone hiding beyond the protective dome. A shadow moved, seeming to ripple as it swelled bigger and bigger.

It wasn't growing, though. It was coming toward us.

The shadow solidified the closer it approached, resolving into the tall and slender figure of a robe-cloaked individual.

I resisted the urge to grab Nevan's hand. We had to portray a strong front, no weakness allowed. Though I didn't consider holding Nevan's hand to be a weak gesture, the sorcerer might. Instead, I let my arms hang loose at my sides.

As the figure neared the wards, it slowed and finally stopped a few feet away. Pale hands protruded from the baggy sleeves of the billowing black robe. The hood concealed the sorcerer's face, though the moonglow shimmered off glimpses of pallid skin.

Nevan took the lead, stepping forward to confront the sorcerer. "If you wish to save your lover—"

The sorcerer laughed. It was a harsh, crackling sound. Far from weak, though, he sounded frighteningly self-assured. "I have no special fondness for my creation. Kill her, and I will make another."

Creation? Make another?

The pendant. Vitality and regeneration. The meaning of the clues dangled so close my mind could almost touch it, but not quite.

Nevan gave voice to my own confusion. "Of what do you speak?"

"My *shabti*, of course." The sorcerer aimed one pale finger at Ceara. "She has served me well, but I can vivify another."

I opened my mouth to speak, but hesitated. *Shabti*. I recognized the term, but couldn't quite summon the information from my brain. *Shabti* was ancient Egyptian, I remembered that much. Something to do with tombs.

Ah-hah. I remembered. *Shabti* became servants to the deceased in the afterlife, an army of slaves to do all the menial labor.

Nevan glowered at the sorcerer. "You gave new life to Ceara in the forging."

The sorcerer sniggered. "No, Your Exalted Majesty, he who assumes he knows all but understands nothing. That is not what I have done. Haven't you wondered why she resembles no known elemental race?"

"You have imbued her with your dark magic. It altered her makeup."

"In a sense, you are correct." The sorcerer sighed, the breath rattling in his chest. "I carved her body from solid alabaster, then vivified it with the power of elemental fire combined with the magic of the papyrus column amulet." The sorcerer pointed at me. "If you don't believe me, ask your familiar. His fire animated her."

Max helped create Ceara? I refused to glance at Max, unwilling to expose my surprise to the sorcerer. I shouldn't have been surprised, though. Max had been enslaved by this being, this purveyor of the blackest magics. My familiar though he may have been, Max couldn't tell me everything the sorcerer had forced him to do—even if he wanted to tell me.

Nevan clenched his fists. "Why create a being fashioned after my wife?"

"Oh, you misunderstand," the sorcerer said. "She is not merely fashioned in the image of your wife. She contains the soul of Ceara. Rather than forging her, at the moment of death I trapped her soul within a *pithos* and then carved a stone form for her, modeled after her former body. This took a great deal of time and effort, but not nearly so long as I required to find the appropriate conduit to vivify my creation. At last, I came upon a forlorn salamander willing to bargain away his freedom, and with his help I vivified this woman."

He raised an arm, sweeping it in Ceara's direction.

"You distorted her soul," Nevan said, "into a reflection of your twisted darkness."

"What I did," the sorcerer said, "merely gave voice and form to the secret recesses of her soul she hid from you."

"My wife was a kind and good woman, not a vicious creature like the one you have created."

More crackling laughter, rife with derision. "You mean she was meek, always deferring to your wishes. You truly understand nothing at all."

"You are blind, Tuathal." Ceara spoke from behind us, causing Nevan and me to both swivel our heads in her direction, to where she hunkered on her knees beside Travis, seated on her heels. "I was meek because it was my duty to please and obey my husband. I did not choose to marry you, it was imposed upon me. Throughout my life, duty to one's husband was hammered into every girl child."

Nevan shook his head, baffled. "We shared, if not love, at the least a friendship."

"Friendship?" She let out a harsh laugh. "You fool, Tuathal. I despised you from the moment we married. I despised your self-righteous insistence upon doing right by your people, marching off to battle the enemy but leaving your wife and child defenseless. Most of all, I despised you for impregnating me, forcing me to endure childbirth and take responsibility for a child I did not want. I would have slaughtered you in your sleep, if not for the surety of my execution for such a crime."

I glared at the other woman. "If you could've gotten away with it, you would've had the courage to murder him in his sleep. You are a slimy little coward."

"Perhaps." Ceara wriggled until she rose up off her heels. "But I am allied with the true power in this world. You lay claim to a band of weak and useless beings."

"Says the woman caught in my trap."

Ceara scuffled forward on her knees until she could glimpse her lover behind us. "Free me, storm-bringer. Free your most faithful servant, your one love."

He spread his hands. "Why should I waste my power on you? I can fashion another bedmate."

"But—" Tears streamed down her cheeks. "You vowed to protect me."

Enough of this crap. It was time for the next stage in our plan. We had the sorcerer, now we needed to trap him inside the wards.

And it was all on me.

Nevan flashed me a look assurance, conferring his strength of spirit into me without speaking a word or touching me. Not a magical transference, but an emotional one.

I concentrated on the wards, on the threads of glittering magic invisible to the naked eye that comprised its walls. Feeding energy into the spell, I commanded the wards to expand. The spell responded, pulsing as it inched outward, still unseen. *Faster.* I needed the barrier to move faster. My whole body tensed as I funneled more energy into the wards, pushing and pushing and pushing, my head pounding from the effort, sweat dribbling down my temples. Pushing, pushing, pushing.

The ward ballooned outward to encompass the sorcerer. He was trapped inside my dome.

With us.

Oh God, I prayed the magic-dampening effect of the wards worked on him.

The sorcerer lifted one hand, scrawny fingers outstretched toward Ceara. "You have indeed served me well and pleased me greatly. Thus, I grant you a swift end."

He jerked his fingers closed.

Ceara's head snapped back. Her mouth popped open, her eyes went lifeless.

She collapsed into a heap on the ground, dead.

Oh shit. A vicious shiver rattled my bones. The sorcerer's magic still worked.

He waved his hand, and everyone except Nevan and me flew backward across the clearing to slam into the wards.

Nevan whipped up a tempest around the sorcerer, working so hard to surround the lunatic with hurricane-force winds that veins in his neck and temples throbbed.

The sorcerer waved a single finger.

Nevan sailed backward through the air and hit the ground with a sickening crack.

I hurled every ounce of my magic at the sorcerer, expending my physical energy and my powers in a frantic attempt to demolish my enemy.

The sorcerer flinched but remained standing.

I staggered backward, swerved my derringer up, and fired.

The bullets bounced off him, hitting a nearby tree.

He moved his fingers, and I flew into his arms.

Shackling me with both arms, he whispered in a hoarse voice, "You cannot defeat me, Janusite. No one is more powerful than I am."

He swept a hand in an arc over his head.

The wards tumbled down.

We vanished, hurtling away through the abyss.

Chapter Twenty-Four

Out of the tunnel we plummeted, into a gloomy and dank space where a draft prickled my skin. My eyes needed time to adjust, spoiled by the bright moonlight in the clearing. While I blinked and struggled to discern my surroundings, the sorcerer placed a hand on my back and shoved me forward. I stumbled over a threshold of some sort, into a colder and darker space.

A door banged shut behind me.

Flickering lights appeared around me, small and not bright, but enough to let my eyes separate out the shapes around me. The lights were oil lamps that seemed to grow out of the jagged rock walls, their flames an odd, sallow shade. I inched forward, tripped over a depression in the floor, and glanced down to note an array of pockmarks in the stone beneath my feet. Water had collected in many of the holes, and it had splashed onto my boot to darken the leather.

The windowless room was small, no more than ten foot by ten foot. Behind me, the black door stood shut. Shackles affixed to the back wall hung open, awaiting a new prisoner.

I had wound up inside the sorcerer's dungeon.

Would I become the next victim, chained to the wall and drained of magic and life?

Screw that. I would only become a victim if I did nothing. Unlike those poor women the sorcerer had murdered, I had multiple weapons at my disposal. My derringer for one. I raised the gun I still held in my hand. He hadn't confiscated it, which made me suspect he didn't know it was endued and viewed it as no threat to him. I also had magic, the full powers of the Janusite.

My confrontation with the sorcerer had weakened me, physically and magically. How much time would I need to regain my strength? Even when I regained it, what could I do to stop the evil bastard?

Think, Lindsey. Janusite powers, Janusite…means you've got the essence of a god inside you. Use it.

Self-inflicted pep talks were great, but I needed information. Since finding out I was the Janusite, I'd delved into the mythology about the god in hopes of learning more about what I'd become. I needed that information tonight.

If I could remember it any of it.

Why was it when you most needed to remember a thing, the knowledge flew out your ears?

The lock clanked, and the door crept inward. Its metal grated across the floor.

Brighter light from outside the room leaked through the doorway. His robed figure revealed in the backlight, the sorcerer stepped onto the threshold.

"Are you prepared to cooperate?" he asked. "You cannot overpower me, so there is no benefit in fighting."

I'd rather die than give in to you. Keeping that thought to myself, I replied, "Sounds like there's not much point in making a fuss."

Sounded like. I hadn't lied but rather obfuscated. Before I rifled my brain for answers, I might as well glean as much from this creep as possible. Play along, that was my strategy—for the moment.

"Come," he said, and shepherded me out into the chamber beyond.

Yellowish-white light poured down from unseen sources in the ceiling, maybe eight feet above us, much like the everywhere lighting in the home I shared with Nevan. In our home, though, the light soothed and warmed. Here, it cast a wan illumination that stained my skin with a jaundiced color and seemed to enhance the damp chill in the chamber, a space roughly carved from the same dark rock as the cell where he'd stashed me.

No furniture in the room. Not one speck of decoration, or any sign anyone lived or worked here. Ennea's spell lab had tables and potion bottles and myriad other items to aid in her magical endeavors. Her lab was a living space. This place was…dead.

Max had mentioned a bedroom. This must not be where the sorcerer lived. Either that, or he used magic to conceal his living spaces.

I made a show of surveying the chamber, swinging my head left and right, up and down. "Not big on creature comforts, are you?"

He turned toward me, but his face remained hidden in the shadows of his hood. "This is a prison, not a palace."

"No duh."

His head tilted to the side. "You speak nonsense."

And he sounded as baffled by me as Nevan had when we'd first met. Nice to know I could confound anyone, even a supposedly all-powerful sorcerer.

"I speak mortal," I said. Stuffing my hands in my jeans pockets, I rocked back on my heels. "Seeing as you're going to suck me dry and chuck me out with garbage anyway, how about you answer a few questions? You know, satisfy my curiosity before I bite the big one."

"Death need not be your end. The forging awaits you."

My first instinct was to shout *hell no*. Instead, I told him, "Not sure about that yet."

He said nothing, moved not one muscle.

The draft raised goose bumps on my arms, making me wonder where the draft came from, since I saw no windows or doors—except the door to the windowless cell. I couldn't detect any cracks or ventilation shafts either.

A rattling sigh gusted out of him. "It is no mystery why Nevan has become weak and confused, unable to defeat a mouse, much less one as powerful as I. Dealing with an insane mortal has destroyed him."

"Your ignorance of human culture doesn't make me insane."

This jackass might drive me batty, though, if he kept prattling on about how powerful he was.

"Nevertheless," he said, "I will answer your questions. Since you will join me or die shortly, nothing I tell you matters. Your acquiescence will give me your loyalty, and your rotting corpse cannot damage my plans."

"Awesome," I said with sarcasm, as I gave him a matching sarcastic thumbs-up. "First question. Who the hell are you?"

He chuckled, low and harsh and dripping with dark pleasure. "Nevan has not guessed, then? Ah, more proof he is nothing but a demi-mortal."

Demi-mortal? Nevan was all strength and masculine power, with or without magic. More than a mortal, more than an elemental, he was…my Nevan. No one held a candle to him.

"You said you'd answer my questions," I reminded my captor.

"And I shall."

He reached up to take hold of his hood, drawing it back and away from his face. The shadows retreated inch by inch to expose the face of…

I jerked my head back, staring at the sight before me. What was I looking at? Not Skeiron. Not Calder. Not really Notus either, I suspected.

The iris of one of his eyes was onyx, seething with metallic ribbons of vile green and orange. The other eye featured a golden brown iris, with no white at all, and a black pupil dilated by the dim lighting in the chamber. Fiery red hair covered his head, the shaggy locks curled and frizzy. His skin shimmered with a faint silvery sheen.

He lifted one scrawny hand and flexed his fingers.

Black claws shot out from the tips.

The sorcerer twitched one finger, and a wind tore through the chamber. It whipped my hair in my face, then died as swiftly as it had begun.

A show of power? No, more like a clue he intended for me to interpret.

I scrutinized his face, chilled by the familiarity of his features. They reminded me not of one individual, but of two. His left eye, that belonged to Skeiron. His right eye and the clawed fingers, that came from Calder. The rest of him was different, from someone I'd never met before.

He couldn't be three people. Could he?

Oh hell, after everything I'd witnessed and experienced I no longer had the option to deny anything was possible.

"Ah," he said, almost purring the word, "I see you are coming to a realization."

"I am, but it makes no sense." I leaned toward him, peering into his eyes. When I focused on the left one, I had the eerie sensation of staring into Skeiron's eyes. When I focused on the other, a shiver of recognition told me I was eye to eye with my ex-fiancé, Calder. I pulled back, doing my damnedest to suppress my revulsion. "You seem to be part Skeiron, part Calder, and part somebody else. Notus, maybe. Never met him, so I can't say for sure."

I really, really wanted him to say I was imagining the similarities.

But he smiled, exposing yellow teeth, and said, "Perhaps you aren't as unintelligent as I'd first assumed."

Rock. In my throat. Cold, hard, and stuck.

He stretched out one long, bony finger to stroke his claw down my cheek with a bizarre and disturbing tenderness. "You are correct, though I gather you have no conception of how this is possible."

"So explain it to me." I swallowed, but my mouth had gone dry and the rock refused to budge from my throat. "How did you even know Calder? How did he get to be a part of you? Are you really Notus?"

"I am what remains of him." He withdrew his claws. "When Skeiron defeated me, I was scattered—but not to the Four Winds. A powerful sorcerer intercepted the remnants and attempted to resurrect me. However, the spell went awry. Instead of being born anew, my previous body regenerated, I possessed the sorcerer's body."

"But your appearance. If you're in the sorcerer's body…"

"My essence was too much for his body to contain." He made a slicing motion with one finger. "Our essences were disassembled and combined into one being. The sorcerer's soul is gone, but I retain his memories, knowledge, and skills—combined with my own, of course."

"Okay, that explains how Notus—how you came back." Sort of, kind of, not really. Maybe Nevan would understand it, but I had trouble with the idea of essences versus souls versus…*Gah.* I was getting a headache thinking about it. "How did Skeiron and Calder get in there with you?"

"The sorcerer had the ability to sense when an elemental has been destroyed, as well as the magic to capture the essence of that being before it reaches the Four Winds." He scratched the bridge of his narrow, bumpy nose. "I despised Skeiron, but he was incredibly strong, thanks to the magics he'd stolen from others. I absorbed his essence and took his purloined power into me."

Stolen power. Stolen essences. A gear clicked into place in my mind.

"That's what you wanted to do to Nevan," I said. "Steal his power. But you didn't want his essence, did you?"

The sorcerer frowned. "Why would I want to take a part of him into me? He aided Skeiron in my destruction, and his power pales in comparison with the former king's. Besides, once I'd absorbed Skeiron's essence, I acquired more than his memories. I acquired his hatred of Nevan." The sorcerer's voice mutated into a growl. "Torturing him, tearing the very soul from his body and corrupting the mortal he loves, it seems an appropriate punishment for the one who assisted in dethroning two kings."

Well, at least that explained why the sorcerer appeared so soon after Skeiron's demise. Infused with Skeiron's memories and power, the Notus-Skeiron-sorcerer being inherited the former king's anger and hatred of Nevan as well. Nevan had, after all, been instrumental in thwarting Skeiron's plan to steal my power and conquer the mortal world.

I couldn't keep calling him the Notus-Skeiron-sorcerer being.

"What do you call yourself?" I asked. "You must have a name, everyone does."

"You may refer to me as Notus. I am predominantly the storm-bringer."

Ceara had used the term storm-bringer. It must've been Notus's moniker, as a wind god.

"I'd really like to know," I said, "how and why you incorporated Calder into your...self. He wasn't destroyed and scattered."

"Your former beloved?" He skimmed his gaze up and down my body, licking his lips when his attention stalled on my breasts. "He wasn't destroyed, no. But he was killed, by an endued weapon. When your new lover and the raven spirited you away for healing, I sneaked into the cave to draw Calder's essence from his lifeless body before it could be snatched away by the soul-taker. Your kind call him Charon."

The Greek myth about the underworld ferryman was true too. Huh. Since it didn't help me at the moment, I set the information aside in my mind.

I screwed up my mouth. "Don't get it. Why would you want the soul of my dead ex-fiancé? He wasn't particularly powerful."

"But he has a connection to the Janusite, to you." Notus lifted a finger, hooking the claw under my chin. "He knows you. And as they say, knowledge is power."

If he believed Calder had ever really known me, Notus was way more deluded than I'd imagined. Nevan knew me on a deeper level than anyone else, especially Calder. My ex-fiancé had believed I'd want to become one of the kerkopes, a monster chained to the eons-old curse that created the first pair of shapeshifting monkey-men.

Let Notus believe that. His misconception might give me an edge, somehow.

"Strictly for curiosity's sake," I said, "what do you plan on doing with all this power once you've collected it? You want to steal mine, but then what?"

His smile evinced pure self-satisfaction. "I will become the most powerful being in the universe. I will conquer the mortal realm first, to acquire slaves and concubines. Then, I will conquer the Unseen. Worlds will fall at my feet, every being in my domain will clamor to appease me. Not even the Oversoul can stop me."

"What then? You'll have two worlds at your mercy. Okay, that's super cool. But what then?"

"I rule. Forever."

A mere mortal like me simply couldn't grasp the appeal of multi-world domination, I supposed. Living forever as the ruler of two subjugated worlds, forcing everyone to kiss your feet, it seemed to me that would get old pretty fast. What then?

He'd need more worlds to conquer.

My shoulders fell. "Let me guess. There are other realms of existence you could access, what with all your new-and-improved magical prowess. You'd keep on enslaving worlds to your heart's content."

Someone like him would never be content, though.

"Yes," he said, "precisely. There are unknown numbers of worlds, which are currently inaccessible. I will have the power of the Janusite, the power to thrust open any doorway to any world I desire."

And there it was. The endgame.

My powers would bring about the destruction of every world, countless souls subjugated or murdered to service the insatiable hunger of one demented being. Three demented beings, actually, crammed into one body.

Oh, this would not do. Not at all. No way would I become the instrument for universal domination.

Time to make use of the tools at my disposal.

I shambled closer to Notus and bent my head back to look at his face. The monkey smell he'd inherited from Calder infiltrated my nostrils. Tapping into all my strength of will, I kept from wrinkling my nose at the stench.

He gazed down at me with crinkled brows, his Skeiron eyes swirling faster, his Calder eye dilating further. It was the creepiest thing I'd ever seen, but I didn't have the luxury of cringing.

"If you really have a part of Calder inside you, then you know what he meant to me." I'd told Calder I loved him, only later realizing it hadn't been love after all. Nevan had shown me the true meaning of the word. "I can feel he's in there, and that's why you haven't killed me yet. Why you insist I'll join you. A part of you doesn't want to let me go."

Calder had believed, until his last breath, he was my true love. Notus had those memories, otherwise he wouldn't have sought to take Nevan away from me. I was banking everything on the strength of his need to possess me.

Notus's lips parted, his breathing grew labored.

"Tell me the truth," I said, floating my arms up to settle my hands on his bony shoulders. "You want me, don't you? More than you wanted Ceara."

His gaze fevered, he sloped his body closer. "She was a creation. It took thousands of years to carve and vivify her body, and yet she meant nothing to me."

"But I do." I zeroed in on the Calder eye, holding his focus. "Haven't you thought I chose Nevan over you, Calder, because his magic was stronger? But now you are the strongest of all. You have the power to protect me. We can be together again."

A ragged breath inflated his chest. The pupil of his Calder eye had blown, while his Skeiron eye churned wildly.

Gotcha.

I slid my hands to his neck. "The question is, what do you want?"

Breathing so hard he was almost wheezing, he slapped his hands over mine. "I will harvest your power and take you as my consort."

Never, ever if I lived to be a thousand would I submit to him.

"First, Calder, I'd like you to bring me a gift. Bring me—" I couldn't say Nevan, as badly as I wanted to. Might tip my hand. "Travis Blackwell. He was your brother once upon a time, and you know he always had a thing for me. Fetch him so he can serve as a sacrifice, to prove your devotion to me. Then I will gift you with my power."

Excitement invigorated his face. "Yes. Punish my brother."

Oh God, I prayed this would work. Getting Notus out of this chamber would give me time to come up with a plan. When Travis arrived, he could distract Notus while I enacted said plan. Nevan would've been better, but I couldn't risk alerting Notus to the fact I was faking my desire for him.

"Find him," I said. "Bring me Travis."

Notus poofed out.

I stumbled, since I'd been leaning against him. Righting myself, I tugged my shirt down and brushed hair from my face. All I needed now was a plan.

Where could I find one?

CHAPTER TWENTY-FIVE

WITH NO CLOCK TO SHOW ME THE TIME, I HAD NO IDEA HOW LONG I waited in the damp and musty prison. The cell door hung ajar behind me, the shackles visible in the deeper shadows within the cell. I started to pace, then decided to preserve my energy for the fight to come.

And it would be a fight. A big old nasty one.

I slouched against the wall, my hands linked over my belly. Maybe Notus would observe, invisible and undetected, but I had no time to waste on worrying about it. Let him watch, if he wanted. As long as he brought me Travis, I didn't give a damn about a peeping sorcerer. Sylph. Monkey-thing. Whatever.

My powers were the key, I felt it in my soul. The Four Winds had, presumably, granted me the magical essence of the god Janus. Why? I had no clue, but why didn't matter. I needed to understand what I might do with these powers.

I needed to understand Janus.

Bob had told me a bit about what being the Janusite meant, Nevan had told a bit too, and I'd learned a lot about the mythology of Janus on my own. Mythology wasn't the best source of information, but often legends held at least a kernel of truth. Based on my experiences with the Unseen, myths had a great deal to tell me about this world.

Resting my head on the wall, I shut my eyes and tried to recall everything I'd read about Janus.

He was the god of doorways and transitions, as well as beginnings and endings. Nevan had told me that much. The mythology about Janus elaborated on his nature and his power. He was a doorkeeper, yes, but he also had a connection to time. Though most often shown as a being with two faces, he could also have four faces to signify his dominion over all lands. All worlds?

A god with dominion over every world, every doorway and gate, every beginning and ending, and even time itself. His temporal association connected him to past, present, and future—though nothing I'd read explained exactly what that meant. One article had mentioned the god Jupiter could travel through time thanks to Janus. From what I'd gathered, it was his dominion over time that gave Janus power over transitions, doorways, and everything else he over which he held sway. Time affected the flow of our lives, and thus the flow of history and the future.

Time was the ultimate doorway. It linked everything else.

Could the doorway go both ways? Janus's dual faces implied it did.

What about his four faces? Maybe that implied time moved in four directions, not merely backward and forward, but also laterally.

Right. Lateral time. What the hell did that mean?

I pushed away from the wall. Lateral movement through time. What would that look like? I began to walk the length of the wall, skating my hand over its rough surface as I traveled. Well, if I dodged sideways I could avoid an obstacle. What, then, constituted an obstacle to time?

To freeze time would create an obstacle. Anyone wanting to travel through a frozen moment would need to sidestep it.

I halted, flattening my palm on the cold wall. The idea made a certain kind of screwy sense, but then, everything about me being the Janusite was screwy. A human with the powers of a Roman god. One woman in all the universe who could open the doorways between worlds and ferry elementals across the boundaries in the mortal realm. One woman with dominion over transitions and…time.

What had Bob said in his prophecy? I pressed a hand to my forehead, willing the memory to return to me. I'd sworn I could never forget the strange and spooky prophecy.

Time to break it down, line by line.

In the twentieth era of the mortal calendar, a girl child shall be born into an enlightened clan.

That part fit me. I came from a family of New Age believers.

She will possess the power of Janus, god of the doorways and of transitions, and like him she will face both ways, belonging to neither but bound to everything.

Okay, I had the powers. How did I face both ways? I'd assumed that meant backward and forward, as in entering and exiting the portals. It might also mean traveling through time.

Boundaries fall in her presence.

I'd assumed that part referred to the boundaries in the mortal realm, the ones that kept elementals from invading our world. Other types of boundaries existed, however—like those delineating past, present, and future.

The veil shall open to her, she who holds the power to converge the worlds, she whose power is beyond any seen before, in any realm.

Converge worlds? Not sure I wanted to do anything of the sort. The veil Bob mentioned had, at the time, seemed obvious. It was the veil between worlds. Maybe time had a veil too, an invisible and intangible barrier preventing anyone from breaching it. Anyone except Janus.

Or the Janusite?

The prophecy ended with *she is the bearer of the key and the staff, the child of the god, she is the Janusite.* In mythology, the Janus key had symbolized "I come in peace." Travelers would use a key symbol to let everyone know they meant no harm. The staff represented Janus's dominion over all lands, all doorways and roadways.

And time?

If I had more time I could've tested my theory. Tried to bend the universal clock to my will, played around with the power if it worked, learned how to control it. Max might've helped me with that. I had no time to spare, ironically.

Two people materialized in front of me.

Notus, his hood still pushed back, gripped Travis's arm.

"Your sacrifice," Notus rasped.

Travis went dead still. "Sacrifice?"

I shrugged.

Notus released Travis, and his mismatched eyes homed in on me. "May I kill him?"

"Why don't we play with him a little first?"

Travis gaped at me, the whites of his eyes seeming brighter in the inconstant light.

I looked straight into his eyes and said, "You better not try anything, sheriff. Your brother never liked you lusting after me."

"Brother?" Travis did a genuine double take, then glanced sideways at our captor. "What the blazes are you talking about?"

Notus turned toward Travis, his stance imperious as he glared down his lifted nose at his ex-brother. "I am Calder Blackwell."

Travis snorted, though he still appeared baffled. "You ain't my brother. I know what he looked like, even as a beast-man whatsit."

"He's telling the truth," I said. "The original sorcerer merged with Notus, who forced out the sorcerer's soul. Later, Notus merged with Skeiron and Calder to absorb their powers and knowledge."

Travis staggered backward, shaking his head slowly. "That ain't right. Three guys inside this...thing? Calder may've been screwed up, but he'd never have gone for this."

"He had no choice. His essence was dispersed, and Notus captured it. The being you see is not just Calder, but an amalgamation of three beings."

Travis rubbed his jaw. "Sure, that makes shitloads of sense."

I'd have to explain it better after we saved the world. For now, I needed to make sure he understood what I wanted him to do. "Remember what I said, sheriff. No funny business, or we'll bump up your sacrifice."

The confusion and shock on Travis's face metamorphosed into a clear understanding.

God, I hoped I was reading him right. If he didn't get my meaning, we were both in big, big, gigantic trouble.

Notus moved closer to me, his lustful gaze devouring me. "What punishment shall we mete out upon him first? I've dreamed of making my proud brother fall to his knees before me and beg for mercy."

Jesus, I could not believe the real Calder felt that way. He might've been weak, giving in to the siren song of power and immortality when it was offered to him, but he'd always seemed like such a decent guy before this craziness started. Nevan had told me the forging was a horrific process and only the strongest souls could survive it intact. Calder's weakness had broken him.

My thoughts backtracked, to the part about immortality being offered to Calder. I'd wondered, more than once or twice, who had forged him. I'd assumed another of the kerkopes had done it. Yet during the ordeal in the cave, when Calder had tried to kill me and make me into his monkey-mate, he'd said a man offered him a new life. A man. The kerkopes looked manlike, but they retained much of their monkey-ness even in human form because, as Nevan said, the curse Zeus had placed on the kerkopes to create them prevented them from shifting fully back into human form.

Calder wouldn't have called his so-called savior a man. He would've called him a being or a creature or…something.

Once I destroyed Notus for good, I'd give up any chance of ever knowing the truth about Calder's transformation.

I gazed up into Notus's eyes, focusing on the golden brown one—the Calder eye. "I'm curious. You must know who forged you, and I've always wondered."

A serpentine smile crept across his face. "Notus did."

Referring to himself in as a separate entity? Hmm. Maybe I'd succeeded in drawing out the Calder part of him, and it had taken precedence.

I laid a hand on his cheek. "I assumed the kerkopes would be the only ones who could make more of their kind."

"One with our level of power knows no limits."

He'd slipped back into the royal "we" mode.

Travis stomped his foot. "Hey! The sacrificial human has something to say."

Notus—Calder—cast a scathing glance over his shoulder at his ex-brother. "Perhaps we should tear out his tongue first."

"Like hell you will," Travis said.

"I will do whatever pleases me."

"You never could best me, Calder." Travis scratched his cheek and smirked. "Bet ya never knew I kissed Lindsey."

Technically true. In the midst of the Skeiron melee, while he was still reeling from revelations about the existence of magic, Travis had gotten drunk and given me a sloppy, awkward kiss.

Notus stalked toward Travis, stabbing a de-clawed finger into his chest. "She would never have let you."

"She did." Travis smirked some more, hands on his hips. "And she liked it."

Outright lie, but so what. If it pissed off Notus enough to distract him…

Time for my lateral move. Time for a miracle.

Notus seized Travis's shirt and hefted him off his feet. "She hates you."

"Does she?" Travis laughed with a derisive edge to it, his feet dangling six inches above the floor. "Then why'd she kiss me back? With tongue?"

Notus roared, shaking Travis hard.

I summoned my power, gritting my teeth against a resisting force. It fired a scorching tingle over my skin that plunged deep beneath the surface to sear my veins and nerves. The force hungered for my power, its phantom claws hard and hot as they tore at my psyche, shredding and consuming me.

Dear God. I recognized this pain, this ravenous energy.

The same thing had occurred when Ennea helped me tap into Nevan's memories. This vile force, it came from the sorcerer. From Notus, Skeiron, Calder. All of them at once, crammed inside a single body and recombined into a new and dark entity. Maybe he didn't realize he was giving off the consuming energy, but I had to shake it off either way.

Thrusting with all my energy, physical and magical, I bore down on the invading power. It slashed and thrashed and burned, frantic to stop me. I gathered my Janusite power, the blue magic crackling and glittering on my skin, and hurled the invader out of my way.

The physical form of the sorcerer convulsed. His hold on Travis broke, and Travis tumbled to the floor. Notus stumbled backward until he hit the wall, his eyes wide and unseeing.

Now, I commanded myself. Summoning every scrap of power within me, reaching out to gather in more of it from recesses I hadn't known existed inside me, I pictured the energy coalescing and condensing into a tight ball of brilliant blue light, it surface shimmering with a mottled white gleam. I grasped the ball in both hands and tossed it into the air.

The globe of glittering magic hovered above my head for the briefest moment, then burst. Sparkling sapphire energy rained down, expanding outward.

I spread my arms wide, directing the power to stretch out its billions of microscopic fingers. The energy suffused the room, the walls, and I sensed it mushrooming out into the world and the universe to fill in every crack in every structure and every infinitesimally tiny gap between the atoms in things and creatures and people.

Everything froze. Everything except me.

I glanced around, hardly able to conceive I'd succeeded. Travis sat frozen on the floor, his mouth open, caught in the middle of pushing up with one arm to raise his body off the floor. Notus hung slumped in the air, in the act of collapsing to his knees, his face rent with fury and agony.

No whisper of a draft. No sound save for my own breathing and the thumping of my heart.

Holy shit. I had stopped time.

CHAPTER TWENTY-SIX

THE PAUSE IN TIME DIDN'T AFFECT ME, UNTIL I TRIED TO WALK. IT FELT LIKE wading through mud. The absolute silence and stillness around me made for a creepy atmosphere, and it seemed as if everything had taken on a grayish tinge. How long the freeze would last, I had no clue. This was my first time halting the procession of time.

Halting time. Just thinking the phrase gave me the creeps.

I moved in front of Notus, kneeling so I could look him in the eye—not that he saw me, or so I hoped. Given the mind-boggling amount of power he'd amassed, nothing seemed impossible. Maybe he'd leap at me any second, having only pretended to freeze.

Oh great. Now I'd keep picturing that.

No, he was frozen. He had to be.

I stretched out a hand to wave it in his face. No reaction. I shouted at him. Nothing. I almost touched him, but pulled my hand away. Since teleportation worked on others when I touched them, I didn't care to find out if laying hands on Notus might liberate him from the frozen timeline.

This creature before me, composed of fragments of four beings, seemed evil at his core. But was he? Staring into the monkey-like eye of Calder, I flashed back to those months with him. He'd loved to surprise me at work by turning up with a bouquet of flowers and whisking me off to a lunch at our favorite restaurant. He'd taken me to museums, even though he hated art and history. I went to Dallas Cowboys games with him, even though I hated football. We'd laughed together, cuddled up to watch movies together, talked about the future together. When he'd proposed, I'd said yes without hesitation.

Neither of us ever could've envisioned our true futures. Him, metamorphosed into one of the kerkopes. Me, gifted with the ancient powers of a god. Christ, we'd planned on buying a little house and raising kids.

My hand flew to my womb. I might be carrying a baby right this moment. A half human, half sylph child. Definitely not the life I'd imagined.

I pictured Nevan, and the truth rushed through me like a sweet, sultry breeze coming off a tropical ocean. This life was better, so much better. I must save the life, the happiness, I'd found.

Yet gazing at Notus, I began to see Calder. His features were different, of course. Somewhere beneath the unfamiliar exterior, though, I sensed the man I'd known—before his forging, before everything imploded and our lives were reassembled into a new and unforeseen present.

Could I really destroy Calder? I'd done it to Skeiron, but Nevan had killed my ex-fiancé. I'd thought I killed Calder three years ago, when he'd attacked me, but even then I'd realized the person assaulting me was not the man I'd promised to marry. I'd never actually faced this dilemma, destroying the soul and essence of Calder. Could I do it? Should I do it? He'd been a human once, a decent guy. According to Nevan, Skeiron and Notus had started out as good kings, corrupted the power they amassed because they believed it was the only way to secure their positions and the safety of their kingdoms.

I covered my face with my hands, letting the breath flood out of me, drooping my shoulders. I was getting damn tired of being the instrument of men's destruction.

Maybe I could save Calder. Maybe I could save them all.

Staying on my knees, I shuffled around to face Travis and placed a hand on his chest.

He flinched, sucking in a wheezing breath. His eyes darted, then stalled on Notus. "What the—"

"I froze time."

"You—huh?"

While I kept my hand on his chest, unsure what might happen if I removed it, I tried for a sympathetic expression. "I know it sounds insane, but I really did freeze time."

"Okay," he said slowly. Still propped up on the arm he'd been using to push himself off the floor before I froze everything, he sat up. "Why am I...thawed?"

"Because I'm touching you. I figured time-freezing might work like teleporting, so I tried putting a hand on you and, voila, you unfroze."

"Uh-huh." His gaze shifted past my shoulder to Notus. "You sure he's frozen?"

"Pretty sure."

Travis flattened his palms on his thighs, his face pinched. "This was your plan? I distract him while you stop time."

"My plan was for you to distract him, yes." I made a sheepish face. "The rest I made up on the fly."

"Now what?"

I moved my hand to his shoulder and glanced back at Notus. "I was going to kill him, but…"

"What?" His gaze searched mine for a few seconds, then he dropped his head and sighed. When he looked at me again, empathy shone in his eyes. "Lindsey, that ain't Calder."

"A part of Notus is Calder."

"Yeah, the monkey-beast part." Travis settled a hand over mine on his shoulder. "The Calder we knew died three years ago."

"But his soul is inside Notus."

"How do you reckon that?"

My jaw began to quiver as I spoke, my voice too. "The forging doesn't create a different being. Nevan became a sylph, but he kept his personality, his memories, his soul. Calder would have too. He wasn't as strong as Nevan, so the forging warped him into a tortured, angry monster. But the essence of Calder, his soul, remained intact."

Travis slumped, though his hand stayed on mine. "Lindsey, I—What are you saying? You don't want to kill him? The sorcerer killed three women, he stripped out Nevan's soul, and he murdered his own girlfriend. He doesn't deserve to live."

"I know. He has to die." Tears streamed down my cheeks, hot on my skin, dribbling their salty tang into my mouth. "Destruction of an elemental banishes the soul to hell, Travis. I can't condemn Calder for all eternity."

Travis's face blanched, his eyes went dull.

Gripping his shoulder, my nails digging into his flesh, I said, "Can you honestly tell me you'd be okay with sending your brother to hell?"

He squeezed his eyes shut, his mouth crushed into a hard line. "Fuck."

If ever there had been an appropriate time for cursing, this was it. As long as I'd believed the Calder we'd known had vanished years ago, I could plot the sorcerer's demise without any guilt. Now that I'd proved to myself something of Calder survived inside Notus, I couldn't blithely riddle him with endued bullets.

"Are you sure," Travis said, nailing me with his cop stare, "Calder's soul is in that thing you're calling Notus?"

"Positive." I swiped my eyes dry with the back of my free hand. "Everyone keeps saying that to scatter an elemental means his essence and powers are sent to the Four Winds. Notus himself told me when the sorcerer absorbed his essence, the sorcerer's soul got displaced by Notus's essence. That means the essence is the soul."

Travis opened his mouth, and from his expression I knew he was about to object.

I silenced him with a shake of my head. "Listen to me. Destruction of an elemental doesn't always eliminate the soul. Your brother's soul might be stranded, or worse, if we destroy Notus."

"Jesus H. Christ. What do we do? Can't let Notus run around with all his superpowers while we try to save Calder's soul."

No, we couldn't do that. Neither could I keep time frozen for as long as we needed to figure out a plan. At least, I assumed I couldn't hold this time freeze for much longer. The magic buzzing on my skin had grown hotter, sharper, almost a stinging pain. My physical energy was siphoning away too, a sure sign I was approaching the limits of this spell.

A solitary idea sprouted in my mind, so I told Travis.

"If I could sap Notus's power," I said, "we'd have a better chance of containing him until we come up with a plan for Calder. I wouldn't have to pump him dry, which I'm not sure I could do. Just bring him back down to the level of an average elemental."

Travis made a face that said he wasn't quite convinced. "What makes you think you can do that? You ever tried it before?"

"No, but I'm confident I can handle the task." Semi-confident. Edging toward confident. "No choice, I have to try."

He lifted my hand off his shoulder to clasp it in both of his. "Lindsey, don't go killing yourself to save Calder."

"I don't want to die, trust me."

"Maybe you should get Nevan. He could help, right?"

"Not sure if—" I swore I saw a light bulb pop on above my head, but I probably imagined that. Probably. "The one whose help I really need is Max."

"The—incubus?" Travis's lip curled. "Don't tell me you're dumping Nevan for that weirdo."

"You used to call Nevan a weirdo. My how times have changed." I patted his hand, which still encompassed mine. "Relax, I'm not interested in Max that way. He's my familiar, remember? I think he can help more than Nevan could."

"Right, your familiar."

Travis's eyes had glazed over, a sign I recognized all too well. I had felt the way he looked on more than one occasion since discovering the hidden world parallel to our own.

"Problem is," I said, gnawing on my lip, "I have no idea what will happen if I whisk away to get Max. For all I know, time will start up again. I could try whisking Notus away with me, but again, I have no idea if my teleporting will break the time-freezing spell."

His brow pinched, Travis regarded the corner of the room and made a clucking noise with his tongue. After a moment, he swung his attention back to me, the tension of deep thought ironing out of his features. "You got your endived gun?"

I stifled a laugh. "Endued, not endived. It's not a salad, Travis."

"Fine, whatever. You got your gun, right? And it can kill anybody, even this Notus guy?"

"Yes. But we can't kill him until we save Calder."

"I know how to shoot a bad guy someplace that'll hurt like hell but won't kill him." Straightening, he reset his expression to cop mode. Determined, confident, sexy. "Give me your derringer. That way you can concentrate on getting Max here."

"Got a better idea. I'll whisk all three of us—you, me, and Notus—straight to the rest of the gang. That way, I can get all the help I might need."

A fae witch, a surly leprechaun, my roguish familiar, and my super-hot sylph boyfriend. We were a dream team, for sure.

The team included Travis.

"I'll have to let go of you for a minute," I said, "so I can get my gun out and reload. You'll probably freeze again."

"Let's get this done."

The instant I withdrew my hand, he turned into a statue again. His hands hovered where he'd held mine.

I pulled out my derringer, flipped the barrel down to expose the twin chambers, and dumped the empty shells. Switching the gun to my other hand, I dug in my pocket for two fresh rounds and dropped them into the chambers, then snapped the barrel shut.

Scrambling to my feet, I touched Travis's shoulder.

He woke up, and without a word, got to his feet.

"Ready?" I asked, offering him the derringer.

Travis accepted the gun, holding it barrel down with his finger on the barrel just above the trigger. "Ready."

We stepped closer to Notus. I placed my other hand on his shoulder.

And I zipped us away in the instant Notus came back to life, roaring his fury.

Chapter Twenty-Seven

Back in the clearing where we'd left the rest of the gang, the second we touched down Notus leaped at Travis.

And froze in midair.

Travis froze in the act of ducking out of Notus's path.

In the clearing around us, the others were paused in various poses. Tris and Ennea seemed to have been arguing at the moment I stopped time, his arms raised and his mouth open on what must've been a snarky complaint, her hands on her hips and her mouth puckered. Max and Nevan were about twenty feet away from me, engaged in a serious conversation, by the looks of it. Nevan wore his stern king face, while Max listened with a strained expression.

My first impulse? To run over there and throw my arms around Nevan.

Second impulse? The right one. To grab Max and siphon enough power out of Notus to make him no stronger than any other elemental.

I sprinted to Max, slapping a hand on his arm.

He looked confused for heartbeat, then grinned at me. "You have temporal powers."

"Yeah, I do. Big whoop."

"It's an enormous whoop, my mistress."

He executed an exaggerated bow, and somehow I kept my hold on him through the whole, silly display.

"Temporal powers mean nothing," I said, "unless I can weaken Notus."

I quickly outlined the plan Travis and I had devised.

Max scrubbed his hands on his conjured pants. "You need Nevan. He can—"

"Both of you would be ideal," I said, "but I can't unfreeze you both and hold onto the time-freeze spell. I feel it slipping already. You're my familiar, and I need your help. Okay?"

"Here to serve, mistress."

"I keep telling you to call me Lindsey."

"Of course, Mistress Lindsey." The twinkle in his eye gave away the fact he was teasing me, the smart-ass familiar.

We approached Travis and Notus, my hand on his arm the whole time. I laid a hand on Travis just long enough to urge him aside, and as he struggled to comprehend the situation, I sent him back into the frozen timeline. No time to explain. No time to waste.

Max and I took up positions in front of Notus. I had to keep one hand on his arm, leaving me only one hand to link with his, maintaining a slight gap between our hands as we'd done before. Energy began to sizzle and glitter within the gap, but he couldn't give me more power. His assistance grounded my power so it wouldn't run out of control, providing—as he'd told me the first time—an anchor for me in the stormy sea of magic.

I had no idea how to drain an elemental's power. With my previous spells, I'd imposed my will on my power, commanding it to perform a task. No words spoken, nothing more than intention and resolve. I did the same now, concentrating on the idea of reducing Notus's power, of stealing the magic he'd stolen from others, and of funneling it into…

A container. I needed a container for the magic, to ensure no one else could snare it out of the ether as the sorcerer had done.

Max's expression evidenced a dawning understanding and an unflinching commitment to the mission.

"Whatever you need," he said, "I will do it."

Christ. How could I ask him to be the container for dark magic? What would that do to him?

"I am your servant," he said.

"No you are not." The magic bridging our hands unified us in a strange and not unpleasant manner—not sexual or romantic, but a strong bond nonetheless. "You are my friend, Max. What I need to do…It requires a container for the power we pull out of Notus."

"Then I will be the container."

"What will that do to you? Can you stay yourself with all that crud inside you?"

"I am stronger than you realize. Perhaps not in terms of magic, but in the ways that count."

"I know you're strong," I said, "but I don't want to lose a friend today."

"You won't." He took a breath, exhaling it in a rush. "I'm ready."

"Max—"

"Lindsey," he said, his tone gentle yet firm, "this is my purpose. To serve you, as your familiar and as your friend. I'll fight the dark magics and survive this, you have my word." He winked. "Why should everyone else get the chance to be selfless and brave, but not me?"

I tried to smile, but faltered. "You are brave, Max. But you're also an amazing friend and an amazing familiar."

"That sounded like goodbye. We're not parting ways."

"No. You're coming back from this, if I have to rip that scuzzy magic out of you with my bare hands and hand deliver it to the Four Winds."

He turned thoughtful. "You will need to deliver me to the Temple of the Four Winds and summon them to remove dark the magics from me. Nevan can lend a hand with that."

"We will fix you. And you have *my* word on that."

I focused on the blue magic simmering between our hands, rising into a rolling boil of power tempered by the anchoring magic of my familiar. Max shut his eyes, his expression strained as if waiting for and dreading the transfer to come. I let the power tingle over my skin, lifting every hair and awakening the Janusite within. Tendrils of sapphire energy snaked out from between our hands, whipping through the air as they sought out the target.

The tendrils latched onto Notus. They coiled around his limbs, crawling over his torso and over his head, engulfing him in a mesh of pure power. It shimmered as sparks erupted all along the tendrils.

Darkness fought back. It clawed and scorched and screamed down the lines of magic connecting Notus to me and to Max. I clenched my teeth, battling for breath, the strain of the spell like a steel corset ratcheting tighter and tighter around my torso. The dark power scrabbled for a foothold, a way to get inside me, but I fought back with every ounce of energy within my body.

A blue fireball raced down one of the tendrils, straight into the grounding space between my hand and Max's. Oily blackness writhed within the ball, searing my skin.

No turning back.

I funneled the darkness into Max and felt it scour down the lines of power connecting us, shy away from me, and dive straight into him.

Max's body convulsed. His eyes shot wide as black threads whipped through the swirling colors of his irises. His chest inflated on a breath that roared like a hurricane wind.

I pushed a wave of my blue energy into him, desperate to bolster his own power with mine, the instant before our connection shattered. The force of the disconnect sent me reeling backward, but Max did not freeze.

He went stone-still, but his chest heaved with each hollow breath.

While I staggered and caught my balance, time resumed its forward motion. The rest of my friends, and Nevan, spun toward the weird sound emitted by Max.

Notus came to life screaming like a sinner pitched into the fires of Hell. His gaze landed on me, and he lashed out one bony hand as if to strike me down with his magic. His power, what remained of it, hit me like a light slap in the face but nothing more. He stumbled, lost his balance, and smacked onto the ground on his butt, breathless from the exertion of magical energy. And likely from having his stolen power ripped out of him.

Travis clapped his boot on Notus's chest and shoved him down on his back, the amalgamated being too weak to fight.

Victory.

Not quite yet. We had to save Calder.

I caught sight of Nevan. He smiled, lips closed, eyes crinkled at the corners, and my heart melted.

The smile disintegrated. He swung his sword up, the moonlight glancing off its blade and shouted, "Lindsey!"

I spun around.

Travis went flying past me, limbs akimbo, a strangled cry bursting out of him. He crashed to the ground a dozen feet away.

Notus threw his body at me, and we tumbled to the grass with him on top. One of his elbows rammed into my gut. His clawed fingers clinched around my throat, but I fired a burst of power into his chest, hurling him off me. He collided with a tree, dazed but no less infuriated.

I shoved up onto hands and knees, winded from the attack.

A feral roar split the air from behind me as Nevan sprang through the air headed for Notus. His massive body sailed down toward the sorcerer, but Notus thrust one foot up to kick Nevan in the chest, punting him backward. The sword popped out of Nevan's hand and wheeled through the air.

Nevan careened to the ground at my left, grunting from the impact.

His sword punched into the ground inches from my right hip.

Notus clambered to his hands and knees. He raised one hand with the fingers curled, as if holding an object though nothing was there.

A thin, curved sword materialized in his grasp.

Everything unfolded in a heartbeat, so fast even Nevan couldn't get to me in time. Notus lunged at me, slashing the sword down toward my neck. I reached for my holster, but the derringer wasn't there because I'd given it to Travis. With no time to think, I grasped the hilt of Nevan's sword, levered myself up, and vaulted over the sword an instant before Notus's blade lanced the air where my throat had been.

He bounded to his feet, hunched but with a firm grip on his curved weapon.

On my knees, I took hold of Nevan's sword with both hands, yanking it out of the earth, imbued with a new strength fueled by adrenaline. I knew the boost wouldn't last, and I'd have one shot at this.

Notus raised his sword with both hands, wielding it high above his head in preparation for a death blow. With a banshee-like scream, he drove the blade down toward my chest.

I propelled Nevan's sword upward.

The blade punctured Notus's stomach, plunging deep, all the way to the hilt. His sword tumbled from his hands.

I teetered backward, about to fall over from the weight of him skewered on the sword.

Nevan appeared beside us. He grabbed Notus's shoulders and tore him off the sword, flinging him aside.

Bent backward at an awkward angle, the sword in my grip, I couldn't move. My body had begun to tremble, as the adrenaline rush flooded out of me and my overtaxed muscles wailed for relief.

Falling to his knees beside me, Nevan snatched the sword away and tossed it onto the ground. He lifted me onto my knees again and hugged me to him for a brief moment before he took my face in his hands and scrutinized me.

"Are you harmed?" he asked, anxiety tightening his features.

"I'm fine." Turning my face into his hand, I kissed his palm.

He touched his forehead to mine. "I will dispatch him."

Nevan rose.

"No." I grabbed his hand, scrambling to get up. "Nevan, we can't kill him yet. I have to save Calder first."

Nevan's brows knit together. "Save him?"

"Calder's soul is trapped inside the sorcerer's body. I have to set him free."

A rustling erupted to our left, from where Notus had wound up crumpled on the ground. He'd pushed up off the ground, blood oozing from his mouth and pouring from his gut wound, his fevered gaze locked on me.

A gunshot detonated.

Notus crumpled.

Halfway across the clearing, Travis held the derringer pointed at where Notus had stood a second ago. A faint wisp of smoke curled up from the gun's barrel.

An endued bullet had felled Notus. What if he was dead? For real?

Travis must've noticed the panic on my face, because he lowered the gun and strode up to me and Nevan. "Don't worry, Lindsey. I told you I know how to shoot somebody where it hurts like hell but won't kill 'em."

Notus lay crumpled on the ground, his legs bent, but his eyes were open and he was breathing, though his breaths were labored. He clutched one hand over a wound on his shoulder. Blood stained his fingers, but the wound didn't seem life threatening. He was weak from the previous attack and from getting a good deal of his magic siphoned out of him.

Travis squinted at a sight past my shoulder. "Is he okay?"

I tracked his line of sight past Nevan, to a figure crouched near the clearing's perimeter.

Max lifted his head to fix his gaze on me.

Unease crawled along my skin and shivered through my veins.

His eyes had become a maelstrom of molten metal shades, with bright red flames licking at the pupils. Tiny flames on his skin burned orange and red. His mouth was open slightly, his expression savage and dark. His hands rested on the ground, the palms flattening the grass. The fire on his skin erupted, flaring high enough to set his hair ablaze and singe the trees behind him. Smoke drifted up from the grass as it blackened beneath him.

"Max?" I said, taking a few tentative steps toward him, until Nevan grasped my arm to halt me.

The salamander's skin had gone crimson, and white flames sparked within the fire engulfing him. He sank his fingers into the earth, gritting his teeth with his lips peeled back.

Oh God. He must've been fighting the dark magics with all his power, all his strength of will. How much longer could he hold out?

I looked to Nevan, who still grasped my arm, but he was staring intently at a spot on the other side of the clearing.

"We have to fix Max," I said. "Get him to the Temple of the Four Winds before that evil crud wrecks him. Can they save Calder too?"

Nevan remained silent, his gaze glued to the empty swathe of earth across the clearing. I turned toward him, and his hand fell away from my arm.

"Hey," I said, pushing on his upper arm in a vain attempt to shake him. His superior strength made him immovable. I waved a hand in his face. "What are you staring at? We have pressing issues to deal with."

"Yes," he said, finally looking at me, "we have extremely pressing concerns. Such as where Ceara's body has gone."

"What do you m—" I flashed back to the sight of Ceara's lifeless body on the ground, in the exact spot Nevan was staring at now. The empty spot. "Maybe Notus took it."

Nevan's jaw worked, as if he were literally chewing on the idea. Then he stomped over to Notus, still prone on the ground, and dropped into crouch straddling the defunct sorcerer.

Notus cringed.

All-powerful no more, eh, Mr. Baddest of the Bad?

Nevan closed one hand around Notus's throat without squeezing. His voice was menacing, but deceptively soft. "What have you done with Ceara's body?"

"I did not take it," Notus rasped, his speech halting.

"Someone did." Nevan shook his captive's neck. "You must have witnessed the taking of her body."

Notus spat blood. "She simply vanished."

I moved up beside Nevan and spoke to Notus. "Was she really dead?"

"Difficult to say." He glanced past Nevan to the vacant spot where Ceara had died by his magic. "She was a vivified statue, after all."

"You killed her with magic," Nevan said. "It takes an endued weapon or a magically enhanced poison to destroy an elemental. Simple telekinetic magic does not kill, unless it's polluted with dark energies. I did not detect the odor of fouled magic." Nevan shot me a chagrined look. "I should have considered this at the time."

I settled a hand on his shoulder, bending over to say, "It's not your fault. We all had a lot on our minds." To Notus, I said, "Did you know you weren't actually killing her? If simple magic can't do the trick, you must have known."

Notus sniffed. "My magic is not simple."

Straightening, I considered the winded and wounded creature slumped at my feet, and a thought occurred to me. "Ah, I get it. You believed you were the most powerful badass ever in the history of badassery. Naturally, your spectacular magic would destroy another elemental where regular magic fails to get the job done."

Nevan sprang to his feet. "Arrogant fool."

"This means Ceara might still be alive."

"The least of our concerns at the moment." Nevan pointed toward the conflagration that was my familiar. "We must take care of that problem first. And then find out if this one can be saved."

He nodded at our prisoner.

Travis held the derringer out to me. "You might need this where you're going. Who knows if these wind people are friendly or not."

Nevan shook his head. "If she arrives at the temple carrying a weapon, she will be ejected from it."

I waved away the gun but dug the rest of my endued ammo out of my pocket. "Travis, you'd better take these. Might need them if Ceara comes back."

Nevan proffered his sword to Travis. "Take this as well. I cannot bring it with me to the temple."

With a small nod, Travis accepted the sword. He held out his hand, and I dumped the ammo into his palm.

"Good luck," he said, stuffing the bullets into his pocket.

Ennea and Tris reached us then, offering their own statements of support and wishes for luck. Tris assured that such wishes "coming from a frigging awesome leprechaun" like himself meant a great deal more than a similar statement coming from an average elemental.

I believed him.

Nevan kissed me, a quick and sweet meeting of our lips, and said, "I will transport Max, as I'm far more fireproof than you."

He assumed I could transport Notus. The silent vote of confidence made my heart swell.

"I've got this guy," I said, kneeling to clap a hand on Notus's shoulder. "You lead the way."

Nevan zipped across the clearing to Max, bending to touch the salamander's shoulder. The pair vanished.

I followed Nevan's warm and brilliant trail of magic.

Chapter Twenty-Eight

A GALE BLUSTERED AROUND ME. I THREW AN ARM UP TO SHIELD MY eyes from the onslaught, but the roar of the wind made it hard to hear anything. I knelt on rocky ground, that much I could tell. The fog that somehow shrouded the landscape in spite of the wind obscured my view of anything further away than the man slumped at my feet.

Notus groaned, sounding as miserable as anyone I'd ever heard.

Keeping my arm up to protect my eyes, I cupped my other hand into a makeshift megaphone and shouted, "Nevan!"

I sensed him nearby but couldn't see a damn thing.

The air around me began to clear within a bubble of calmness, expanding outward to form a protected dome perhaps ten feet in diameter. Beyond the bubble, the wind raged and the fog obscured everything.

Nevan stood before me, his expression grim.

Though his body blocked most of my view ahead, I saw the flames raging behind him. Leaning to the side, I peered around him at the man-size mass of flames. Max's skin and face had vanished into the conflagration.

"We have to hurry," I said to Nevan. "He doesn't have much time."

"I know." Nevan grasped my upper arms. "Listen to me, Lindsey. I may not be able to accompany you into the temple."

"What? Why?"

"I've been here once before, shortly after Skeiron and I defeated Notus. To enter the temple, one must be deemed deserving by the Four Winds. They ejected me."

Nevan always said what he meant, which told me he'd been tossed out of this place—ejected, rather than simply rejected.

"Why would they do that?" I asked.

"I aided in destroying the king of the sylphs. The Winds deemed me a traitor and therefore unworthy of their assistance."

We had so little time, but I had to know. "What did you want from them?"

He avoided my gaze, his darting everywhere except to my face. "It does not matter. You must hurry to save these two."

"What if I'm not deserving?"

Nevan looked at me then, his grip tightening on my arms. "You are."

My throat had grown tight, thick with emotion. I gulped, but couldn't quite shake the disturbing sensation of weight bearing down on me. The weight of responsibility. The weight of so many lives riding on my success or failure. If the Winds denied me entry, I had no idea how to save Max or Calder.

If Max lost his inner battle, the darkest powers would consume him and turn their voracious eyes on the rest of the universe.

"Summon them," Nevan said.

"How?"

"Request an audience. In not words, but intention."

I rolled my eyes. "Thanks for the unambiguous instructions."

"Close your eyes and concentrate on your desire to meet with the Four Winds." He squeezed my arms, his expression turning gentled. "You will be admitted. Because you, my love, are the most worthy being in any world."

He loved me, so of course he'd have to say that. But I believed him. I believed he meant it.

I shut my eyes and let his grounding presence, the calming effect of his touch, draw me into a kind of trance. The noise of the wind outside our bubble faded into silence.

The ground rumbled and shuddered beneath my feet.

If not for Nevan holding me steady, I would've toppled onto my ass on the hard rock ground. As I scanned our surroundings, I realized the wind hadn't faded because I'd been in a trance. It had just…stopped. The fog retreated away from us as if sucked up by a gigantic vacuum cleaner, sweeping up and up and up the rocky slope ahead of us. The sun emerged from the retreating fog, and the sky cleared in its wake.

Soon the earthbound clouds had gathered above us, at the top of the now-exposed mountain. The fog condensed into a vaguely rectangular shape, rotating around a central point.

We had landed on the side of a mountain, a barren peak amid a field of barren, craggy peaks with steep slopes and only a smattering of grass and the occasional bush to interrupt the pockmarked rock surfaces. The mountain range extended to the horizon in all directions. Above us, the sky shimmered such a deep blue it was almost purple, with nary a cloud to mar it.

"You are worthy," Nevan said.

I tapped his chest. "So are you. Otherwise, you'd be tumbling down this mountainside, wouldn't you?"

His brows lowered and crinkled. Then, with all the brilliance of the sun dawning after a month of storms, he smiled.

Motion above us attracted my gaze, and I discovered the condensed fog bank had begun to rotate with more vigor. Nevan followed my gaze, turning toward the mountain peak some hundred feet or so away.

A burst of wind dispersed the fog.

In its place, perched atop the summit, hunkered an imposing structure with Corinthian columns and enormous wooden doors. A steep set of steps carved out of the mountain led up to the structure's portico, where a shallower series of steps approached the doors. The entire building appeared to be fashioned from white stone that glimmered in the sunlight as if dusted with the essence of stars.

Nevan stared at the huge building, starstruck. "The Temple of the Four Winds."

I slipped my hand into his, lacing our fingers. A sense of awe, mixed with fear, overtook me at the reality of what was to come. The Four Winds, those avatars and guardians of power more immense than anything I could imagine, awaited us inside the temple. My gaze shifted to Max, his body aflame with wicked power, and I wondered. We had been deemed worthy of entry, but would the Winds help us?

Max disappeared.

"Nevan—" Before I could finish my exclamation, Notus poofed out too. I latched onto Nevan's arm with my free hand, the other still clutching his hand. "Where'd they go?"

He patted the hand I'd clamped onto his arm. "Easy, love."

A horrendous grinding noise made us both look to the summit.

The doors of the temple crept open.

"Our invitation," Nevan said. "Or the closest we'll come to receiving one."

He tucked my arm under his and guided me to the steep steps embedded in the slope.

I let my gaze skim up the narrow steps. "Can't we zip up there?"

"Unfortunately, they have wards around this peak. I cannot zip us anywhere."

But the Winds could poof Max and Notus away to wherever. *Not fair at all.*

I sighed. "Trudging up these steps is probably a test of our commitment, or some baloney like that."

Nevan threw me a sideways glance. "Perhaps you shouldn't think of it as baloney when you seek their aid."

"Point taken." I shouted up the mountainside, "Excuse me, your eminent windinesses. It's not baloney, it's a perfectly reasonable test."

Nevan groaned.

We ascended the steps side by side, mounting step after step until my legs started to ache, soon joined by my stomach muscles. I couldn't quite catch my breath, probably because the air was thinner up here. Five times, Nevan paused to breathe clean air into my lungs—and that wasn't a metaphor. He sealed his open mouth over mine and exhaled, feeding me oxygen-rich air that tasted like him.

At last, we made it to the top, to the base of white stone stairs that accessed the temple doors. I bent over, panting, my hands on my thighs and my knees bent.

"Need a sec," I huffed.

Brawny arms lifted me off my feet. Nevan cradled me to his body, and his mouth descended on mine for another life-giving lip-lock. As the sweet, clean air filled my lungs, I wrapped my arms around his neck.

"Better?" he asked.

"Yes."

Nevan carried me through the massive wooden doors. They dwarfed us both, their ornately carved panels towering at least five times as tall as Nevan. He halted just inside the temple and set me on my feet.

The room was vacant—of life, of furnishings, of decoration. A smooth floor made of marble-like rock stretched away from us in three directions. I estimated the building measured about a thousand feet in breadth and half that in width, though I had minimal confidence in my ability to gauge the size of such a vast and empty space. It was huge, period.

High up on the walls, sixty feet overhead, intricate friezes depicted winged beings dressed in flowing robes.

A delicate, tepid breeze wafted around us. It seemed to investigate us, brushing over my skin, ruffling my hair, touching me with the sensation of soft fingertips. From Nevan's look of mild surprise, I knew he was experiencing the same exploration.

Four beings materialized before us.

They wore white robes that dragged on the floor, their arms and heads exposed. Two were women, two men. At least, they appeared to be male and female. Since they served as avatars of magical power, who knew if their current appearances bore any resemblance to their actual forms. If they had real forms.

All of them had white hair and pale skin, but their eyes shone glossy black.

I sidled closer to Nevan.

They watched us, unmoving, expressionless.

Unnerved, I gave a curt wave of my hand. "Hello there."

Nevan tensed. He was probably cringing inside at my silly greeting.

Well honestly, I'd never met an avatar of power before. How did one introduce oneself to such a being?

You didn't. *Duh.* You waited for them to say howdy.

One of the females glided toward us. She halted a foot away from me, her body bobbing the tiniest bit, as if she floated barely above the floor. Her black eyes drilled into me, and she canted her head.

"Lindsey Astrid Porter," she said, her voice as ethereal as the wind and as alien as her appearance. "We have received your request."

"I—I didn't make one yet."

She flourished one slender hand.

Max and Notus winked into view behind her—Max a pillar of man-shaped fire, and Notus sprawled on the floor. The erstwhile sorcerer moaned, his head lolling.

The wind-being in front of me reached out one pale finger to touch my jaw. "You wish us to save these two. Of what benefit is it to us?"

"Isn't it your job to collect scattered powers and guard them?" Despite the knot in my stomach, I looked directly into her spooky eyes. "You're supposed to keep a destroyed being's power from being misused, right?"

She drew her head back, as if surprised or maybe annoyed.

Not sure which option would've been worse for me.

Her nose lifted, and she sniffed. "You dare question us?"

I glanced at Max, his body covered in fire thanks to the evil crud stuffed into him. His brave and selfless willingness to take in the discarded powers had put his very soul in danger. And he'd done it for me.

Separating from Nevan, I confronted the wind-being. "Yes, I question you. It's your job to pick up scattered powers, but a sorcerer got his hands on the essences of three elemental beings. He became so powerful, he might've destroyed two worlds."

"Yet he did not." She looked way too smug about that statement.

"Because my team—two fae, a salamander, a sylph, and two humans—risked our lives and our eternal souls to take him down." I flapped a hand toward her ethereal buddies. "You guys screwed up big time. Dark power got stolen, and you don't seem to have done a damn thing to get it back."

She stared at me, her eyes wide, her nostrils flaring. The black in her eyes pulsated.

Nevan tugged my hand.

I glanced at him, expecting to see his dismayed look. Instead, he smiled with his lips closed, his eyes gleaming with pride.

The wind-being narrowed her gaze on me. "We gifted you with great power, Janusite. Are you not grateful?"

"Honestly, I'm not sure yet."

The black in of her eyes shrank into a dark pupil, rimmed by a wide iris of shimmering emerald green. "You are forthright and courageous, but without arrogance. We admire this, especially from a mortal imbued with the essence of a god. Power of that magnitude can and often does corrupt the bearer."

Was that a compliment?

She curled a lock of my hair around her elegant finger. "You remain pure of heart, despite the sorcerer's attempts to blacken your soul."

"I—" Lying to this being seemed like a very bad idea. "I gave in to the darkness, for a little while. I'm not pure."

Her pale mouth curved into a smile. "You never succumbed to darkness, child. You gave in to anger in a time of desperation, but that is not the same."

"Um…How do you know what I did?"

"We are one with the Oversoul. The connection grants us far-reaching knowledge." She let go of my hair, settling her hand on my cheek, the touch barely perceptible. "You are worthy of our intervention. We will remove the unwanted power from the salamander."

The other three wind-beings nodded in unison.

I could've hugged her, but I restrained myself. "Thank you."

Nevan made a strangled noise somewhere between a groan and gasp.

Oops. I'd said the T word—to a hugely powerful being, at that.

"Be at ease, sylph," the female said. "Your soul mate owes us nothing in return. We owe her a unpayable debt for retrieving the lost magics."

She'd called me Nevan's soul mate. I wanted to ask why, what that term meant to someone like her, but I had other concerns.

"What about Calder?" I asked. "Can you save him and send his soul to a good place?"

"I am afraid saving him is beyond our purview." She stepped back, sweeping an arm in the direction of Notus. "Only you can liberate his soul."

"Me?" I shook my head. "I wouldn't know how. Not very adept with my magic yet."

"No magic is required. Make use of your humanity."

Sure, that sounded way easier than magic. "I don't suppose you could explain what that means."

"The answer lies in your heart." She glided toward Max, and her three companions floated up to encircle the incubus. "We shall render aid to this one, while you consider the other."

As the Four Winds raised their spread arms, a wind erupted around Max. It spun around him in wild torrents of air that doused the flames on his body. The wind mutated into a whirling fog so dense it obliterated my view of Max, and even the Four Winds became indistinct figures at the periphery of the cloudy tempest. A pillar of glittering black energy punched through the fog, shooting straight up to the ceiling. An opposing current of pure white power coalesced out of the roof, seeming to emanate from the stone itself, and wound its tendrils around the blackness, swallowing it whole.

The white energy receded. The fog dispersed.

Max huddled on his knees, doubled over with his forehead on the floor.

I rushed to him, laying a hand on his shoulder. His skin was hot, though not scorching.

He raised his head to look at me. "Lindsey. It is…gone."

The female Wind who had addressed me before moved closer to us. "Yes, the darkness has been stripped from your being. It is now quarantined."

I bit my lip, contemplating the wind-being. "Shouldn't dangerous magic be destroyed?"

She gave me an empathetic smile. "Magical energy cannot be destroyed, only contained. This is the reason we exist, the purpose of the Four Winds."

Max pushed up onto his knees, facing the female. "You have saved me. I owe—"

"You owe us nothing," she said. "We removed the dark magics from you, but we could not have done, if your mistress were not the Janusite."

I leaned toward her. "What does that have to do with anything?"

"Your power protected him." She must've noticed my confusion, because she gave me another empathetic smile and explained. "Janus had dominion over transitions, and this includes changes in condition. When you transferred the dark magics into your familiar, your Janusite power protected him from the brunt of the intrusion. You maintained his condition, defending his innate magic. He needed to fight the invading energy, but he could not have survived without the shield of your magic and your desire to protect him."

Max swerved his gaze to me, his expression one of utter astonishment. "You saved my life, Lindsey. Thank you."

I was astonished too, by the revelation I'd shielded him from the dark energy and by his gratitude. A tether of magic snapped taut between us, cementing the debt.

Shit. I hadn't wanted anyone owing me, but now two men had sealed a life debt.

"Aw, Max," I moaned, "why did you go and do that?"

"Because you saved me." He rose to his full height, his skin coppery skin seeming brighter compared to the white of our surroundings. "I accept debts when I owe them. And I know you will never misuse the debt."

"Still wish you hadn't done it."

"You can always absolve me later."

The wind-being swept an arm toward Notus. "To save this one, Janusite, you must demonstrate his worthiness."

"Me?" I stared at the prone figure in black robes and his ashen complexion. "How on earth do I do that?"

"You are not on Earth," she said with a hint of annoyance. Then she paused, as if to regain her composure, and continued in her serene tone. "You knew the mortal whose soul you wish to spare. Only you understand how to do this."

Great. Vague instructions for something I had no idea how to accomplish.

Nevan turned toward me, splaying a palm over my cheek. "You cared for Calder once, and he cared for you. Speak to him. You do not need magic, only your strong and good soul. If the man you knew is truly there, he will respond."

"I'll try."

"You will succeed."

"Because I'm the Janusite."

"No." He smiled, stroking my cheek with his thumb. "Because you are Lindsey Astrid Porter."

"I really love you, Nevan."

"And I love you." He stepped back. "Now save that man's soul, as only you can."

Only I could do it. He meant it as encouragement, that I would this my way, but I felt the burden of salvation for Calder's soul bearing down on my shoulders. The wind-being had told me only I could do this. If I failed, it was all on me.

"His weakness condemned him," Nevan said. "If he can be redeemed, you will succeed. If he cannot, you bear no responsibility."

Sometimes I swore he could read my mind.

But he was right. And I had to try.

To the wind-being, I said, "Will he be destroyed if I can't help him? The bullet was endued, but he was shot in the shoulder."

"Endued weapons always kill." She eyed Nevan, then returned her attention to me. "Unless there is extreme intervention, that is. Depending upon the location of the injury, death may come slowly or quickly, but it will come. And his body was already weak from the strain of housing three essences."

The body would perish. The soul might be saved.

Approaching Notus, I knelt beside him.

His bleary, mismatched eyes rolled up to look at me. Sweat dampened his gray skin, and blood stained his hands from his attempts to staunch the bleeding. His face was slack, and his arms had slid down to the floor.

I picked up one of his blood-stained hands. "Calder, I know you're in there."

His brows twitched faintly, as if he couldn't quite draw them together.

"You're dying," I said. "Nothing can stop it. You have a choice to make, between condemning your soul or saving it. I want to help you, but you have to help me do that."

His mouth opened, then closed. He pulled in a slow, rattling breath and tried once more to speak. "We are doomed."

"Cut the 'we' crap." Keeping his hand in mine, I leaned down to gaze into the Calder eye. "I know you can speak as individuals. You've done it before, when you took me prisoner and Calder came out to talk to me. Please, I need you to come out. This is your last chance."

"We..." He coughed, the sound wet and crackly. "Cannot."

"Yes you can." I grasped his face in both hands, staring hard into the eyes of this being, possessed by a powerful certainty I could find the man I'd once vowed to marry buried somewhere inside this creature. "I know you cared for me, Calder. I know you're a good man at heart. The forging brought out your weaknesses and messed with your head, turning you into a tortured, confused soul. That part of you is gone. You can become yourself again. Please try, please."

His mouth opened, his jaw quivered.

What more could I do to convince him? I glanced back at Nevan, and in his eyes I saw the answer.

"Please, Calder," I said, "give everyone who cares about you the peace of knowing you died with salvation. Travis loves you, he wants you to be safe. I care about you, and I can't stand to watch you die this way. Fight for you salvation, Calder. Do it for me."

I pressed my lips to his cold and clammy mouth. I held the kiss, willing him to see the truth and fight. The change was impossible to describe, impossible to pinpoint, but I sensed it happening. Something deep within him shifted.

Pulling back, I searched signs of the change.

The Calder eye, once the golden color of a monkey, roiled and altered. The pupil shrank, and the iris turned a very human shade of lustrous brown.

Tears stung my eyes. My throat grew thick, almost choked with the emotion surging up inside me. I recognized that eye. It belonged to the man I'd once wanted to share my life with, the man who'd made me laugh and made me feel wanted. The monkey-man had crumbled away, and the human had reasserted himself. Calder Blackwell had come home.

"Lindsey?" he said, his voice weak but familiar. His face might've looked like someone else, but I was hearing Calder's voice, complete with the Texas twang. He coughed and tried to lift his hand, but it dropped back to the floor. "Why are you here?"

"Don't you remember? You're dying."

"Meant why are you trying to save me." His cast his eyes downward. "After what I did to you…I killed a man, and I tried to kill you."

"You weren't yourself, I understand that now." I swiped away the tears that escaped my eyes, rolling down my cheeks. "The forging made you crazy. I'm not excusing what you did, but I believe you can redeem yourself."

Again, he struggled to lift his hand.

I clasped it in mine, holding our hands on his chest, over his heart.

"God, Lindsey." His own eyes teared up, the whites reddening. "I'm so sorry. What I did I can never take back, but it's almost like it was a dream. A nightmare. Can't believe I did those things."

"I know."

He grimaced, summoning enough strength to raise his other hand and brush his fingers over my cheek. "I love you, and I always will. I know you don't love me, but we had a good thing and I trashed it. Don't expect you to forgive me, won't ask for it. I just need you to know I'm sorry."

Tears streamed down my cheeks, my throat burned with a sharp pain, and I had trouble speaking at all. I bowed my head, and the tears dripped onto his face.

Despite everything he'd done after his forging, I believed him. Maybe it was crazy. Maybe I should've hated him. I couldn't, not anymore. His behavior after becoming an elemental shapeshifter had made me question whether our relationship had ever been real, and at last I knew the truth. He had cared for me.

Calder glanced at Nevan and managed a rueful laugh. "Hey, I'm glad you broke my neck. I deserved it."

"Yes," Nevan said, tall and stiff, his face unreadable, "at the time, you did."

"Take care of her," Calder said. "She deserves to be happy—and loved."

Nevan T's gaze veered to me, branding me with its intensity, and then he returned his focus to Calder. "As long as I live, Lindsey will never want for love."

Calder let his hand fall away from my cheek and settle atop our linked hands on his chest. "Tell Travis I'm sorry. I may not have shown it, but I was always grateful to have him for a big brother."

"I'll tell him."

"One more thing before I…go." He hesitated. "Don't feel sorry for me. Doesn't matter what happens to me now, all I care about is that you stop blaming yourself for what happened to me. I did this to myself. I wanted you, and that need turned into an obsession, to the point I was willing to kill you to keep you."

"The forging changed you, I know."

He sighed, his eyes closing briefly. "The seed was there before I died and turned into something else. Travis knows what I mean. He probably thinks he'll become like me, but tell him not to worry. He's stronger than I ever was, and a better man."

I couldn't speak. Had no idea what to say.

"Be happy, Lindsey," Calder said, "and have a good life. That's the only salvation I need."

I squeezed my eyes shut, but the tears leaked out anyway. My heart hurt for what we'd once had, but I'd done my grieving years ago. This was closure, for both of us.

His chest stopped rising and falling under our hands. His hands went limp around mine.

My eyes popped open, and I stared at the lifeless face of a dead man.

"Look," Max said.

I followed his gaze to a spot behind the group of wind-beings.

There, Calder stood tall and straight, wearing jeans and a T-shirt with cowboy boots covering his feet. His mouth spread into the boyish grin I remembered so well.

And then he was gone.

I jumped up. "Does that mean he's okay? His soul moved on to a good place?"

The female wind-being smiled with beatific grace. "You succeeded. The soul of Calder Blackwell has been redeemed and welcomed into eternal peace."

"Oh thank God." I slumped, swaying a little.

Nevan rushed to bolster me with his body, one strong arm around my shoulders.

The body on the floor twitched.

I startled, sidling closer to Nevan. "What was that?"

The wind-being floated closer to the body, regarding it with detached interest. "The other essences will attempt to revive the body."

Maybe saving Calder had made me mushy, but I had the sudden to impulse redeem a couple more souls. "Can I save them too? Nevan said Skeiron and Notus used to be good men."

"Indeed they were," the wind-being said, her spooky eyes zeroing in on me. "But they squandered that goodness of their own volition. They sought power in order to subjugate others, to enforce their own wills rather than serving their people justly. Calder Blackwell became corrupted by his forging, which amplified preexisting weakness. These two—" She gestured at the body. "—were not forged, but born as elementals. They had no excuse for their greed and lust for power."

I tilted my head up to meet Nevan's gaze. "I'm sorry."

"Don't be, love." His gaze darted to the body. "They sealed their own fates."

To the wind-being, I said, "Do what you have to do. Their powers should be locked up forever, where they can't do any harm to anyone."

"They shall be." She clasped her hands before her and lowered her head. "Let it be done."

Her airy friends gathered around the body, all bowing their hands and clasping their hands as she had done. Wind whipped around them, growing and roiling, lashing the women's hair around their faces and tearing at the dead sorcerer's clothing.

As the gale picked up speed, Nevan and I backed away to the doorway, and Max joined us there.

The sorcerer's robe billowed and flapped. The wind latched onto the fabric, ripping it asunder, but a dense fog rushed in to conceal the sight of his exposed flesh. Soon, the gale and the fog encompassed the wind-beings.

A gust ripped through the entire temple.

The wind snuffed out in a puff of fog, the clouds dissipating swiftly.

Both the body and the wind-beings were gone.

We lingered in the temple for a moment, silent and awestruck. What we'd experienced here seemed like a weird dream, but none of us could awaken from it. Finally, we exchanged uncertain glances and turned to leave.

The female wind-being popped up in front of us.

She looked at Nevan. "You wish to know why you were turned away the first time you came to us."

Nevan didn't move or blink, but arm around me tightened a fraction.

"You were worthy then," the wind-being said. "Shortly before you came to this temple, an oracle visited us. He foresaw your visit to the temple, as well as your bond with the Janusite and that you would need your powers to aid and protect her. We rejected your request for this reason and this reason alone. You have never been deemed unworthy in our eyes."

Though I wanted to know more about Nevan's previous visit to the temple, I had the feeling the wind-being wouldn't stick around much longer. So I asked the question that had plagued me for weeks.

"Why was I chosen to be the Janusite?"

Her lips formed a faint smile. "You must ask Janus."

She blinked out amid a puff of air.

I laid a hand on Nevan's chest. "What was she talking about? Why did you come here the first time?"

"When I visited this place before," he said, "I had already realized Skeiron would become a tyrant like Notus. And I saw but one way to be free of the madness."

My fingers crooked against his skin. "What way?"

"To be stripped of my powers and made human."

"Oh." I bit my lip. "You don't want that anymore?"

He tugged me closer, dipping his head to nuzzle my nose. "I don't care if I'm human or elemental, as long as I can be with you."

"I don't care which you are either. I want you, not your powers."

"And I want you, Lindsey, not your powers." He smirked, his eyes glittering with humor. "Though perhaps it's best I keep my powers for the time being, considering how much trouble you get into."

Max chuckled. "She is a challenging mistress."

I glanced at the spot where the sorcerer had died, and where Calder had been freed from damnation. "Ceara might still be out there."

"Better get home, then," Max said, "and make sure the bloody woman is gone for good."

We marched out the temple doors, headed back to our friends.

Chapter Twenty-Nine

THE CLEARING STOOD EMPTY AND DARK, THE MOON HAVING SET IN preparation for sunrise. The first rays of dawn cast a meager light on the vicinity. I disengaged from Nevan, and the loss of his heat enhanced the chill of the predawn air, triggering a flurry of goose bumps. The chill stemmed from more than the air temperature, though. It came from deep inside me too, from a primal part of me that recognized the inherent wrongness of the scene around me.

"Where are they?" I asked, turning in a circle, squinting into the gloom.

Nevan scanned the area in full warrior mode, his body taut, his gaze narrowed and sharp, his mouth compressed.

Max, his body as taut and ready for battle as Nevan's, flexed his fingers and released a small burst of flames from the tips.

Kind of like cocking a gun, I supposed. I'd never seen him do that before, but then, I'd known him for barely a day. It felt like so much longer.

Nevan's gaze locked onto something on the ground, near the clearing's edge. He stalked toward the object, and I trailed behind him with unease shivering down my nerves.

This was wrong, all wrong.

He bent to nab the object. The sword glistened in the ever-increasing glow of sunrise, its blade cast in the pink and yellow shades of the burgeoning dawn.

"You gave that to Travis for safekeeping," I said. "He wouldn't ditch it."

"Here!" Max called from our left.

We hurried to him, arriving as Max rose and showed us the object seated in his palm.

He held my derringer.

Max ducked down to dive his hand into the grass. When he straightened, his fingers were damp with a dark liquid. With a shake of his hand and a puff of fire, he cleansed the stain from his skin.

"Blood," he said.

Nevan latched a protective arm around my waist. "Someone has attacked our friends. We must find them at once."

I snatched the gun from Max's hand. "It's Ceara, it has to be."

"I agree," Nevan said.

A storm of cracking and rustling erupted in the forest ahead of us.

Nevan removed his arm from my waist and gripped his sword in both hands, raised before him.

Max flexed his fingers again and emitted tiny flames, each like the pilot light on a gas stove, from their tips.

I checked the derringer's chambers, finding a fresh round snug inside each barrel. As the racket drew nearer and nearer, louder and louder, I raised the gun and sighted in on the vicinity of the noises.

Tris and Ennea barreled out of the forest, stumbling to a halt a few feet from us. Ennea grasped her belly with both hands and struggled to catch her breath, her face flushed from exertion. Tris, his cheeks just as red, bent to slap his palms on his thighs as he gasped for air and held up one finger in the universal gesture for *wait a damn minute, please.*

Nevan couldn't wait, evidently. He demanded, "Where is Travis?"

Hold up. Why were they breathless from running?

"Why didn't you zip here?" I asked. "Didn't think elementals ever sprinted."

"More like stampeding," Tris said, still breathing hard. He rose from his bent posture, though his shoulders stayed slumped. "Couldn't travel the usual way. She did something to us."

"She?" A shiver raced down my spine. "Ceara found you."

"Yeah, and that broad is pissed." Tris shoved a shaking hand through his red hair. "She hit us with some kinda spell, and wham, we couldn't do any magic. Had to skedaddle the mortal way. Totally humiliating."

"But how..." I looked to Nevan. "Her powers came from the sorcerer. Shouldn't they have gone bye-bye when he bit the dust?"

"Yes, they should have." Nevan lowered his sword to his side, the blade horizontal to the ground. "Ceara should be no more dangerous than a mortal."

"Then how—" A realization rushed through me. "The pendant she wears. The papyrus column amulet."

Nevan arched one brow. "Notus must have instilled his own magics within it, to enliven her stone body. The pendant connects them, which allowed her to absorb enough of his power to continue on and make use of his powers. We must vanquish her with an endued weapon."

Tris snorted. "Good luck, pal. The broad's wacko, threatened to wipe out all life in both worlds one by one to get back at Lindsey."

"Me?" I lodged one hand on my hip. "What'd I do that nobody else did?"

Nevan canted his head at me. "The sorcerer snapped her neck and took you away with him. He made it clear to her he always wanted you, above all others."

"Oh great. This is a supernatural cat fight." I bent my arm, the derringer aimed at the sky. "Fine. She wants to throw down with me, she'll get her wish."

Tris flapped his head wildly. "You can't do that. She'll take away your powers too."

Nevan puffed up, but not out of self-pride. He moved a touch closer to me and said, "Lindsey is the most powerful being in either world. More than that, she is the most intelligent and resourceful being I've ever met."

Wow. I loved it when he waxed complimentary about me.

"Thanks, honey," I said, patting the bulging bicep of his sword arm. I asked Tris, "Where did you guys go? And why?"

Both leprechauns looked sheepish, but Ennea spoke. "That broad tricked us. We heard you shouting for us, and we ran to help. Turned out it was Ceara doing a bang-up imitation."

Tris gave a sour laugh. "She oughta be doing Vegas, with impersonation skills like that."

"I'm sorry, Lindsey," Ennea said, her shoulders deflating and caving in toward her chest. "Ceara took Travis."

"Took him?" I said. "Where?"

She shrugged.

The five of us exchanged glances, none of us sure what to do next.

We got our answer anyway.

"Help me!" a male voice cried from further into the woods. "Lindsey! Help me, please, she's crazy."

The voice mimicked Travis's drawl and twang.

Ennea made a bewildered face. "Does the broad think we're so stupid we'll fall for the same trick again?"

"No," I said. "She doesn't care. She's taunting me."

Tris threw his hands up. "What the hell do we do?"

Nevan's watchful gaze, trained on me during this whole conversation, flared wide and then narrowed into slits. "No, Lindsey."

"Yes, Nevan." I closed my hand around his, the one gripping the sword. "It's the only way and you know it."

He sighed, his body deflating for a moment before he went taut and erect again, ever the ancient warrior.

"Uh, excuse me," Tris said. "What did we just decide?"

I answered. "We're sneaking up on the evil bitch, with me as bait."

CHAPTER THIRTY

I TRACKED THE FALSE TRAVIS VOICE THROUGH THE WOODS UNTIL I reached a small waterfall that poured its waters into a small—but deep, judging from its color—pool at its base. The trees closed in around the pool and the cliff that formed the waterfall, leaving a narrow path around the periphery.

Nevan and Max prowled the forest behind me, somewhere, though I could neither see nor hear them. Ennea and Tris had gone back to her magic lab, against their complaints they didn't want to leave us. Without magic, they were too vulnerable.

Despite having two stealthy and powerful men as backup, I felt nothing close to secure. Ceara could've been hiding anywhere.

"Here I am," I called out. "Come and get me, you lifeless hunk of rock. I brought my hammer and chisel."

"Your attempts to goad me are wasted."

Ceara's smooth voice sounded behind me.

I turned around, poising my finger over the derringer's trigger, though I kept the gun aimed at the ground.

She stood a few feet away, at the pool's edge—with Travis.

He was on his knees, clothes and hair unkempt, dirt smudged on his face. Blood dribbled down from his scalp. He seemed unable to move, as if an invisible force bound him.

"Do not worry," Ceara said in her saccharine voice, "he will survive his current wounds. Whether he survives beyond this depends on you."

"What do you want, Ceara?"

She smiled with feral hunger. "Your powers, of course."

"Can't give them to you even if I wanted to. No idea how to do it."

"You will discover a way, given the proper motivation." She conjured a knife in her hand, turning it this way and that so its wide and long blade glinted in the light of the newly woken sun. "Do it, or I will end this mortal's life."

She held the blade to Travis's throat.

He made a disgusted face. "Don't do it, Lindsey."

I couldn't move, my thoughts a tangle of conflicting needs. I had to stop Ceara. I had to protect the people I cared about. I needed to end this now, with Ceara's destruction. But I couldn't let Travis die because of me.

"Do you bother to think," Ceara said, caressing Travis's throat with the blade, "how many have died in your name? Three young women, whose only crime was their resemblance to you. The man you were to wed, who became a monster because he longed to be with you forever. Two kings. And how many sylph soldiers, in the battle to dethrone Skeiron?"

I realized what she was doing, but that didn't lessen the blow of hearing the death toll recounted aloud.

Ceara smiled again, with a vicious edge to it. "Nevan almost lost his eternal soul because of you."

No, he'd almost died because her magical mashup of a boyfriend thought it would be fun to torture Nevan. And Ceara had helped the sorcerer do it. She wanted to shame me into giving up, but I'd had enough of this bullshit.

"Nice try," I said, "but I'm canceling my reservation at the guilt trip hotel."

I swung the derringer up and pulled the trigger.

The shot bounced off her.

Dammit. She had a personal ward, like the sorcerer.

And I had one bullet left.

Ceara's smile twisted into a nasty grin. She yanked Travis's head back and slashed the knife across his throat. Blood streamed from the wound as she let go of him, and his body crumpled, his head slumping over the pool's edge, his hair touching the water.

"No!"

I barreled toward Ceara, slamming into the wards that encased her, throwing both of us to the ground. The wards shoved me away, but I sprang forward to pin her to the ground. I pounded my fists on the barrier, and shockwaves of white magic erupted through the wards. Blue sparks exploded from my hands, punching into the wards like glittering steel spikes.

Ceara screamed, thrashing to get me off her.

I punched and punched and punched, hitting the wards over her chest, her stomach, and landing a wicked hit directly in her face.

The wards fractured.

Ceara shrieked, part anger and part terror. She lashed out with one foot, punting me in the knee. She slugged me in the shoulder, and the derringer popped out of my hand, flying through the air to splash down in the pool, sinking into the dark depths.

I punched her in the gut. "You fucking bitch!"

The breath exploded out of her.

"Lindsey!" Nevan's voice roared from the edge of the woods.

He was banging his fist and his sword on the solid wall of another ward.

Ceara hauled in a wheezing breath.

No time to think. I flung up one hand and conjured Nevan's sword.

My arm shook from the weight of it, but adrenaline gave me more strength than I'd known I could summon. I rose onto my knees, aimed the sword straight down, and drove it into Ceara's chest.

Blood coated her chest and soaked through her clothing. She let out a choked gasp and went limp, her eyes staring up but seeing nothing. She would never see anything again.

I wrenched the sword free of her flesh, wedged its tip on the ground, and heaved myself to my feet.

Her body hardened, her skin growing paler and smoother, her posture locked in the final moment of horrific awareness that she was dying.

My legs weak, I braced my body with the sword.

Ceara's body metamorphosed into stone, then crumbled into dust.

The wards crashed down, and Nevan and Max bolted toward me.

I dropped the sword and ran to Travis, falling to my knees beside him. His eyes were closed, his body limp. One hand dangled over the pool's edge, and the blood accumulated under his head oozed over the edge to drip onto the water. The droplets spread out in the water, carried away by the spinning current. I laid a hand on his back but detected no sign of life.

My eyes stung. I sucked in a breath through my nose, not wanting to cry. Not here, not now. We'd won the battle, saved the worlds. We couldn't lose one of our own. Dammit, this shouldn't have been happening.

Nevan knelt beside me, his arm coming around me.

"We have to save him," I said. "Must be a vortex around here somewhere, we have to find Tris—"

"No, love, it's too late." Nevan pulled me close, burying my face against his neck. "There are no healing vortexes on this side of the falls."

Over his shoulder, I glimpsed Max a few feet away. He watched us, lines tightening at the corners of his mouth and eyes. The flames at his fingertips had snuffed out.

Tris and Ennea appeared just behind him, at either side.

When their eyes fell on Travis, Ennea bit down on her lip and Tris scrunched his mouth.

"But we can take him through the portal," I said, my voice hitching and rising to a higher pitch. "Tris can heal him."

Nevan cradled the back of my head with his hand, murmuring to me with his cheek against mine. "He is gone, it's too late."

"But—"

"Shh." He kissed my temple. "You can't feel it, but the rest of us can. Ceara coated the blade that cut his throat with poisoned magic. Nothing can bring him back. I'm sorry, my love, I would do anything to spare you pain but there is nothing I can do. Nothing anyone can do."

Max cleared his throat. "Not entirely true."

I jerked my head up. "What? There's a way?"

The incubus aimed his steady gaze at the sylph, but spoke to me. "There is one way."

Nevan's jaw hardened, a muscle ticking there. "No."

I glanced from Nevan to Max and back again. "You have to tell me."

"Travis wouldn't want it," Nevan said gently. "He saw what became of his brother."

A shiver of understanding whispered over my skin. I scuttled backward on my knees, never taking my eyes off of Nevan. "You're talking about the forging."

"Yes." He ran a hand over his mouth. "But we cannot put him through it. I have never and will never forge another, you know this and you know why."

"But you and Max came through it fine."

Nevan stared at the swirling pool for a moment, his eyes half closed. When he faced me again, his eyes had taken on a haunted look. "I survived the forging with my sanity intact, but only by a hair. This is nothing I would inflict on another, no matter the situation."

"You wouldn't do it to save me."

His features hardened into a steely resolve. "No."

Though his answer should've warned me off this path, I couldn't accept it. Refused to believe it. Desperation obliterated reason, and all I could see was Travis lying dead on the ground in a pool of his own blood, murdered by an evil mirror image of my lover's dead wife.

If Max and Nevan could survive the forging intact…

My familiar told me he'd forged somebody once before.

He'd also sworn he would never do it again.

If I ordered him to do it…

Nevan grabbed my hands. "Do not do this, Lindsey."

"Calder was weak, Travis is strong. He can come through it okay."

"You can't know what will happen. The risk is too great. I will not do it."

Max strode toward us, crouching alongside me. "I will do it."

Nevan squinted at Max, forcing words out between his gritted teeth. "Don't encourage her. She is grieving and has no conception of what she asks."

"I know what's involved," Max said, his voice calm but his face pinched. "And I understand the consequences. If Lindsey wants this, I will do it."

"You would forge another without his consent?" Nevan sat back on his heels, his hands slipping free of mine. "I will not allow it."

My gaze wandered over the pool, the falls cascading into it, the foaming water that swirled in eddies. Nevan had lain beside a pool once, ages ago, dying and desperate to live. Notus had offered him a new life, but left out the details of becoming an immortal and an elemental. This world, the Unseen, was harsh and strange and unforgiving. Magic lurked in every nook and cranny of this realm, some of it benign, some deadly. How difficult would it be for Travis to learn the ins and outs of the Unseen?

I'd had six weeks to adjust, and I still didn't understand everything. Travis would be hindered by the forging, by a kind of change I couldn't fathom, a change that would alter him from the inside out and mold him into a different man.

Not a man. A salamander. An incubus.

Tears flowed down my cheeks, searing my eyes and moistening my skin. They dripped off my chin onto my hands. Could I really do this to another person? Without his permission? What gave me the right? Nevan swore he wouldn't even do it to spare my life, yet I was willing to force it on Travis, my oldest friend, my ally in these crazy supernatural battles, a hero in his own right. And I would destroy him, in hopes he'd be reconstituted into something I might recognize.

Oh God, what was I doing?

Sobs burst out of me, wracking my body. I flung my arms around myself, rocking as I wept and wept.

Nevan dragged me into his arms, frisking his hands up and down my back, murmuring wordlessly.

"Time is short," Max said. "If he's dead too long, even the forging won't bring him back."

My head on Nevan's shoulder, I waited a few more seconds until the sobbing faded. Then I swallowed, sniffed, and told Max, "We can't do this. It isn't right. We may have won the battle, but Ceara gets her revenge on me. She took away someone I care about."

Nevan stroked my hair, combing his fingers through the locks. "She has not won. Travis died for a good cause, for the safety of two worlds."

"I wish that were true." Pushing away from Nevan, I mopped my eyes dry with my shirt. "But he was held captive, couldn't move or fight. She tried to convince me all the deaths that have happened since we met are my fault. I denied it, but in this case she was right. Travis got lured into Ceara's trap because of me, and he died because of me. The blame for this death is squarely on my conscience."

"It was not your doing."

"Doesn't matter." I got to my feet, every muscle aching, my heart aching. "Travis would never have gotten involved in any of this insanity if he hadn't followed me. He was always trying to protect me. His death is my fault, and I have to live with that."

Nevan rose but didn't touch me.

Max stood too, glancing at Nevan. "You should take her away from here."

I balked. "We can't leave Travis lying there."

"Of course not," Max said. "I'll bring him back to the mortal world. You have my word."

"Thank you." Considering he owed me a life debt, my gratitude couldn't enact any kind of debt on my part. It only scratched the surface of the monumental debt he owed me. To Tris and Ennea, I said, "I appreciate your help. You're my allies and my friends, so if you need anything, all you have to do is ask. Okay?"

"Goes both ways," Tris said. "Like you said, we're friends."

Ennea nodded. "We're Team Lindsey."

I couldn't muster a smile. "See you later. Be safe."

They left in a blink.

At the instant Nevan whisked me away, my eyes met Max's and something flickered on his face. Regret? Determination? Dread? I had no time to puzzle it out before Nevan took me away.

We landed at our usual portal, the small pond in front of a burbling boulder. He moved his hand toward the water splashing up out of the rock, about to open the portal for us.

He froze, an odd look on his face.

"What is it?" I asked.

Muttering a curse in his ancient language, he threw an arm around me and teleported us back to the falls where we'd left Max. We wound up on the other side of the water from Max, where he stood beside Travis's body.

Max chanted in a language I'd never heard before, his voice infused with a rumbling intensity, and the sound of it skittered a cold prickling down my spine. This was a forbidden language, something inside me whispered. Where the idea had come from, I had no clue, yet I recognized the truth of it. No mere mortal was meant to hear the tongue Max spoke.

He raised his hands, palms out. Glowing, shimmering orbs sparked to life inside the forest—fairy lights, I recognized—and swarmed out to surround Max and Travis, sheathing them both in a cloak of glittering brilliance. The illumination intensified into a blinding whiteness.

I flung up an arm to shield my eyes. Energy crackled over my skin, the backwash of whatever Max was doing.

Nevan zipped to the other side of the pool. He tried to approach the mass of energy that engulfed Max and Travis, but every time he got close he flinched away. Nevan gave up and returned to my side.

"We should go," he said. "You do not want to see this."

"He's forging Travis, isn't he?"

"Yes."

When he reached for me, to take me away again, I shrugged away from his hands. "I'm staying. This is my fault, I have to see it through."

"Max decided to do this. You told him not to, which means it is not your fault."

"Don't you get it?" I twisted the hem of my shirt in my hands. "Max owes me his life. He thinks this is how he can repay me."

Someone screamed.

Not Max, I sensed that much. No, someone else. I shut my eyes, afraid to breathe or move.

Travis was screaming, from an agony I could never comprehend, as the forging tore him apart and remade him.

I forced my eyes open, focusing on Nevan and only Nevan. "Tell me what it's like, the forging."

He covered his face with his hands as the screaming went on and on.

"Tell me," I said, seizing his hands to tear them away from his face. I felt sick, I didn't want to know, but I had to know. "Please, Nevan."

His eyes shut, he told me. "The forging will rend his limbs, his mind, every particle of his body and soul, crushing and melting them. A power beyond imagining will reshape his form, and he will be born anew through the scalding agony. He might wish for death with his last coherent thought, before the pain and fire consume everything that made him human."

"Everything?"

"Only his soul and his memories will remain."

I collapsed to my knees, unable to process the information, unable to look at anything except the boiling, amorphous mass of supernatural energy on the other side of the pool.

The screaming cut off.

Nevan hauled me to my feet, one arm around me, ready to spirit me away.

The cloud of energy dissipated, revealing Max hunched beside a naked man who lay facedown in the dirt. Smoke, or maybe steam, wisped up from the coppery-skinned figure.

I gulped but couldn't dislodge the lump in my throat. My heart raced, my pulse thundering in my ears.

Travis lifted his head. His gaze zeroed in on me.

A soul-deep anguish wrenched my gut. His eyes had become burning red coals.

Max bent to lay a hand on Travis's shoulder, and they vanished.

CHAPTER THIRTY-ONE

In the days following the longest day of my life, the day we defeated the sorcerer, we did our best to tighten up the loose threads dangling in the wake of the sorcerer's vendetta. Three young women had died. Their families needed answers and closure, but we couldn't exactly tell them a sorcerer with multiple personalities had murdered their loved ones in order to torment me. With the sheriff missing, the undersheriff took over the investigation—and he knew nothing about the Unseen.

Although Nevan and I both hated it, we'd agreed he must enchant the acting sheriff and the medical examiner to convince them only one woman's body had been found behind the rock shop. Since Travis had kept the other two bodies under wraps, no one questioned the story the American girl had died of dehydration after getting lost in the woods.

Nevan had taken the other bodies back to the women's respective home countries. No one knew they'd wound up in Michigan, and their deaths were ruled accidental, due to dehydration.

We needed to explain Travis's disappearance too. Nevan and Max worked together to concoct a car accident that killed him and, thanks to a fiery explosion courtesy of Max, his body had been burned to ash. There had been a funeral, and I had cried as if Travis was actually dead.

Not dead, but gone. I hadn't seen him since his forging, though Max turned up at least twice a day every day to reassure me Travis was doing okay. The transition took time. That's what both Max and Nevan kept telling me.

We'd covered up everything. What a victory.

I felt sick every time I thought about it, but I understood we'd had no choice.

Seven days after the thwarted apocalypse, Tris waylaid me when I was getting out of my car in the shop's parking lot.

"You gotta take me over the boundary," he said. "Come on, Lindsey, I helped save the worlds twice. Don't I deserve a break?"

"We've been over this." I shut the car door, bracing my butt against it. "I have no idea if I can take anyone other than Nevan over the boundaries. I won't be responsible for your destruction."

"Your powers are way stronger now. Please?" His tone had turned wheedling. "If you're worried I'll rat on you about being the Janusite, I won't. You got my word."

"That's not what concerns me."

He raised his hands, palms together. "Please? I wanna meet a hot mortal chick, like Nevan did."

"A hot mortal chick?" I caught my lips between my teeth to stave off a laugh. "That's why you're so dead-set on crossing the boundary. To meet girls."

He shrugged.

"Tris, you're risking annihilation. You know, getting ripped apart molecule by molecule until nothing of you is left, except a thin cloud of atoms." I clapped my hands on his shoulders. "Why don't you find a nice elemental girl?"

The leprechaun made a whiny, groaning noise. "They're so boring. Even the busty little undine."

What could I say to that? The Unseen was far from boring in my estimation, but then I hadn't grown up over there. Maybe a compromise was the ticket.

"Tell you what," I said. "Let me practice my powers some more, and when I'm confident I can control them, I promise to take you over the boundary. Deal?"

"Awesome. It's a deal."

I could rest easy knowing I wasn't bound by magic to keep my word. When and if I felt confident in taking him over the boundary, I would do as I'd promised.

Tris left then, satisfied one day he might meet a hot mortal chick.

Although I'd absolved Nevan of his life debt to me, Max absolutely refused to me do the same for him. Three times I tried to do it anyway, and three times he absconded before I could finish. The next time I saw him, I ordered Max to stay put and tell me what his problem was. After grousing a bit, he sank into one of the chairs in the underground home I shared with Nevan and finally told me the truth.

"You may remember," he said, "I mentioned I forged someone once."

"Before Travis. Yeah, I remember."

He squirmed in the chair. "Her name was Aurelia. We had fallen in love before my forging, as humans, and a decade after my change I found her again. She was ill, dying from an incurable disease. I couldn't find a fae to heal her through a vortex, but I told her everything about me, about what I am. On her deathbed, she begged me to forge her so we could be together."

"What happened?" I asked.

"The forging was not kind to her." He leaned forward, elbows on his knees, and clutched his head in his hands. "It happened gradually, over many centuries. She went insane little by little, became a wild thing addicted to the sexual energies of any male she encountered. Many of her lovers were not willing. She used her powers to force them into wanting her, and many of them died from her attentions. She took more than she needed to survive, more than any being could give."

Jesus. I wanted to comfort him, but I had the feeling he wouldn't have accepted it. Instead, I asked, "What happened to her?"

He looked up at me through his spread fingers. "I bargained with the sorcerer to end her life. I became his slave to stop her. Three young women have died, and I am partly to blame for that."

"Max…" Nothing I might say seemed appropriate, so I let my words trail off.

"Don't you see?" he said. "I deserve to be enslaved. At least you're a compassionate mistress. Please let me keep this debt to you."

I relented then, unable to force him to relinquish something that made him feel he'd atoned in some measure for the sins he believed he'd committed. Later, when I understood him better, I could convince him to give up the debt. The fact he'd said "please," here in the Unseen realm, proved to me this was the right course.

"The debt stands," I said. "For the time being."

He rose shakily and teleported away.

On the tenth day, I was lounging in the home Nevan and I shared on my day off. With Ennea's help, Nevan had installed a TV that somehow received satellite signals from the mortal realm, letting me watch all my favorite shows in the secluded comfort of our underground lair. Nevan was spending a lot of time with the tribunal, this time around trying to mend the badly torn fences between king and traitorous tribunal. The old members had resigned, replaced by new members chosen for their diverse backgrounds. One was a high-ranking soldier in Nevan's army, another was a metalsmith, a third was an elder of the kingdom, and the fourth hailed from a family of sylph witches.

Yep, the sylphs had witches too.

Today I reclined on the red sofa Max had given me, my gaze aimed at the TV but not really seeing anything on the screen. When I glanced at the two clocks on the wall—an addition I'd brought to our home, with one clock for mortal time and a second for elemental time—they told me Nevan had left his latest tribunal meeting nearly three hours ago. Nevan had balked at the presence of clocks, but he'd finally accepted I'd never be cool with not knowing the time. The dual faces ensured I wouldn't be late to work.

And I'd know exactly how long Nevan had been gone.

The aftermath of the sorcerer's plot had lasting effects. I couldn't help getting a little anxious whenever Nevan met with the tribunal, even knowing it was a new and improved group. Every day, I worried a little less—but I didn't know if I'd ever stop worrying. About Nevan. About being the Janusite. About Travis.

The last time I'd seen him, seconds after the forging, he'd looked so…alien.

Why wouldn't Max give me details about Travis's condition? I deserved to know. For that matter, why wouldn't Nevan? He'd seen Travis since the forging.

I shut off the TV. No relaxation for me.

Pushing up off the cushy sofa, I began to pace the room with my hands linked behind my back and my gaze directed at the floor. Thoughts bounced around in my mind, a mishmash of fears that set acid to churning in my stomach.

"You're ruining my hard work again."

I yelped at the sound of Nevan's voice.

He'd materialized no more than an arm's length away, watching me with an amused little smile.

I poked him in the chest. "You scared the crap out of me."

"How could I do that," he said, moving closer, "when you can sense my approach?"

"Kind of distracted at the moment. Not sensing much of anything."

"Mm, yes, I can see how tense you are." He slid his hands down my arms, following them to my hands behind my back. Those large, muscular hands of his settled over mine, and he drew me snug against his body. "And you are ruining my hard work. I spent so much time convincing you to relax and stop restraining your emotions. But you've reverted."

"Not totally." I looped my arms around his neck, and his hands draped over my buttocks. "I won't be anxious if you vanish our clothes."

"Ah, darlin', I'd love to but not yet." He lifted me with his palms on my ass, raising me until our eyes were level. "What are you worrying about today?"

"You were gone an awfully long time."

"I had an errand to run after the tribunal meeting."

"Errand? Since when do you run errands?"

He skimmed one hand up my back and around to my breast, cupping it in his hot palm. "I'll explain later. What else are you fretting over?"

"The old tribunal aided and abetted the sorcerer."

"The newly convened tribunal has no connection to the old one. From now on, the tribunal will be restricted to its original function of mediating disputes and will stay out of the business of ruling the kingdom."

"Sure you can trust them?"

"Positive." He pecked a kiss on forehead. "You, my love, should know better than anyone how trustworthy the new tribunal is. You employed your lie detection spell on them, after all."

"Hmph." I threaded my fingers through his hair absently. "Just means they didn't lie when I interviewed them."

"Your paranoia is endearing but unnecessary." He scrutinized me for a moment, then asked, "What else?"

Even if I could've lied convincingly to him, I didn't want to deceive Nevan. "Can't stop thinking about Travis."

"He is doing well. As well as can be expected."

"Not super comforting." I wriggled out of his arms. "I want to see Travis."

Nevan groaned, a sound of frustration I knew all too well.

I planted my hands on my hips. "You really want to *Lindsey* me, don't you?"

"But I've learned it will do no good." Nevan scratched his jaw. "You are the most stubborn being I've ever met."

"And you're the king of evasion." I nailed him with my hardest stare. "What aren't you telling me?"

He placed his hands on my arms, frisking them up and down. "Leave it alone, please."

"You said the P-word. This must be really bad news you're trying your damnedest not to tell me."

Nevan glided his hands up to my shoulders. "You cannot see Travis, because he has expressly forbidden it."

Taken aback, I could do nothing except make huffy, gasping sounds. When I found my voice again, I managed only to stammer. "I—wha—that—no."

"It's true."

"He wouldn't say that."

"You must understand." Nevan squeezed my shoulders gently, his eyes full of love and understanding. "The forging is a brutal process that doesn't end with the physical transformation. One must adjust to a new existence with new powers."

"I get that, but—"

"Lindsey, he has become an incubus." Nevan slanted his head to bring our gazes nearer to each other, and his voice took on a grave tone. "Travis is experiencing urges he cannot yet control. Max will teach him how to cope, but the adjustment will take time. For now, he must stay away from females—especially you."

When Max had told me what he was, I'd called him a sex demon. He'd scoffed at the demon part, but then he'd been born an incubus. Travis underwent a massive and agonizing transformation to become a completely different kind of being. The human version of him died, and he was reborn a salamander. An incubus. A being who thrived on sexual energy.

A being who needed sex to survive.

Max had flirted with me in the beginning, even making a minor attempt to seduce me away from Nevan. When I'd called him on it, he'd said seduction was an innate instinct for him. He couldn't help it. If he hadn't learned to control his urges...

My scalp prickled. Did I really want to find out what uncontrolled incubus urges looked like?

Nevan brushed hair from my face, tucking it behind my ear. "You understand, I can see it in your eyes."

"You said he can't see women, but especially not me."

"He is in love with you," Nevan said. "Travis admits he has not yet moved past his feelings for you, though he understands you don't love him in that way. But his incubus urges will have enhanced his physical reaction to you, and they might drive him to, ah..."

"You think he'd attack me?"

Nevan cradled my face in one hand. "That is his greatest fear at the moment. Give him time, and he will want to see you again."

I nodded, clamping my bottom lip between my teeth.

He pulled me into his arms.

After a moment of blissful intimacy, I propped my chin on his chest to gaze up at him. "You haven't told me about your errand."

"Later, when the time is right."

I let him lead me to the bed, knowing he would make love to me and banish all my worries with the exquisite pleasure of our joining. Afterward, my fears would resurface—but for this precious time with him, I would enjoy the bliss of forgetfulness.

He settled me onto the plush bed, our clothes suddenly gone, and pressed his warm, soft lips to my throat. I sighed my pleasure, my body melting. He kissed his way down my throat, tracing my collarbone to my ribs, dragging his mouth lower and lower until his hair tickled my breasts. Just as he shifted his head, opening his mouth to seal it over one nipple, I laid a staying hand on his cheek.

"What is it?" he asked, his brows adorably crinkled.

"I love you, with all of my heart and soul, and I never want to be without you."

His dark brows cinched tight, rising over the bridge of his nose. "I love you, Lindsey, you know this. What is it you truly want to say?"

"Do you remember the conversation we had right after Ceara showed up, before we knew she was working with the sorcerer? I wondered if you were tempted to go with her, to have an immortal queen."

Nevan levered up on straight arms, appraising me with a tight expression. "I told you, I have no wish to be with anyone but you."

"I'm not sure you've really thought about the consequences." I folded my arms over my breasts, oddly self-conscious all of a sudden. "You love me as much as I love you, and I know from experience how devastated

I'd be if something happened to you. I don't want to be the cause of your suffering."

He bent his arms, dipping his head to feather a kiss on my lips. "Nothing will happen to you. I will not allow it."

"But one day I will die. I'm a mortal, Nevan. You can't stop the natural course of life and death."

"We've had this discussion before." He dropped onto his side next to me, one hand spread over my belly. "I will take whatever time I have with you and be grateful for it. Believe me when I say I have watched many I cared for die, even immortals. We have no guarantees. I want my life to be with you, for as long as the fates allow."

I diverted my gaze to the ceiling, following the lines in the grain of the stone.

Nevan placed a hand on my cheek and turned my face toward him. "Do you believe me, love?"

"Yes. I believe you." Of course I did. He wouldn't lie about this, and he was right. An immortal could die. Death wasn't the exclusive domain of humans. "I'll take you for as long as I can have you."

His hand on my belly drifted lower, moving in circles over my womb. "There is a chance we've created a child."

Oh damn. With all the chaos surrounding the murders and Travis's disappearance, I'd forgotten to tell Nevan. "I'm not pregnant. I had my period last week, which means no little sylph on the way."

"You're certain?"

"Uh-huh." I slapped my fingers lightly on his chest. "I explained the menstrual cycle to you weeks ago, when you wanted to have sex and I said 'not tonight, I've got cramps.' You were going to pout all night if I hadn't explained."

He focused on his own hand drawing patterns on my belly.

I tapped his chin. "Are you disappointed?"

Though he stilled his hand, he kept gazing at my lower abdomen. "It's for the best, given the dangers involved in a mortal bearing a hybrid child. But I must admit, I looked forward to creating a new life with you."

"Me too."

His head came up, his swirling eyes incandescent in the gentle glow of the house lighting. "You wished to have a child with me?"

"Yes, you silly boots. I love you, and I would love to make a family with you."

For the first time since I'd known him—and, I suspected, the first time ever in his millennia-long existence—Nevan got choked up. Not the way I would, of course. Being a manly sylph-man, he pinched the bridge of his nose and squeezed his eyes shut, determined to stave off the tears glistening in them. He took a few stuttering breaths, his head down, then rubbed his eyes with the heel of his hand.

"Wow," I said, ruffling his hair. "Never seen you so emotional before."

His clear eyes met mine. "Never before have I envisioned a future of true happiness."

"I'm happy too." Laying a hand over his on my belly, I couldn't tear my gaze away from his, away from the depth of emotion sparkling in his eyes. I also couldn't stop myself from saying, "About this errand of yours…"

A glorious smile enlivened his face, lending him a younger and more innocent air, sweeping away the pain of past losses. "Perhaps this is the right time."

"For what?"

"You shall see." In the actual blink of an eye, he repositioned us with him on his back and me seated astride him. "Close your eyes."

"Why?"

"Because you adore and trust me."

I grinned. "Do I?"

"Yes." He gave my rump a playful slap. "Eyes closed, or I'll make you wait another day or two to find out what my errand entailed."

"Playing on my impatience. That's a dirty trick."

"You know full well how many dirty tricks I have at my disposal."

I closed my eyes, hands on my thighs.

He skated a hand up my inner thigh. "You may look."

My lids fluttered open, and I giggled. Seriously, I giggled. It was all his fault, because he held up a small jewelry box with its lid flipped up to reveal the diamond ring seated within the velvet interior.

He took hold of my left hand, raising it between us. "Lindsey Astrid Porter, my sweet and precious love, will you marry me?"

"Yes." I lunged down to shower kisses over his face. "Yes, yes, yes."

Nevan laughed. "I've never heard you say yes with such fervor except when I'm inside you."

Hands flat on his chest, I grinned down at him. "You will be in a minute."

"Indeed I will." He wagged the box at me. "Your finger, if you will."

Proffering my hand, the appropriate finger extended, I giggled some more as he slid the ring into place. He tossed the box aside. It hit the floor with a soft thunk.

A hard object prodded my belly.

I glanced down at his erection. "Ready to go, eh?"

"For you, always." He thrust a hand between my thighs, feeling the slickness there. "You seem ready as well, in record time."

"I got wet the second you asked me to close my eyes. I was expecting a sexy surprise, though." I rocked my hips as he stroked my sex, setting off a wave of liquid heat and burning need. "Oh, Nevan…oh yes."

His eyes had gone hooded, his breaths heavy. "Your sexy surprise is still to come. As are you."

I let my head fall back, riding his hand, gasping when his thumb found my rigid nub and rubbed it in vigorous strokes. One of his long fingers plunged inside me. I rose up on my knees, moaning and pumping my hips to make his finger thrust in and out of my depths. The pleasure of my climax hit me hard and fast, my body milking his finger like it never wanted to let him go, even as his thumb get rubbing. I doubled over, my hands on his chest and my fingers digging into his flesh as the spasms of my orgasm subsided.

Nevan withdrew his hand and gave me his most devilish smile. "Your move, my love."

"Which of my moves do you want this time?"

He opened his mouth, but I silenced him with a finger on his lips. "Never mind. I'll surprise you."

I took hold of his shaft, positioning it with the head at my opening, and impaled myself on his engorged length. He hissed out a breath and secured my hips with his hands. I clapped my palms on his chest, bent forward with my breasts dangling above him, and began to move. The delicious sensation of his hardness gliding through my slick, inflamed sex had me moaning again and grinding my body into his, craving the deepest connection imaginable.

He surged his head up to capture my nipple and suckle it.

Pure ecstasy. Hot and molten and firing down every nerve.

"Oh, Nevan." I bent lower to grant him better access to my breast and moaned yet again as he took the entire areola and nipple into his greedy mouth. His tongue laved the rigid tip, his teeth nipped at my flesh. "Oh God, yes. I love the way you feel inside me, I love you so much."

Poof. I lay on my back with Nevan stretched atop my body, his weight a wonderful pressure as he thrust deep and slow, over and over, his shaft gliding out and driving back inside me until I was writhing under him, shoving my fingers into his hair, ravishing his mouth with a kiss of mind-altering passion. Our tongues lashed each other, our bodies moved together, our souls merged.

I locked my legs around him.

"Lindsey," he growled into my ear, thrusting harder and faster, "I love you more than life."

He pounded into me, bouncing us both on the bed, his knees wedged into the mattress to give him incredible leverage. I came again, screaming with the abandon of a woman being loved by the only man I ever wanted to love. My fiancé. My soul mate. My Nevan.

With a feral cry, he succumbed to his own release, his shaft pulsing inside me. After two more powerful thrusts, he collapsed on top of me, spent.

I laced my fingers through his hair, his head on my chest. "No rude unleashing of sperm this time, hey?"

"Did you want me to?"

"Not right now. We need to understand what an elemental-human pregnancy means for us before we go that route." I kissed the top of his head. "We'll find a way, though. After all, we are two pigheaded people."

"That we are." He rolled off me, tucking me against his side with one arm around my shoulders. "We've earned a good night's sleep."

"Mm, yes." I cuddled into him, one arm across his body. "I'd love to sleep with my fiancé."

There, ensconced in his arms, I realized a truth I'd doubted since the moment I met Nevan. We belonged together. Not as the Janusite and her protector, but as Lindsey and Nevan. I belonged with him, and he belonged with me.

I couldn't wait to marry him.

CHAPTER THIRTY-TWO

A FEW DAYS LATER, NEVAN STOPPED BY THE SHOP DURING MY SHIFT. HE was dressed in his human-friendly attire and had altered his appearance into a mortalesque version of his true self, as he always did when consorting with humans in the mortal realm. Despite his toned-down body and his human eyes, he took my breath away.

I trotted out from behind the counter, seized his hands, and bobbed up on my tiptoes to kiss him. "Hi, honey."

He smiled. "Hello, darlin'."

We strolled hand in hand down the nearest row of wooden bins, each filled to the brim with various types of rocks. At the bin of moonstone, Nevan stopped us.

He picked up a polished rock. "Do you recall what this stone signifies?"

During our early acquaintance, he'd told me the answer. "Love and passion."

"I should make you a necklace of these," he said, rotating the stone in his palm, "to remind you of how much I adore and desire you."

"Don't need a rock for that. Speaking of rocks…" I dug in my pocket, pulling out the soul stone. "Been meaning to ask you. This thing seems to have stopped working."

He plucked it from my fingers. "Because you purged it when you restored my soul. I can recharge the stone, if you like."

"Not necessary." I leaned into his side, nestling my head against his shoulder. "Got my own way into our house, and I don't need a stone to remind me we belong together."

Nevan hooked his arm around my waist. "Neither do I."

We lingered there, relishing the comfort of each other, for several minutes. Tourists wandered by, ignoring us. Stan caught sight of us, but he only smiled and rolled his eyes. We'd told everyone about our engagement, and the planning had begun for our wedding. Yep, we were going to have a real, mortal-style wedding. My mom insisted on it.

She'd threatened to shoot us, actually, if we denied her the privilege of harassing her only daughter and her future son-in-law about cakes and napkins and table settings.

The guest list would be limited, since Nevan wanted to recite his vows while in his native form. I concurred with that decision. I'd met and fallen in love with him as a sylph, and I was proud to marry my half-naked, bronze-skinned, swirling-eyed king from the Unseen realm.

"I talked to my mom this morning," I said. "There's a bit of a hitch in your let's-get-married-quick plan. My mom really wants to spend the week before the wedding with us, getting the final prep done. But Ash can't get off school until Thanksgiving break."

"And that would be when?"

"Late November." I tilted my head back to peek up at him. "Can you wait two months?"

"Your brother must be here, and I wouldn't wish to disappoint your mother. Of course we will wait." He gave me a quick squeeze and winked. "As long as I don't have to wait until our wedding night to make love to you again."

"Oh God no. I couldn't possibly wait that long."

"Glad to hear it." The playful gleam faded from his eyes, and he stepped back to face me, holding my hands in his. "I did interrupt your work day for a reason."

"What's that?"

"Travis wants to see you."

Something like eager dread rippled through me. I wanted to see him, but it had been only a couple weeks since his forging. "Are you sure he's ready?"

"Max assures me Travis can handle a brief meeting." Nevan stroked his hand over mine, warming my skin. "Both I and your familiar will be present in case of…mishaps. You can deliver your message from Calder without undue risk."

A sylph and a salamander as my guardians. No girl could've asked for more.

I glanced at the clock on the wall, above the checkout counter. "It's almost my lunch break. Let's see if Stan minds me leaving a little early."

Nevan trailed me back to the counter, waiting there while I ducked into Stan's office to inform him of my early departure for lunch. He grunted and shrugged, his way of saying it was A-okay with him.

When I returned to Nevan, the shop was vacant. He wrapped an arm around me and whisked us away to the falls, carried me through the water, and ushered me through the portal into the Unseen. He spared a moment to dry our clothes with a flick of his wrist, then zipped us to our destination.

I took in the surroundings—a short waterfall cascading into a deep, if small, pool hemmed in by the forest.

Stumbling backward a step, I grabbed for Nevan's hand. "Is this…"

"The place where he died and was reborn."

My gaze flew to the spot where I'd driven an endued sword into Ceara's chest. A dark stain on the earth snagged my attention. The blood stain. Where Travis had died.

"Easy," Nevan said. "You must be calm when he arrives."

I nodded, taking a deep breath to cleanse my psyche of the memories. Concentrating on Nevan helped, and I took several more long breaths.

"Are you prepared?" he asked.

"Yes. I'm ready." Was I? How could I answer the question with any certainty? I'd never met a newly forged…anything.

Nevan whistled.

Max appeared first, naked as he preferred. He muttered something I couldn't make out, and another figure materialized beside him.

I choked back a gasp, determined not to expose my shock.

Travis…Well, he resembled the man I'd known, but his hair had darkened to a glistening ebony and his skin bore the same coloring as Max's, tanned but tinged with a coppery sheen. His muscular physique had expanded, and he'd grown several inches taller. The forging had remade him into a mountain of masculine power rivaling both Max and Nevan. Unlike those two, however, Travis wore a pair of jeans that fit his new body like a glove. Max or Nevan must've conjured those for him, or else he'd learned that trick already.

But his eyes. Christ, those eyes. They flamed bright red, with yellow and orange tentacles spinning within the fiery color.

Travis's gaze snapped to me, and his eyes erupted with pure white fireworks. Lips parted, he stared at me with the intensity of a starved man presented with a steak dinner he couldn't quite reach.

I fought the urge to back up closer to Nevan. Strength and calmness, that's what I needed to portray for my friend, the man who'd died in defense of me.

Rolling my shoulders back, I managed a smile. "Hi, Travis."

He flinched, averting his gaze. "Lindsey."

His voice was gravelly, as if his throat was parched.

I clasped my hands in front of me, trying for a nonchalant pose. "It's good to see you. Max says you've been doing okay with the, uh, adjustment. Are you feeling better?"

He nodded once.

What was I supposed say now? I had no idea.

Travis's gaze reeled back to me. His lips worked, as if he struggled to form the right words. "I—am sorry."

"For what?"

"Everything. I—harassed you for—three years."

Like I cared about that anymore. He'd believed I killed his brother, but he'd followed me from Texas to Michigan in a misguided effort to protect me.

"All in the past," I assured him. "Forget it. Besides, you've proved what kind of man you really are, fighting alongside the rest of us and—" I'd almost said *giving your life for me*. Not the way to maintain a calm atmosphere. "Well, the point is you've made up for any past transgressions."

His attention zeroed in on left hand, and his eyes widened.

I covered the ring with my other hand.

"Married?" he asked.

"Not yet. Engaged."

His lips twitched into a near smile. "Congratulations."

Not awkward at all, no sir. "Uh, I appreciate that."

Travis glanced at the blood stain on the ground and his lips flattened. "Should've died."

"I'm really glad you didn't."

"But Calder." Travis covered his eyes with his hand. "He turned into—a monster."

"You won't."

"Don't know that."

The pain in his voice made my chest ache. Oh, to hell with this standing idly by nonsense. I couldn't watch my friend agonizing over what he'd become without doing something.

I took a step.

Nevan laid a hand on my arm.

Glancing back, I said, "I have to do this. Trust me."

He withdrew his hand.

I walked straight up to Travis and took his face in my hands.

Travis went rigid, his eye unblinking.

"You are not Calder," I said. "He was weak and gave in to the lure of power. Still, in the end he realized what he'd done and he atoned for it."

Travis shook his head—or tried to, but my hands stayed him.

"Calder gave me a message for you." I boosted myself up on my toes. "He said to tell you he's sorry, and he's grateful he got to have you for a brother. He also said not to worry, because you're stronger than he ever was and you're a better man too. You will never become like him."

Travis swallowed visibly, his face wrenched with a myriad of emotions.

I felt for him, more than I could ever have explained. Turned into an incubus, forced to deal with powers and instincts he didn't understand and couldn't control. I could relate to having uncontrolled powers.

"You are my friend," I told him, "and I will never give up on you."

He closed his eyes, struggling to control his erratic breathing.

I let my hands fall to my sides as I backed away a little. "You'll be fine. I believe in you."

Max cleared his throat to gain my attention. "We should go."

He indicated Travis's pants with a motion of his eyes.

That's when I noticed the growing bulge inside Travis's jeans. *Oh lord*. He couldn't control it, but this seemed like the appropriate time to split.

I returned to Nevan's side.

Max told me, "There will be more visits in future. It's good for him to test his willpower. A salamander needs a great deal of it."

Travis and Max disappeared.

Nevan took me back to the mortal world, but not back to the shop just yet. I had more than forty minutes of my lunch break left. We ambled past the healing vortex, with its stone benches, and veered off the path to head for my favorite secluded spot. I used to eat lunch here every day to avoid other people, and I'd had my first real conversation with Nevan here, under the bows of a maple tree.

We sat down beneath that same tree, side by side, nestled against each other with my head on his shoulder and his arm around me.

A man appeared before us.

Nevan and I both jumped.

I gaped at the visitor, speechless at the sight of him. "Bob?"

The oracle I'd thought was dead grasped the lapels of his navy blue suit, the one that appeared tailored exclusively for him. The sun made his gray hair seem lighter and glinted off his bright green eyes. They once again glowed with an eerie light, the same shade as the illumination in the creepy dark forest.

I scrambled to my feet, kneeing Nevan in the gut in the process. He didn't seem to feel it, or maybe he was too shocked by our visitor.

"How are you alive?" I asked, my wonder evident in my voice. "I watched Ceara plunge a sword through you. Why aren't you dead?"

"Told you before, I've moved beyond all designations." He moseyed over to a tree to lean against it. "The sword wound took me out of commission for a while, but I'm back."

Nevan sprang to his feet. "Why have you sought us?"

"Got a couple messages for you two."

I sidled up to Nevan, and he looped an arm around my waist. What messages could be so important the oracle would set foot in the mortal world to deliver them? I flattened a hand over my stomach, suddenly queasy.

Bob smiled up at the sun. "First, you can stop fretting about whether you and Nevan will ever conceive a child. You'll have several."

"How? A hybrid pregnancy is dangerous."

The oracle chuckled, his smile broadening. "Have faith, Lindsey. A way will present itself."

He'd called me by name. Back in his lair, he'd called me "Janusite" or "mortal." Might he have decided he liked me? What would it mean if he had?

"Oh dearie," Bob said, giving me an empathetic look, "you worry about everything, don't you?"

Nevan piped up. "She does."

I elbowed him gently in the side.

He smirked.

"Yes," Bob said, "I like you, child. You have spirit and courage."

Though I appreciated the words, I restrained myself from thanking him. We might've been in the mortal world, but for all I knew he carried the magic of the Unseen with him wherever he went. Better not to risk it.

"What's the other message?" I asked.

"Trust in Janus."

"Um…Not to sound ungrateful, but what the heck does that mean?"

Bob smiled, tapped his head, and vanished.

I stared at the place where he'd stood, flummoxed like never before. "Ohhh-kay. I'm clearly not enlightened enough to understand that one."

"Neither am I," Nevan said. "But we'll concern ourselves with that later."

He scooped me up and poofed us back to where we'd been sitting before the oracle arrived. This time around, I perched on his lap with my legs outstretched and my arms around his neck.

"Hungry?" Nevan asked.

"Well, it is my lunch break. So yes, I'm hungry."

"Since I had no time to cook you a sumptuous meal, I'll conjure one instead." He held out his free hand, palm up, fingers spread.

A takeout pizza box poofed into his hand.

I laughed. "You could conjure anything you want, and you chose pizza?"

He set the box across my lap. "You enjoy pizza. This one has extra cheese, the way you like it."

"You are hands down the awesomest fiancé ever." I kissed his cheek. "I love living with you, and I can't wait to marry you."

"But you'll have to wait." He flipped the pizza box open and extracted one gooey slice, the cheese stretching beneath it. "Can you survive two months until we wed?"

I opened my mouth as he held the slice of pizza for me to bite. My teeth sank through the crispy crust, and I tore off a mouthful. "Maybe I can talk my mom into a shorter prep time and less planning. We don't need a big-deal wedding. Just you and me—and our friends and my family."

"That's all we ever need."

As usual, he was right. I couldn't have done better than to find a man who loved me and my incessant questions, who adored my stubbornness and my family, a man who taught me to embrace my passions and find my courage.

Let the future unfold as it would. I had everything I needed right here.

ANNA DURAND IS A BESTSELLING, MULTI-AWARD-WINNING AUTHOR OF contemporary and paranormal romance. Her books have earned bestseller status on every major retailer and wonderful reviews from readers around the world. But that's the boring spiel. Here are the really cool things you want to know about Anna!

Born on Lackland Air Force Base in Texas, Anna grew up moving here, there, and everywhere thanks to her dad's job as an instructor pilot. She's lived in Texas (twice), Mississippi, California (twice), Michigan (twice), and Alaska—and now Ohio.

As for her writing, Anna has always made up stories in her head, but she didn't write them down until her teen years. Those first awful books went into the trash can a few years later, though she learned a lot from those stories. Eventually, she would pen her first romance novel, the paranormal romance *Willpower*, and she's never looked back since.

Want even more details about Anna? Get access to her extended bio when you subscribe to her newsletter and download the free bonus ebook, *Hot Scots Confidential*. You'll also get hot deleted scenes, character interviews, fun facts, and more! Plus you'll receive the short story *Tempted by a Kiss* and mutliple bonus chapters in both ebook and audiobook formats.

VISIT ANNADURAND.COM TO SIGN UP.